THE LOST TRIBES

Safe Harbor

C. TAYLOR-BUTLER

MOVE BOOKS

To Albert Taylor for showing me warriors can dance. RIP
And my "family" Ken, Alexis,
Olivia, Delfina, Johanna, Kimberly & Isaiah
— *C. Taylor-Butler*

To Mina, Silas and Petey. They are the best of me.
— *Patrick Arrasmith*

Text copyright © 2016 by C. Taylor-Butler
Illustration copyright © by Patrick Arrasmith

Book design by Virginia Pope

Library of Congress Control Number: 2016915085

10 9 8 7 6 5 4 3 2 1   11 12 13 14 15 16
Printed in the U.S.A.
First edition, November 2016

MOVING BOYS TO READ
P.O. Box 183
Beacon Falls, Connecticut, 06403

Contents

PROLOGUE

Great Sphinx of Giza
29.9753° N, 31.1378° E

"Enter those who have proven worthy."

Deep beneath the Sphinx, Kurosh glanced at the hieroglyphics carved thousands of years before by ancient ancestors. After years of research the teams were no closer to opening the Hall of Records. Soon the work might all be in vain.

His device vibrated to indicate an incoming transmission. He laid it on the white altar and answered. "I have the formulas you requested."

"Indeed," said a male voice, the words curling out of the device like smoke. "That is welcome news."

"I propose an exchange," said Kurosh. "The coordinates and precise frequencies."

A sigh erupted. "Unfortunately, the target has been elusive."

Kurosh narrowed his eyes and gestured for his lead warrior to join him. Kavera walked toward the altar, careful not to step on the shallow troughs that cut through the stone floor and terminated at eight towering canopic jars. The once dormant channels pulsed with electromagnetic activity. Static electricity crackled in the air yet barely registered on their scanners.

"SOSUS detected the whale's unique signature," Kurosh continued.

"At 52 hertz in the Earth year 1989. That may not be the frequency now. One can only hope it is immortal."

"There are those who think WE are immortal."

"Would that it were so. I would like to offer my condolences on the loss of your brother and his wife."

Kurosh twisted the strands of his white prayer beads into a figure eight, then let them unwind again. "And for yours. May their souls nourish the universe and watch over us."

"Thank you, old friend," said the voice. "I look forward to our meeting tomorrow."

Kurosh logged out and studied the sparks flashing inside the canopic jars. "The children are never to enter this room."

"Understood. But may I speak freely, Jemadari?" Kavera asked.

"Permission to speak has never been an issue,"

"It concerns the children. Whatever destroyed their home and breached our facility remains a threat."

"And your point is?" Kurosh opened a small box and slipped a device into a gap in the cloth lining. It was no wider than the threads themselves and easily hidden by the vials of liquid contained inside.

"You risk their safety and the mission by removing them from the Harbor."

"It poses a greater risk for them to remain here while security protocols are reinforced."

"They are worried about their parents. Perhaps if we assigned more teams—"

"That is not possible. Completing the mission will take every remaining resource," Kurosh said.

"And the children?"

"Will adjust to their new reality."

"Jemadari!" Kavera paused and softened his voice. "Kurosh. You will be unprotected. A triad can—"

Kurosh's eyes narrowed. "The matter is settled. You have your orders."

Kavera hesitated, wanting to question the wisdom of taking five unseasoned children to a meeting with their most frightening ally, but before he could protest his commander, a man the children referred to as Uncle Henry cut him off.

"There is no one I trust with this task more than you, Kavera. Consult with Aurelia, then assemble a team and find my brother. Volari and I can protect the children. "

Kavera frowned and nodded. "Akoosh sakur, sha ka don fur."

"Askar," Kurosh replied. *Confirmed.*

—

It Begins

∴

"Wouldst thou," so the helmsman answered,
"know the secret of the sea?
Only those who brave its dangers,
Comprehend its mystery."

—*Henry Wadsworth Longfellow*

PART I

CHAPTER ONE

The Triangle

Bermuda Triangle
26.38695° N, 69.395142° W

•⁘ Ben stood on the bow of the 138-foot Brigantine yacht, the wind clawing at his many layers of borrowed clothing. He could barely hear himself think over the sound of the pounding surf and his own chattering teeth. Last night, the twin-masted research vessel set off in calm Caribbean waters as dolphins raced beside them. Now there were no other signs of life beyond the perimeter of the hull. Even the seagulls had abandoned them.

The storm intensified sending Carlos, Serise, Grace and April scrambling into the cabin for safety. Ben felt his uncle's hand on his shoulder, restraining him as he tried to join them.

"*Stay*," Uncle Henry commanded, steering the ship towards some unknown destination.

Ben stared at his friends, their eyes wide in horror, and tried to process the situation. It had been two days since their parents had sent them to safety at the Harbor outpost after their homes had been attacked. Only a day since finding out the truth they'd been hiding.

That none of them were human. At least by Earth standards. And now they were traveling alone with the scariest person on the planet, his own uncle. What about the concept of safety did his uncle miss in the memo?

Volari, the deep-sea intelligence agent, emerged from the cabin, his webbed feet slapping the deck as he walked to the starboard side of the ship. He placed a diamond-shaped box on the railing then aimed a trident at the sky. It was instantly hit by a bolt of lightning. Volari pointed the staff towards the Atlantic Ocean, discharged the electrical energy then started over. Each impulse grew in intensity as did the waves.

The ship banked right and steered into the wind, its eighty-foot masts creaking and groaning as the sails tugged against their rigging. Even so, the ship, which had been traveling at twice its rating of nine knots, picked up speed, cutting effortlessly through the angry surf. Ben squinted. The sails should have billowed towards the bow of the boat—in the direction of the wind's gusts. Instead they pushed towards the stern.

Struggling to remain upright, Ben gripped the brass rail tightly. *"Where are we going?"* he shouted telepathically.

Uncle Henry pointed towards the horizon. *"There."*

Ben saw nothing out of the ordinary. The waves swelled and surged in an attempt to capsize the boat. Queasy from the violent rocking, Ben hoped the journey would lead back to someplace warm and tropical.

"There where?"

"We'll be met at the agonic line."

Ben was growing weary of his uncle's cosmic mumbo jumbo. He studied a compass on the ship's console. The dial fluctuated wildly. "I don't think this thing works."

"Correct. This is one of two places in the world where the Magnetic North Pole and the Geographic North Poles are in perfect alignment."

"Where's the other place?"

"Devil's Sea off the coast of Japan," his uncle replied.

Ben was sorry he asked. He longed to be with his friends, safe inside the dry, warm cabin. A quick look from his uncle killed that idea.

"How big is the Bermuda Triangle?"

"Roughly a half million square miles," his uncle said.

"So if we get lost—,"

"It is unlikely the Coast Guard would find us," his uncle said.

Ben's stomach turned sour. He rubbed his arms and was drawn to a disturbance in the distance. A tornado hurled in their direction bringing with it more crashing waves and the sound of a speeding freight train.

"Right on time, Volari," Uncle Henry shouted, his prayer beads vibrating in the wind.

Volari raised a single webbed digit in affirmation but continued to concentrate on his control panel.

"What is that?" Grace shouted, as she poked her head out of the cabin door.

"Waterspout," Uncle Henry replied. "Think of it as the subway to our next destination."

"You've got to be kidding!" Ben screamed. "We'll be killed!"

"That's pretty much what's going to happen if we don't complete this mission," his uncle said. "So, now . . . or later . . . what's the difference?" He gestured for Ben's friends to rejoin him on the deck. They complied, but only after what looked like an animated debate.

The wildly flapping sails caught Ben's attention. Six Hayoolkááł team members materialized on the booms; four at the square sails on the foremast, two on the mainmast. They saluted to Uncle Henry before spreading their arms and dissolving into the mist.

"How long have they been up there?" asked Serise, her mouth gaped open.

"Who did you think piloted the boat from Woods Hole?" Uncle Henry said as if the answer were obvious.

A feather fell from one of the masts and lightly brushed Serise's cheek. It hovered a minute, unaffected by the violent wind. A young Hayoolkááł warrior materialized, winked, then dissolved into the mist. Grinning sheepishly, Serise blushed, caught the feather in her hand and placed it in her pocket.

Uncle Henry scowled. "It seems I will have to review Harbor protocol with his superior officer."

"Aren't they going with us?" asked Grace.

"No," said Uncle Henry. "The trip gave them an opportunity to study trade winds in this region. Their mission is complete. They are returning to the Harbor." He passed a pill to each person.

"What's this?" asked Ben.

"The key to your survival. Wait for my command before putting it in your mouth." Uncle Henry walked across the deck to join Volari.

A brief flash of light appeared as Ben held the pill with his wet hands. "Think this is green glob with a purple coating?"

"Your mother's habitat formula made us appear human, not impervious to death by hypothermia," Grace said.

"Might be cyanide." Carlos turned the pill over and over in his hand. "Your uncle could dump our bodies in the ocean and no one would be the wiser."

"Get real," said Ben. "He's fine. I mean he hugged me. Remember? When he found out we didn't blow up with the transport ship?"

"And that right there should tell you he's not in his right mind!" Serise said pointing at Volari. "Look at the Gila monster with the trident. Does he strike you as normal? Do you see that storm? We're going to be killed and your uncle gives us a pill? Am I the only one here who thinks this isn't normal?"

"Stop it!" April yelled. "I trust Uncle Henry. And Volari too, even though I can't understand anything he says."

Uncle Henry gave Volari a pat on the back, opened a gate in the railing, then gestured for the children to join them. He raised a single eyebrow when they hesitated. "Is there a problem?"

Grace and Serise huddled against Carlos. His eyes bugged out as he shook his head in disbelief.

"We're going to turn the boat around, right?" Carlos asked. "I mean, no wonder no one comes back from this place. That thing is going to kill us."

"I believe Ben has already covered that subject," Uncle Henry said, scowling. "Have faith. Take the pill, chew hard and get it soft. You will feel a slight discharge of static electricity against your tongue. Don't be alarmed. When I give the command, blow the biggest bubble you can and jump into the base of the wave."

"Blow a bubble and jump?" asked Carlos. "He can't be serious."

Ben looked to his uncle for confirmation, but he was busy studying Volari's console. The waterspout spun towards them, pulling a massive wall of water from the ocean the height of Mount Kilimanjaro. It rose above the boat with a thunderous roar.

"Get ready," Uncle Henry shouted.

Serise stared at the pill in her hand, screamed then leapt into the air as if trying to fly away with the long gone Hayoolkááł warriors. Grace clutched the pendant her father gave her as she and Carlos dropped to their knees in desperate prayer. April soon joined them. Ben's uncle chuckled and shook his head from side to side before returning his attention to the waterspout. At its base lay a frothy, foamy brew. Uncle Henry touched his watch. The wave paused. The sound muted. Although the waterspout and gathering storm clouds blocked the sunlight completely, flashes of swirling neon light filled the air providing the illumination they needed.

Volari pointed his trident one more time. A silver star appeared in the center of the storm's funnel, then stretched to form two vertical strands that separated like elevator doors opening.

"It's time," Uncle Henry shouted. "This gateway won't last long."

No one moved.

"Jump!" Uncle Henry ordered. "If you stay, you will not survive."

Ben thought about Grace climbing into a sarcophagus in the Sunnyslope Museum when they were on escaping the explosions that destroyed their neighborhood. She had mastered her fear of the unknown. What was he? A basketball jock with basic swim skills. And what were the choices anyway? Jump and drown, or stay on a boat as it was torn to pieces?

"I could push you but this is only one of many tests you will be facing. You wisely chose not to go home with the transport. The fates have kept you here for a reason. Now, when all else has failed you, your only hope of survival will be unwavering faith in yourself and in your team."

Ben blew a bubble which popped immediately. He pulled the gum back into his mouth, chewed furiously, then blew another. Success. It stayed intact. April clung to Uncle Henry. She pointed at her bubble and gave Ben a thumbs up.

Volari dove gracefully into the water, leaving no ripple or splash in his wake. Fear frozen on their faces, Grace and Carlos blew gargantuan bubbles and disappeared into the surf. That left Serise. She was struggling to blow a bubble but couldn't get it started. There was also her fear of heights. The deck was at least ten feet above the surface of the water.

Houston, we've got a problem!

Without hesitation, Ben blew a new, much larger bubble, tackled Serise and hurled them both through the opening in the rail.

We're going to die!

CHAPTER TWO

Lampocteis Cruentiventer

Sunlight Zone: 20 feet below sea level

•ᵔ• Ben gasped from holding his breath and dared to suck in a lung full of air as they plunged downward, then came to a gentle stop. Serise kept her hands firmly gripped over her eyes and her head pressed into his shoulder. They were encased in a capsule, like the inside of a giant soap bubble. Water rippled around them, and glorious sweet-smelling oxygen filled the space. A small hieroglyphic readout flashed on the transparent surface before changing to English:

24 C° ∫ 6 atmospheres external.
24 C° ∫ 1 atmosphere internal

This isn't so bad. The water was calm as they hovered not far from the hull of the yacht. And then Ben remembered. The waterspout was on pause when they jumped. Before he could get his bearings the water began to churn violently.

What did that mean for—

Suddenly, the capsule was sucked through a tunnel that twisted and turned at odd angles. A kaleidoscope of colors raced past them as it spiraled out of control. With nowhere to sit and with no safety devices to hold on to, Ben struggled to remain upright. Losing all sense of direction, he gripped Serise's arms tightly as they rocketed through the vortex.

Blood curdling screams reverberated off the walls. Ben had no intention of opening his eyes to see what had caused them. He wondered if they were dropping down into some deep sea trench. Serise's fingernails dug trenches of their own into his shoulder.

Twilight zone: 2500 feet below sea level.

$$12 \ C^O \ \int 76 \ \text{atmospheres external.}$$
$$24 \ C^O \ \int 10 \ \text{atmospheres internal}$$

"Are we there yet?" Serise asked as the capsule came to a stop. It expanded to accommodate her distance as she backed away. Ben wondered if it could stretch the length of a city block in case of more danger. He didn't have much skin left on his shoulders.

"Gosh, Webster. Think you could have gripped me any tighter?" She winced, rubbed her arms, then tried to blow pressure from her ears by squeezing her nose shut. "And did you have to scream in my ear?"

Ben frowned then heard a muffled sound. Uncle Henry and April were together in a single capsule, closely followed by Grace and Carlos who each had their own. The interiors glowed from some unseen energy source. Volari glided alongside them, checking for leaks, then swam off into the blackness. The temperature inside the capsule remained steady. Breathing became easier as the panel showed the inside pressure, which had risen slightly, was quickly returning to 1 atmosphere.

"Wonder where are we?" Ben asked. He didn't expect an answer.

"In a vortex." Uncle Henry's voice boomed through an invisible speaker. "Your shell will provide the air you need. Volari has gills. He doesn't need one."

Beacons on the top and bottom of each capsule activated. They scanned in all directions of the water like searchlights. Besides the other capsules Ben still couldn't see anything.

"Wonder how far down we are?" Serise pressed her hands against the capsule's surface, now solid and shimmering.

"Don't know," said Ben. "But as long as we're in here we're safe."

"Ya think?" Serise said sarcastically. "The spaceship was supposed to be safe too and you see how well that worked out."

Ben sighed. He didn't want to revisit the space ship, the explosion, and all those scientists whose escape to their home worlds ended abruptly. It just made him think about how close they'd been to joining them. And then his mind shifted to his missing parents. He wiped away a single tear. He wasn't going there.

Serise frowned, sighed and dropped her arms in defeat. "Sorry. That was rude. I miss my parents. Never thought I'd hear that come out of my mouth."

Ben gave her a half-hearted thumbs up. He couldn't help feeling like he had dragged his friends into this mess and that being dead was surely less scary than where they were now: in an endless void of dark water. "I'm sorry too."

He tried to get Carlos's attention, but Carlos was on his hands and knees probing every inch of his capsule in rapt fascination.

His little sister chattered away while Uncle Henry listened patiently. April had one hand on her hip with the index finger of the other waving and making circles in the air to punctuate her comments. Ben couldn't hear what she was saying.

Instead, he waved at Grace who waved back tentatively but Ben knew her fear of the dark was kicking in. The directionless void offered little in the way of hope except for a glow that appeared in the distance. Nothing in the Woodland survival challenge at school could come close to this bit of scariness. In the challenges you had to depend on your team, have faith in them to guide you. He'd given anything to be back in the woods— blindfolded.

Specks of light winked on in the distance until the water was saturated—like an endless sea of stars surrounding him. Ben wondered if this was how astronauts felt on a space walk. Except Earth, the moon and the International Space Station were missing.

"Are we in space?" Ben shouted. "Was that a jump gate to another galaxy?"

If his uncle heard him there was no acknowledgement. April now had both hands in the air as if she were telling an exciting story. Uncle Henry just nodded, but kept his distance, hands folded in his lap.

"Space?" said Serise. "Where have you been? A T L A N T I C ocean! Get it?" Serise waved her hand around in a sweeping motion. "Water! None in space." She banged her hand against the side of the capsule causing the water to ripple around it. "Ergo O C E A N!"

"I wasn't talking to you!" Ben groused and wondered how his uncle had created a bench in his capsule.

"Well, who else is in here with you?" asked Serise. "Geez, those aren't stars. They're probably bioluminescent plankton!"

Ben rolled his eyes. "Hey! Uncle Henry! What's all this white stuff floating around us?"

Uncle Henry looked up, cleared his throat and said, "Phytoplankton, zooplankton, and debris."

"Debris?" asked Carlos. "What kind of debris?"

"Dead animals, decayed bits of plants, regurgitated food, fish waste," Uncle Henry said dryly.

"Fish waste?" asked Grace.

"I think he means we're surrounded by fish poop," said Carlos.

"Thank you for that colorful interpretation," said Uncle Henry. "Your description is both adequate and reasonably accurate."

"Thanks Webster. I was happy thinking of it as glow-in-the-dark plankton." Serise brushed her clothing as if their brief encounter with the water had actually deposited something on her.

Ben frowned. "Wonder how we're going to get to that light? How do we steer this thing?" Ben followed Carlos's lead and felt the surface of the capsule looking for hidden controls. "Think we need to just start running? You know, like this is a hamster ball and you're the giant rodent?"

He waited for Serise's response so he could zing her again. Instead, Serise's eyes grew large as saucers. He braced, winced, then reluctantly spun around. A massive translucent blob headed in his direction. And then another. And another.

Soon the capsule filled with screams again. This time it wasn't Ben. His own terror caught in his throat despite his best efforts to release it. He choked and swallowed hard.

Hundreds of alien spacecraft appeared. Shaped like beating hearts, the towering crimson and black vehicles stopped short of the capsules, holding their position as they swayed back and forth. Pulsating lights alternated on and off along the spines of their jelly-like surface. It was only then that Ben realized he was looking at living species.

"Remain very still," said Uncle Henry. "We've arrived at our first destination. We must wait for Volari to return with an escort. Don't make any sudden moves and you should be fine. They are lightning fast and quite deadly."

"What are these?" Ben heard Carlos ask.

"Lampocteis cruentiventer," Uncle Henry said.

"Huh?"

Uncle Henry cleared his throat. "Bloodybelly combs. They guard the outer marker."

"The outer marker of what?" asked Ben, not sure he wanted to know.

Uncle Henry's eyes flashed. "Atlantis."

CHAPTER THREE

Outer Marker

•°• Ben was stunned. Serise spoke the words that froze in his mouth.

"Atlantis? As in the Lost City of Atlantis?"

"Since Atlanteans are still living there I don't think they consider themselves 'lost'," said Uncle Henry. "Just voluntarily unavailable for Earth-based human discovery. I admonish you to choose your words carefully while we are their guests. The Atlantean Council is not fond of land-based, bi-pedal creatures and are easily offended."

Ben was skeptical but kept his mouth shut, careful not to make any sudden moves that would antagonize the jellyfish or his uncle.

"I saw these things at the Monterey Bay Aquarium," said Carlos. "The sign said they only grow about five inches long."

"And your point is?" asked Uncle Henry. "Until a few days ago, you didn't believe in life forms from outer space. I suspect we're going to be debunking a few more myths in the ocean depths."

As if on cue, more creatures appeared, led by Volari.

"Ahhh! It appears the escorts have arrived," said Uncle Henry.

Remembering his uncle's warning, Ben tried to remain motionless. If five-inch jellyfish could grow to ten feet out here, then what was coming for them now?

As Volari circled each capsule the lights dimmed considerably. The surface deformed to create a bench that ringed the circumference. Volari had a heart. Ben took advantage of the situation and sat down.

Twelve ghost-white squid swam closer, each with enormously long spindly legs and large unblinking eyes. Ben drew in a breath. Like elephant ears, the wings of the creatures folded in and out in an aquatic ballet. They looked like a cross between Daddy Long-legged spiders and butterflies only they had ten legs not eight.

What were they?

"Magnapinna talismani," Uncle Henry said without waiting for the question. "Rarely seen by people on Earth and they prefer to keep it that way."

Four creatures broke formation and gripped a capsule as if their legs were the metal claw fingers of an arcade game.

"Steady," cautioned Uncle Henry. "They will take us the rest of the way but their legs are fragile. Stay as still as possible. It won't be long now."

Four squid followed Volari to the front capsules. The remaining squid flanked the rear as the bloodybelly combs swam away to resume their patrol.

Swimming in unison, the squids flapped their massive wings and glided downward towards a distant light.

The Abyss: 19,000 feet below sea level.

$$3\ C^{\circ}\ \int 579\ \text{atmospheres external.}$$
$$24\ C^{\circ}\ \int 1\ \text{atmosphere internal}$$

Ben did a double take at the digital read-out. At this pressure the capsule and everything in them should be crushed, but the internal pressure continued to hold at sea level.

Hundreds of ships lay ahead on the ocean floor. Modern yachts, submarines and ancient schooners came into view. Ben squinted into the water for a closer look. Airplanes lay scattered across the landscape including six Navy bombers sitting side by side as if they were ready to take flight again. It was surreal. Their hulls were covered with coral and plants. Fish swam in and out of the openings as if the long forgotten relics were condominiums.

The squids swam closer to a three-masted ship bearing a tattered flag with a skull and cross bones. Ben wondered what treasures would be found inside. He remembered watching a documentary about the Titanic. Explorers found a lot of it intact. The giant carved staircase, dishes from the dining room. But here, other things littered the deck of the pirate ship. Not treasures but bones.

Human bones.

A skeleton stood at the stern of the ship, hands tightly gripped at the wheel, swaying back and forth. A ghost ship with a captain or first mate steering it to nowhere.

Ghost ship.

They were seeing something never witnessed before by humans unless you counted the Sonecian team. Hundreds of skeletons hanging out of cockpits and windows or clutching the ground. Lost to the world, never to be found by their loved ones. No one would ever know where they were buried.

He pushed his head against the surface of the capsule. Somewhere his parents were out there alone. He still felt a connection to them. He couldn't explain it but he knew there was still hope. If his uncle wasn't worried, Ben knew he shouldn't be. Uncle Henry had insisted the new team leader, Aurelia, was the best tracker in the universe, except for himself of course. Apparently she had special skills no one else had. Nothing Ben could do, nothing he could try, could possibly match the resources of a trained Xenobian warrior. So he tried to relax and focus on the bizarre landscape surrounding him.

He felt like he was sitting in the front row of an amusement park ride. They'd already braved a waterfall, then the deserted ships. Next would be what? He wracked his brain. The town, and merry frolicking! Yeah. After all the horror he had faced he was ready for some merry frolicking.

The squids continued towards an even larger ship. It, too, was littered with hundreds of skeletons and discarded treasure. The capsules were aimed toward the lower section with cannons poised for battle and sharp, possibly lethal, pieces of hull jutting out.

Ben held his breath. Serise was speechless but her bugged out eyes matched his own.

"Have faith," his uncle had said earlier. *"When all else has failed you, your only hope of survival will be unwavering faith in yourself and in your team."*

The ship and its doomed crew grew faint as a familiar silver beam appeared. It lengthened and split to create a portal. The squid escorts passed easily through the barrier. Ben hoped it wasn't another giant marble chute.

"A cloaking device," Uncle Henry said dispassionately.

"Ooh!" Ben heard his sister squeal in delight. Looming in the distance, a city sparkled in the middle of a liquid landscape.

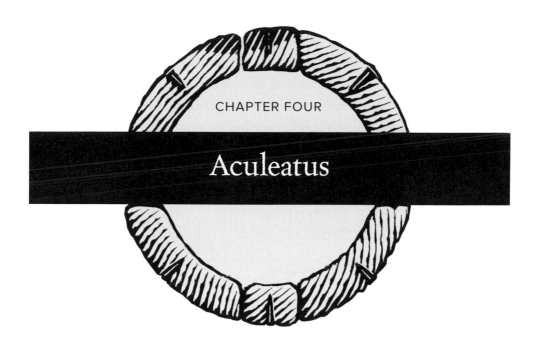

CHAPTER FOUR

Aculeatus

Location: Classified.

•ᵃ• Protected beneath a clear dome, Atlantis stretched far into the distance. Towering stone and crystal buildings dotted a landscape of concentric circles and causeways surrounding a massive central core. Gleaming crystalline structures sprang up along the outer rings.

Volari swam to Uncle Henry's capsule and aimed a laser.

"Stop!" Ben yelled.

Ignoring Ben's plea, Volari pierced the surface of the capsule creating an opening. Uncle Henry gently guided April to one side of the capsule as water seeped through. He braced against the opposite side just as the force of the water became a torrent. April seemed fascinated but didn't utter a word.

Volari looked briefly at Grace and Carlos's capsules but didn't stop. Instead, he headed directly for Ben and Serise.

"Hey! What are you doing?" Ben shouted.

Volari pierced through the surface. The digital readout showed the temperature plummeting and the pressure rising fast. Ben's ears popped as the pressure changed.

"Get away from us you freak," shrieked Serise.

"Serise!" Uncle Henry growled.

Volari flashed a murderous look at Serise before transforming into a massive sea dragon complete with gigantic wings and long fangs that extended past his muzzle even when his mouth was closed. His tail curled around the capsule and shook it angrily before letting it float freely again.

Ben wondered if his internal organs had been rearranged as he picked himself off the now wet floor of the capsule.

"Serise! Apologize . . . before he rips . . . us apart!"

Volari placed his face against the side of the capsule where Serise cowered in terror. His irises formed black starbursts in the center of blood red eyes. Eyes bigger than both Ben and Serise combined. Volari's mouth stretched back into a wide grin as he used one of his massive talons to split the capsule at the top. Water poured into the center separating Ben from Serise.

"Serise!" Ben pleaded. "Now would be a good time to apologize.!"

Serise's screams grew ear splitting as Volari grabbed the partially separated capsule in one claw. Drawing back his long, scale covered arm, he hesitated—like an Olympian gathering strength and momentum before launching a shot put. Ben wanted to beg for mercy.

"I'm so sorry," said Serise, kneeling as her hands clasped in a prayer position. "I take it back. I was just nervous. I think you're really, really, REALLY cute in a scaly kind of way. I know a bunch of girls who would think you were hot! You know—an underwater supermodel kind of guy."

With sizable force Volari launched their capsule towards the city.

Have faith, Ben muttered to himself as they rocketed towards the Atlantis dome. *Oh please, oh please, oh please, let me have faith.* Ben tried to conjure one of his mother's prayers but all he could think of was, *"I'm a dead man!"*

Breaching the barrier, the capsule split and formed a tight seal around each of them. The self-contained suits felt like soft plastic wrap. Ben's terrifying free fall was slowed by large fronds of seaweed that covered the ocean floor. He could still breath. He could move his arms and legs freely. And if he could stop shaking in terror it would be possible to swim as naturally as if he were in a swimming pool. He pinched himself and felt the material stretch in his fingers. "Whoa! Aqua survival suit."

Serise sobbed and tried to compose herself. Grace, Carlos and April swam over to assist her but she was tangled in seaweed and swinging combatively making things worse.

Volari sent an unintelligible sound into the water. Serise screamed as the seaweed rose and carried her aloft as if they were Olympic sprinters.

Everyone froze.

"What were those things?" asked April.

"Aculeatus," answered Uncle Henry with an appreciative nod. "Visiting octopus delegation from Australia. Often mistaken for seaweed. Quite marvelous aren't they?"

The creatures deposited Serise at a temple in the center of the city before going inside. She was still screaming.

An odd vibration pulsed through the water then transformed into a loud chorus of bass-toned laughter. Reverting to his original size and shape, Volari gave Ben's uncle a webbed thumbs up before swimming off towards the city, flipping and spinning joyfully.

Ben had gotten the message and hoped for their sake that Serise had too.

CHAPTER FIVE

Atlantis

•̈ Almost recovered from the terrifying entry, Ben had a chance to get a better look around. Atlantis reminded him of ancient Mesopotamian temples. Much of the stone surface was covered in coral and sea plants. Light was provided by bioluminescent materials on its surface and in the water surrounding them. A fish floated by, blinking on and off like a firefly.

The channels between the "islands" of Atlantis were punctuated with vents that flashed orange and emitted hot gaseous bubbles. Ben figured they acted like an ocean floor furnace. Every horizontal surface was littered with gemstones.

Manta rays, jellyfish, seahorses, lionfish, longnose batfish, and stingrays swarmed around him. A large Napoleon fish swam closer and examined him. It briefly bared a mouth full of sharp teeth, then disappeared into the temple.

A stern look crossing his face, Uncle Henry raised his index finger to his lips then went inside. Stone steps flanking the entrance reached high up into the liquid sky. The protective barrier was at least a mile above him. Large stone fish flanked the doorway, their tails curved upward like the ones decorating the Sunnyslope park fountain.

Once inside, Ben and the others floated downward so they could walk instead of swim. The temple walls were built from massive stone blocks with no visible mortar in the joints. Along their surface chiseled sea creatures swam immortalized in a landscape of stone and coral. The carvings were more curved than Mayan hieroglyphics but more angular and than Egyptian or Rongorongo. Sea creatures swam in and out of the levels overhead as if this were the inside of a giant aquarium decoration.

Everyone followed closely behind Uncle Henry and Volari as schools of neon fish swam around them. Serise eyed Volari with suspicion and stayed as far away from him as possible. Occasionally, Volari would stop, look back at her and wink. That caused Serise to hang back even farther. Even Ben wondered what the nature of Volari's dragon transformation had meant. He had a lot to learn about the Sonecian teams. A whole lot.

After a few minutes they stopped at an entrance that loomed two stories high or more. Volari spoke to Uncle Henry in his foreign underwater language. Uncle Henry nodded and stopped short of the door. Volari swam to the rear of the group and held out his arm. Serise looked terrified and backed away.

Volari waited patiently, his scaly turquoise arm chivalrously extended with a slight bend at the elbow. Uncle Henry raised his fingers to his lips but pointed towards Volari. Serise reluctantly looped her arm in his and allowed him to guide her through the door.

Her knees shook violently. Ben was surprised she could walk at all and wondered why Serise had been selected to go first. Maybe Volari was offering them all as human sacrifices to the Atlanteans with Serise picked to be first. After a moment's reflection he conceded that Serise was part of the team and he had a moral obligation to defend her if she got in trouble.

Darn mom's endless lectures on personal ethics and civic responsibility!

The doors swung open as Volari approached. Serise's aqua suit dissolved as soon as she stepped across the threshold.

The room contained an air pocket just big enough to encompass the inner third of a chamber. The space beyond was almost the size of a basketball arena. At the center of the void was an elaborate dining room table covered in white linen and silver vases filled with exotic green plants. Flanked by eighteen high-back chairs draped in velvet and silk, the table was set with silver, china and crystal.

Serise raised her hand to her mouth, careful not to make a sound, then looked from Volari to Uncle Henry to her friends, her eyes ablaze. Volari kissed her cheek, said something in his native language and bowed as he guided her towards the table. He even pulled a chair out for her. When he spoke again it just sounded like bubbles popping.

Serise blushed. "What did he say?"

"He said you're not a bad looking human specimen yourself." Uncle Henry sighed with disinterest. He studied a series of small boxes he pulled from his cloak. "That is for someone lacking scales and gills. But he is thousands of years old and you're young enough to be his great, great, great, great granddaughter. However, he appreciates the compliment and the apology even if offered under duress."

Ben looked at Volari with newfound appreciation. Thousands of years old? That caused him to wonder about his uncle's age. Uncle Henry looked like he was in his forties, but that probably didn't mean much in space years.

Volari gestured to Grace and April, seating them at the table and chivalrously kissing each on the hand.

"Where'd all this stuff come from," asked April. She gently picked up a silver chalice and sniffed the liquid inside it.

"It was salvaged from shipwrecks all over the world," said Uncle Henry. "On rare occasions they have human guests and prepare appropriately."

Ben's plate was rimmed in gold. Beneath a red flag the words, "White Star Line," were printed inside a gold ribbon. His salad plate read, "Mary Celeste." His concentration was broken when Uncle Henry began passing tiny silver disks to each person. Demonstrating their use like an airline steward, he held the disk high, pointed to the bottom, pulled a small strand from it, then placed the disk in his ear.

Ben was the first to try it. The disk fit comfortably as he adjusted the rod so that it bent towards his mouth.

"Is that better, young warrior?" a voice said in Ben's ear.

"Is what better?" asked Ben. Then he stopped. Volari was grinning. He had spoken to Ben in English!

"Heck, yeah! What are these things?"

"Shakrarian translators." Volari's voice sounded as though he was still submerged in water. "The Harbor teams have implants. You've seen them. The Sonecian star earrings."

Ben gestured to the others. "Hurry up! This is slick!"

The others rushed to insert their devices and gave a thumbs up.

"The translation is instantaneous," Volari continued. "For instance your phrase 'Heck, yeah!' translated as, 'Why, yes it does!' "

Ben laughed and relaxed in his chair. This intergalactic spy stuff was amazing.

"But I caution you," Volari said. "When the Atlantis delegation arrives, choose your words carefully. The current Atlantean ruler is a bit eccentric and will translate your words literally. Watch Kurosh and me for appropriate patterns of behavior and you should survive this trip unscathed."

Ben looked to his uncle for confirmation. But Uncle Henry was nowhere in sight.

CHAPTER SIX

Calamar

•• Ben's panic was short-lived. Uncle Henry sauntered back into the room, the heels of his boots clicking on the dry stone floor. The bubble of air closed behind him.

"Restrooms are down the hall about twenty meters," he said. "The plumbing is similar to what you'd find at home and heated for your comfort. The void will expand as needed to accommodate you, but no farther, as the area beyond that is off limits."

"Does home mean Sunnyslope or Safe Harbor?" Ben shuddered to think it was the latter. The Harbor bathrooms were the equivalent of torture chambers.

"Sunnyslope," said Uncle Henry dryly. "As I said, the Atlanteans are eccentric but accommodating."

Ben joined his friends in a mass sigh of relief. He hadn't thought much about bathrooms since arriving but it was good information to have given the circumstances.

Uncle Henry looked at his watch and then at Volari who shrugged. Suddenly, hundreds of creatures edged close to the barrier, crowding into the arena-sized area like anxious spectators. They sprinted away just as the doors to the chamber swung open.

A collective gasp rose from Ben's friends, followed by a stern cough from his uncle. Everyone quickly clamped their mouths shut and softened their expressions.

"Don't say a word, Ben," said Uncle Henry. *"I can't send a signal to the others, but I am expecting you to conduct yourself as a Xenobian warrior and set the tone for your sister and your friends."*

The lights dimmed as a procession of creatures floated into view.

"What's happening?" Grace whispered, her eyes darting around the room nervously.

"The light was temporarily increased to help you become oriented to your surroundings," said Volari. "Many of the Atlanteans do not venture near the surface of the water and their eyes are unaccustomed to the intensity."

A long serpent-like creature was the first to enter. It bore the head of a dragon but—unlike Volari's alter-ego—lacked wings, arms or talons. Instead, its body was covered with shiny, six-sided scales. A row of light emitting scales stretched along the length of its belly and long tongue. As it breached the void its body transformed into human form but the dragon head remained intact. The serpent's elaborate green robes were veined in silver and puddled on the floor as it walked. It stood at the far side of the table and nodded in Uncle Henry's direction.

"Kuuuuuroshhhhhh, Vooooooolaaaaaariiiiii, my ooooold friends. A pleaaaaaasurrrrrre to be graaaaaaced with your coooooompany once again."

Uncle Henry smiled briefly and nodded.

Next through the barrier swam a fat, silverfish with enormous bulging eyes and a large tooth-filled overbite. Like the first creature it had light emitting spots on its belly. And like the dragonfish, it transformed as it passed into the void. Its silver robes shimmered with red and black scales as it walked forward on fat webbed feet. Ben tried hard not to stare at the bubble-like eyes that protruded out from the top of its head.

Once he got past his initial shock, Ben decided the procession was even more fascinating than the space teams that with the Sonara transport ship. That was saying a lot. To think all this cool stuff was going on under his nose while he was stuck in boring Sunnyslope figuring out useless math problems. He could tell it was as much of a struggle for his friends to remain silent as it was for him.

Creatures continued to stream into the void and transform into half-human, half-sea monster hybrids. A hammerhead shark, a fish that looked strangely like the coelacanths—the creatures that first crawled out of the sea during evolution (at least according to Ben's science teacher)—and a dolphin. A blue whale hovered at the entrance too big to fit in the space between the massive open doors. He shrank to human size before breaching the barrier.

Ben's stomach lurched as a multi-tentacled creature with bulging eyes crossed the void and transformed. The octopus retained its head and its eight sucker-covered legs, two extending from each sleeve of its pink and orange robe. The arms were similar to those of the Kraken that provided transportation for Ben's mother and Dr. Hightower in Antarctica.

Last to enter was a large, black creature whose body was tight and compact like an egg. Its eight legs were connected by webbing. Its head reminded Ben of a partially opened umbrella. The creature took a place at the far end of the table.

"What is that?" Ben smiled nervously as the creature looked in his direction.

"Vampire Squid," Uncle Henry replied.

Ben gulped and regretted asking the question. He studied the delegation, all standing silently at the table. Some bowing to Uncle Henry, some looking at him with apparent distain before appraising Ben and his friends as if they were items on the menu.

Ben heard the roar of something big being propelled through the water. The barrier rippled behind him. He looked up half expecting to find a submarine and barely stopped a violent gasp as he stared into the face of the gargantuan squid towering above him. Dwarfing everything in the room, its head nearly reached the ceiling. Its arms and tentacles stretched out in both directions and spanned the length of the space. It had to be at least 50 feet long. The squid swam closer to Ben, the water barrier moving with it. It made no effort to breach the void.

"Is this the boy?" The creature said in a deep raspy voice that sounded like he was wheezing.

"He is my brother's son, your Excellency," said Uncle Henry.

"Don't move a muscle Ben. It's a test," Uncle Henry transmitted.

Ben held his breath as the creature rubbed a water-covered tentacle over his head.

"Steady," said Uncle Henry. *"It lasts only a moment. Set a tone for your sister. Fear is not an option today. Am I understood?"*

"Yes," Ben answered. Not an option? Who was he kidding? Fear was shooting through every inch of his body but he isolated and froze each muscle and waited for further instructions as water dripped down his cheek.

Uncle Henry and Volari both shot a glance to the others. His friends seemed to understand and were rock still.

"And the others?" the squid asked.

"My charges," Uncle Henry said. "Casmirian, Shakrarian, Hayoolkááł."

The squid shot an appraising glance at each child then hovered over Carlos. "You are Casmirian?"

Carlos looked to Uncle Henry who nodded to indicate that Carlos should answer.

"Bey," said Carlos in a Mayan dialect. "Carlos, in k'aaba'e."

The squid's eyes lit up but he said nothing as he moved on to April.

Ben flinched instinctively. He'd been so protective of his sister he couldn't help reacting now.

The squid abruptly glided back to Ben. "Are you afraid?"

"Don't lie Ben. He'll know it," cautioned Uncle Henry. *"He is not aware of our telepathic abilities. Follow my instructions to the letter."*

Ben nodded.

"Is that a yes?" asked the squid, unleashing a torrent of tiny bubbles from his tubing.

"Tell the truth," said Ben's uncle.

"No," Ben flashed a look at his uncle. "I am not afraid."

"You are lying young warrior in training. I can smell your fear as it permeates the barrier between us," the squid said in a low halting growl.

"Tell the truth," repeated Uncle Henry. *"Don't bluff him."*

"I was temporarily on guard," Ben answered, keeping his gaze directed at his uncle. "I am trained to protect my sister until I am sure danger has passed."

Uncle Henry's eyes narrowed but he said nothing.

"And at your size who would you protect her from? Me?" The squid unleashed a loud, deep laugh and was joined by several others around the table. "You are but an insignificant guppy. A mere appetizer for my dinner guests."

"But I will die defending her like a warrior," Ben said, thanking the bootleg comic books he had once stashed in his pillowcase for the corny language.

Uncle Henry's eyes suddenly lit up in surprise or horror. Ben couldn't tell which. He swallowed hard and willed himself to stare up into the face of the giant squid.

"Perhaps I should put you to that test." The giant squid leaned close enough for Ben to feel the vibrations of its words against his face. The squid's eight arms gripped Ben's shoulders as two long tentacles emerged from behind and settled on the table in front of him. Rotating hooks on the ends of its tentacles looked like claws.

Ben nearly wet his pants.

"But not today," the squid continued before swimming to the head of the table, breaching the barrier and pulling out a chair. Like the octopus he retained his head and tentacles, but the remainder of his body transformed to make him look like the bulked up wrestlers on television. His robes were the most magnificent in the room—jewel and shell encrusted, flashing with iridescent threads that caught the light. Everything about the Atlantean ruler screamed *"Power"* and *"Don't mess with me!"*

"I am Calamar," said the squid nodding in Ben's direction and gathering his considerable robes about his body before sitting. "Welcome to the Atlantean High Council. Members may be seated."

The squid gestured for Uncle Henry to take the seat beside him. Volari took a place at the opposite end of the table near the Vampire squid.

"Impressive!" Uncle Henry shot a quick almost imperceptible glance in Ben's direction before returning his attention to Calamar.

Ben's heart soared even as he forced every permanently tensed muscle in his body to relax.

One test down. Three gazillion more to go.

CHAPTER SEVEN

What's For Dinner?

•ᵗ• Calamar leaned towards Uncle Henry but spoke loud enough for everyone to hear. "Your charges are impressive specimens. Are they all as outspoken as your nephew?"

"I'm afraid so," said Uncle Henry with a loud sigh.

"Then you have your work cut out for you," Calamar said. "And the makings of a glorious team."

"Thank you, your Excellency." Uncle Henry opened a box revealing a stainless steel interior and several vials. "I would like to present you with a token of our appreciation for your help these many years."

The giant squid extended his two tentacles, taking a vial in each. He stared appreciatively at the dark indigo liquid which sloshed against the sides of the glass. "Magnificent!" Calamar growled in a softer tone. "May I?"

Uncle Henry nodded.

Calamar passed the box to a council member who extracted a vial then passed the box along. Each vial was a different color, from deep forest greens to vibrant yellows to royal purples. A murmur of satisfaction rose from each delegate who drew something from it.

The rule about silence was killing Ben. He was dying to know what was in the box and how a container that small could hold so many vials.

Calamar leaned forward, one tentacle resting against his head. His gaze fell upon Serise. "You are Hayoolkááł?"

Serise gulped. One hand fell to her lap. Ben glanced and could see that she was using it to grip Grace's hand for comfort. "Yes."

"You cannot answer me in your own language?"

Ben felt sorry for her. He had no way of warning her about how to act. No telepathic way to send information.

"I can use it if you request," said Serise, clearly trying to keep her voice from shaking.

"No need," said Calamar. "I only meant to thank you, the young warrior in training and his fortunate sister. These vials contain a precious life-giving fluid. A mere drop of the liquid will restore entire sections of our ecosystems destroyed by the land dweller's waste."

As the box reached Ben —empty—he noted it was labeled with rows of hieroglyphics. He reached in as far as his elbow before he felt the bottom. He stared at the tiny exterior and wondered how his uncle had managed that magic trick.

"Synthesized by your mothers," Calamar continued, still admiring one of the vials in his tentacle. "Medie and Cheryl - as they were known on Earth - have done us a great service. We grieve their loss and have pledged our assistance in locating their remains."

The color in Serise's face drained.

"I don't believe they are dead," Ben said defiantly, not waiting for a dirty look from his uncle. "My connection to them remains strong."

"Yeah! Mine too!" said April suddenly. She took Ben's hand and gripped it tightly.

"And mine," said Carlos, taking April's other hand.

"And mine," said Grace, taking Carlos's hand.

"Me too," said Serise retaining her death grip on Grace.

Calamar unleashed an even louder belly laugh. "Yes indeed, Kurosh. Very fine specimens you have presented today. I feel their fear and am intrigued by their impudence. But they are strong warrior material. They meet with my approval."

He raised a glass in the air. "As you would say on Earth's surface, let the festivities begin. We feast to our alliance, to future good fortune and an end to the reign of terror from the enemy above and below."

Eighteen seahorses appeared at the barrier carrying enormous platters in their snouts. As they stepped into the air pocket they transformed into mermaids and mermen. Ben knew it was likely an optical illusion but his mouth dropped open nonetheless as a merman with raven black hair placed a covered dish in front of him and clear containers of liquid. Ben was grateful. The liquid wasn't green which meant Danine hadn't shipped an advance batch of his mother's disgusting breakfast formula to Atlantis.

The mermaids and mermen stood at attention behind each guest, their eyes on Calamar. He nodded. With a flourish they removed the silver domes covering the plates then retreated behind the barrier and floated away.

Ben looked down at his plate. Arranged on a bed of lettuce lay a row of bizarre, pale sausage. Then he looked closer. There were nails on the ends of the sausages.

Fingernails.

One finger still sported an engraved silver ring around its circumference.

Ben stared in horror at his friend's plates. Carlos had a foot. April had two ears and an eyeball. Serise's meal still had goggles and hair attached. And Grace? She looked close to retching on a foot that was probably a match to the one on Carlos's plate.

Ben dropped his fork, but caught it tightly in his grip before it clattered to the table. He glanced at Volari who devoured a plate of greens sprinkled with tiny shrimp. Served the same meal as Volari, Uncle Henry ate with gusto as did the other council members. The table was filled with animated conversation, the sound of clinking glasses and loud slurping. Ben blocked out translations of treaties, border disputes and a raucous argument about sonar waves and Naval testing sites. He stared at his food unable to comprehend what he was seeing.

"What ails you, young Sonecian warriors in training? Does the food not suit you?" Calamar tilted his head to the side. With no visible mouth it was hard to read his expression but his tone was clearly mocking.

Uncle Henry looked up abruptly.

"It's a person," Ben said. "Or what is left of one. Is this a test?"

"Isn't everything?" asked Uncle Henry. "Not all is as it appears. Eat the food with relish. Do not insult our host."

"Is something troubling you?" repeated Calamar.

"No," Ben lied. He stared at the fingers and tried not to let his horror show on his face.

"To honor your arrival we are serving only the finest sushi," said Calamar. "It took great effort to obtain these items. We hope it meets with your approval."

Ben looked at his friends whose faces were now the same shade of sickening green.

Uncle Henry continued to shove salad in his mouth while watching Ben closely. "Eat!" he demanded. "Set an example for the others!"

Ben poked gingerly at the finger on his plate. As he did, the food morphed into a plate of sea greens and tiny shrimp. The others followed suit and breathed a collective sigh of relief.

The council delegates laughed and nodded in approval.

Ben chuckled in relief. "I thought these were fingers."

"Would it have mattered if they were?" asked Calamar. "Quite a bit of human meat comes our way. If it is food we eat it. We do not waste."

"You eat humans?" asked April.

"Does that surprise you?" asked Calamar. "Tell me, what did you eat for dinner last night?"

The other delegates grew silent and listened with interest.

April hesitated.

"Kitty got your tongue?" asked Calamar before turning to Uncle Henry and saying, "And how is Aris these days? I owe him something."

"I know," sighed Uncle Henry. "He was appropriately disciplined for the transgression."

"As I was saying. What did the young humans eat for dinner?" He shot a glance at Serise. "Young Hayoolkááł? I monitored your approach to the city. If I remember correctly you referred to my cousin as a freak. On what did you dine last night?"

Serise shook violently.

Volari rose from his chair. "Cousin. That is past us. I received a proper apology. She is a protected class human."

"Indeed," said Calamar. "Does that prevent her from revealing the contents of her dinner?"

Calamar leaned forward. His voice dripped out in a slow, hypnotic cadence as he tapped his suckered tentacles together in tempo with his words. "Young Hayoolkááł, please enlighten us. On what did you dine? I can smell it in your system. Why not reveal it? I promise, I will not harm you for telling the truth."

Serise looked to her friends for help. Ben was grateful the heat was off himself for a change, but felt uncharacteristically sorry for her. Serise had bragged about being the only person with the courage to try the house special at the waterfront restaurant. Uncle Henry had tried to talk her out of it. But she had insisted. Gave the order to the waiter before Uncle Henry could object. She had eaten . . .

"Fried seafood," Serise said, her face streaming with tears.

Now all the delegates leaned forward. The room fell deadly silent.

"Could you be more specific?" asked Calamar.

Uncle Henry closed his eyes and bowed his head.

"Calamari," she sobbed. "I ate fried squid."

The room filled with laughter again as the delegates returned to their dining. Calamar leaned back with an air of satisfaction. "Thank you for your honesty, young Hayoolkááł. I trust it was adorned with an appropriate tomato and horseradish sauce."

Ben's mouth gaped open in surprise.

"You see," said Calamar. "Each of us at this table knows our role in the food chain. But humans don't appear to appreciate the sacrifice. Those squid you ate? Distant relatives. But all life is sacred and dependent upon all other life. Break the chain and we all die. That is why your mother's chemical formulas are so important. It helps us undo the damage done by top dwellers. Eradicates the disease caused by invaders. Restores our reefs and ecosystems. Until now you thought yourself a superior race."

"Superior?" exclaimed the Vampire Squid. "We had jet propulsion when their kind was still living in caves."

Calamar gave the vampire squid an angry look. The vampire squid scowled and resumed eating.

"As I was saying," said Calamar. "Now you know you are part of a vast food chain just as we all are. Mind you remember that on future excursions to the beach. To my shark friend here, you are just an appetizer on the way to his next meal."

The hammerhead shark gave each person an appraising glance as if determining their protein content and calorie count. Grace continued to pick at and under her salad looking for other strange items.

"Now, eat!" Calamar continued. "Build your strength! We have many battles to come. You'll find that the greens are composed of plankton and seaweed. Adorned with small shrimp from our zooplankton feeding stocks. No human meat is served here for State dinners. And like most sentient beings, we don't eat our own kind."

CHAPTER EIGHT

Tale of the Beast

•⁚• Ben picked at the salad greens, then stuffed a forkful in his mouth. He braced for the taste and found it was surprisingly good. He settled down, took a sip from his glass and relaxed. The liquid was an exotic fruit juice with just enough fizz to pass for a soda. Volari nodded his approval as Ben began to eat heartily.

"So cool being in the lost city of Atlantis," said Carlos.

Ben winced along with Carlos as they both recognized the mistake.

The vampire squid grunted and emitted an inky black liquid from beneath his collar. "Lost City? Who has lost us? Only those whom we did not wish to find us. We prefer the term 'hidden city'."

"The myth of Atlantis is to keep tourists busy," explained Volari. "It was once a ship used as a floating island upon our ancestor's arrival. Now submerged to prevent detection."

"Thanks to the departed Plato for writing a description of both our landmass and our location," said the Dragonfish. "He put what we hoped would remain legend to paper. We moved to prevent unwanted visitors."

"Outside of the Sonecians and the Dogon of Mali," grunted the Octopus, "no one was meant to know of its existence. We momentarily breached protocol by speaking to delegates from Eastern and Northern Africa. Our understanding is that Plato recorded stories passed down by Egyptian priests."

"We were listed as human!" The coelacanth sniffed. "That is the unfortunate consequence of giving tours to bi-pedal trash."

"Those who seek to discover our location are surely disappointed," explained Calamar. "We manufacture storms to keep the curious away."

"For all the good it has done us," huffed the shark. "Land-dwellers are as interminably curious as they are stubbornly clueless. But then again, my kind eat well in those circumstances."

Ben choked on his salad. April reached over and squeezed his hand. The salad greens cleared his throat quickly.

"You seem shocked, young outspoken Xenobian," said the dragon-fish. "Why? This environment belongs to us. Humans continue to ruin the land, soon the sea will overtake the land, and we will rule. They cannot live here, yet they poison us with their waste."

"There is a phrase in your realm," said the vampire squid clearly trying to fuel the conversation. "Finders keepers. Losers weepers."

"Yes!" said the shark. "We are happy to abide by human rules! Whatever falls off the land and into the water is ours to keep!" He smacked his lips greedily.

"Enough!" Calamar grunted impatiently. "It is time to start the meeting!"

A holographic projection rose from the table and spanned its entire length. Earth's continents and oceans rotated in the center, their three-dimensional form extending beyond the flat plane. Highlighted areas and points of light appeared all over the map.

The whale delegate rose from his seat. "We've noted seismic activity in these regions and increased tectonic plate movement. It appears that activity at the Earth's core has accelerated."

"Indeed," said Calamar. "The temperature from the vents has risen by 10 Celsius degrees."

"Is that a lot?" asked Ben.

"It's a shift of almost twenty degrees Fahrenheit. Enough to kill off an entire species and upset the food chain," said Carlos. "And if there is methane gas in the vents the increased temperature may cause it to explode."

"You are wise, young Casmirian. Perhaps you would like to train here with us. We have many interesting things we can teach you," said Calamar. "I have always admired your people."

Carlos shot a fearful look at Uncle Henry.

"He is required at the Harbor. As are all our charges. But thank you for your kind invitation." Uncle Henry eyed Calamar with suspicion.

"The tectonic plate activity is disruptive. Many of Earth's native aquatic species are beaching themselves: colossal squid in New Zealand, whales near Japan," said the whale.

"More troubling are the increased helium emissions near the Los Angeles basin. They are primordial in nature."

"What does that mean?" Ben asked.

"They date back to the origin of Earth," Volari said. He studied the readings and frowned. "This means . . . "

"Yes," said Calamar. "The helium originates in the Earth's mantle. The explosion in Sunnyslope may have worsened . . ." He looked at the children then continued. "Even with Rapa Nui terraformers coming online, we predict the western coast will sever from the continent within the next decade if we do not find a way to activate the others."

"Mudslides will be a problem for members of our alliance. We've relocated some species to the Marianas trench but the cold temperature and pressure at those depths poses a problem," said the giant octopus.

"Open a vent to stabilize the region, Barakas" ordered Calamar. "Tell teams to migrate toward the equatorial region."

The octopus nodded.

"We believe the beast is moving expeditiously to complete its plans," said the whale.

"Beast? What Beast?" Grace asked suddenly, her fork in mid-air, the salad on her plate barely touched.

"Perhaps you know of it as 'the devil', young Shakrarian."

"You've seen him?"

"Why do you assume it is a 'him?' Some of the worst beasts I've encountered are female," The shark winked. "Present company excepted."

"So is it a her?" Grace pressed.

"Perhaps. Perhaps not." Calamar tapped his tentacles together in a steady rhythm. "Why define something of that immense power in terms of such limited scope?"

"But you've seen him, her or it?" asked Carlos tentatively.

"No. We merely catch glimpses of the markers long after it is gone."

"It's old," said the dragonfish. "Older than civilization. Older than the planet. Perhaps as old as time itself. We believe it makes its home in the core of the Earth. Humans act as batteries for its power."

"As do many creatures," said Uncle Henry shooting a look at the delegates.

"Indeed, many have been seduced by the beast," Calamar confirmed.

"I'm sure you've seen the results on your news broadcast," said the shark. "Perhaps in one of their many thirty-second sound bites. Where WE are cast as the villains."

"We ordered the Hammerhead delegation to discuss our requirements with the Great Whites. The human killings off the Great Barrier Reefs were not authorized—," said Calamar.

"I am acutely aware of that," the shark retorted, cutting him off. "We had ordered the Great Whites to Florida to scare off the tourists with their fast food waste and their plastic amusement park trinkets."

The whale became agitated. "Aquatic parks are a disgrace."

"That has been resolved," Volari said quietly. "There is no need to revisit it."

"What do you mean resolved?" asked Grace. "What's been resolved?"

Ben wondered why Grace couldn't take a hint.

The whale unleashed a wide grin.

"The whales in Florida and California parks are animatronic," Volari answered. "When the Atlantean Council heard of the Sonecian rescue at Roswell's Area 51, they asked for similar dispensation in exchange for extensive data on ocean currents and tectonic plate movements."

The whale grumbled. "A killer whale turned into a docile creature performing circus tricks for money. What sort of role is that for such a powerful beast? They are denied their hunting birthright. Their connection to their tribe."

"We offered assistance," said the Shark, laughing. "We had an abundance of volunteers. To our disappointment, the Sonecian delegation declined."

"Land-dwellers hunt us, we should hunt them," shouted the whale, as the conversation continued to deteriorate into an angry exchange. He leaned in Grace's direction. Her face blanched. "For instance, the people of Japan increased their hunting of my kind to intolerable levels."

"But I'm from Tibet," Grace protested. "Why does everybody think I'm from Japan? Just because I like . . ." She froze in horror and didn't complete her sentence.

"Like what?" asked the whale. "By all means don't hold back now. Your righteous indignation is quite refreshing."

Grace buried her head in her hands. "Tibet isn't anywhere near the ocean," she said barely above a whisper. Serise patted her on the back and lowered her own gaze.

Ben groaned silently. *Here we go again.*

The whale left his chair, walked towards Grace and took a sniff. "As I suspected. Fresh octopus. Four days ago. Mixed with wasabi, pickled ginger and seaweed. Watch your back, Barakas. Seems some of your relatives are no longer with us."

The octopus grunted and narrowed his eyes.

"Who knew Sonecian females were so lethal?" said the Vampire squid.

"The octopus in her system is synthetic," Volari protested. "Mei-ling created seafood replicants from a soybean-based compound with some modifications at the molecular level to simulate the real thing."

"Ahh," said the vampire squid. "But Mei-ling has departed this Earthly plane. With her mother gone, this young Shakrarian may develop a craving for the real thing. Perhaps we should all watch our backs."

The squid rose and sniffed April. Ben tensed but held his reaction.

"This one is clean," said the squid. "Primarily vegetarian. At least for now."

Both Volari and Uncle Henry held their heads in their hands. Uncle Henry remained expressionless, but Volari appeared to be laughing — hard. His chest vibrated violently as his head shook back and forth in his palms and he emitted what seemed like chuckling sounds.

Grace and Serise clutched each other. Carlos froze as if he expected to be next up for attack.

"Have no fear, young warriors. You are Sonecian - there is a difference," continued the whale as he returned to his chair. "You are protected class. Your Earth-based human counterparts? Well, we can't eat them. I, for instance, am limited to krill for sustenance. But we are often happy to pinpoint their locations for our friends the sharks."

"At one point," said the vampire squid, clearly delighted with the direction of the conversation, "most of the whale species—represented so competently by our friend here—were much like many of your Sonecian teams — live and let live. They took the less effective non-violent approach."

"We are coming to see the wisdom in adopting that of our brethren the Killer whales as they are known topside," said the blue whale. "They are similar to Casmirians and so it shall be for my kind as well."

"We seek only a single ancestor," Uncle Henry said. "One whale."

"No," said the Blue Whale.

"We wish only to present a proposal," insisted Volari. "The whale shall not be harmed."

"No!" said the whale delegate. "I will not reveal his location. On this matter, my tribe is firm."

"Him?" said Uncle Henry, his eyes growing a bit wider.

The whale huffed and shifted in his chair. "Unfortunate choice of pronoun. Regardless, our decision is final."

"As you can see," said Volari, "the rise in the Beast's influence is causing ruptures in the natural order of things. As its power grows, wisdom and logic become corrupted. The council is committed to restoring order in their territories."

"Not that of the bi-pedals," the vampire squid quickly added. "We shall not help them."

"But you will die," said April. "If Earth blows up won't you blow up too? Doesn't seem logical to me. Shouldn't we join forces to defeat this evil thing?"

Uncle Henry coughed in protest.

"No," replied Calamar. "Let the young princess speak her mind."

"If we help land-dwellers and they end up destroying us what will we have gained? We prefer a quick death to endless torture by harpoon and fishing nets," said the bubble-eyed fish which, up until now, had remained silent. "Or disruption of ocean harmonics from military exercises and sonar wave disbursement."

"Oh." April said quietly.

The whale snapped, "It was decided after lengthy debate these many years. We shall not help land dwellers with certain exceptions made for Sonecian teams."

"But if the planet is destroyed, all life everywhere will cease," said Serise, her voice shaky.

"There are other alternatives. Earthquakes can be very effective in destroying life topside while leaving our kind reasonably intact," the whale said.

"And if that doesn't work? If the earth goes kaboom and takes out the universe too?" April waved her hands in a wide arc to simulate a massive explosion.

"So be it," answered the whale, his anger evident as sound waves shook the table. "Whales have their own hierarchy. Whales will have their own summit. Your naval sound waves are killing our kind even as you've eaten our flesh and burned our oils to stay alive. We are closer to your kind than any here at this table and yet your Earth counterparts exploit us. We will not help them in repayment for their disrespect."

Ben looked to his uncle for a reaction but he and Calamar were huddled in negotiation. Ben's uncle fingered a small, jewel-encrusted box in his hand then pushed it in the direction of Calamar but kept a tight grip on the prize. The squid reached into his lavish robes, produced a tiny box of his own and pushed it forward. Maintaining a grip on the first box, Uncle Henry reached for the one offered by Calamar. It dissolved. Uncle Henry shot Calamar a look of reproach.

"Perhaps Aris should return," said Uncle Henry, his voice dry and monotone. He cocked his head to one side. "Bastet is with him."

Calamar froze then dipped his two longest tentacles into the barrier behind him and clapped them together. A servant breached the barrier bearing a silver box that looked very old.

Uncle Henry relinquished control of his box and took the other into his grasp, a satisfied smile briefly crossing his lips before his stoic expression returned.

Calamar opened his newly acquired possession but only a centimeter or so. A blinding light shot out of it causing the other delegates to wince in pain. Calamar snapped the box shut and bowed his head appreciatively to Uncle Henry.

"What's in the box?" Ben asked out loud.

"Strategic advantage," said Calamar before Uncle Henry could respond.

"What does that mean?" asked April. "And is there any more of this stuff? It was deeeeelish!" She pointed to her now empty plate.

"Sometimes conflict is about tipping the scales, young Xenobian princess. And yes. We have nourishment in abundance. You need only ask." He leaned four of his elbows on the arm of the chair, emitted a high pitched sound and a merman appeared with a fresh supply of food for April.

Ben noticed an unusual twinkle in his uncle's eyes as he gazed at the polished silver box. That rare occurrence told him Uncle Henry had gained the upper hand, but there would also be no prying the secret out of him.

CHAPTER NINE

Danine's House Of Horrors

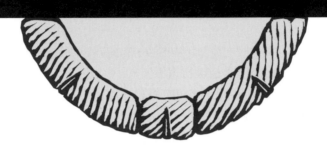

•ᵒ• Ben materialized in the Harbor's control room. Disoriented, he gasped, coughed and dropped into a crouch using his hands to steady himself until the room stopped spinning. He was not alone. Everyone fell to the floor as they came out of the transport beam.

Having completed their business in Atlantis, Uncle Henry had asked Calamar to assist him with a "ride home." Ben assumed that meant something fun like a ghost pirate ship, rides on the back of giant sea turtles or in bubble capsules towed by a whale.

Instead, a beam of light appeared in a chamber off the Atlantean dining room. Once inside, Ben expected the whisper soft tickle he heard the Harbor transport beams created. In reality it was like being spun in a blender and reconstituted at the final destination. As it turned out, Atlantis was state of the art for 500 BCE—its last known upgrade. Apparently transport to other water-based sites was easier on mammals than transport to land. Remembering Calamar's near-threat, he felt lucky to be back at Safe Harbor in one piece.

Uncle Henry and Volari had business in the Devil's Sea. Having suffered enough weirdness to last him a lifetime, Ben didn't ask to tag along. Grace and Serise looked as if they were thankful to be away from the Atlantean's scrutiny and were probably swearing off seafood for life.

As usual, the control room buzzed with activity with every holographic monitor streaming images of natural disasters, NASA updates and team activities around the world. No one seemed to notice that the kids had arrived. Ben could barely move from sheer exhaustion. Aris sauntered over to inspect him, then moved to April, leapt into her arms and purred.

Ben yawned. "I don't know about you guys, but I'm ready for some shut-eye."

"Me too," said Carlos. "Think we're supposed to hang out at your uncle's apartment until he gets back?"

"I'm afraid not," said Mansurat. The tall green man towered over them and obliterated most of the ambient light. It took a moment for Ben to realize he still wore a translator and could understand him. "While your quarters are being readied, Danine has requested your presence in Medlab."

"For what?" said April.

"Tests and a dermal scrub." Mansurat sniffed in disapproval.

"Maybe we should wait until my uncle gets back," said Ben. His friends nodded in agreement.

"Right," said April. "I don't feel sick."

"Apologies, young Sonecians. Danine is the final authority on medical issues. Only the Commander can overrule her and he rarely does it"

Ben sighed. He had never been sick. The only real doctor he'd ever met was Danine in disguise. But his visits had been short and pleasant so he figured he had nothing to fear.

"Okay," he said. "Let's get it over with so I can get some sleep."

"Many blessings, young warriors," Danine chirped as they trudged begrudgingly through the door. Her cheery demeanor reminded Ben of his mother.

Nothing in the all-white medical facility looked familiar. Gone were Danine's holographic projections which, in retrospect, looked like the sets on TV medical dramas. In fact, the only color in the room were the kids themselves and Danine's deep maroon skin. Her outfit and leather thongs were white, like everything around her. If Ben squinted, Danine's head looked as if it were floating in air.

"Come in. Make yourself comfortable," she said. "I need to take new baseline measurements for each of you."

"How come?" Serise asked wearily. Her face still looked ashen from the trip and she and been uncharacteristically quiet ever since she was forced to admit she'd eaten a relative of Calamar's for dinner.

"In case you need further assistance," said Danine. "Do not worry. Even in our holographic simulations we went to great lengths to spare you the agony of traditional Earth medicine. Now there is no pretense and we can dispense with what Earth people refer to as 'the ruse.' Sonecian science is much less invasive than primitive human techniques."

"Kind of like Star Trek," said Carlos.

Danine stared at him. "I do not understand the reference."

"Old TV show," Carlos explained. "People made a bunch of sequels, movies and reboots."

"I see," said Danine, still looking confused. "You will not need new boots during the exam but I will have some fabricated and delivered to your quarters if you would like." She pressed something on her tablet and five round platforms rose from the floor. She gestured. "If you please."

"No, thanks!" Ben yelped and stepped backwards. "Been there done that!"

"Yeah," said April, her arms crossed against her chest. "I'm not standing on that."

Danine frowned. Her skin tone shifted to light purple. Her cheery attitude evaporated. "It was not a request."

"Gosh," said Grace. "You sound like my mother. You have kids?"

"I have not yet been blessed with offspring," said Danine. "I have, however, heard your parents talk of their experiences many times. It has been enlightening. I believe the proper response for this circumstance is 'Don't make me say it again,' and 'I'm sure I made myself clear the first time'. Those are the correct parental phrases are they not?"

"Yes, Ma'am." Ben choked on his laughter and gingerly stepped on to the platform. He knew better than to argue. And he still wasn't sure what her changing skin colors really meant.

"Many thanks," said Danine, her skin returning to its maroon shade and her mood lifting. "Put your mind at ease. These are not stasis tubes. I did hear of your brief introduction to them. As I said, Kurosh lacks finesse with children but he does manage to convey his points efficiently."

"So what's next?" asked Ben. "What do we do?"

"Nothing is required," said Danine. "Simply stand quietly and allow the process to proceed."

Five tubes descended from the ceiling and encircled them. A familiar blue mist rose from the floor then turned the same purple shade as Danine's previous skin tone.

"Hey!" everyone shouted.

"This is a trick," said April. "I knew it!"

"Quiet please," ordered Danine. "I need accurate readings."

Ben banged on the glass tubing. "But you said—"

"I am sure I was speaking English," Danine said in a curt but distracted voice.

Ben shut right up. Danine had clearly done her homework on human parenting. He noticed that the mist was not cold this time. Actually, it smelled like the Freesia's in his mother's garden. Not lavender though. He almost wished it did. It was his mother's favorite scent.

Within seconds the thick purple mist reached Ben's head. He closed his eyes and waited for it to rise, but it stopped short of his chin. He opened his eyes and scanned his friend's tubes. The mist frosted the glass and obscured their bodies below the head.

"Ugh oh," said April "What's going on?"

"Shhh!" said Danine as she sat at a console.

"This is not right," said April, ignoring Danine's instructions by moving around. "Where'd my clothes go?"

Ben felt his thigh. His own clothes were also gone. He hadn't noticed them dissolving. The warm mist felt soothing.

"Biodegradable," said Danine. "The tank is maintained at body temperature. You should be comfortable."

"You mean we're ALL naked," said Carlos looking extremely distressed and red-faced.

"You are in your natural state," replied Danine. "Are you embarrassed?"

"Well yeah," said Serise in alarm. "I mean there are boys in here."

"And what can they see?" asked Danine with disinterest.

She had a point. The tubes were now solid below their chins.

"That's good," Grace joked. "Seeing Ben naked is sure to turn us to stone."

Ben growled.

"Well, I—" said April.

"Silence young argumentative ones! Extend hands and arms out to the side please." Danine had Uncle Henry's drill sergeant routine down cold.

Ben wanted to ask how they would accomplish that in the narrow tubes, but decided against it. He raised his arms until they were parallel to the floor. The tube widened temporarily to accommodate them.

"Now," said Danine, "Hold your breath and be perfectly still. The scan will only take a few seconds.

Across the room the white walls lit up with five human forms—a digital representation of each child. The names above each panel were in alien codes but Ben could still make out who was who.

He took in a lung full of air and held his breath as red beams streamed from the tops, bottoms and side of his temporary prison. A pleasant relaxing sound, like wind chimes, rang inside his tube.

On the far walls, near Danine's console, data and images streamed past. First the image of Ben's skeleton rotating in two dimension. Then lasers shot out of the screen. Five miniature skeletons rotating in three dimension materialized in front of Danine. The skeletons completed seven rotations before organs were added – fully beating hearts, a brain, stomach, kidneys and other things Ben should have recognized but forgot to study in class. A circulatory system soon filled in. The models looked like the ones in his school's science lab.

"Gee, Ben," said Grace. "You've got a spine after all!"

"Shhh!" said Danine. "If you are unable to comply with my instructions, I will be forced to inject you with a paralysis agent."

"Yes, Ma'am," Grace said.

Within minutes the skeletons were fully covered with muscles. A thought occurred to Ben. The next layer would be skin and its many layers of epidermis. Soon the miniature models would be anatomically correct.

Danine seemed to sense his discomfort. The models stopped rotating just before the skin was applied.

"Gross," said April. "Looks like that traveling show where you could see what real people's insides look like."

"Oh yeah," said Carlos. "The Body Exhibit. It was kind of cool and gross at the same time."

"Zip it!" Danine shook her head and let out a light chuckle. "One more moment, please and you can relax."

The monitors streamed with data. Limb measurements, height, weight, body mass—or so Ben guessed. Red blood cells flashed on the screen. Danine paused, then pressed something on the console, sending a stream of gold mist into April's chamber.

"Hey! That tickles. What is this?"

"Confirming your genetic coding," said Danine. "Xenobian patterns are a bit complex."

The gold mist entered Ben's chamber before turning blue, then black. Danine calibrated her equipment, looked at him a moment, then allowed the mist to dissipate. Every monitor filled with spinning lengths of double helix. A computer simulation rapidly unwound the strands, marking each rung with symbols Ben didn't recognize.

"That our DNA?" asked Carlos?

"It is," Danine said.

"I learned that only two percent of our DNA does something. The rest is junk, according to my teacher."

"That is an unfortunate and incorrect Earth conclusion," Danine said. "Nothing in life occurs by chance."

"Whoa!" said Serise. "So you know what the other genes code for?"

"I do." Danine continued watching the monitors, a smile creeping up her face as the genetic sequences completed their download. "Thank you, young warriors. We are done with this phase."

"So are you going to tell us?" Serise pressed.

"Perhaps another time," Danine said.

Ben waited for the tubes to recede. They didn't.

"I thought we were done."

"That is correct," said Danine, her eyes twinkling like a mad scientist. "The exam is complete. But you are each in need of a bath. I've ordered a dermal scrub. When the goggles lower, please place them on your eyes and nose. They will provide oxygen. If you are brave, you may watch the process. However, I would advise you to keep your mouths closed unless you want your teeth cleaned, in which case, open wide and clench them together. Don't be alarmed by the small lifeforms entering the tubes. As I am sure your uncle explained everything in the complex is recycled."

CHAPTER TEN

Home

•• "That was gross." Grace sulked as they followed a silent escort to their new quarters. "I mean, she could have warned us."

"She did." Serise hugged herself, wrapped her cotton robe tighter and shuddered.

"Yeah, but she withheld critical information," said Ben.

"I started panicking when she mentioned the life forms entering the tube." Carlos brushed himself as if still trying to detach them. "That was a clue to try to break the glass and escape. Wish I had a copy of my mom's combination car remote and laser gun."

"I'm not doing that again," said April. "It may be natural, but it was just wrong."

Ben shivered as his body involuntarily recalled the experience. The tubes had filled with a marvelously warm water. It was like taking a bath standing up.

"So far so good," he'd thought.

He had waited as the water rose above his head. The goggles had provided oxygen mixed with the appropriate amount of nitrogen— according to Danine. She also said something about infusing the mixture with antioxidants to lower the number of free-radicals detected in his body.

He should have been grateful.

He WAS grateful.

The soothing bubbles made him feel as though he was in a whirlpool spa or a hot tub. He had finally felt as if he could relax and drift off to sleep.

That is until the first black-striped fish entered the tank and began to pick at his skin. April had screamed something about being bitten by piranhas. Danine gave information in the same clipped way Uncle Henry did.

"Harmless fish . . . "

"Symbiotic relationships . . . "

"Can learn a lot from coral reefs . . ."

"The cleaner wrasse eat the dead skin and any parasites they find on the body . . ."

"The host in turn protects the fish from predators . . ."

Ben and Carlos both covered their privates as they walked down the hallway. Ben had to admit his body felt tingly clean. But the process was gross. And he was going to insist on underwear next time.

"I don't know about you," said Carlos, "but I'm thinking fish fry!"

Another first. Passive, non-violent Carlos was turning into a ruthless Casmirian piscivore.

The group arrived at a plain wooden door. Not having been at the Harbor long, every hallway looked the same. Ben wasn't sure where in the complex they were.

"How close are we to Uncle Henry's apartment?" asked Ben.

The almost transparent sentinel—a race Ben hadn't seen before—simply waved its hand, opened the door and gestured the kids inside. He didn't enter with them, but turned on his heels and vanished.

Into thin air.

Everyone's mouths gaped.

"Okay, we've got a lot to learn," said Ben. "But right now I'm exhausted. I've got to hit the hay."

"Hay?" mocked Carlos, imitating Danine. "Are you a horse?"

Ben walked across the room, grabbed a pillow and threw it at Carlos. "I could sleep like one. Standing up! Wonder where we bunk for the night?"

"That's easy," said April, peeking through a doorway. This room has three beds. That one over there has two. Three girls. Three beds. Two boys. Two beds."

Ben took a quick moment to survey the surroundings. Leather couches with fuzzy chenille pillows on one and tribal tapestry pillows on the other. A large round table with six chairs. A few abstract paintings hung on the walls. No television. No video games. No computer.

Ben sighed and wished he could use Serise's computer or his father's PDA to dial himself to an electronics store. But their devices had been confiscated and returned with the necessary transport software removed.

A bank of bay windows looked out to a view of his own backyard in Sunnyslope. A small button on the left caused the scenes to change: Venice, Hawaii, a mountain view and planet landscapes they didn't recognize. The selection seemed endless. They could pretend to be anywhere on Earth or in the universe. He was tempted to use Saturn, but instead he stopped at a Caribbean landscape.

"NO!" shouted Carlos. "I've had enough of those views."

"How about this," Ben mocked as he chose another.

"Atlantis? Be serious," said Grace.

"By the way, Serise," said Ben. "Want some calamari?"

"I'm sick of being the butt of jokes." Serise walked over, shoved him out of the way and scrolled through the menu of options. She chose Sunnyslope, their old neighborhood.

"Why there?" asked Grace.

"Because it's gone," said Serise before storming towards the girls' bedroom. "And I miss it. And at least the people there cared about me."

Ben picked himself up off the floor, winced and saw the shocked looks on his friends' faces. "Sorry. It was a joke."

"You can be such a jerk when you want to be," said Grace. She and

April rushed into the bedroom where Serise could be heard sobbing.

"Nice timing, Webster," said Carlos.

Ben sighed. He wondered if he should try to talk to Serise, but her anguished sobs told him he should wait. More than his wisecracks were at play. He understood how she felt. It was getting harder to mask his hurt than to give into it. There was still no word about his parents. And no way off the planet. Stuck with a weird assortment of space travelers who were no closer to solving the mystery of how to keep the Earth from blowing up. They were doomed.

"I'm sorry. Guess we're all stressed," he said through a weary yawn. "I'm going to get some sleep."

He wandered into the other bedroom and collapsed on the first flat surface he encountered. His first apartment and he was too tired to enjoy it. "We'll figure out our next moves in the morning. And I'll apologize to Serise."

CHAPTER ELEVEN

Get Up

•⁚• Harsh lights pierced Ben's closed eyelids. He peeked through narrow slits and allowed his gaze to focus. Kavera stood by the door with a bemused look on his face, a new strand of prayer beads coiled around his wrist like a bracelet. Aris, in house cat form, entered and sat beside him.

"Welcome back, brave warrior. I hear you spoke up to Calamar and survived unharmed. That's a Harbor first."

Ben looked at the clock. 6 a.m. A noise startled him. Carlos's snores were louder than a sonic boom.

"What happened to the last person that talked back to Calamar?" asked Ben, not sure he wanted the answer. His words slurred and he closed his eyes again.

Kavera laughed."Calamar ate him. Or at least he tried to. I was there, it wasn't pretty. Young, rash Casmirian warrior. Called Calamar an aquatic slime ball. Aris and Carlos's father tried to pry him out of Calamar's beak while thirty Sonecian team members held his arms and tentacles. The rest of the Atlantean Council stood to the side and took wagers. Aris bit off one of Calamar's arms in the process."

Aris blinked and bared his teeth. Ben could have sworn he was grinning.

"Danine helped Calamar regenerate a replacement," Kavera continued, "but it took years to restore diplomatic ties with Atlantis after that."

Ben's eyes popped open. His stomach wrenched as he remembered how close he'd come to suffering the same fate. Xenobian warrior? Forget it. The only safe place on Earth right now was this bed.

"Rise and shine," Kavera sang as he shook Carlos gently, then returned his attention to Ben. "Be of good cheer. The Casmirian warrior fully recovered and you have a full day of work ahead of you."

"No! I'm never leaving this room," Ben said, his words a groggy slur. "You people do stuff that's scary. I take it back. I don't want an adventure. I want a boring life."

The modified futon that served as Ben's bed featured controls to adjust the firmness. Ben adjusted his level to 'extra soft.' It was like sinking into a giant pillow. "Go away," he groaned.

"Time for calisthenics, young warrior. We allowed you to sleep in an extra hour."

"You've got to be kidding," Carlos groaned. "Glad it doesn't apply to me."

"Oh, but it does," said Kavera. "Pendon is expecting you. In fact, all the tribes have requested to train their own progeny. Although I've heard Calamar has offered Carlos the opportunity to train with the Colossal squid army."

"This is a democracy," Carlos groaned. "Ben votes to stay in bed. I do too. That's two votes to one. Majority rules. We studied it in Civics class. 'And to the Republic for which it stands' blah, blah, blah, etcetera, etcetera. It's the law. You're out voted. Go away."

"Yeah," said Ben. "We're endowed by our creator with certain inalienable rights." He curled into a ball and pulled the woven tribal blanket over his head.

"Perhaps I should convey that message to Kurosh?"

"Sure. Go ahead," said Ben "He's at some Devil's Sea place near Japan."

"Yeah," Carlos said through a yawn. "Too far away to yell at us. Even for him."

"He is in his apartment. Next door. Arrived late last night. In a good mood, I might add. Do you wish to be the one to ruin it?"

Ben lifted his head and glowered.

"Says right here on the duty roster. One Benjamin Webster and Carlos Lopez to report to calisthenics, then to the library for educational period."

"What about the girls?" asked Carlos. "How'd they get out of it?"

"They didn't. They got up as soon as I knocked."

"That figures. They're always sucking up," said Ben as he willed his legs to move. They didn't obey his mental request.

Kavera walked over to Ben's futon control and turned the dial. It inflated rapidly and pitched Ben on to the floor.

"Ahh! You're up!" laughed Kavera. "Nice of you to comply. I've brought food for you. Made a side trip back to Audrey's on the way home from Afghanistan. It is the last trip to that location. All future meals will be prepared in the galley. For today I secured homemade Belgian waffles and an array of breakfast meats. But if you aren't dressed and ready in twenty minutes, I'll have it removed and replaced with double doses of your mother's habitat mixture. I hear it's a gastronomical treat. What do you call it? Hmmm . . . let me think. Green glob?"

"You're evil," groaned Ben.

"Oh, you don't even know the half of it!" winked Kavera as he turned to leave. "I'll return in twenty minutes with escorts."

Ben peeled himself off the floor and used the edge of the futon to hoist himself up. He felt hot air on his neck, turned, and found himself staring into the eyes of a panther. He wondered how many shapes and sizes the cat had. Aris licked Ben's face with his sandpaper tongue before leaving to join the girls. Ben yawned, wiped at his wet cheek and reconciled himself to the inevitable.

"You awake?" he asked.

Carlos nodded but didn't utter a sound. His head remained buried in a buckwheat pillow.

Disoriented, Ben shuffled around the room. Two doors punctuated the rear of the chamber. He opened the first - a bathroom. But at the

Harbor, bathrooms were more like an evil scientist's laboratory than a residential comfort stop. It had holes to put "things" in or stoop over. A mirror hung over the modified sink. Activating it required the user to step on a small scale. It sent bio-data back to Medlab while the occupant brushed their teeth. Ben's mouth felt pasty. He found toothbrushes but no minty fresh toothpaste. Only a small jar marked with a scientific notation engraved on the jar.

"What's $NaHCO_3$?" yelled Ben.

"Sodium bicarbonate," said Carlos, his voice groggy.

"Is it safe?"

"Yeah. It's baking soda," Carlos mumbled.

Yuk!

Ben pulled up instructions on a panel near the door. The alternative was to partially submerge his face and allow cleaner shrimp and other small "biological agents" to do the work and remove the plaque.

No thanks!

The shower looked too much like Danine's cleaner wrasse torture chamber for Ben's comfort. He had wondered why there weren't any shower heads or controls. Now he knew.

Then there was the toilet. Too horrible to describe, his first inept attempt at peeing without properly reading the instructions nearly required bandages afterward. Ugh! He needed to go, but not that bad. He shut the door to the chamber of horrors and looked to the right.

The second door lead to a more pleasant discovery: a closet stocked with plain clothes, socks, shoes and underwear. Names woven inside the collars and waistbands indicated the intended owner. Ben's clothes were on the left. Carlos's were on the right. Apparently Danine's full-body scans served a dual purpose.

"What'ya find?"

Ben jumped before realizing Carlos was behind him.

"Uniforms. Look." Ben peeled back the waistline of a pair of soft white cotton pants. "Name tags."

"Good," said Carlos. "Was wondering what we were supposed to wear." He pulled out a sleeveless red tunic, black pants and a pair of soft leather boots. He checked to make sure the label bore his name then tossed them on the bed.

"Those are cool. Are you sure that's what you should wear to a work-out?"

Carlos nodded. "It's what my dad wore when he and my mom were working out." He yawned again and allowed himself to fall backward on the futon. "Want to go to the bathroom first? I got to go, but I'm not looking forward to it."

"I hear ya," said Ben. "Having things reach out and grab me is not my idea of a fun experience either. I say we hack some transport software, get those hotel codes from Serise and sneak out when we need to."

"It's a plan," said Carlos, eyeing the bathroom with trepidation before stepping inside.

Ben could smell the aroma of breakfast coming from the living room. His stomach growled. He dressed quickly. The white pants and tunic looked like the ones his own parents wore during morning exercises. The clothes moved like second skin, comfortable and soothing against his body. Better than anything he could get in a store. He wondered how they were made so quickly then decided he'd let that be just one more mystery to solve later.

He could hear the girls attacking breakfast out in the living room. For now getting his fair share of the food was his only priority.

CHAPTER TWELVE

Morning Calisthenics

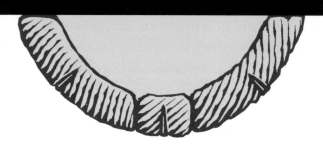

•᛫ Ben followed Kavera through a labyrinth of corridors. He was curious to see what the space teams did for a work-out. His basketball training would give him an advantage. He could play for hours without breaking a sweat.

They arrived at the far end of the complex. Like the courtyard near the living quarters, this room was massive, round and covered with a skylight. The room contained no weight training equipment or machines of any kind. Just rings and iron bars suspended above a wood parquet floor.

Ben couldn't believe the teams had been working out for more than an hour. Legs curled over the iron bars, warriors rose effortlessly at the waist. With each lift they twisted and touched an elbow to the knee on the opposite side before lowering back towards the ground. Ben groaned. He could feel the burn in his own abs even though he wasn't participating.

Others completed chin-ups with their legs folded in a yoga tuck, a teammate sitting in the folds for extra weight.

"We don't carry extra weight on the transports," Kavera said. "It's a waste of limited storage and burns much needed fuel. The team acts as its own weights and resistance."

"Am I supposed to be able to do that?" Ben asked.

"Make a muscle," said Kavera.

Ben flexed, proud of the rock-hard lumps he produced.

Kavera poked and laughed. "Not now, but perhaps sooner than you think. We are about to do a simple exercise. That will be enough introduction for today."

Aurelia entered the room wearing a sleeveless white tunic tied with a sash woven out of African Kente cloth. Her stern, unblinking expression was different from the friendly one she wore when she first arrived on Earth. She almost looked Casmirian. Her ceremonial knife hung from a sheath connected to the belt along with white prayer beads that matched his uncle's but now included the violet bead he'd given her.

Ben felt grateful that he had picked the correct uniform and had been complimented by Kavera for understanding protocol. Ben hoped his friends had fared as well. The Casmirian escort looked Carlos up and down, grunted then shoved him out the door of the apartment. The girls were still waiting for their own escorts when Ben left. April had to return to Medlab. A power surge had corrupted her medical data and she had to repeat the tests. Ben didn't envy her.

The warriors snapped to attention as Aurelia approached. Kavera produced a digital device which she reviewed without expression. Pursing her lips, she shook her head and returned it. "Adimu."

Kavera walked to the front of the room and shouted an unintelligible word. It sounded like "Mistari fomu!"

Ben realized he'd left his translator on the bed. He got Kavera's attention, gestured towards his ear and mouthed the words *"sorry!"*

Kavera seemed confused by Ben's gestures. He furrowed his brow, then brightened and nodded in understanding.

"Just follow my lead," he said telepathically. *"I said, 'line up!'"*

Aurelia stopped her inspection. "Benjamin?" There was no warmth in her tone. "You are unprepared? Where is your translator?"

"On the bed, Ma'am." Ben braced for a tongue lashing.

Aurelia didn't smile, but her gaze softened from a reprimand to simple resignation. "I trust this will serve as a learning experience.

I will allow Kavera to make appropriate accommodations this time only."

Kavera smiled broadly and winked at her. Aurelia winked back then returned to her "all business" demeanor. Ben wondered what that meant.

"Tunaanza!" Kavera shouted, then translated, *"We begin."*

Four warriors took places at drums placed near a stained glass window. They started with a simple rhythm. The remaining warriors followed by executing equally simple stretches.

Piece of cake. Ben touched his toes, raised his hands high in the air, then returned them to his toes. Only, as he looked around, everyone else had placed their palms flat on the floor. He grunted with the stretch and barely made it the whole way but missed the signal to rise. Now he was out of synch with their rhythm.

Kavera laughed. *"Piece of cake, huh? I wouldn't make assumptions young warrior in training."*

Ben scoffed and caught up. Two more repetitions were followed by a rise and arc to the side. The warriors swung from the waist, like pendulums. At the top of each arc their outstretched arms seemed like praise to the universe. Ben's stomach ached after the twentieth swing. He was using muscles he didn't even know were in his body.

The exercise repeated, only now the warriors bent their knees in a progressively lower stances. Ben gripped the floor with his toes to keep his balance. He was getting dizzy.

Left . . . Down . . . Right . . . Down . . . Left . . . Up . . . Over . . . Right . . . Down.

Five reps later they added side leg lunges.

Lunge left . . . straighten and down . . . lunge right . . . straighten and down . . . lunge left . . . straighten up . . . over . . . lunge right and down.

Ben could barely catch his breath as the speed of the drumming increased. He'd never make fun of his parent's stupid Tai Chi exercises again.

The drumbeats stopped. Everyone dropped to the floor.

"*Rest break,*" thought Ben, relieved.

"*Don't think so,*" transmitted Kavera, smirking. He remained upright, scanning and taking readings of the team as Aurelia walked up and down the line inspecting them.

"Kukaa juu!"

"*Sit-ups,*" Kavera translated.

Ben placed his arms behind his head. "*Piece of—*"

Kavera chuckled and Ben knew he'd just made another mistake.

The drummers beat their instruments forcefully sometimes switching instruments with their neighbor. They danced as they drummed, their massive muscular arms suggesting they were getting a work-out of their own. Ben wondered if he could do that instead.

After a few more reps of Xenobian torture, the rhythm changed. Slow, fluid and a lot of instruction from Kavera about keeping legs bent, toes pointed and arms strong and powerful as they stretched out. Ben felt like he was in a ballet class. Kavera demonstrated a stretch. He stood on his toes then tilted and lifted his right leg until it rose one hundred and eighty degrees and pointed toward the ceiling. The team followed effortlessly. The best Ben could achieve was ninety degrees, his right leg barely horizontal to the floor. Kavera appeared behind him, adjusting his torso into proper alignment. His muscles burned with the stretch. His leg rose only another ten degrees. Ben assumed the Xenobian rule was that if it didn't hurt, he wasn't doing it right.

Kavera laughed. "*That would be an accurate analysis for your current state of conditioning. Mild discomfort is normal for a beginner. But if it starts to be painful, then we'll reassess.*"

"*It's—*"

"*Not bad enough to warrant concern,*" said Kavera showing him a data monitor. Danine's Medlab readouts showed Ben's current activity levels still in the green zone.

Aurelia continued her inspection, occasionally straightening an arm here or there or pushing on a spine to straighten a back. The team's expressions were of intense concentration. Aurelia's appraising gaze, however, became even more critical.

Ben, on the other hand, didn't understand the rhythm and not just because he was a music lesson drop-out. Their movements didn't always fall on the beat. Parts were syncopated, requiring a sudden stopping of forward momentum to switch to a different direction. Ben's legs were forced to follow one beat while his hands and arms followed another. It was like trying to rub his head and pat his stomach at the same time.

"You're working parts of your brain that appear to lack previous activity," said Kavera, grinning. *"A mind is a terrible thing to waste young newbie warrior."*

Ben just glowered. He was too whipped to think of a snappy comeback. But Kavera was funny and seemed like he had "bud" potential.

Kavera grinned broadly. *"Don't worry, young rhythm challenged warrior. You'll get used it. And no one here will judge you."*

Aurelia watched his efforts with expressions ranging from alarm to amusement. No one would judge him? Yeah right. Only the head of the Xenobian elite squad. Ben felt grateful his uncle wasn't there to witness his failure.

Ben couldn't think of anything but going back to bed after drinking three gallons of water to replace what he'd lost in sweat. Sucking in a lung full of air, he prayed for a quick end to his misery and wondered how his other friends were faring.

CHAPTER THIRTEEN

Trials of Casmir

•⁰• Carlos entered the Casmirian arena and was immediately hit with air so hot the room might as well have been a blast furnace. The bright lights made him wince but he held his reaction in check as he walked past rows of Casmirian warriors lined up in military formation. He glanced back and found their commander—he supposed the guy was also his own commander —glowering at him. Pendon's face glistened with sweat highlighting a long scar that ran from his goatee, across his cheek, ending at the edge of his ear.

"You are late," Pendon barked.

Carlos was grateful that his father had insisted he study unusual dialects claiming one belonged to an obscure Central American tribe. Now he knew. He'd been studying his native language and as a result could respond with a flawless accent.

"I am here now," grunted Carlos as he worked to mask his fear and sound sufficiently tough.

Pendon growled. "Get in line with the others. Calisthenics is almost complete, then combat. You do know how to defend yourself, don't you, boy?"

"I am my father's son," said Carlos, lying through his teeth and grateful his tribe did not have the same telepathic skills as Ben's. He marched to the back of the line, attempting to mimic his father's macho swagger. It wasn't convincing—even for Carlos—but no one complained.

One of the warriors gave him an appraising glance, not unlike the one he received from the Atlantean hammerhead shark. She shoved a thick metal rod into Carlos's hand. It looked like the one his father held the day their home was destroyed but it had to weigh at least fifty pounds. His arm dropped in response to the sudden load. Carlos wondered how his parents had been able to handle it with a single grip. It took both hands to keep it at waist height. No wonder his mother traded up to a tiny laser beam gadget.

He studied engravings along the shaft, a mixture of Mayan, Incan and Aztec but with other variations. He wondered if he was related to all three cultures. After examining the rod for hidden controls, Carlos was mystified.

"Do you need a female to help you?" asked Pendon impatiently.

Carlos wasn't sure what comeback he could throw at the leader that wouldn't get him killed. He considered mimicking his father's gruff sarcasm, or even Ben's uncle, but decided against it. Both of those men could defend themselves in mortal combat.

Instead he shook his head, strained his muscles to lift the rod and gripped it until the carved patterns pressed deep into his flesh. He felt his thumb catch in a groove which moved as he bore down and revealed rotating channels. Carlos spun the channels in opposite directions as he lifted the rod. The blades extended. The Casmirian team completed the action in a single smooth motion with one hand. Carlos had a lot to learn.

"Where is your translator?" Pendon barked.

"On my bed where it belongs," growled Carlos.

Pendon grunted in approval, then proceeded to inspect the line. He pushed Carlos forward until he was surrounded on all sides.

"Proceed!" Pendon yelled.

Calisthenics consisted of ear-splitting chants about battle as the warriors walked through an odd series of kata. They used their rods to obliterate invisible opponents. Despite their gruff demeanor, their exercises were synchronized and matched the pattern of their battle recitations.

The warriors lunged forward to spear the enemy. Carlos moved quickly but not quickly enough. He felt a jab in the back.

"Hey!" He turned and saw one of the warriors glaring at him.

"You are soft," the man grunted. "Next time you will move more quickly or be disemboweled."

"And I will take you out with me," Carlos growled back, hoping the man wouldn't detect the fear in his voice. He figured if that worked for Ben when he spoke to Calamar, it might work for him too.

Carlos felt a jab to the right as another warrior grunted in frustration that Carlos was in the way.

"Perhaps you should return to the back of the room," he said. "That is where we put the babies and the daydreamers."

Carlos took two deep breaths, concentrated on keeping up with the exercise, and waited for an opening.

Lunge left. Plunge.

He willed his body to move with more speed and distance. He remembered Grace saying something about ballet lessons and Tai Chi. Stay in plié. It was a French term for keeping the knees slightly bent.

He shifted the rod in his two hands so that it was better balanced, dipped slightly and found that the lowered position allowed him to cover more distance on the floor.

Lunge forward. Plunge.

Carlos grunted and shoved the rod forward, tripped and narrowly missed the warrior in front of him by a mere two inches.

Turn sideways. Jab backward.

He was sweating with the effort. His legs felt like rubber but he remained upright and kept the rod from slipping out of his hands. He did manage, however, to slightly nick the first warrior who insulted him.

The warrior growled in anger. "You clumsy fool!"

"Surely a little nick is not an issue for such a strong specimen as yourself," Carlos grunted. He was trembling. "Perhaps it is you who should move to the back of the room." Okay. Now he was now mimicking the Atlantean leader. It didn't take much effort to copy Calamar. He began to think training in Atlantis was a preferable alternative to this brute force.

Lunge right.

He willed what little remaining strength was in his arms and poked the warrior to his right on the side in payback for his previous insult.

"And take this fool with you," Carlos grunted.

He winced and waited for what was surely going to be a violent response. Instead the warriors broke out in a hearty laugh.

"It appears the little mouse has a mighty roar," said the tall one.

"So it seems," said the other laughing as well. "Just stay out of the way and keep up. We'll try not to kill you before the exercise is complete."

As the warriors ended the mock battle, they waved their rods in victory and twirled them rapidly as if they were performing a half-time show at the Superbowl. Carlos's arm almost dislocated from his shoulder. He couldn't keep his rod lifted high enough let alone make it twirl in his hands. He felt the hydraulic pressure failing him as the muscles and nerves in his arms refused to obey the electrical impulses streaming from his brain.

His energy waning, Carlos found himself being smacked in the head, arms and sides to a rousing refrain of "Idiot! Get out of the way!" He dropped to the floor and tried catching his breath. Humiliated, he now understood why the armies in his father's computer games had deserted him. He wanted to raise a white flag. Surrender. Get it over with.

But he couldn't. It would be considered a disgrace to his father. He willed his aching body to move. It declined the invitation.

Through a sea of legs he could see Pendon staring at him in disgust. "Do you need medical attention, boy?"

"No," Carlos said. Closing his eyes, he summoned power from some untapped internal source and, ignoring the screaming pain from his bruised knees, rose to his feet. He brought the rod up to his chest, then above his head. About now he was wishing he could trade places with Ben. At least Kavera had a sense of humor, although the jury was still out about that Aurelia woman.

He waited for the end of the exercise then drove the spear into the floor with the others.

Pendon peered at him with a sly smile. "Calisthenics are complete. Pick a partner. Time for one-on-one combat."

Carlos froze in horror and considered asking to be locked in a stasis tube when a warrior twice his size tapped him on the shoulder and gestured to an open spot on the floor.

Carlos sighed. There was no white flag in sight.

This was going to be a massacre.

CHAPTER FOURTEEN

Wings

•⠂• Serise stood ten feet from the precipice, watching as other warriors swooped and soared across the sky. Her friends were training at the Harbor, but she'd transported to a remote island in the South Pacific. She fingered the lapis lazuli necklace that was given to her just before they left the control room. A tiny blue tear drop on a silver chain.

"Come join us, young princess," said a team leader who identified herself as Kyloria. "First leaps are always hard."

Instead, Serise took in slow sips of air to mask her fear. "I never learned," she admitted. "I don't know how."

"Such a burden for your parents," said Kyloria, her brown eyes sparkling in the sunlight. "To not be able to reveal their true nature. Or course they should be the ones to teach you. I am sorry for your loss and pray they are found soon. You may watch for now."

Relieved, Serise sat on a rocky outcrop and watched the graceful flights in front of her. In the distance, some warriors looked like kites, buoyed on currents of air but staying fixed above the ground instead of moving away. Whoops of joy erupted. She waited until Kyloria had flown to inspect someone's progress on a nearby cloud before allowing a stream of tears to escape.

"The gravity here is different than on our home planet," said a voice behind her. She quickly wiped her face with a sleeve and turned to find the young warrior she'd seen on the yacht before he flew away. She still had his feather at the apartment.

"You are in distress?" he asked as he sat beside her.

Scrise wiped a straggling tear with her thumb. "No. Just allergies. I'll be fine."

"I was curious why you chose to stay at the water's edge, but Kyloria explained. I thought I'd join you for a moment."

"What's it like?" Serise asked. "Home, I mean?"

"It is lush and green. Not unlike this place," he answered. "Earth's gravity is less than on our planet making flying effortless. But here the currents of air are also unpredictable. We enjoy the challenge. The Earth's rotation sometimes varies." He thought a moment. "I believe the term is 'wobbles' about its axis. It is not enough for humans to detect, but enough to provide great training for us. For instance, Dazal there to the right." He pointed toward a woman whose hair was drawn into a single braid, balancing beneath a cloud and allowing a gust of wind to move her backwards and forward, her arms outstretched. "She is studying what your people refer to as the Coriolis effect."

Serise frowned. "I don't know that term."

The warrior shifted his weight. "The way the ocean currents are affected by wind current." He pointed. "Chotze will move higher and try to catch a jet stream. One could say he enjoys speed and acceleration. Perhaps more than is prudent. But we indulge him. We've asked the Harbor to replicate a solar pulse to see what changes occur when the electromagnetic energy in your atmosphere changes. Perhaps we will travel north to study the Aurora Borealis. I hear the light shows are magical to view in the night sky."

Serise studied him intently and shrugged.

"You should try," he said gently. "It will become second nature in time."

She shook her head. "Everyone's so strong. I'd just get in the way."

"I see." He held out his hand. "I am called Micique. May I?"

Serise eyed him curiously but did not take his hand.

"Close your eyes," he said.

She hesitated. He waited patiently. "Trust in your team, young princess."

Trust. That seemed to be a theme these days. She'd trusted her parents and her life had been a lie. Her friends trusted her and they'd gotten lost looking for the Harbor. Trust ended in a life filled with doubt and uncertainty. She'd lost all connection to her family and now, here were the replacements doing something she could never do in her wildest dreams. Ben's mother's habitat mixture had taken care of that.

She felt a gentle tap on her shoulder.

"Close your eyes, young princess." Micique waited patiently for her hand. When she complied, she felt him place her palm on his own.

"Keep your eyes closed," he said, closing his hand to create a firm grip.

Soon she felt a rush, a kind of tickle, in the center of her stomach that flowed up through her and out her shoulders. A breeze lifted the strands of her hair.

"Keep your eyes closed," Micique repeated. "That is the most important part. This is about letting other senses guide you."

She felt her feet leave the ground and tried to jerk her hand away but Micique's grip was firm. Someone else took hold of her other hand and suddenly her arms stretched out at ninety degree angles to the side. More hands held her upper arms for support.

"Patience," Micique insisted. "I will tell you when you can look."

The breeze intensified, even though she was hovering only inches over the ground. She'd felt no movement except for the slight lift from her resting place. But she wasn't scared. She felt safe with them. Suddenly she lifted higher. Only a few inches, she was sure. She'd flown on a plane once, with her eyes closed the whole way, and even then she could tell she was thousands of feet above the ground. The pull of gravity is a reliable gauge of proximity.

"Keep them closed," Micique repeated.

She remained still, balancing on a current of wind, the tips of her toes pointed down but not touching the ground. "We're going to tilt your body. Feel yourself float as if you are in a pool of water. But don't open your eyes," a women said.

The roar of the wind grew louder as the temperature dropped. Serise felt mist settle on her face and hands.

"Is a storm coming?"

The woman holding her other hand laughed. "No. Just the nature of the wind to be arbitrary on its way to its destination."

Serise tilted backwards and felt as if she were back at the Harbor resting quietly in the harmonic hammock Ben's uncle provided on her first night. She relaxed and sank into the cool jets of mist flowing around her. She let her breath flow in and out as she rocked on a gentle breeze and felt the tension release. This was no scarier than being blindfolded for the Woodland Challenge. Or in the cave beneath Rome. But this time she would wait to open her eyes.

She was gently guided into a vertical position. In seconds her shoes felt the resistance of solid ground. The exercise was over.

"Open your eyes," Micique said.

Serise wasn't sure she wanted to let go of the feeling. As frightened as she was of heights, she wanted to maintain the illusion she'd been with the others, high above Earth. Untethered. But she couldn't remain in this fantasy forever and she did as she was told.

Micique stood next to her smiling. "That is a good start for today. Not as intimidating as you believed?"

Serise smiled sheepishly. "No," she said. "Not so bad. But I don't think I'm ready to go up to the clouds, though."

He chuckled.

Serise grew guarded and a little hurt. "What's so funny?"

The young warrior shrugged and pointed to a cumulus cloud where Dazal hovered, waving at them. "You were there flying with us only moments ago!"

CHAPTER FIFTEEN

Shakrarian Princess

•• Grace sat cross-legged in the middle of a dimly lit room. All around her, white cloaked figures loomed and prayed. She closed her eyes and breathed deeply as instructed. She brushed her hands against her calves to make sure her fingers still felt like flesh and blood and not the skeletal bones she saw the day her tribe arrived.

A gentle vibration flowed through her. Again, as instructed, she opened her eyes. The room was dark. She was alone. Or maybe not. A shape hovered in the shadows. She assumed it was her tutor, Tenzin, observing her reaction to the changing environment. She fought to overcome her intense fear. She'd survived the spooky environment of the underground Vatican outpost. She'd gone through the secret opening of a mummy sarcophagus first. She was strong. She could do this. All she had to do was concentrate. Become one with whatever image presented itself.

She imagined this exercise wasn't much different than what Ben and Carlos had to go through during their vision quest in Sunnyslope. They survived. There are no ghosts she told herself. No monsters. Only what lurks in one's own subconscious mind.

The wait was interminable. She began a sequence of meditation. She tensed every muscle in her body and then, slowly, relaxed them in sets. First her shoulders.

There are no ghosts.

Then her arms.

No monsters.

Then let her fingers go limp.

Only what lurks in one's own subconscious mind.

All the while she controlled her breathing.

Slow deep breath in through the nose.

Long, slow exhale out the mouth.

Repeat.

Something brushed past her. She looked up hopefully, expecting to see Tenzin standing there.

Instead she let out a scream and collapsed.

CHAPTER SIXTEEN

The Librarian

•• Done with training, Ben stumbled into the library. He turned to find his holographic escort had evaporated. Once inside, he expected a futuristic environment. Digital devices were, in fact, scattered around the room, occupied by members of various tribes all streaming data at superhuman rates. But the library looked more like a cathedral with its buttressed ceilings, ten story stone columns, archways and iron balconies. Books were crammed into every nook and cranny.

Sitting at a round table to the left of the doorway, Carlos held an icepack on the top of his head while Serise rubbed his back. April scampered through the door behind Ben.

"What'd I miss?" she asked. "Something good? Or maybe not from the way Carlos looks."

Ben groaned. "A lot of exercises, dancing and drumming. Xenobians can go for hours without breaking a sweat. Their idea of fun must be twenty-four hours of Cross Fit." He groaned again and collapsed in the nearest chair. "What did Danine do to you in her lab of horrors?"

April laughed. "Nothing. She just took some blood tests. She's good. I didn't even feel the stick. She said something about analyzing my chromosomes and my mitochondrial DNA, whatever those are, then she told lame jokes and kept cracking herself up while she ran the samples through the computer. You know, like, 'What do you call a futzul that when launched as a projectile fails to complete a return to its origin. A bartog!' I had to get her to translate that into English to figure out what she was talking about. It's supposed to be, 'What do you call a boomerang that doesn't come back'."

Ben blinked.

"Well?" April asked. "What do you call it?"

Ben groaned again. "I have no idea."

"A stick," April said. "Once I got it, I laughed to make her feel better, then I told her some knock-knock jokes. She didn't get why a person would ask 'who is there?' if they were standing in front of the person telling the joke. She is so nice but so weird at the same time."

Ben groaned. "Lucky duck. Carlos? You okay?"

Carlos answered Ben's question with a grunt, shook his head, then moved the ice pack to a ripe red bruise on his leg. "I lived to tell the tale. I guess that's something. They're like Klingons and Predators, only without the honor," he said, before slumping and letting his head rest on the table.

"Serise?" Ben asked.

Before she had a chance to answer, the door opened and Grace walked in. Her face was pale but otherwise a blank slate.

"We were just sharing today's fun adventures," Serise said. "Ben's team dances nonstop like the Twelve Dancing Princesses fairytale, Carlos's team tries to see who can hold off death and injury the longest, and my team imitates kites and plays with wind currents."

"And you did it?" Grace said, her voice quiet and distant.

Serise laughed. "Not voluntarily. Think cave, eyes closed, and Woodland Challenge at school. Think scariest thing you can imagine with or without a blindfold and no, I'm not doing it again."

Grace nodded and sat at the table. "Good luck with that."

"So you going to spill the beans?" Ben asked.

"About what?" Grace asked.

"Training. Team stuff. What happened in your session?"

Grace shrugged. "I don't want to talk about it." She sighed and looked away. "Are we going to get some lesson plans or what?"

Ben shot his other friends a look. Even Carlos looked concerned. There was silence for a few minutes. Finally, April spoke up.

"Anything we can help with?"

Grace eyed her thoughtfully, then shook her head. "No thanks. I can handle it."

"You sure?" Serise asked.

One tear hovered in the corner of Grace's right eye. Then she nodded.

Now Ben was alarmed. While Grace studied the library, head raised to scan the top level, he grimaced and then gestured to Serise and April. "Find out later?" He pantomimed falling to sleep then pointed out the door.

Serise gave a quick thumbs up and got a fist bump from April.

A hologram appeared at the middle of the table. "Greetings, young Earth warriors!" said a cheerful woman dressed in a robe with more colors than a box of crayons. Her bright white hair coiled in an enormous bun on top of her head. Bits of paper and writing tools poked out from the many pockets. "I will be your tutor until we are able to return you to your home planets."

Ben groaned and wasn't alone.

"What's your name?" asked April.

"Name?" asked the woman. "One has never been necessary. You may choose one that you makes you most comfortable."

The librarian fumbled around in one of her pockets and pulled out an old notebook. "It says here that Earth protocol is to first administer an assessment test to determine the proper level of instruction. Let us start with rudimentary avionics."

A new hologram appeared, projecting a three-dimensional image of a triangular spacecraft in a solar system Ben didn't recognize.

"Please use the position of the stars to identify the ship's location in the Sonecian galaxy then calculate the approximate distance from the nearest star."

"Uh, what?" asked Carlos.

"Identify the ship's location and calculate the distance from the nearest star."

No one moved.

"Do you need assistance?"

Everyone sat in stunned silence. Finally April spoke up. "We don't know this stuff."

The librarian seemed perplexed. "My apologies. It appears I was programmed using Sonecian curriculum. I suspect the teams wanted to quickly get you up to speed." She rumbled through her holographic pockets and produced a red notebook, this one much newer than the other. "I have reset my program for Earth related lessons." She wet her index finger and flipped through the pages. "Ah! Let's try this one. Human aircraft can travel at an average of 510 knots. Please translate that into parsecs per hour."

No one moved.

"Hint," the librarian said. It would be an extremely small number. Very close to zero."

"What's a parsec?" asked April.

"You are younger than the others. Perhaps your companions can explain?"

When no one answered the librarian frowned. "A parsec is used to measure large distances between an astral body and its sun."

Silence.

"Perhaps it would be easier to state your answer in kilometers or miles per hour?"

Ben shook his head.

"Hmm!" the librarian said, fumbling through her notebook. "Perhaps this question will be easier. Earth people once invented a vehicle that could travel at twice the speed of sound. Name the aircraft."

Laughing, Carlos raised his hand.

"Ahh. Much better," the librarian said, her cheeks flushing pink. "Young Casmirian?"

"I prefer Carlos," he said. "It was the Concorde. It had to fly in the upper atmosphere because its speed caused sonic booms. They don't make it any more after one of them crashed."

"Correct!" the librarian said beaming. "Now tell me its average rate of speed at twice the speed of sound……"

Carlos frowned and sagged, but Grace and Serise waved their hands like parade flags.

" ….and how that changes based on Earth's ambient air temperature. Feel free to use Celsius, Kelvin or Fahrenheit for temperature calculations."

Grace and Serise's hands quickly fell to their laps. Ben wondered if he could hide under the table until the test was over.

"I see. Perhaps this is a bit much given your exhaustion and adjustment to your new environment."

"It's a bit much," said Ben, "because Earth schools don't teach this stuff to kids."

The woman cleared her throat. "What do they teach?"

"Stuff like one plus one equals two, things like that," said April. "Or i before e except after c. But not airplane stuff. Kids here aren't allowed to fly or go to outer space."

"How unfortunate," the librarian said. "Your parents were already piloting crafts at your age. Both the Webster and Lopez vehicles were modified to look like automobiles. The outer skins drew energy from the sun. Did your parents not teach you how to fly them?"

The look on everyone's face could best be described as shock and awe.

"So that's how we were getting to school early even when we left late," said Ben, closing his eyes and conjuring memories. "Once Dad drove so fast it felt like being launched into space. And that explains why I never saw him go to a gas station. But no, Dad and Dr. Lopez kept that whole 'my car is a rocket ship' thing a secret."

"My apologies. You must miss them terribly. I shall skip avionics for now and focus on math." There was a flurry of activity from beneath the librarian's robes. More arms flew out and stretched toward shelves behind her. Finally, a bound manuscript flew down from a shelf and landed on the table with a thud. Calculus by Gottfried Leibniz, dated 1684.

"Nope," Ben said. "Too advanced. This is your first time handling Earth kids?"

"I must confess it is," she said. "But not to worry." Her hands reached out again and she found a text book dated within the last year.

"Where'd you get that so fast?" April asked.

"I have access to every book on Earth," said the woman. "Given the proper requirements I can find anything."

"Down here?" April pressed. "I mean this library is humongous, but it can't have every book."

"Down here," the woman replied, "it does not. But the books that surround you are not, as you say, down here."

There was silence as everyone stared around the massive space. Balconies ringed the room and there were at least ten stories, each with racks of books extending as far as he could see.

"I don't get it," Ben said. The air on each level seemed to vibrate. But that wasn't possible. Unless . . .

"Those levels are gateways," April shouted with excitement. "The books aren't here, you just transport to where they are."

"Correct," said the woman. "It would not be practical to store a copy of every book ever printed. The rooms on the lower two levels contain what we could salvage from ancient libraries. They are sorted by civilizations. Our earliest teams were able to retrieve half the scrolls and parchments housed at the Great library in Alexandria before it was destroyed. Contemporary books on the upper levels are accessed through portals."

"So I could walk into the Library of Congress," said Carlos.

"Correct!" said the woman. "Or the Vatican archives, and the Smithsonian. Those not open to the public are accessed after hours to minimize detection and we always return what we borrow. That is a Sonecian rule."

"Slick!" said Carlos, his eyes popping. "I might just live in here."

"We never close and I am always at your disposal," the librarian said. "Now, it is time to return to our lessons. Let us start at the beginning and advance until we determine your individual levels of proficiency.

She opened the book and, using her finger, wrote out a number in the air which formed as a glowing mist. "This is?"

Ben laughed. "Zero."

"Correct! And this?" The librarian wrote out "1."

"One," said April. "This is kindergarten stuff. We don't have to start back this far."

Ben kicked his sister underneath the table. "Easy A," he said telepathically, not sure she was able to hear it.

"I see," said the librarian. "One more, please to verify your statement of 'easy'." She wrote "10."

"Ten," Grace groaned.

I'm afraid not," said the librarian

"Yes it is," said April. "Even I know that."

"It is not," the librarian repeated.

"I think your program is broken, on Earth THAT is a ten!" Ben said. "If it's not, then what is it?"

The woman looked perplexed. "You honestly don't know? It is the most basic of languages. The number represents 'two' in Earth language."

While everyone shook their heads, Serise sighed loudly. "She's asking us about machine language. It's binary code."

"That is too simplistic an analysis. This code and math are the universal language of the universe!" The librarian beamed. "Let us begin!" She opened a portal and a large code appeared. "What is the meaning of this?"

01000001 01110000 01110010 01101001 01101100
01000010 01100101 01101110 01101010 01100001 01101101 01101001 01101110
01000011 01100001 01110010 01101100 01101111 01110011
01000111 01110010 01100001 01100011 01100101
01010011 01100101 01110010 01101001 01110011 01100101

Ben groaned. Sick of codes and clues, he suddenly longed for the days of basic math and a life as a real boy.

CHAPTER SEVENTEEN

What's for Lunch?

•ᵒ• "I would like some meat," Ben said, staring at a short green life form that was a dead ringer for an Oompa Loompa from a Willie Wonka movie or a Munchkin from the Wizard of Oz.

"You are vegetarian," he, she or it replied as it heaped a third mound of steamed vegetables on Ben's plate, most the same shade as the cook. Those servings were followed by a heap of casserole filled with bland beige cubes that looked suspiciously like tofu. Ben stared at the grotesquely large hunk of grilled meat on Carlos's plate. A trade was in the making.

"I would like some meat," Ben repeated.

The alien cook seemed confused. It stopped as if accessing an internal database, its red eyes going blank for a moment. "Unauthorized. You are vegetarian."

"Carnivore!" shouted Ben, exasperated. A hush came over the dining hall as team members across the room looked up. Across the aisle, the Casmirians nodded in agreement and a particularly large warrior raised his glass and an even larger rib of meat in salute. Ben lowered his voice but remained firm. "I am a carnivore. A meat eater. There must be a mistake in your files. I'm not human.

I'm a Tyrannosaurus Rex." He pointed towards the corner of the room where Aris and Bastet in panther form were tearing apart a heaping mound of raw meat twice their combined height, their loud growls punctuating their joy. "I want some of that yummy goodness, only cooked well done with french fries on the side! Oh, and vanilla ice cream for dessert."

"You are vegetarian," the cook repeated as if that were the sum total of its English vocabulary, then added two ladles of unidentified purple berries and two cherry tomatoes to Ben's plate. "Dessert and garnish." It blinked once, then twice as its long fingers curled around the ladle and a pair of tongs. "More?"

"No," Ben grumbled. "I have MORE than enough, thank you!" He stomped over to a long stainless steel table where his friends were gathered. Grace and Serise had well balanced food pyramid selections and were slipping steamed fish onto April's plate. She looked grateful even though she might be eating relatives of the Atlantis delegation.

"Got your back bro," Carlos said, giving Ben a quick nod. "I think that thing put an entire cattle ranch on my plate. I'll trade two sides of sirloin for some of that broccoli and a few sprigs of parsley." They scooped food onto each other's plate.

"Is it me, or is life at the Harbor about as exciting as my little finger," said Serise eyeing a waxy yellow plant snared on the tip of her fork. "Almost everyone is on a mission and we're stuck here with the skeleton crew."

"Perhaps we can fix that!" Kavera slid onto a bench at the head of the table, his long braids cascading around his shoulders. His plate was filled with the same bland choices as Ben, only he had twice as much. "What ails you, young restless warriors?"

"The librarian is nuts," said Ben. "Look at the homework." He put a digital tablet with the binary code in front of Kavera.

Kavera laughed. "Easily translated. Much easier than the game clues I created for your uncle. There is little challenge in that code."

Ben glowered. "Wanna give me a hint?"

"If I remember correctly, Grace once said a clue was as plain as the nose on your face when you played the digital game meant to lead you here."

"You were watching us?"

"I was listening," said Kavera. "For your safety and to give a tiny push when your uncle wasn't looking. And so, with my hint, you should be able to decode the homework. And I will add another. From one friend to another. It is an alphabetical list."

Serise groaned, looked at the code again, then mimicked writing in the air with her index finger. Finally she said, "April, Benjamin, Carlos, Grace, Serise."

Kavera nodded. "It appears your problem is solved. Let us rejoice with this fine repast the new chef has prepared!" He took a bite of the tofu casserole, grimaced in horror and put his fork down.

"We have a list of demands," said April. "Like normal bathrooms that don't try to attack you when you use them. And a tub with jets and maybe some bubble bath. And a television, some computers, ice cream, and clothes that don't look like pajamas, hospital scrubs or yoga outfits. That last part is NOT negotiable."

Kavera chuckled. "I'll see what I can do. Perhaps a tub in exchange for the answer to a riddle? I have several that went unused when designing the game."

Everyone groaned.

Finally, April said, "Go ahead, give it your best shot."

"I get wet when I dry."

Grace dropped her fork. "What?"

"You have all you need to decipher the riddle," Kavera said. "I'll arrange a tub when you figure out the answer. And no, the librarian will not reveal it. Are there any other requests?"

"No red shirts when you get us decent clothes," said Carlos. "I'm kind of superstitious. I wore one to training and almost didn't make it back alive."

"Understood," Kavera said. "No red shirts if you answer the following: There are two men wearing backpacks in the Libyan desert. The Xenobian whose backpack is open survived. He is wearing a blue shirt. The stubborn Casmirian whose backpack remains fully packed but unopened has died. He is wearing a red shirt. What is in his backpack that could have prevented his death?"

Carlos laughed. "What?"

"Determine the answer and I will provision clothing in any shade but red."

Carlos grinned. "I already know the answer to mine. What's in the unopened backpack? He was late arriving with Pendon's dinner."

Kavera burst out laughing. "I am tempted to reward you for that clever solution. But no, that is not the answer. And now, young warriors in need of a fashion makeover, is there anything else you require?"

"I need something to do," said Serise. "My mind is a terrible thing to waste and no, I'm not answering riddles. This whole place is one big riddle."

"You are training with your team, are you not?" Kavera grinned and tilted his head. "I hear you've recently explored the density of a cumulus cloud in the South Pacific."

Serise frowned. "How much did Micique tell you?"

"He revealed nothing of your outing. Danine monitored your progress remotely."

Serise groaned. "Does she have eyes everywhere?"

Eyes still twinkling, Kavera leaned forward and placed his elbows on the table. "It often seems that way. But no, she monitors only in rare instances and only for medical purposes."

"So what are we supposed to do while we're here?" asked Ben. "How about we go check out those giant canopic jars in the Guardian room?"

"Afraid not," said Kavera. "There has been a development and the area is now off limits except for authorized personnel."

"What does that mean?" asked Grace. "Something happen after we were attacked?"

"There have been unusual electromagnetic fluxes in the jars," said Kavera. "As a precaution, Kurosh has ordered that you not return to the chamber."

"They moved when we walked by them. Is that normal?"

Kavera pursed his lips. "It was an anomaly. We prefer to restrict access only to authorized members until we can insure there is no risk to the Harbor or to the Sphinx above it."

Ben looked around the sterile dining hall with its gleaming metal walls, all streaming with binary data and Sonecian codes. Monitors silently streamed volcano eruptions, earthquakes, and other natural disasters around the world. Others showed NASA briefings and news channels. There was no escape from the mission, even during meals. Most of the teams were in the field but there were still a hundred people seated for lunch, all segregated by tribe. The Saavarian shrouded in dry ice because they preferred the cold. The Mondavi huddled in conference having returned from Easter Island. A race of beings that looked like giant praying mantis, but who weren't Sonecian, clicked and chirped over plates of live insects. And many others. Only his own table was a mixture of cultures. Ben frowned. So much for diversity and the myth about being one big happy space family.

"What's up with everyone staring at us?" April asked.

"Probably not used to seeing kids at the Harbor," Grace said.

Ben glanced at Kavera who showed no reaction to the question. "That's not it, is it?"

Kavera pursed his lips and took a long slow sip of the purple juice in his glass before he answered. "No, it is not."

"So what's up?" Carlos asked, seeming braced for bad news.

"Your tribes requested that you remain in their care until the mission is complete," Kavera said.

"You're not going to let that happen?" asked Grace, her voice rising half an octave. "I mean. You can't!"

Ben shifted his gaze to his other friends. He wasn't alone in his concern about Grace and what was going on in her training sessions.

Kavera placed his hand on her shoulder. "Are you in need of assistance, young warrior? Kurosh has jurisdiction and can speak to Tenzin to address any concerns you might have."

"No," Grace said, avoiding his gaze. "I just mean these guys are kind of my family now. That's all. Don't want to break up the team."

"As it should be," said Kavera. "To lose family and then be separated from each other seemed cruel. Kurosh concurs and vetoed the requests, although it did cause a temporary rift at the Council meeting." He gave Ben a fist bump. "The matter is now closed."

Ben searched Grace's face for answers but she refused to look at him. Instead, she scanned the room. Ben followed her gaze, trying to listen in to the muted conversations but unable to separate one voice from another.

"Where's Uncle Henry?"

"He takes meals in his quarters," said Kavera.

"Does he get meat?" Ben grumbled.

Kavera laughed. "That, my young vegetarian warrior, is classified!"

Ben continued his visual sweep of the room, fixing his gaze on a team of translucent people who weren't eating from plates of food but were, instead, consuming sparkling strands of steam directly from the air. He pointed, "What are they doing?"

"Ah. The Solai. They thrive on the high nitrogen content of Earth's air. They also enjoy methane and helium and are not in agreement with the Tribal Council's decision to bring terraformers online. They consider global warming to be a welcoming gift from Earth inhabitants. We chose not to explain that it is the result of reckless human behavior. Instead, they are marvelous trackers so we use their dietary preferences to our advantage. We point them toward problematic helium vents near the Los Angeles basin, and toward hog farms in Kansas where methane is manufactured in abundance inside the massive ponds where excrement is stored. It is, as you say, a win-win for Earth and for us!"

"Ugh!" said April. "Pig poop! In ponds? Losing my appetite. Switch the subject, okay? Like, where are the teams?"

"In places to numerous to say," Kavera said. "Angor Watt, Olmec, Deception Island in the Antarctic. It would take all day to cite them all. I can ask the librarian to provide you with an alphabetized list, if you wish. It might make for interesting research."

"And those keys you need to unlock the Guardian?" Ben asked. "Can we at least see the ones you've found?"

Kavera grew quiet, then said, "We are still analyzing them and your uncle has . . ."

Ben shook his head. "Don't bother. We know the drill. It's classified." Back to his old ways, his uncle could strip the color from a rainbow.

"But we're going to get bored living down here," whined April. "We're kids. We need something fun to do."

"Fun? Well, why did you not ask sooner? I have a solution for that!" Kavera passed out five digital tablets. "Duty rosters for five bored warriors in need of stimulation. After lunch each day, Carlos will report to tech lab. In reading your debriefings we were quite impressed with your electrical improvisation at the Vatican outpost."

"It was just a potato battery," said Carlos, poking at his food and frowning at the bloody juices that flowed out of a steak.

"Exactly. And it helped you determine your exact location when you were lost, did it not? That type of ingenuity is impressive." Kavera winked. "As I was saying, Carlos, there will be many gadgets to hold your attention. Ben will report to the Xenobian training compound to assist with equipment maintenance. April will report to Sanctuary as well as assist in the hydroponic gardens. Serise will report to the control room and assist with monitoring team activity. Grace will provide Shakrarian mission support and help with translation."

"I'd rather go to the Libyan desert facility and see what's up with all those stasis tubes," said Ben. "Can I be assigned there instead?"

"Unable to comply," said Kavera, brushing his long dreads out of his face. "That facility is locked and off limits except for . . ."

"I know. I know," Ben groaned. "Authorized personnel. But can you at least tell us what those tubes are for? It looks like there are thousands of them and since there's no more ships coming to rescue us before the planet blows up I was thinking—."

"It's classified, young warrior. I am sorry I cannot be more forthcoming." Kavera's expression grew serious, his jaw tightening slightly then released.

"How about we go with you on a mission?" April asked, a broad grin spreading across her face. "We found that metal thing for Easter Island. Bet we could open up the Chinese Emperor's tomb and find another one. You know, the one guarded by those Terra Cotta soldiers! Bet there's some good clues in there!"

"Are you kidding?" said Ben. "Was that deadly water tornado, Volari the underwater dragon and that giant squid dude's creepy fish council not enough excitement for you? Grace said that Terra Cotta tomb is booby-trapped. Even the Chinese government won't open it. So my vote is no, no and add an extra no on top of that!"

"I'm with Ben. No spooky tombs and no ancient booby traps," said Grace, fingering the jade necklace her father gave her.

"But we got practice playing the game," said April. "Wasn't that the point? To find clues?"

Kavera let out a chuckle. "The game has served its purpose. It is safer for you to remain at the Harbor, young warrior in training. For everyone involved. I'm sure you understand."

"No! I don't understand!" grumbled April. "But fine. Okay."

"But Serise was allowed to——," Grace started.

"Serise wore a prototype device that created an anti-tracking shield around her." Kavera gestured for the rectangular lapis stone she wore around her neck. "The experiment was successful and the device will be returned to tech lab."

Serise scowled, unclasped the silver chain and handed the necklace to Kavera. "So what do we do for free time?"

"Free time? I'm afraid there is too much work for that. We will schedule recreational periods on occasion. But it is important that you stick to your routine. We don't want to disrupt the warrior's work, do we?" He grinned.

"All work and no amusement park . . ." Ben said.

"Will get this mission completed quicker," Kavera interrupted, his smile growing wider.

"That's not what I was going to say," said Ben.

"Oh, I believe it was," said Kavera. He laughed, then shifted his gaze over Ben's shoulder and straightened his posture as his face suddenly went blank.

Aurelia walked past them then stopped, her eyes narrowing at the sight of meat on Ben's plate. It was the same expression his mother used to give him when he ate steak prepared for his uncle. Instead of snatching it away, Aurelia said, "I trust you will exercise moderation in this choice of protein, young warrior," then continued towards the tables where her team was gathering. Kavera quickly picked up his tray and followed but turned and winked at Ben before he sat down.

"Don't tell her about the Belgian waffles and bacon," Kavera said telepathically. *"That's our little secret!"*

Ben smiled and gave him a quick thumbs up.

"What's up with those two," asked Grace.

"Don't know," said Ben. "But I'm going to find out."

CHAPTER EIGHTEEN

The Grays

•⁖• "You sure this is a good idea?" Grace asked.

"I saw Kavera and Aurelia go in there with a team, and both cats," Ben said. "Just want a peek. What they don't know won't get us in trouble."

They casually walked through the control room, nodding and smiling at technicians as they went. The door to the Libyan hall opened and closed quickly as Xenobian team members entered with equipment and boxes of supplies. Ben caught glimpses of endless rows of tubes stacked many stories high.

"Did you see anything that time?" asked Grace.

"Not much. Just tubes. Did you?" asked Ben.

"No," said Grace. "The suspense is killing me. There's got to be a way to fake a pass code. They do it all the time in the movies."

"Well, we can't be caught hanging out by the door trying to guess the combination," said Ben, watching as the lock alternated patterns and colors that changed every time someone entered or exited. "That's some complicated alien technology on the door. We can't break that, even with a brute force method. Too many variables. Probably a trillion possible combinations."

Grace thought a moment. "Let's go upstairs."

Ben frowned. "That's even farther away. Do you have binoculars?"

"I'm not going to honor you with an answer to that question, Mr. Higher Order Thinking. Give that brain some exercise. How can we get into a room without a key or passcode?"

"We'd need to find a door without a lock," said Ben. He paused then his eyes grew wide. "Without a lock! The deserted corridor!"

"Now that's the genius brain I know and love," said Grace.

They sprinted out of the control room as if headed back to their apartment, then backtracked to the balcony from the second floor. They crept down the walkway looking for the wooden door they'd come through the day they first arrived at the Harbor. A door that would lead to an abandoned mezzanine directly above the Libyan facility. As luck would have it, the door was gone.

"I knew it wouldn't be easy," said Ben. "They think of everything."

"I wonder," said Grace. "Your uncle said that gateway hadn't been used in thousands of years. They certainly didn't expect to find us hiding there. Maybe it's not gone, just sealed or cloaked. Remember that day we escaped the explosion? My father was feeling the garage walls like he was checking for weaknesses?"

"Yeah?"

"Maybe he was checking for portals instead. So, lets do the same thing. Like the computer game. Don't leave clues undetected."

"Ok," said Ben. "You go high, I'll go low. And watch out for anyone coming down the hallway. Don't want to have to explain ourselves."

Ben and Grace moved their hands back and forth in wide arcs feeling every inch of the wall as they went. They stopped and jerked backwards as their hands passed a warm spot and a door appeared then disappeared.

Ben grinned. "Guess they don't know anything about child-proofing a spy outpost!"

"Yep," said Grace. "Score one for nosy teens."

Gingerly placing his hand on the wall, Ben found the spot again. The door opened with a loud creak. He and Grace froze then popped their heads inside the dark corridor. The noise from the main floor most likely masked the sound of the door opening. Torches on the columns ignited and the cat heads above them rotated towards the door. Ben remembered they held hidden cameras. He whistled a tune his uncle had used there. The torches extinguished. The columns returned to their starting point. Safe for now.

"Nice work, Webster!" Grace whispered as she tiptoed into the darkened corridor.

Staying low, they crept forward, peering through the stone railing. The Libyan facility stretched well out of sight. Tubes nearest the doors glowed in alternating hues.

Dressed in parkas and goggles, Aurelia's team of three protectors, her triad, stepped onto a transport pad at the far end of the room with Bastet and Aris. Aurelia touched her palm to Kavera's forehead, then hugged him before he joined them. "Akoosh sakur vera inna," she said as he disappeared, then turned on her heels and returned to the control room.

"Aww man, we missed them," said Ben slumping. "Wonder where they are going?"

"A better question is if they're using a normal dialing platform to travel, then what are all those stasis tubes for?" said Grace.

"Think, maybe, they're expecting casualties and use them for the wounded? Kind of like putting 'em in cryogenic freeze until they can find a medical cure or get them home?"

"Works for me," said Grace. "But that can't be a good thing they've got so many."

Ben nodded. "There's got to be thousands and it looks like they're adding more." Something out the corner of his eye caught his attention—a body in one of the tubes. A man dressed in overalls. Ben struggled to get a closer look. Another next to him dressed in a business suit. "Look. They've got people in those tubes down there. They don't look like warriors. Unless they were undercover when they got hurt."

Grace craned her neck. "Something looks familiar about that one in the suit."

"Probably cause he's one of the warriors," said Ben.

"No," said Grace. "It's something else. He's . . . Oh! I've got it. He's a weatherman on cable. Mom used to yell at the television every time he came on."

"Why?"

"Made a sarcastic comment about people who died in a storm. Accused them of being stupid and not listening to his newscasts. She said no wonder, since he couldn't predict the end of a year let alone the rain in the middle of a monsoon."

"Then what's he doing here?" asked Ben.

Grace shrugged. "I guess he got on the other warrior's nerves too."

"So maybe he's a Sonecian working undercover. Like our parents posing as college professors and U.N. translators. Probably got hurt and couldn't make it to Medlab."

Grace gasped. Ben gasped. Two aliens walked out from behind a row of tubes. They resembled the creatures on TV movies and science fiction magazines. Large heads. Large almond eyes. Thin grey-green bodies cloaked in white robes with tool-filled belts attached. Their long spindly arms extended to check the tubes with scanners, then extracted the newscaster and placed him face down on a slab.

The man didn't move as straps were placed around his back, legs and arms. Metallic objects rose from beneath the table and positioned themselves over the man's body. The table pulsed with electric lights and streaming hieroglyphic symbols. Danine entered the room, scanned the man's body with a handheld tablet, then nodded her approval.

"Ondana," Danine ordered. "Nala."

Long needles extended from the devices. Grace gasped again, only a lot louder this time. Unfortunately it occurred during a lull in the activity. The two aliens looked up to the balcony, then pressed something on their consoles. All around Ben, light erupted. Not torches this time, but scorching white beams as the cat head columns rotated into alignment. A holographic screen appeared above the aliens, complete with a two story image of Ben and Grace in glorious technicolor, shown crouching near each other with nowhere to run or hide.

Suddenly, they felt a presence behind them. Towering over them, was a very angry Uncle Henry.

"It appears you did not choose wisely," he growled.

CHAPTER NINETEEN

Namaste

•ᵒ• Ben tried to concentrate on his work, cleaning the equipment and keeping the floors spotless since the teams worked out in their bare feet. His friends had cool assignments. His sister was frolicking with flora and fauna in the Harbor's hydroponic garden. And for sneaking into the Libyan facility he was stuck as a glorified Xenobian space janitor. Just like the Karate Kid movie.

Wax on. Wax off.

He tried opening the wall of weapons but didn't have security clearance. But he did find a large stack of metal crates in a storage room behind the wall and was about to open one when he heard the training room door open. In a panic, he slipped back into the training center before he got caught.

At the far end of the room, Aurelia began a workout beneath a simulated window. Bathed in light, she moved fluidly across the mat, breathing in a deep but controlled way as she fought against an invisible opponent. Mindful of her ability to hear his thoughts, he tried to think about cleaning one of the benches and not his resentment at the menial tasks he'd been assigned. But he couldn't help being drawn to the beauty and grace of her kata. Each movement resembled an elaborate tribal dance instead of a training exercise for the head of a military operation. It reminded him of his mother's morning exercises before she disappeared.

Ben's uncle entered the room but stopped just inside the door. Accompanied by ten warriors, he leaned against a limestone column, partially obscured in the shadows, his massive arms folded tightly across his chest. His eyes followed Aurelia as she moved from one side of the room to the other. From his rigid expression and narrowed eyes it was clear he wasn't pleased a woman was leading the military team. Ben had seen that same look of disapproval aimed in his direction more than once.

Uncle Henry raised his index finger toward Aurelia. Each guard took up a weapon, entered the training area and formed a circle around her. Aurelia stopped abruptly, glared at Ben's uncle, then walked to a small table where she retrieved a long black cloth. She wrapped it across her face like a blindfold and returned to the center of the room . . . with no weapon. Uncle Henry shrugged, then nodded to the tallest guard who seemed confused but stepped forward. He attacked with a metal rod which looked like the ones carried by the Casmirians only this one was longer—at least six feet.

Even blindfolded, Aurelia was lightning fast—and accurate. Within seconds the guard was pinned to the ground, her foot on his chest, his weapon now in her possession. Muscle's rippling, her expression was fierce and resolute. She reminded Ben of a mythical Amazon. He gulped and covered his own neck.

Ben's uncle clapped his hands. The nine remaining guards attacked in unison wielding weapons that looked razor sharp and lethal. That hardly seemed fair to Ben. But Aurelia exploded into action. Nine, eight, seven, six . . . Ben counted as the guards fell to the mat like dominoes. Ben couldn't understand how Aurelia was able to disable each guard without injuring them or removing her blindfold. At times he could see only a blur on the floor as Aurelia crouched, sprang, reacted, whirled and deflected blows as if she were surrounded by an invisible force-field.

Once all of the guards were down and their weapons lay at her feet, Aurelia removed the blindfold. Ben was both paralyzed and awestruck. He stifled the urge to yell, "All Right!" Aurelia bowed to each guard and helped them regain their footing. Her defiant gaze returned to Ben's uncle.

Scowling, Uncle Henry bowed and turned to leave the room. Aurelia's expression hardened. He stopped in his tracks. The guards suddenly marched out of the room in single file formation. Uncle Henry slipped off his shoes and walked towards her. He was twice her size.

"You doubt my skills to handle this mission, Kurosh. I have never doubted yours."

Ben's breath caught in his throat. He could hear her! He strained to see if he could tune in to both of them.

"On the long journey I was captivated by Earth tales of the legendary Dahomey warriors. Were you aware that it was the women who protected the king?" she continued.

"Irrelevant as there is no king for you to protect," growled Uncle Henry, a weapon in his hand. It was shaped like a template for drawing French curves but with multiple sharp points jutting from each end. He swung it rhythmically through the air in every direction. The weapon hit nothing but air. Ben blinked and somehow, Aurelia had slipped behind his uncle. She stood with her hands to her side, a smile creeping up her face.

"You are slipping, Kurosh."

Uncle Henry dropped the weapon and tilted his head as if listening for something. He drew in a long slow breath and closed his eyes. Aurelia did the same.

Ben could barely comprehend what happened next. His uncle attacked with a ferocity that seemed beyond human ability. Aurelia successfully blocked or dodged each move but did not return his blows. She possessed super human agility. Her expression remained fixed in extreme concentration. The faster Uncle Henry moved, the faster Aurelia responded until they were just a blur moving across the room.

Ben was scared to blink for fear he would miss something. It was like they were moving at subatomic speed.

Without warning Aurelia changed tempo. She sprang into the air, twisted mid flight, and landed behind Ben's uncle without making a sound. In a flash, he pivoted to face her as his arm rocketed outward. The fight stopped abruptly, her left palm on his forehead, his left palm on hers, both with their right hands held high in the air as if to strike. Ben clamped his hand over his mouth to keep the sound from escaping.

"Do not worry Kurosh. I am still Shaman. I can heal you if you sustain an injury." Aurelia dropped her hands and offered one in friendship.

Uncle Henry softened his expression, returned her gesture and said out loud, "You are a worthy opponent Aurelia. You have become quite good."

"No," she replied, keeping his hand firmly in her grasp. "I am the best."

"Indeed. I am honored you have chosen to serve." Uncle Henry bowed respectfully, and left the room.

Ben knocked over a pile of cleaning supplies. Aurelia did not look in his direction. Instead, she picked up a flask of water and drank heavily.

"Your uncle spoke English for your benefit," she transmitted quietly. *"As did I. Did you learn anything while you were spying on us?"*

"Can you teach me how to do that?" Ben asked struggling to contain his excitement over what he'd witnessed.

"What is it you wish to learn that you don't know already?" Aurelia returned the flask to the table.

"To fight."

"I do not fight. I react to an opposing force. There is a difference."

"But you are a warrior."

"Correct."

"How can you be a warrior and not fight?"

"Ah! I see your confusion." She tapped Ben's head with a long slender finger. "The most powerful tool you have is in here. Xenobians use force only as a last resort. We are trained to be constantly aware of external influences. I train my mind and my body to peak efficiency. In combat we do not attack or strike the first blow—ever. We have attained a higher state of consciousness."

"But what happens when you are attacked first?"

"Basic scientific principle. Your planet calls this discipline 'physics.' I believe the saying is that for every action, there is an equal and opposite reaction. We are trained to deflect the enemy efficiently and effectively. The first strike from our opponent is usually the only strike they are able to initiate. And the last."

"And you don't hurt them."

"I am well trained in alternatives," said Aurelia.

"Don't you ever get angry?"

"I cannot control what happens around me, young warrior. Only how I react to it. It is one of our most basic tenets. To choose wisely."

"So you're a warrior but you've never hurt anyone?" Ben asked.

"It has never been necessary."

"But what if it is necessary someday?"

"I hope it will not come to that, my young prince. The highest state of attainment is to see the divine even in the face of an enemy. I can restrain my opponent until he or she becomes more—let's just say—enlightened."

"But if there was no other choice except to save your life or the life of someone you cared about," pressed Ben. "What would you do?"

Aurelia smiled slyly. Her eyes narrowed, her nostrils flared. The same scary animal-like fierceness Ben often witnessed in his uncle, pierced through her calm demeanor. She cocked her head slightly and examined every inch of Ben as if he were a lab specimen. "If that comes to pass . . . " She paused to reflect on his question. "Then I will choose to free the troubled spirit to go where it can serve a greater purpose."

Aurelia bowed, turned silently on the mat and left the room.

Ben almost felt sorry for her enemies. They didn't stand a chance.

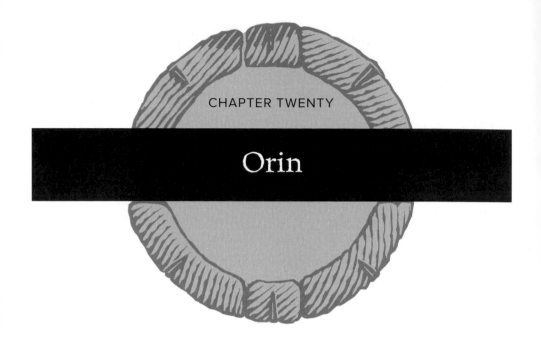

CHAPTER TWENTY

Orin

•⁘• Tech lab turned out to be a cavernous room filled with electronic debris. Chaos was everywhere. Weapons, crates of mechanical parts, and discarded machinery littered the floor or was placed randomly on iron racks lining the walls. Carlos was tempted to turn around and tip toe back into the corridor."

"Something you need?" barked a man with short cropped hair and a few scars across his cheek. He was shaping an iron rod with a hand held torch.

"I'm assigned to help organize the equipment, or whatever," said Carlos. "Are you Orin?"

The man grunted, looked up from his table, then down again. "Aye. I am Orin. But I am not in need of assistance."

"I think it's to get me out of Pendon's sight for a while," Carlos confessed. "What'ya doing?"

"Weapon," Orin grunted. "Top secret. So close your eyes."

"How am I supposed to work with my eyes closed?" Carlos asked.

"You're a bright specimen. Use your other senses," Orin growled. "The blind are quite proficient without eyes. The young and untrained seem to be deficient even with them."

"Well, if you don't need help, do you mind if I just hunt around and find something to do?" Carlos asked.

"Organize and catalog the items in the back if you insist on remaining here. My predecessor did not leave this place in proper order. He was in a hurry to leave this planet. A decision that proved a fateful error."

Carlos frowned as his mind slammed back to the explosion that had killed all the evacuating teams. He shook it off and picked through the bins of debris and discarded equipment.

"What's all this junk?"

"Unnecessary distraction," said Orin.

Okay, thought Carlos. *This is going to be a long day.*

In the corner, he spotted a familiar piece of equipment. An ancient iMac computer like his father's.

"This yours?" Carlos asked.

Orin looked up. "No. It is not."

"Can I have it," Carlos asked, noticing the arm that held the monitor was broken. The base looked like the guts had been cannibalized for parts.

"What do you have to trade?" Orin asked.

Carlos didn't have to think about that. Everything he owned had blown up with his neighborhood and the transport ship. He had only the clothes on his back. Even his old clothes, which were rank after a day of being lost on the way to the Harbor, had been burned by Danine as a biohazard.

"If it's not yours, why does it matter?" Carlos asked.

"You find something I need, I give you something you want. That's how it works, boy."

"Fine," Carlos spit and kept rooting through boxes. Buried under coils of copper wire, he stumbled upon two gold canisters. Each held identical gold disks marked with line drawings and codes and measured about a foot across.

"Hey! I've seen these before. These are copies of the golden records NASA made."

"Not copies," said Orin, seeming disinterested in Carlos's new line of inquiry. "I have work, boy. Best get to your own."

"NASA made more than two?"

"I am not aware of others," said Orin.

Carlos laughed. "Then these can't be them. They were sent up with the Voyager probes."

"That is correct," said Orin, a sly smile creeping up his face, making his scars seem more prominent.

"So how'd you get them?" Carlos asked, fingering the disks and studying star patterns that looked a lot like ones he'd seen on his father's computer.

Orin stopped tinkering and looked disappointed. "I shall allow you one guess. Choose wisely."

Carlos frowned. The Voyager probes were supposed to go as far as Jupiter and Saturn then quit, but for some reason the power cells kept operating and now they were headed out of the solar system.

"You stole them?"

Orin scowled. "I am not a thief. I took what was intended for an extraterrestrial being to take. I replaced them with something else. It was an even exchange."

"Like what."

"Boy, you test my patience with these endless questions." Orin put his experiment down and turned to face him. "New disks."

Carlos shrugged. "What was the point?"

"You have heard of extraterrestrial abductions?" he asked.

Carlos nodded. "Just people having nightmares."

Orin's left eyebrow raised slightly.

"Not nightmares?"

Orin didn't answer. It took Carlos a few minutes to process his conclusion. "We were abducting people?"

"Humans make interesting test subjects and zoo specimens," Orin said dryly.

Carlos froze.

"But we have no time for such distractions," Orin continued.

"Alpha Centaurians are human's chief predators. They've shown great interest in harvesting this planet. Obviously we could not allow that to happen, given our mission priorities. We could not risk other civilizations visiting Earth. On a previous mission we stopped to repair one of the arrays anchored on Jupiter. As the probe flew past the moon, Io, I upgraded the power cells and provided new disks coded in hundreds of languages."

"Saying what?" said Carlos. "Don't come to Earth?"

Orin smirked but kept his attention on his work. "Inviting them to visit Alpha Centauri. A rough translation would read, 'We welcome you to a most bountiful planet. Come share our abundance in minerals and technology. We gladly offer ourselves as sacrifice for your dining pleasure'." He chuckled again. "Warding off intergalactic pirates in search of treasures and rare exotic meal ingredients will keep the Centaurians occupied for some time."

Carlos was both fascinated and horrified. It took him a minute to realize he was, in fact, no longer living his human reality. Alien was his new normal.

Orin returned to his tinkering. He seemed dissatisfied as he aimed his device at a small bronze statue of a buffalo. It disintegrated. He studied the digital readout on his console, frowned, and disassembled the weapon.

"Can I ask what you are working on?" Carlos asked.

"I apparently have no way of stopping you," said Orin.

When Orin didn't finish his response with an answer, Carlos figured he was a literal thinker and changed the phrasing of his question. "What are you working on?"

"Strategic advantage," said Orin.

Carlos groaned. "Can you be more specific?"

"Weapon," Orin grunted.

Carlos rolled his eyes, tossed the golden disks back in their canisters and walked to the console. "Seems like it works pretty good to me."

"I suppose humans have a low standard for this type of thing," Orin said, wiping his nearly black hair out of his face and scratching his short beard. Carlos walked to his side then stopped. Orin was missing both legs below the knee.

"What are you looking at, boy? My missing limbs? I can still best you from across the room."

"No doubt," said Carlos trying not to stare. "No doubt."

Orin relaxed a single facial muscle.

"So the laser isn't strong enough?"

Orin frowned. "It's strength is adequate for the task. However. I am in need of a better crystal. The ones synthesized in the lab lack the irregularities of a volcanic one. Too much symmetry in their internal architecture. The beasts we may encounter are hard to defeat."

Carlos froze. "Beasts?"

"Aye! Perhaps you saw one the day the Harbor was attacked."

Carlos remembered briefly seeing the grey creature Uncle Henry beamed to the sun to be incinerated. "There's more of them?"

"Aye. It is a certainty." Orin didn't elaborate.

Carlos frowned and looked at the blue rocks in his hand. "Are these sapphires?"

Orin shook his head. "I believe they are diamonds replicated by my predecessor. I would prefer one with imperfections. Makes the weapon harder to defeat. The light signature modulates."

"Like one where the mineral deposits are not uniform?"

Orin tapped a command into his console and brought up holographic images of diamonds and their energy readings. "Perhaps you are not as uninformed as initial reports had me believe. Yes. We have tested a number of Earth diamonds and none have been sufficient in size or composition. So I am, as you might say, improvising a solution."

"How big does it have to be?" asked Carlos.

Orin held up his fingers. "About this big. In Earth terms, approximately forty carats"

"Can I see the diamonds you used," asked Carlos.

"Nothing will come of it, but I grant the request." He pointed Carlos towards the back of a room and nodded towards a large chest. Inside, Carlos found the largest cache of uncut diamond rocks he'd ever seen, in various colors. He searched through them, looking for the one type of diamond he'd thought might work. But of course it wasn't there. Orin had said he tested all of them.

But he knew where one was. Carlos smiled. He finally had a bargaining chip.

"Will you give me the computer if I tell you where you can get a diamond to use?"

Orin looked sideways at him. "Go on. Speak up. Where is such a diamond lying around?"

"Smithsonian," Carlos said. "It's called the Hope Diamond. I've seen it. It's big enough and it glows orange after scientists hit it with a laser."

"Hope Diamond, you say?"

Carlos nodded. Orin searched through his database, reading volumes of hieroglyphic pages until he stopped and honed in on a page describing the diamond. The room filled with scientific schematics of the diamond's energy output.

"Go get it," he said. "It appears to have the appropriate boron composition."

"Carlos threw up his hands. "How am I supposed to do that? It's locked in a museum. With lots of guards."

"You get me the diamond, I give you computer. Fair trade."

Carlos nearly lost it. "That's not even close to a fair trade! And there's no way for me to get it. The Smithsonian is like a fortress. Besides, I'm not allowed out of the compound."

"On whose authority?"

"Uncle Hen—, I mean Commander Kurosh."

Orin sniffed like he'd smelled something foul. "That is the downside of living with your Xenobian playmates. Perhaps this will teach you to live with your own kind. Kurosh? His rules do not apply to us. You are my apprentice, are you not? I desire this Hope Diamond. Prove yourself and go get it. Then we shall discuss what supplies you can have."

Unsanctioned

⁖

**"We will never solve our problems
by using the same thinking that created them."**
—Albert Einstein

PART II

CHAPTER TWENTY-ONE

The Plan

∴ "Are you crazy!" Carlos shouted.

Ben smiled and thought of his father's planned heist of the British Museum before he disappeared. "You said you needed that diamond and I think I know how we can get it!"

Carlos backed away from the table. "Last time you had an idea—"

"But it worked out, right? Kinda sorta?" Ben said. "So what do we have to lose? We could be there and back before anyone misses us."

Grace shook her head. "Let me get this straight. You want to break into the Smithsonian Museum and steal the Hope Diamond."

Ben nodded. "Not exactly steal per se. Just, umm, make it temporarily unavailable for viewing by other land-based bipedal animals." He laughed at his Atlantis joke.

Grace groaned, then added. "It's only the most guarded diamond in the world with the exception of the ones at the Tower of London. I'm with Carlos. You ARE nuts!"

"I'm hoping Orin will get tired of waiting and ask a Casmirian team to get it," said Carlos. "You know—people with skills and tools and clearance to leave the facility."

Ben grinned. He'd been to the Smithsonian. It was huge and did have a lot of guards. On the other hand, he'd been to the British Museum and it was huge too. He had walked the floors after hours without tripping off any alarms. So yeah! Why not?

"Your team would just blast their way in and take it. But us? We can just borrow it long enough for Orin to duplicate it, return it, and it won't even be on the evening news," Ben said. "This will prove we can be as valuable as everyone else. Plus, Dad was planning to get something from the British Museum. I saw what he was going to use to do it." Ben pulled out a digital tablet and drew a crude picture of a disk with his index finger."

"Are you planning to copy Carlos and make one of those out of a vegetable?" April asked. "Because we don't have anything like that, plus I'm still trying to figure out Kavera's riddle so I can get us a bathtub and decent clothes."

"I saw those disks," said Carlos. "They're sitting on a shelf. Orin didn't build them. He said he didn't know what they were for. Guess the guy he replaced kept sloppy notes."

"Then it's a plan," said Ben. "We need four. Maybe grab some extra just in case."

"No," said April, sounding adamant. "Something is hunting the teams, right? So here is safer than out there. SAFER. Plus, you and Grace are still in trouble for peeking into that tube place. And on top of that we don't have a dialer."

"Yep. That don't have a dialer problem is a deal breaker," said Grace.

Serise remained quiet.

"What's up, Serise?" Ben asked. "I can usually count on you to say something sarcastic."

"Just thinking," she said. "We might not need a dialer."

Grace's eyes narrowed. "You're not really going along with this scheme are you?"

"Why not?" she said. "I'm bored too. Honestly. Being chased on the way here was way more interesting than eating alien rations and flunking endless problem sets meant for a PhD Astrophysics major."

"You found a way to get the dialer software back?" Grace asked.

"No. The game software is gone and they wiped the back-ups on all three flash drives including the one I hid in a fake tube of lip gloss. But I don't think we'll need it."

Carlos coughed. "Hello! To get there we need a dialer or a transport pad and the only ones are out in the open."

"Not all of them." She grinned. "I'm thinking we need to get serious about our studies and put in some extra time in the library after hours."

Ben paused. Then he grinned too. There was a portal directly to the Smithsonian Archives and with Serise assigned to the Control Center she could charm her way into having access to all the Harbor programs that controlled them. A little reprogramming and they might be able to access the Museum of Natural History close by.

"Okay," said Serise. "Here's the deal. The barriers were reinforced to keep anything from getting in unless you're on a team. But we've got Harbor ID badges so there's a chance they'll unlock for us."

"You sure it will work?" asked April.

"Only way to find out is to test them," said Grace. "While I was in training, someone said there was an original Copernicus manuscript at Linda Hall Library in Kansas City. Kept under lock and key. I'm working on translations so I'll tell the librarian I want to borrow it and promise to put it back before the library opens."

"It's probably in a vault," said Carlos. "It's not just going to be laying around out in the open."

"Yes, but did she or did she not say that with enough time she had access to every book everywhere?" said Grace. "Well, we want that book. For an hour. That will let us know if we can get all the way to the states and back to Egypt without getting caught."

"She's not going to go along with it. You and Ben are on lock-down," Serise said.

"But does she know that?" asked Ben. "Carlos, can you get Serise's lucky no-tracking necklace back?"

"Yep," he said. "Orin scowled and then threw it in a bin. He said Casmirians don't hide from danger. So I'm pretty sure he won't miss it if I, umm, temporarily make it unavailable for Casmirian viewing." He laughed.

"Sweet!" said Ben

"There's one more hurdle. The library portal logs who is coming and going just like all the others. Our badges will let them know we're not at the Harbor. They won't know where we are, but they'll know we're not here."

"I can get replacements," Grace said, suddenly growing serious.

Everyone froze.

"You can?" Serise asked. "How?"

Grace shrugged. "Don't ask questions. You won't have to lie if you get caught, okay? What do they call it?"

"Plausible deniability," Carlos answered. "That's what they called it in that Independence Day movie with Will Smith."

"Yeah, that's it," Grace said. "Plausible deniability."

"We'll leave our real badges on our beds," April said. "But we still need to figure out how to plan the mission without getting caught."

"Easy," said Ben. "We'll use library books. They don't leave a digital footprint. Stay off the Harbor's computers and just do a manual search for copies of the Smithsonian blueprints."

Carlos groaned. "Hello! I don't think those are going to be easy to get. If they were we could just ask for the security blueprints too."

Ben laughed. "Sorry, I meant floor plans. Like from a visitor brochure. They're on the website but we can't let anyone know what we're up to so an internet search is a no-go. If we can each use a tracking blocker to make a side trip and snag some tourist copies, we can put the plan together faster."

"You can use the computers if you get stuck," said Serise. "No one is going to worry if you are looking at the Smithsonian. It's a kid friendly site and won't raise suspicions. Plus it's got a virtual tour so you can walk it in cyberspace before you go. But if you're planning to do more than that tell me first. I might be able to erase the searches off the servers. It would be risky. So don't do too much unless it's an emergency."

Carlos's eyes grew wide. "Whoa! They let you have access to the servers?"

Serise's eyes sparkled. "Not yet."

CHAPTER TWENTY-TWO

The Copernicus Test

Taking one deep breath and then another, Grace stood just inside the doorway to gather her courage. One slip and she'd ruin the mission. Getting to Linda Hall library would be simple. Getting past the librarian? Not so much. Sipping one more lung full of air, she grasped the borrowed access badge that she'd tucked into the sleeve of her borrowed white robe and walked inside.

"Greetings," said the librarian, hovering above the floor. She wore the same multi-pocketed robe which made sense since she wasn't a real person, just a digital projection. "How may I assist you."

"I have need of a reference," Grace said, keeping her mind clear and focused as she'd been taught in her training sessions. The effort however gave her a sharp headache.

"I am here to serve," said the librarian. "What is the reference, and how soon is it required?"

"I desire a copy of Nicolai Copernicus's The Revolutions of the Heavenly Sphere. First edition, circa 1543. Printed in Nuremberg."

"I am happy to send a digital copy directly to your station. Or perhaps on a portable device if you prefer."

Grace coughed to clear her throat then said, "Thank you. I prefer the original. In Latin. As you know, Copernicus was the first European to accurately describe the precise nature of this solar system. Perhaps he held other clues to the materials we seek. Similar to Plato's unfortunate discussion of Atlantis in his own writings."

"Yes," said the librarian. "That was unfortunate. But it yielded little in terms of scientific discovery. I am told the Atlanteans remain safe for now."

"Indeed," said Grace. "As for the Copernicus edition, I am told there may be coding embedded in the margins of this specific copy. There is also a volume by Galileo at the same location that may be of interest."

"I will obtain them," the librarian said. "Certainly."

"I prefer to get them myself," said Grace, keeping her language as formal as possible and her voice deeper and more adult like. She reminded herself not to fidget but her splitting headache and rising temperature was making it difficult. She couldn't maintain this pretense for long. "I am eager to explore that region of the country."

"As you wish," said the librarian. "I will scan the vault's security protocols and open a portal." She paused, her multiple hands dipping into pockets as holographic windows opened with streaming video feeds and pages in binary code. "Ah!" she said finally, "It is a weekend, the library is closed, so we don't have to wait. I can access it now. How much time will you require?"

"One hour," said Grace, fingering the necklace in her pocket Carlos got from Orin. "Perhaps less."

"I am happy to serve," said the librarian. "It appears that the books are not in the vault."

Grace froze. "On loan to another location?"

The librarian smiled. "They are on display in the rare book room. No need to access the vault. That will reduce the energy needed to gain access. Steel vaults are often many feet thick and moving flesh and bone through such material is not impossible, just a drain on Harbor resources. When you arrive I'll arrange to have the book out of the case. I will replace it when you are finished. The Galileo as well. I thought you might be interested in a da Vinci. Such a rare treat to see his backwards writing."

Grace stopped a minute. "How are you able to remove the books?"

The librarian seemed perplexed. Grace suddenly realized her mistake in asking the question. Sonecian teams had invented the technology and would already know the answer.

"The same way the Harbor moves its teams around. Glass, like all matter, is just an arrangement of molecules held by electrical bonds. Energy is used to temporarily rearrange them to create a portal. Are there any other documents you require?"

"No," said Grace, tempted to ask for brochures for the Smithsonian but feeling lucky she'd gotten this far. Why push her luck? "Access to the reading room is sufficient."

Linda Hall Library, Kansas City, Missouri
39.0342796° N, 94.5801818° W

Grace opened her eyes and found herself in a windowed room filled with glass cases. She gasped for air and relaxed, feeling her core temperature dropping as well. She chanted a few lines of prayer and focused, tensing each muscle and then releasing them one at a time. The headache began to fade. She hadn't been training long, but it was physically draining. She'd be punished if she got caught. The Shakrarians were very kind, but also very strict. And from what she'd seen on the first day, there were worse things than being grounded. Grace allowed her eyes to focus in the dim light, happy that an interior glass wall revealed a deserted corridor on the other side. The idea of appearing in the middle of a dark vault with limited oxygen had scared her. This was much less claustrophobic.

As promised, three books were placed on the top of glass cases. The librarian had thought to provide white gloves. At first Grace thought they were to prevent fingerprints in case of an investigation. But that was stupid. Even if the book were dusted as part of a crime scene, it wouldn't lead to someone hiding in a secret space outpost in Egypt.

No, the gloves were because the Harbor's librarian, like all librarians, wanted to protect the book from the oils and secretions on Grace's hands that might ruin the pages.

Slipping a pair of dark glasses out of her robe, Grace put them on then tapped once. The glasses began converting the Latin text to English. Strategic advantage. No other team had access to them. She couldn't understand why but she was told not to talk about Tenzin's technology in development. Still, she hadn't been told not to borrow them. Nor had she been told not to use them. So technically, she was within the rules, even if skating along the outer boundary of her tribe's intent.

Reaching for the Copernicus, she opened to the first pages. The glasses streamed in binary code then stopped once it began its translation. Elapsed time: 2 seconds. It would get faster as it learned, or so Tenzin had said when showing them to her.

> *Diligent reader, in this work, which has just been created and published, you have the motions of the fixed stars and planets . . . You also have most convenient tables, from which you will be able to compute those motions . . . Let no one untrained in geometry enter here.*

She laughed at that last line. But the glasses worked. And now she had to get them back before Tenzin missed them. She'd convinced him to go to the galley and ask them to prepare a traditional dish for her. She'd said she was curious about Shakrarian delicacies especially if it was a scrumptious desert. With enough flattery, he'd offered to do it for her. Although she cringed at the thought of the little green head chef making anything for human consumption. It was a toss-up whether the result would be edible.

Losing herself in the fragile pages, her eyes caught Copernicus's pleas to the Pope. At that time, suggesting that Earth was not the center of the universe was punishable by imprisonment. Or worse.

> " . . . *I can imagine, Holy Father, that as soon as some people*

hear that I have written about the revolutions of the spheres of the universe, that I attribute certain motions to the terrestrial globe, they will shout that I must be immediately condemned together with this belief . . ."

She paused, thinking she heard something. But it was just the sound of her own breathing echoing against the glass case. Having forgotten to pause the translation, she returned to find it partway down the page. The text was fascinating. The first European to get it right and dare to write about it. More than six thousand years after the first transport ship arrived. How surprised he'd be if he'd discovered there were many solar systems supporting life. She certainly was.

She looked at the clock and scowled. Class was due to start in fifteen minutes. She needed to get the glasses back to the Shakrarian section of the compound before she was caught. But she'd done it. Distracted, she put the gloves in the pocket of her robe and closed the books. The library portals worked. At least for her. Moving through them was much easier than the Atlantis beam had been. And with Tenzin's glasses, she could translate anything, anytime as long as she could pry the prototype away from him.

Safely back at the library, she saw her friends filing in, glumly holding the results of their homework.

"Greetings," said the librarian. "I trust your mission was successful,"

"Indeed," said Grace. "Quite productive. You may return the books to their original locations." She brushed past her friends who parted to make an opening but didn't give her a second glance. She could get to the Shakrarian science lab and back in ten minutes if she sprinted.

On the way out she heard Ben say, "Anyone seen Grace?"

"I have not," said the librarian. "But I am sure she will be here soon. She is a most punctual young woman."

CHAPTER TWENTY-THREE

Midnight Oil

"Two minutes on the clock! The score is tied with the home team in posses-sion of the ball."

Footsteps slipped quietly into the room. Ben kept his eyes closed. Across the way, he heard Carlos shift and yawn.

"Ben Webster pivots to middle court, dribbling the ball with a sweet cross-over from one hand to the other as his opponent attempts to rush in for a steal."

The footsteps moved forward, pausing at his bed, then walked out again. Even through his closed eyelids Ben could see the room fade to darkness.

"He takes the shot. It's going . . . ,"

The outer apartment door whooshed open and then closed.

"Going . . . ,"

He waited.

Waited.

"Score!"

Silence returned and the apartment was still.

He bounded out of bed. "Okay! Coast is clear."

Carlos slipped out of his own bed, tossed the experimental disks he'd been hiding to Ben and they headed to the front room where he knocked on the girl's door. Seconds later April, Serise and Grace were at the table as well.

"That was close," said April. "Is Kavera going to check on us every night? Blocking my thoughts is getting hard."

"Yep," said Ben. "I think he's under orders from Uncle Henry to make sure we're tucked in."

"But that's a good thing," Serise said. "A very good thing."

"How do you figure that?" asked Grace.

"Think about it. It's like prison. Every night there's a manual bed check. Then the guard leaves and doesn't come back. "

"So?" said Ben.

"So," she said, grinning like a Cheshire cat. "No hidden cameras. Otherwise why come in? Plus, if your uncle could scan your thoughts from next door, he'd be here right now scolding us."

"Good point. That means privacy. One problem down, four bazillion to go." Carlos rubbed a welt on his arm.

"You okay?" asked April. "That's a pretty big bruise,"

"I"m fine," he said. "Didn't duck fast enough in training."

"Maybe you should see Danine," said April. "She could fix you right up."

"I'm fine," Carlos said, tugging his shirt down. He didn't seem angry. "So what's the plan?"

But Ben wasn't so sure about that. "What's going on with training? You were limping yesterday."

Carlos sighed. "They kind of play rough. I think their motto is, 'Whatever doesn't kill you makes you stronger'."

Ben laughed. "Want to trade?"

Carlos chuckled. "Be careful what you ask for. I think they're the ones that introduced the concept of human sacrifice to Earth people. So Grace, going to spill the beans on your training?"

Grace looked up, her face suddenly a blank slate, and shrugged. "It's no big deal. And no, I can't talk about it. So move on. We've got a mission to get to. What's the plan?"

Ben narrowed his eyes. Grace had been his friend longer than anyone else in the room and she never held back. But at least she was now coming back from training sessions with color in her cheeks. Still, even Serise and April couldn't break her silence. And they'd been persistent.

A light breeze brushed across the table. Ben turned to see Aris walking through the locked door as if it weren't solid. His mouth dropped open. "Aris, how many other things can you do?"

Aris, didn't answer. Not even a growl. Instead he shrank to cat size, pounced on April's lap and studied the map on the table. His orange eyes narrowed, then he yawned and began grooming himself. He purred as April stroked his ears.

"You're not going to say anything, are you, Aris?"

The cat let out a quiet growl and pawed at April when she stopped petting him.

"Spoiled kitty," she said, her voice dropping to a whisper. "Have a hard mission today?"

The cat stretched, then licked her in the face before curling into a ball.

"He was on a mission with Uncle Henry. Wish he could talk so we'd know what he was up to," April said.

Grace scratched his ear affectionately. "He's kind of growing on me. Okay, back to the plan!"

Ben gestured at Aris. "The cat?" he whispered.

Grace waved him off. "If he was going to turn us in, he'd have done it by now."

Ben frowned, then nodded, still thinking about how his mother's cat could walk through closed doors on a whim and how he could use that to his advantage.

"So when can you test the portals?" Ben asked.

"Already tested," said Grace. "Did it during training."

Serise frowned. "Today? The librarian said she hadn't seen you."

Grace bit her lip. "She didn't. But they work. I know for sure."

Everyone stopped.

"You going to tell us how you know?" asked Carlos. "I mean this is a high risk mission and you know where guessing got us last time."

She smirked. "Here. Eventually. So yes. They work. I asked Tenzin to go get something for me and piled on the flattery until he said yes."

Ben noticed Grace tapping her fingers against the table. She looked him straight in the eye but there it was: her tell. She was lying, or as close as she could get to a lie. And he knew he wasn't going to pry it out of her.

"I made these," April said, tossing five round paper disks on the table. Each contained two concentric wheels marked with letters. They were held together with a small bent pin.

"What's this?"

"When we played the game," she said, "we had to solve codes, right? We need a way to communicate with each other that the team can't figure out."

No one talked.

"So, we made these in Girl Scout camp one year. Secret decoders called ciphers. Think about it. The people on this mission can translate every language in the universe so the Egyptian symbols won't work. Or any other symbols and I don't know that many. We can't use those pigpen codes, even though Serise was a genius at solving them, because they'd take too long to figure out unless we had a PDA, which we don't have. It's not a device so they can't track it. It's flat so it can hide under our beds. And if we have to slip notes to each other we can use the decoder. Just keep the messages simple."

Silence. Ben looked around and everyone was as stunned as he was.

"That's genius!" Grace said giving her a fist bump. April beamed.

"I can get PDAs from Orin," Carlos said. "I'll tell him I can't get the diamond without them. Then we send messages using April's decoder. That way if they're connected to the computers here, no one will be able to translate the messages. And I'll wipe them when we get back."

"There's a problem," said Serise. "Using the wheel is brilliant, but it will take forever to type out the code."

April looked dejected.

"But," Serise continued, "what if I program your decoder into the

PDA's. It will code and decode the messages without us having to manually spin the wheel."

"Works for me. And we can use the paper ones in emergencies to leave each other messages if the PDA gets taken away. Because you know, if we get caught, they're gonna be!"

Carlos burst out laughing. "That's been our track record. So it's a plan!"

"Okay," said Serise. "We're in luck. I downloaded the virtual floor plans for the Smithsonian. But we've got another problem. The diamond isn't in a vault. It's on display on the second floor in the mineral section. Right in the middle of a room on the same floor as the IMAX theater and the butterfly exhibit. So there's going to be a lot of people around."

"Not if we get it at night after the museum is closed," said Carlos.

"Won't work," said Ben. "I'm betting they've got security on at night. You know, like the movies where the room is crisscrossed with invisible laser beams."

"So we have to go during the day?" asked April.

"Why not?" asked Ben. "A bunch of kids in the Smithsonian isn't a big deal and we'll blend in with the crowd. We can use the virtual software to practice a walkthrough so we won't get lost or distracted while we're there."

"Don't forget the time difference between here and there. Six hours. And we have to go when it opens. If we wait until 9 am East Coast time, it will be 3 am here. We'll be exhausted during training unless we go to bed super early which given my training isn't going to be hard." Carlos picked up the holographic disks and placed them on the table at ninety degrees apart. After a bit of fiddling, he found their hidden switches and turned them on. When he ducked his head inside the field generated, everyone gasped.

"What happened?" he asked.

Grace shrugged. "Your head disappeared even though your body was still outside. Like a hologram. I could pass my hand through it."

"Then these things work," Carlos said. "But I still have no idea how we're going to get that diamond. It will be locked in a glass case. Did you hear your dad talking about that little detail?"

Ben deflated. "No. I guess he figured Serise's Dad would know, that's who he was talking to when he planned it out."

"So, Sherlock," said Serise. "How are we going to get through a glass case without setting off alarms or getting caught?" She sat a glass of water inside the forcefield. It was still solid and fell over when she pulled it out, spilling water on the table. April mopped up the water with a hand towel from the bathroom.

Dejected, Ben said, "I guess we're back to square one."

"But we're getting a bathtub!" April yelped, holding the now wet towel up in triumph.

Ben gave her a high five but his mind was still on the problem at hand. How to get the diamond out of the case. He stared at the cat who was snoring softly. Then it hit him. When his father was planning the heist, Aris had been sitting on his shoulder watching it all. And the shape shifting cat could walk through solid walls. Suddenly his mood brightened. In his mind, their Away Team just grew by one more member.

CHAPTER TWENTY-FOUR

Temple

∴ On the mandatory day of rest, Kurosh stood outside the door of the sanctuary, inspecting everyone who arrived as if taking attendance.

"Coming in?" asked Ben.

"No," said his uncle. "But it is a good thing for you to do. Be with your people."

"They're your people too."

"Yes," he answered. "They are. But I have work to do. Right now, attending meditation is your work. Tend to it please." Uncle Henry turned and walked towards the control room.

∴

For thirty minutes, Aurelia guided the team through meditation while Bastet sat at her feet. Aris rested next to April. Ben sat with the others, hands folded, while hearing of their connection to the universe. That the souls that nourished their bodies were made of the same stuff as stars and would one day return to the universe where their energy would blend with all others.

They were asked to visualize their bodies as gifts of the divine. And their deeds should be ones that would help humanity. Every action should be in joyful service to others.

Ben fidgeted, not used to sitting this long. His mother had said similar things. But her meditations—which Ben had thought were time outs because they always came right after he'd been caught doing something he shouldn't—lasted ten minutes at the most.

Peeking through a transparent section of the stained glass window, Ben saw his uncle sitting in quiet meditation on a bench outside of the sanctuary. His eyes were closed, his head bowed, his hands clasped in his lap. Ben wondered why his uncle would listen but not participate.

Kavera nudged him. *"Benjamin. Tend to your own meditation,"* he said gently. *"Let your uncle tend to his."*

"What's going on?" Ben asked.

Kavera didn't answer. Just pursed his lips as if having an internal argument with himself.

"Kavera. Besides April he's the only family I have left here. What am I missing? I'll keep it to myself. Promise."

Kavera sighed.

"Your uncle has received divine dispensation to perform a difficult task. He does not enjoy this part of the mission. He has merely come to accept it. If he wishes, the community will heal him before and after the mission is complete. If not, he will carry his pain inside of him for the rest of his life. I hope he chooses the former. He is a kind and gentle man."

Ben thought about all the arguments he and his uncle had at family dinners in contrast to the hug he received when his uncle realized Ben hadn't died in the ship explosion. It was like two parts of a puzzle that didn't fit.

Still, Ben wondered if he and Kavera were talking about the same person.

When meditation was over, Ben whipped his head toward the window. The bench and the courtyard were empty.

CHAPTER TWENTY-FIVE

Stealing Hope

It took a week but Carlos came through with PDA's as promised. They were old, crude and not used anymore, but they worked. Grace had ID badges but wouldn't say how she got them, only that they had to be back in the Shakrarian compound before calisthenics. After April told Kavera towels get wet when they dry, and Carlos figured out the red-shirted Casmirian had an unopened parachute in his backpack, Kavera came through with street clothes. Three sets for each person including Sky Jump sneaks for Ben. His favorite. And while the kids were in training he'd had their bathrooms retrofitted to human specifications. Complete with a normal shower for the boys and a bathtub with jets for the girls.

"I'm staying behind," said Serise, yawning and flipping the hair out of her face. She and Grace were the only ones still dressed in white Harbor uniforms. "The only way for this to work is for me to change the portal settings from the control center. The only other person who can change them is the librarian. I'll just say I couldn't sleep because I'm jet lagged. It's kind of true anyway. If something happens and our voice link goes down, send me a coded message. I programmed in April's decoder sequence like I promised. Otherwise I'll be able to hear you. Just use the PDA's like a cellphone.

She passed them tiny earphones. "Don't ask me where these came from," she said, giving Grace a fist bump. "Just doing my part in gathering supplies."

Aris growled, then yawned too.

"Remember, Aris," Ben said, "if you get the diamond out of the case. Carlos will give you half his share of steak."

The cat's eyes glowed, but his expression was otherwise unimpressed.

"Where's Bastet? Is he going to be an issue?" asked Carlos.

"Nope. Saw him leave with Aurelia's team," said Serise. "He's in the field."

"Then we're all set," said Grace. "I'll distract the librarian. She's going to take me to the Library of Congress. I told her I was curious about the Jefferson collection."

"What's there?" Serise asked.

"Just his books," Grace said. "He studied other governments and civilizations before he helped write the Constitution. So I said I was curious. Especially the ones about the Roman Empire. She's so cute. I told her I'd love to have a buddy so she's going to get them out of the display cases for me. She said it was tricky because it was daylight. But honestly, how else are you going to get to the Smithsonian without her hovering every time someone walks in? We're lucky there's only one of her and the others were decommissioned when the teams evacuated. There used to be twenty just like her. But she needs to be gone so you can get into another portal without her seeing you. When she comes back, she'll just think a Shakrarian team went to the Smithsonian. If you get into trouble, I'll be close by in the same city."

"And if you send coded messages, just set the PDA to transmit messages starting with AW. That corresponds to the letter A on the big wheel to the letter W on the small wheel of April's decoder," Serise said. "It will scramble and unscramble the messages so no one can decode it but us."

"Are we ready?" asked April.

"No, but it's now or never," said Grace. "See you on the other side."

+38.891239 +77.030198

Ben, Carlos, April and Aris materialized in the middle of a barren rocky plain. A mountainous range loomed in the distance. Aris roared so loud Ben thought his ear drums would split. Something thundered in the distance but there was nowhere to hide beyond a few low lying scrub bushes. It was cold. Freezing cold. And wherever they were it wasn't in a museum. From the looks of the location it wasn't even in Washington, D.C.

Ben shouted into the PDA. He had an eerie feeling he was being watched. Above him, four large condors similar to the one he'd seen while playing the game suddenly appeared. An ominous cloud appeared in the distance.

"Serise! Can you hear us?"

"Yes. Are you there yet?"

"We're somewhere," said Carlos. "But not where we're supposed to be."

"You have to be," she said. "I got the codes right off their website."

"Then someone is playing a trick on us," said Ben. "Check again."

"Oh, hi!" Serise said suddenly. "I couldn't sleep so I thought I'd run some test simulations and get some practice in. Is that okay?"

"Who are you talking to?" asked Ben, watching the condors circling overhead. Aris's tail twitched as he watched too.

April made a slashing movement with her hand. "I think she's talking to someone in the control room," she whispered. "We have to wait."

"Okay, guys. I'm back. That was Mansurat. Who knew he was taking the night shift today. Ugh. I may have to be offline a few times because he's in a teaching kind of mood. But don't worry. I got it."

"Uh, where are we, Serise?" Ben said in a panic. "Did you send us to Washington state?"

"No! Let me check. Oh. Wait. I made a mistake. You're in southwest China. I think it's called the Kashi Prefecture. It's near Tajikistan. My bad. It's confusing using numbers without the compass directions on the end. I typed in a positive instead of a negative. Honest mistake. I'll fix it. Hang on. Do you see a portal opening?"

"Yes," said Ben. "It better be right this time."

They stepped back into the library just as a group of horseman and a herd of cattle thundered by scarring off the condors. Once Serise signaled she'd made a program change, they stepped through the portal again.

-38.891239 +77.030198

They stood, huddled together, on a small island barely big enough to fit the four of them. Ocean waves lapped at their shoes. Ben could swear he saw fins circling in the water.

"Are you getting the feeling this mission was a really REALLY stupid idea?" said Carlos.

"Yep," said April, "I say we quit now and go back to bed. What do ya say, Aris?"

The cat glared at them, then whipped his tail angrily at Ben as if trying to push him into the water. Ben knew the cat couldn't grow in size. There was no extra space on the tiny speck of rock.

"Okay, Aris," said Carlos. "You can have my entire portion of beef if you let us live. I'm on meat overload anyway."

"Sorry!" said Serise in their earpieces. "I told Mansurat I was learning about Earth navigation and he used his console to show me how the numbers can be the same but the locations change based on the direction. I didn't punch in that last code. He did. He didn't know it was linked to people instead of a simulation. I think he put you in the Pacific Ocean off the coast of Argentina."

"Ya think?" said Ben. "A few digits off on the coordinates and we'd be drowning or something's dinner right about now."

"It's okay," she said. "He got called to send an emergency team to Iceland. Something about a temporary stop in volcano eruptions and teams going to study the lava dome before it starts up again. Are they nuts? I looked at the read-outs. It's still like a thousand degrees Fahrenheit up there."

"Serise!" Ben screamed. "We're in the middle of nowhere. Stay focused."

"Oops. Sorry. I'm on it. And he'll be occupied long enough for me to fix this. I SWEAR I'll get you to Washington, D.C. this next time. I'm working on a few hours sleep and still don't have the hang of these weird controls. Nothing is in English."

While they waited a pod of whales swam by, one larger than the others, its song a much lower pitch. The ocean began churning violently in every direction. Inky black liquid splashed onto the already slippery rock.

"This isn't good," April said. "There's something down there and I think we're on the menu."

"Hang on," Serise shouted. "Almost there!"

The pod of whales suddenly breached and Ben swore the largest looked right at him as it returned to the water. It charged in their direction, followed by the other whales as enormous tentacles rose out of the water.

"Serise!" Carlos yelled.

"Got it!" she said.

A slimy gray tentacle slithered on to the rock just as they returned to the library.

+38.891239 -77.030198

The portal opened a third time. Aris hesitated, looked at Ben and bared even longer fangs than he'd shown in the past.

"He may be right," Carlos said. "I think we should quit and stop pressing our luck."

Ben shook off the image of aquatic doom at their last location. They were safe now and they still needed the diamond.

"Are you sure this is it, Serise?"

"Positive," she said. "I double checked the numbers by asking Mansurat about the Air and Space Museum. They're both on the National Mall so the numbers were almost identical. I'm sure."

"Then let's go get our prize." Ben shook the last drops of water off his shoes.

Aris didn't budge.

"Kobe beef. Raw. For a week." Ben didn't know how he'd manage that since he only got tofu, salad and berries from the alien green beans in the galley but it worked. Aris was the first to leap through.

Landing outside a line of parked school buses, Ben, Carlos and April were instantly swept forward in a wave of bodies streaming into the building and up a flight of stairs to the IMAX theater. Aris was nowhere in sight.

"I want to see the butterflies," said a freckled girl in a lime green shirt that read, "Faulkner Elementary."

"Me too!" said another girl in the same shirt.

"No!" protested a young boy from the same school. "Rocks first. Or dinosaurs! I hear they've got a T-rex over there!"

"IMAX first," said a woman, firmly. "Then we'll split up into groups. First count off." She looked at April and noticed her lack of school uniform. "Honey, you're not one of our students. Where's your teacher?"

April pointed in a random direction. "Over there, Ma'am. I'm just looking for the bathroom."

"Well, get with your class and find your bathroom buddy first," the woman said before she started herding her own students into the theater like cattle. "The little girls room is over in the corner by the dinosaurs."

As students poured into the theater, April headed towards the bathroom then made a detour, doubled back and found Ben and Carlos in the corner of the mineral room. The jewel case was surrounded by a crowd of people

"What's wrong?" she asked, standing on her toes to look over someone's shoulder.

Carlos fumed. "It's gone. It was taken out last week. This one is a fake. The real one is on its way to the British Museum for a special exhibit."

"Let's go there," April whispered. "We have time."

"We can't," said Carlos. "London is only an hour difference from Harbor time in Egypt. It's two in the morning."

"So?"

"Remember? When Ben went there Kavera was waiting for him pretending to be a guard. He had disabled the alarm systems."

Ben pointed. "Yes. But look at all these people. We can't go during the day. No way to get it with a crowd like this!"

"Serise?" Carlos whispered into the device. "Can you check the British museum? Is the security on? They sent the diamond there."

"Awe man! Okay, back in a minute," she whispered back. "Got to go schmooz with a tall bald guy. He's got security clearances and likes to show off."

"If she can get Mansurat to turn them off, then Aris can walk through the walls, right?" April said. "Where is he anyway?"

"Maybe," Carlos said, looking around and under things as if searching for the missing cat. "But it would still be risky. Of course taking it in the dark means they won't discover it's gone until daytime. And what if it's not there yet? That would be tragic."

While April and Carlos talked strategy, Ben continued staring at the case.

"Ben? You okay?" asked Carlos.

"No one told me the diamond was blue," Ben said.

"Huh? I thought everyone knew that," said Carlos.

"I didn't know," said April. "I always thought they were clear. It's pretty though." She studied the information cards on the wall. "I like this new necklace better than the old one it was in."

Ben kept staring at the photograph of a blue diamond in the center of smaller white ones. *It couldn't be this simple, could it?*

"Hey Carlos. Is this the right size? The one Orin needs?"

"Yeah. The sign says this one is an exact replica. The real Hope Diamond will be back in two months. Why? We can't use a fake. Orin needs to duplicate the boron distribution in the real one."

Ben smiled. "I know where we can get a bigger one. I gave it to the

Dogon Priest while we were playing the game. Aris! Akoosh!"

Aris sauntered in from the direction of the dinosaur exhibit, just as a young boy came screaming towards the IMAX theater. Aris hid behind a large quartz crystal display on the opposite side of the room.

"Mrs. Silverspoon! One of the dinosaurs moved. Honest. It's alive! It bit me when I pulled its tail!"

"That's nice," said the teacher, shooing him into the theater and shaking her head. "I've got to talk to your mother about your active imagination."

Frowning at the cat, Ben said, "Didn't you get in enough trouble when you bit Calamar?"

Aris purred and his orange eyes narrowed.

"What?" Serise said. "Did you say something?"

"Yeah," said Ben. "Don't worry about the museum. Just bring us home before security sees our man-eating cat on the monitors. I've got an idea. Send a coded message to Grace that we're headed back."

He turned to Carlos and April. "Okay team, let's bounce!"

CHAPTER TWENTY-SIX

Detour

Bandiagara Escarpment
14.2318° N, 3.5950° W

∴ With Serise's assistance, Ben and Carlos landed in the Dogon village halfway up a steep sandstone cliff. The girls had stayed behind to stall in case Kavera made a surprise inspection. But Ben knew they also needed to sleep.

"Okay," said Carlos. "Which hut?"

Ben frowned. It was dark and all the thatched roof huts looked the same to him. He ruled out the ones tucked beneath an overhang in the cliff, and those farther down the hill.

"Don't know yet. It was below the cliff. That's all I remember. It was a hologram inside of a hologram."

Carlos blew air out of his lips, then winced and rubbed his arm again.

"You okay," said Ben. "I'm worried about you."

"I'm fine," Carlos said. "Just dead on my feet, if you know what I mean. Let's just find this guy and get the diamond so we can get a few hours of sleep before exercise period starts. You think the one in the game wasn't real? Everything else was."

"Except Easter Island heads don't really move," Ben said. "So we can't be sure." Scanning each structure, he hoped they'd gone to the right location. They'd gotten these coordinates from an online encyclopedia and were lucky Serise was able to distract Mansurat long enough to get the codes right otherwise they'd be shark bait. Still, looking for the Hogon—the village elder—suddenly didn't seem so easy.

"You are lost?" said a voice behind him. A man Ben didn't recognize stepped out of the shadows. Tall and thin, the man wore a blue tunic with white print and a cloth hat with tassels hanging from each side.

"We were looking for someone," Carlos said.

The man paused, then pointed to the star on Ben's badge. "My apologies. You seek our elder?"

"Yes," said Ben. "The Hogon."

"He is not here," said the man. "He has traveled to see the Nommos."

"Oh. Okay," said Ben feeling like he'd reached the end of the road. "I don't know what a Nommo is."

The man seemed confused. "You are Sonecian, correct?"

Ben and Carlos nodded.

"Then you know of them. They who live in the ocean."

Ben's mood brightened. "Atlantis?"

"Shh!" said the man. "Although many are sleeping, we do not speak the name of their city state here. Just their ancient name. Nommos. You will find my father in their company."

Ben smiled. "I remember your father talking about you."

"And I, you," said the man. "He claims we are both stubborn. I believe that makes us perfect candidates to be elders in the future. I can show you the portal, if you like. It is in the village tonuga, our place of gathering. The Nommos have kept the portal open to allow his return." He gestured a hundred feet to the west. Ben and Carlos followed, careful to maintain their footing on the narrow path.

"We wanted to borrow something Ben gave him," Carlos said. "But we don't want to disturb his meeting."

Ben agreed. The thought of going anywhere near that giant squid and his aquatic council made his spine crawl. Uncle Henry wouldn't be there to protect them and there was only so many ways they could bluff creatures that saw them as a potential evening snack. That vampire squid? Something was pretty creepy about him. Even more than the others. And there was no bringing Aris with them for protection given his history with Calamar.

"What is it you seek?" asked the man.

"A blue diamond," Ben said. "Think he left it here?"

The man's eyes lit up. "No. He carries it with him. But you should ask him. I'm sure he will loan it to you. Let us go seek him out! I will take you there myself!"

"You're not supposed to go are you?" Carlos asked.

The man hesitated. "Perhaps. Perhaps not. But as my father has deemed me stubborn, I feel I must not disappoint him by acting contrary to his expectations. You are Sonecian. Who is to say you did not invite me to join you?"

"Man after my own heart," Ben said. "Thanks!"

He stepped into the portal and hoped this wasn't a giant ruse. Serise had set the library portal to allow them to return without her help. They could be out the door and into the corridor before the librarian appeared. But it was set to return him from the Dogon village.

They had to get the diamond first, though. So how would they get home if he went to Atlantis?

CHAPTER TWENTY-SEVEN

Unauthorized

Atlantis I: Location classified

⁂ The main building appeared deserted. No fish, random lights, or servers carrying dishes entered the corridor even though Ben's stomach was starting to grumble and he'd be happy to have more of the fruit drink and shrimp. They'd walked into a pocket of air so the Dogon elder had to be close. Ben was tempted to turn around when he saw the Hogon walking towards him, his long staff tapping on the floor as he walked. Clearly startled, the elder shot a disapproving glance at his son then paused to compose himself.

"What a treat to see you again, Benjamin. I trust my help was sufficient for you to complete your uncle's game and find your way to the Harbor."

"Yes, thanks," Ben said, suddenly thinking this was a bad idea. "This is my friend, Carlos."

"You have an audience with Calamar?" the elder asked, rubbing his white beard.

The sound of the Atlantean leader's name made Ben's body temperature drop. "No sir, I was looking for you. Your son showed us how to find you."

"So it appears," said the elder showing no further emotion.

Just then, the air pocket compressed as the giant octopus, Barakas, appeared. He didn't bother to transform but remained his original length of about fourteen feet. He curled his tentacles until he floated eye to eye with Ben.

"Welcome, young Sonecians. Such a pleasure to see you both so soon after your last visit. You have business here?"

Ben stammered, then composed himself. "I was just—."

The Dogon elder stepped in. "I was late for our meeting at the village. Such a treat to be afforded an audience with his Excellency. I lost complete track of time. Forgive me. I'm afraid my impetuous son brought them here rather than have them wait at my village."

"No need to worry," said Barakas. "We are always willing hosts of Sonecian tribal members. Calamar extends his thanks for your counsel and has departed the facility to negotiate a treaty. Ben, Carlos, we were just finishing our tour. Would you like to see the control room?"

"Sure," said Carlos, shooting a worried look at Ben and then pointing to his watch.

"Ah! Time. I shall be quick, as you say topside," said Barakas. "I'm sure you'll find the tour enlightening and we can send you back to the Harbor in fifteen of your land-based minutes if you'd like. I just need the codes."

Codes? Ben didn't know any codes. Did he mean the GPS locations? Serise had them.

"Thanks," Ben said, "but we have one more errand at the Dogon village before we go back. But I appreciate your offer."

Barakas nodded. "As you wish." He floated towards a corridor on the right and gestured for them to follow. "What is it you seek from the Dogon?" he asked.

"A blue diamond," said Carlos. "We just want to borrow it."

"I see," Barakas said, "I can supply one if needed."

The Dogon priest held up his hand. "No need, Barakas. I am happy to lend them my own. I know it will be returned in good condition." He pulled the stone from his leather pouch and gave it to Carlos.

"As you wish." Barakas led them out of the building, down a causeway and into another. Like Danine, the color of his outer skin changed; from reddish brown, to black to whatever color was nearby as they passed through, almost like camouflage. At times Ben could barely see him as he blended into his surroundings.

The Atlantean control room looked very much like the Harbor's facility. Only their monitors displayed no news streams, only three dimensional holograms of tectonic plate activity, analysis of ocean currents, wind patterns, sea levels and temperature readouts. One showed volcanic activity and magma flow into the ocean near Iceland.

"Open vents on the western edge of the South Atlantic," said a small octopus swimming near a console on the far side of the room.

"South African vents near the Cape up ten percent," said another. "Opening two percent of the vent capacity in the Southern Ocean."

"Confirmed," said a voice on the other end that sounded human. "Weather alerts now show three eyes forming."

"Three eyes? As in three hurricane eyes?" asked Ben, marveling at how the octopi could manage the consoles as well as any human and with eight arms each, they could get more done faster.

"The Sonecian teams need to search the area so we're manufacturing a storm to force human water craft to detour out of the area," said Barakas. "The Hayoolkáál are shifting wind currents around the Cape of Good Hope. Combined with a rise in water temperature, we sought to create a minor hurricane in the area. Manufacturing storms is a delicate operation and it appears we miscalculated as the action has spawned three."

"This is so cool," said Carlos. "Wasn't that area once called the Cape of Storms?"

"Indeed! I am impressed," said a technician with giant ears like an elephant.

While the technician explained the logistics of storm management to the others, Ben was distracted by a monitor at the far end of the room. Barakas followed him. "Something catch your eye, young warrior?"

Ben looked at the readouts. "You're tracking your teams?"

"Always. And Harbor teams when they're in our domain."

"Domain?" Ben asked.

Barakas tilted his head. "The water of course. We track most activity below sea level which is significantly more vast than Earth's topside landmass." He pulled up a globe and set it to spin on the monitor. "For instance, we track the impact of SOSUS on whale migration." Four tentacles pointed to data points around the world.

"So's us?" Ben asked, confused.

"Pardon," said Barakas. "Sound Surveillance System. Underwater listening posts established by topsider military. The sonar vibrations wreak havoc on our ocean environment."

"My uncle asked about a whale at the meeting."

"Indeed he did," Barakas said. "Is he any closer to locating the specimen?"

Ben shrugged but kept staring at the monitor, searching for something that would spell hope. Pointing to a location near Japan, he said, "Can you stop there?"

Barakas complied. Points of light appeared a hundred miles off the coast.

"Is that the other Atlantis outpost?"

"It is," Barakas said, zooming in on a stretch of ocean but no further. "I am impressed. The Devil's Sea facility which is known as Atlantis II. That region is also known as The Dragon's Triangle."

Ben froze. Eight stationary beacons blipped in the area. Each a different color from the others.

"What are those?" Ben asked, afraid to be hopeful.

"Anomaly," Barakas said, suddenly changing the screen to another location farther south. "Ghost signals. There is nothing there to be concerned about. Perhaps you would be interested in the Marianas Trench."

"No! Go back!" Ben tried to keep his excitement in check. Aurelia had also said there was nothing there shortly after she'd arrived. But what if she was wrong? The phrase "ghost signal" gave Ben pause.

"Any chance of looking again?" Ben asked as Barakas navigated back to the signals. They were gone.

Barakas eyed him thoughtfully. "You thought it might be your parents?"

Ben nodded. "You have any kids?"

Barakas shook his bulbous head back and forth. "No."

"Why not?" Ben asked. "Oops. Sorry. That was kind of personal."

"No offense taken," Barakas said. "I don't have offspring because giant octopi die after we mate. So that's not something high on my to-do list. Dying that is." He slipped a tentacle under the console and produced a tiny thumb drive a half inch long. "This will be between you and me. The codes to Atlantis II should you decide to check for yourself at the Harbor. I assure you, there is nothing there to find. Whatever made those signals is long gone. Perhaps locators left behind when the teams evacuated in a panic."

Ben tucked the flash drive in his pocket. "Thanks. I might check it out for myself if I get the chance."

"As you wish," said Barakas. "Atlantis has strict security protocols. But as Kurosh seems to trust you so shall I trust you also. We believe the whale your uncle seeks was last seen in that area. But let's keep that between us. Don't want to get anyone's hopes up unnecessarily until it can be verified."

CHAPTER TWENTY-EIGHT

Why?

⋮ "That was so much fun!" Ben said, dancing around the apartment and trying to avoid the morning ritual of drinking his mother's "make kids look like humans" formula that sat on the table. "Where are we going next?"

"Don't push our luck," said Grace. "We only got a few hours of sleep. I'm exhausted and still in trouble for sneaking into the tube factory. Plus we've got to meet our teams in thirty minutes." She grabbed the flask labeled with her name and downed the contents in a single draw.

Ben stared in horror.

"Better if you just chug it," Grace said. "A few seconds versus a few minutes on your tongue is like a lifetime."

Ben grabbed his flask and tried it. He got halfway through when he began gagging. "You're a superhero, Grace. That's all I've got to say." He held his nose and got the rest down in a single disgusting gulp. Kavera had slipped a note on to the tray:

> *"For young warriors in need of homework practice. Translate these three sentences and I might be persuaded to visit a comic book*

store on my way home. To aid in your discovery I have eliminated punctuation, numbers but not capital letters. Have the librarian transmit the answer to me while I'm in the field. :-)"

01010100 01101000 01100101 01110010 01100101 00100000 01100001 01110010
01100101 00100000 01110100 01100101 01101110 00100000 01110100 01111001
01110000 01100101 01110011 00100000 01101111 01100110 00100000 01110000
01100101 01101111 01110000 01101100 01100101 00100000 01101001 01101110
00100000 01110100 01101000 01100101 00100000 01110111 01101111 01110010
01101100 01100100

01010100 01101000 01101111 01110011 01100101 00100000 01110111 01101000
01101111 00100000 01110101 01101110 01100100 01100101 01110010 01110011
01110100 01100001 01101110 01100100 00100000 01100010 01101001 01101110
01100001 01110010 01111001 00100000 01100011 01101111 01100100 01100101

01000001 01101110 01100100 00100000 01110100 01101000 01101111 01110011
01100101 00100000 01110111 01101000 01101111 00100000 01100100 01101111
00100000 01101110 01101111 01110100

Ben groaned loudly. "Serise?"
She threw up her hands. "What? I don't want any comic books."
Ben pouted. "But I do!"
"Just mark the ones that say 00100000. Those are blank spaces. Then it's just figuring out the letters from the cheat sheet the librarian gave us. Just remember capitol letters code differently than lower case."
Ben glowered but after fifteen minutes he had the solution to Kavera's sick choice of a joke:

> *There are 10 types of people in the world*
> *Those who understand binary code*
> *And those who do not*

Carlos walked into the room with a box of parts, a slight limp and a huge grin on his face.

"Is that it?" asked Ben, ignoring his vegetarian breakfast burrito with its soggy flavorless wrap and snagging ham from Carlos's plate instead.

Carlos slid the box on the table. "Yep! Orin came through with his end of the bargain. By the way, the diamond worked perfectly. I could tell he was happy. His smile was only slightly bigger than your uncle's. At least a millimeter long. I didn't tell him you got it for me. Hope you don't mind."

"No problem. I know how your team rolls." Ben frowned when he looked inside the box. "It's all in pieces."

"But I think you'll recognize it." Carlos pulled out the dome of the ancient white computer, a silver arm and a lot of mechanical parts. Chips. Circuit boards. Cords. Even a mouse. "This one's regular. It's not like my dad's so we'll need a power source. Got any lemons or grapefruits in the garden, April?"

"I think we'll need more than that to get enough power," she said.

"And there's no electric plugs in here. What do you say, Serise? Want to help me put a computer together and come up with a power source?"

"We don't need to do all that," said Serise. "I've already got a working computer. Maybe there's some software on it that we can use. They probably didn't bother to wipe the hard drive. Who's going to hack into their system down here? If we find some stuff, we can load it on mine. They installed a self-contained power cell in the battery compartment. And Harbor teams will never think to look at my laptop because they've already wiped it."

Carlos narrowed his eyes, looking frightfully like his Casmirian teammates. "But you're the only one with a computer so now we've got two. That was the whole point of going out to get a diamond. So I'd have a computer that reminds me of my father's! I'll just get a power cell from somewhere else."

Serise blinked. "Sorry. You're right. I'll help you rebuild it."

Carlos's expression softened, then he held out his hand in a high five and got one in return. "Okay. Thanks. So now. What's the plan? Where are we going next?"

"I believe Ben has just covered that topic," said Grace, imitating Uncle Henry's voice almost precisely.

"Whoa!" said April. "That was amazing, Grace. You sounded just like him! Okay, so the teams are looking for tribes, but we don't know which ones. Do you think it's the same clues as in the game? You know Uncle Henry. He is always trying to teach us something and the man doesn't like to waste."

Serise pursed her lips and cupped her chin in one hand. Her eyebrows creased as if she were thinking it through. "We can probably bet they're related to the teams that came down from the ship. Just look at where they're going. Norway to look for Laplanders called Saami. New Zealand to check out the Moari. Southwest in America. But we already know that, because my parents were working with the Navajo Nation."

"Okay," Ben said. "We can rule out Africa, Central America, Tibet, and what, New Mexico and Arizona?"

"No, we can't," Grace said. "Because we don't know what artifacts they're looking for. And with migration those artifacts could have ended up anywhere on the planet."

"Let's ask the librarian," April said.

Everyone stopped and blinked at April. Ben groaned at the obvious nature of that comment.

"Good point, but she might not tell us." Carlos said, picking through the box and trying to fit parts together.

"Unless we turn it into lesson plans," said April. "I don't know about you but I can't decode machine language. It all looks the same to me without a decoder. One zero one one one zero zero one. Repeat. Get one thing wrong and the whole thing is wrong. Could blow up a planet if you get the code wrong. So yeah, let's go find some more keys as long as there aren't any booby traps because there's no 'start over' button if we make a mistake."

"Wait!" Carlos said, "That day we were attacked, our parents said they already had some of the keys. I mean, that's what I would be looking for first if I were one of the teams. The keys that belong to our own tribes. They don't even sit together at meals. So why wouldn't they be looking out for their own self interests?"

"Because the world is going to blow up if they don't," Grace said, sarcastically.

"Okay. Let's ask Kavera again if we can see the keys," Carlos continued. "I asked Orin and he said they haven't found any yet. So someone is lying to someone and I don't think it's Orin. He's a straight shooter."

"Maybe, but we all heard our parents say they'd figured out some of the clues so I'll try to wear Kavera down until he gives us a hint." Ben said, his excitement growing. "Then we can help find them." He pumped his fist up and down and started dancing again. "I mean, after all, we did find the key for the Easter Island terraformer."

"By accident," said Carlos. "I don't think lightning is going to hit us twice."

Ben kept dancing to silent music only he could hear. "It would if we could get our hands on Volari's trident. It's a giant lightning rod."

Serise groaned. "Ha ha. Let's not go there, okay? That's a trip I want to forget even if we are protected class humans."

"Any chance there's game software on Carlos's new old computer," asked April. "That Smithsonian trip WAS a lot of fun, if you leave out the part about almost freezing, drowning and being attacked by a whale. Think we could use the GPS dialer to get out of here without going through the library? That way Serise could come with us."

"I doubt it," said Ben. "The game was programmed just for us and not by Carlos's dad or any of the other parents. It was a one time only deal so we'd end up at the Harbor. And there probably won't be transport information on it because who lugs around a big computer to dial themselves around the planet when they have remote access on their tablets?"

"But it might have other stuff we can use," Serise said. "Maybe it's got floor plans of the Harbor. They must have other transport pads otherwise all the equipment would have to come through the Control room. And it doesn't. If we can look at the programs on the hard drive without tapping into the server, that would give us a head start. It would give us some clues."

"And maybe it will tell us what else they're doing," said Ben.

"Maybe," said Grace. "But remember the teams were supposed to be evacuating the planet. They didn't know a new team was coming down. Whatever they're doing now isn't going to be on this computer unless something was sent in advance and I doubt it because your uncle seemed surprised about the new mission. So we still need Serise to help us get access to the new information."

"I could try negotiating with Orin while he's in a good mood," said Carlos. "He's happily replicating blue diamonds with the new boron configuration. Plus, Casmirians don't hold back much, so they must know something."

Ben shook his head. "Maybe, but it was a Xenobian team that installed the tubes and put that giant lock on the door. And it's only my team and some gray space aliens working in there. Plus Danine and you know she's not going to tell us anything."

"Well, the tubes aren't human abduction experiments. Orin said they don't do that anymore."

Ben choked. "Anymore? You mean they used to?"

Carlos shrugged. "Guess it was mostly Alpha Centaurians. I don't think those gray aliens are them because they're too preoccupied defending their planet to come to Earth."

"Focus people. We're on a mission. If we can get extra parts," said Serise, "I could probably hack the Mac with Carlos to make it work on my computer. They don't use wi-fi in the complex. Everything is wired with the outer space version of high speed fiber optic. If we don't connect to it, we won't leave a trail."

"Then we need two things," said Ben. "Find out what artifacts they're searching for, and get extra parts. Shouldn't be that hard."

"Parts are easy. It's that information thing that's going to be tough.

Every time we ask a question someone says it's classified. The operative question is how are we going to get information out of the teams?"

"That's easy, said April. "We'll just play the 'why' game."

"The 'why' game?" asked Grace. "What's that?"

"Come on," said April. "Think like a kid. You just keep asking a question and when adults answer you say 'why?' until they wear out and tell you what you want to know or give you something. Might not work on Orin, but the other teams might be easier. We are kids. They know we weren't trained by our parents. So anything they tell us isn't really going to be something that they think we'll understand. Or can use. They don't think we're as sophisticated as they are. So play the 'why' game. Why is this? Why is that? Why does it work that way? And add a lot of flattery. It works on parents. It's probably going to work on these teams. We are kids. They like us. They want us to spend time with our tribes."

"April!" said Ben, "You're brilliant. That's what I used to do to Mom when I wanted something. But I'd wear out before she did because, well, she's our mom so she was immune to our charms. I'm betting from the way the teams looked at us when they came off the ship that they're dying to get to know us as much as we are trying to get them to spill some secrets. Plus Kavera said they wanted us to live with them. Maybe this is the next best thing."

"Then let's do it. Even Danine will crack if you act cute around her." April crinkled her nose as if to look extra adorable.

"For you, maybe," said Grace, grumbling. "For the rest of us she's all business. But I like the plan. Spend time with the teams outside of the training sessions. Learn everything we can about them, even the ones we don't belong to. And then use it to get out of here. Because I'm telling you. I'm bored. And I'm too young to be trying to learn binary code and calculus. Especially from a librarian made from that code."

"Okay. Game on!" Ben said, "And while we're playing the "why" game let's see if Kavera will tell us what the tubes under the Libyan desert are for."

CHAPTER TWENTY-NINE

Library Redux

The team shuffled into the library in single file. No one wanted to be the first to find out they'd failed their homework. Ben wasn't fast enough and ended up at the head of the line.

The librarian appeared right away. "Greetings, young warriors. I look forward to this next chapter in your learning!"

Ben eyed her with suspicion as his friends sat down. "You're not mad at us?"

"Mad? For what reason?"

"Using the library portals to go to Washington," Carlos said.

The librarian appeared perplexed. "Not at all. I applaud your ingenuity. The portals are now closed to all but authorized adults with security clearance, but I trust the adventure was fruitful."

Everyone relaxed. Grace beamed and nodded. Ben wondered what that was about.

"We have a question," said April. "We were wondering, instead of math homework and coding, could we talk about Earth history?"

The librarian's eyes lit up. "But of course. What period of time would you like to start with? For instance I find the dinosaur period to be fascinating. We could start with their first appearance in the Triassic period and trace their evolution through the Jurassic and Cretaceous periods. That would take us through roughly two hundred million years."

"That sounds interesting," said Carlos, sitting up straighter.

Ben elbowed him in the side. "Ickstay with the ansplay," he whispered in the clumsiest example of Pig Latin he'd ever tried, then said out loud. "We've already seen the Jurassic Park movie, so we were thinking of something else."

The librarian seemed perplexed and searched her database. "That cinematic feature is fiction and does not serve has a substitute for scholarly research."

Grace kicked his leg. "He's just joking."

"I see," said the librarian visibly relaxing. "Perhaps we could start earlier in Earth's timeline. For instance when Earth's land mass consisted of a single continent Earth scientists call Pangea. There are fascinating theories about how it broke apart due to tectonic plate movement. Land is much more stable on all but a few Sonecian planets so the contrast might be a good research paper. Did you know the fragment of Earth's crust containing India and Nepal collided with the land mass now containing Tibet and China thus forming the Himalayan mountain range. If the portals weren't closed we could mount an amazing field trip to the top of Chomolungma."

"Huh?" asked Ben? "Chomo what?

"Chomolungma, the indigenous Tibetan name for the mountain unfortunately renamed Everest by the British to honor one of their own surveyors."

"Or Sagarmatha," said Grace, "which is the Nepalese name."

"Correct!" said the librarian, beaming. "A glorious treasure trove of prehistoric sea creatures buried in the limestone at the summit. Imagine, finding fossils almost nine thousand meters above sea level!"

"Stick with the plan!" Ben repeated through a cough while smiling at his friends.

"We'd like to start with the Sonecian's coming here," said Serise. "We know the teams are looking for artifacts. And we know they sent ancestors down to blend in with people already here. But we're curious about the canopic jars in the Guardian room and what the teams are looking for that can open them. And can you give us a hint on why they have all those glass stasis tubes under the Libyan desert?"

The librarian's face went blank. "That information has been encrypted by Danine. I have no access to it."

"So it IS in the database?" asked Ben.

"It appears so," she said. "Encrypted. I am not authorized to access it."

April winked. "But why?"

The librarian furrowed her brows. "Because I have not been given access."

"How come?" April pressed, her eyes as wide as saucers.

"Because they don't want me to have access," the librarian said without getting annoyed.

Ben made a slashing motion. The 'why' game clearly didn't work on a hologram made of binary code.

"Okay. How about telling us what keys they've already found?" He braced for another round of *"no access"* or even *"classified."*

Instead she said, "That information has not been uploaded into my database. However, to understand what the teams are attempting to find you would need to understand creation myths of the various civilizations on the planet."

Her many arms reached out to levels in the library and dumped a large pile of thick books. Popol Vue, The Bahane Diné, the Bible, The Koran, The Talmud, and on and on until the table towered with volumes.

Ben's head sagged. "Is there a Cliff Notes version of all of that?"

The librarian laughed so hard her bun unraveled. The virtual white braid was almost as long as Rapunzel's. "Perhaps," she said, seeming embarrassed and flustered about the hair malfunction. "But how does one find treasure in something that has already been sifted and filtered? The journey is as important as the discovery." She hastily coiled her braid and repinned it to the top of her head.

"Okay." said Serise. "What if we just start with one."

"Mayan," said Carlos, pulling Popol Vue from the bottom of the pile.

"Why?" said Ben.

"Because one of the stories involves superhero twins, a ball court, and bringing their father back from the underworld," said Carlos.

Ben straightened. "Now that's what I'm talkin' about!" He reached for the book. "It's got my vote if it's got basketball!"

The girls groaned.

"Basketball? Really?" Grace leaned back in her chair and rolled her eyes.

Ben stuck out his tongue. "Well, you got a jacuzzi with bubble bath. I think we deserve to get first dibs on a request."

April laughed. "You got three pairs of four hundred dollar sneakers. So we should at least vote on it."

Carlos coughed. "Four hundred dollars? Each? Do they shoot baskets for you?"

Grace grumbled. "Enough with the sports talk. I think it would go faster if the girl's picked a second book. In some religions the girls rank pretty high. I mean, you don't get twins without some female, somewhere, having the power to create them.

"First Woman," said Serise.

"Eve," said April.

"Nintu in Sumerian lore," the librarian chimed in. "The Sun Mother in Australia."

"And in Tibet it's an extraterrestrial woman who mated with an Earthly being to create the human race," Grace taunted as if declaring check mate.

The girls exchanged high fives.

Grace smirked. "There are three of us and two of you. So I say, yes, let's vote!"

Carlos frowned and shot a pleading look at Serise. She softened her expression, then shrugged.

"I think I'll vote with Carlos this time. We played the game separately back home and, okay, the girls were faster—"

Ben threw up his hands. "Why do you have to go there?"

Serise laughed. "My bad. What I mean is, I kind of think we work better as a team. When we got lost on the way here we worked together. No more girls against the boys. What do you say, Grace and April?"

"Okay, I'm in," April grumbled.

Ben looked at Grace who remained silent. "Please?"

She frowned, pursed her lips, then turned her scowl into a smile. "Fine. Friends forever."

"Not just friends," Ben said. "Family."

"Then Mayan legends are a perfect choice," said the librarian. "Because all creation stories are grounded in some truths. The legends are just a people's way of trying to describe what they've experienced or to give meaning to their environment. The Bahane Diné tells of powerful twins just as the Mayans believed. The same themes show up in a number of myths, for instance those of Tibet which suggest twins become the Sun and the Moon. Other's suggest twins defeat a great evil. But many cultures believe their first origins came from somewhere beyond the planet. Perhaps from the same spring as your ancestors. For instance, in many cultures females are revered as a spiritual heart for a people, just as it is seen with the Hailookail and Xenobians. The power to heal and the spiritual center for the Xenobian tribes is passed down through women."

April scrunched up her nose and beamed. "Like my mother?"

"Precisely," said the librarian. "For Sonecians, the difficulty in finding the keys needed to unlock the Guardian is that over time people have migrated and their traditions began to commingle. The stories are similar but different, making it difficult to find threads the Sonecian ancestors may have left behind. Items are lost or buried. The original codes and texts are no longer accessible. Even to me. When there were more of us, here at the library, we worked tirelessly to locate clues or fragments of clues in texts, museum exhibits, private collections and sheets of music."

"Music?" April asked.

"Indeed yes. You are skilled, are you not?"

"I'm just okay on piano," she said.

"She's actually pretty good," said Ben, giving his sister a fist bump.

"Then you understand that music is another type of math formula or coded language. We scan it looking for patterns that may be seeded there. The fact that so many people respond instinctively to patterns in music is considered a clue. Even patterns in the landscape cannot be discounted as random events. Or ruins left by ancient civilizations. The heads of Olmec bear a striking resemblance to both people of Asia and of Africa. The Moai of which you are familiar harbor mysteries of their own. Earth scientists are only now discovering what we have known for years, that the heads are attached to bodies that extend deep beneath the ground. Even these pyramids that shield the Harbor and other large structures on Earth occur across the planet with some regularity. Often along the same geographic plane."

"So things like the Nazca lines in Peru are clues?" asked Carlos.

The librarian laughed. "No. Those are landing fields built by your ancestors. Conspiracy theorists are correct. The reason they can be seen from the sky is because they are meant to be viewed from a high altitude."

Carlos nodded appreciatively.

"As for the multitude of other mysteries," the librarian continued, "we leave—as you say on Earth—no stone unturned. We start by aligning Sonecian tribal cultures with those most closely mirrored on Earth. Even references to serpents may actually be clues to DNA markers."

She opened a hologram of a DNA strand, its double helix spiraling in front of them.

"If we were to assume the references are literal, then we must analyze genetic patterns. But there are now more than seven billion people living on Earth compared to five million when teams first arrived. Despite the Harbor's substantial computing facilities, it is a daunting task. No different than searching for a single grain of sand in a desert. But as we have time, and because your files say that as a team you were able to recover a programming rod for Rapa Nui, I think you will find this research enjoyable. It is certainly clear from your often half-done math and coding homework that your hearts are not in it."

"I just don't see the point," said Ben. "If everything is going to end in a year or so."

The librarian pulled out a virtual chair and sat at the table for the first time. Her tone grew serious. "It is said that the leading cause of death is birth. All life ends at some point after that. It isn't how long you have that is important. It is how you choose to spend that time that matters. That if it ends, you lived a life worth remembering and you died doing something honorable."

Silence.

The librarian frowned. "I did not mean for this to sound so glum. Life and death, as is the custom in each of your tribes, is to be celebrated. Let us celebrate starting with Mayan myths and work our way through the others step by step. The Maya were a technologically sophisticated and advanced civilization at a time when Europeans were still living in the dark ages." She pulled up a holographic display, complete with videos. "Let us begin."

CHAPTER THIRTY

Accommodations

Braced for another fight, Ben walked up to the counter for lunch. "If you say I'm a vegetarian one more time I'm going to have you melted down for scrap metal."

"That statement is not logical," the green chef said, tongs reaching in the opposite direction of the vegetables. "I am not made of metal and you are not vegetarian."

Ben blinked. "What?"

The chef put a small portion of pink fish on his plate. It measured about four inches in length and width and was about an inch thick. "You are not vegetarian. You are Casmirian on a diet. Limited portions."

Carlos started laughing, then coughed as the server heaped the usual half continent's worth of beef and fish on his own plate.

"Can I have some more?" Ben asked.

"Not authorized. You are Casmirian on a diet."

Ben looked down at the fish which occupied the part of his plate normally heaping with tofu and said a silent prayer. "Okay. Thank you!"

The server nodded, then plopped a spoon full of red berries and a small ceramic container containing something dark and brown on his plate. "Dessert and garnish," it said. Ben groaned. The contents of the container were the color of poop. That wasn't going in his mouth.

"More?" the server asked.

"No. I want ice cream. I really miss ice cream," Ben said, walking towards the table where his friends had already gathered. Everyone had the container of poop filled custard sitting on their plates. It was cold and topped with a crusty substance and tiny pebbles.

"I'm not touching that," said April. "No, nyet and not a chance. Their cooking is worse than my mother's."

"What ails you now, young never satisfied warriors?" asked Kavera, accompanied by Berko, a member of Aurelia's triad. Kavera sat his tray on the table but continued standing. Aris sauntered by, sniffing at the table and letting out a growl of approval when he got to the meat.

"Something is wrong with the server," said Ben. "He gave me the wrong menu."

"Me too," said April, pointing to the fish on her plate.

"He did not," Kavera said. "He was simply persuaded to accommodate your dietary needs."

"And how'd you manage that?" Carlos asked.

"We added Earth-based disability requirements to his database. You have been granted, what we like to call, special accommodations. I did not want to risk our team leader's ire by reprogramming galley software to provide meat on a Xenobian diet, so I modified the accounts to show you are Casmirians in need of weight loss. This is temporary so don't get used to it. I secured a sampling of steelhead trout on my most recent outing. I thought it had your names on it. But I am happy to remove it if you request."

Ben took a bite and sighed in relief. It was light, moist and seasoned with lemons and fresh basil. Almost tasted like salmon. He thought he'd died and gone to heaven.

"Can he put me on the same diet?" Carlos asked. "Because my portion is larger than the state of Nebraska."

"I believe so," said Kavera. "But Pendon would likely disapprove.

In the alternative, I would recommend giving your extra portions to Aris and Bastet. We've found that they are much more affectionate to people who give them table scraps."

Carlos tipped his plate. Aris increased in size, snatched the largest portion of meat available and began tearing it apart on the floor.

Berko growled. "Aris? Table manners. Act like a sentient being or you don't go with me to Java to hunt with your Earth-based panther friends."

Aris glowered, flicked his tail against Berko's leg hard enough to make a slapping sound, then took his prize to the end of the galley where his trays were stored.

"Keep that up, spoiled kitty," Kavera said. "I can program the cook to give you instant oatmeal and canned cat food from the convenience aisle of a gas station!"

Aris turned and let out a reverberating growl so loud it startled everyone in the room. He sounded like a T-Rex.

Kavera laughed and slapped hands with Berko. "Now, back to the meal. What is your concern about your dessert, young demanding warriors?"

"Look at it," said Ben. "Does that look natural to you?"

Kavera frowned and sighed. "I thought, perhaps, with Aurelia in the field, I could ask the cook to indulge you. But I am happy to take it back." He took Ben's dish, scooped out a portion, and then raised the spoon to his lips.

April jumped up. "Don't eat that! We don't know what it is!"

Kavera shrugged, winked and put the spoon in his mouth. "Tastes like Belgian chocolate to me. What do you think, Berko?"

Berko took his spoon and scooped a large portion into his mouth. "Yes. Belgian chocolate. Extra fine grade. Forty Earth dollars per half kilogram."

Ben's mouth dropped. "Chocolate?"

"We are strict. But we are not heartless. We stopped in Brussels and Zadra had a chance to taste an unusual creme brûlée. She thought you might like it, so we smuggled some home."

"You did that for us?" Serise snatched up her bowl and dove in. "It's so good. You're like gods!"

"Not quite," Kavera said. "But I am flattered by the compliment. Now I suggest you scarf—is that the word—that portion down before Danine finds out. It is a limited supply. And as Aurelia will not be back at the Harbor until this evening, you will not be chastised for this breach in protocol. Eat up, and she'll be none the wiser. It was also modified to clear your system before Danine's next physical."

Ben snatched his desert back from Kavera and saw it was half gone. Kavera exchanged his own uneaten portion for Ben's. Berko put his on the table as well.

"For the young skeptical food warriors to share. But we shall not speak of this to our leader. She insists on a certain food protocol during missions."

"It's a plan!" Ben said, his mouth full of creamy goodness. "Aurelia is kind of strict."

"Indeed, yes. My sister is very strict." Kavera, grinned broadly and winked as he picked up his tray and headed for the door with Berko.

Sister? Ben's mouth dropped to the table, and he was not alone in that reaction.

CHAPTER THIRTY-ONE

Shut Down

⁘ "Screwdriver," said Carlos. "Or whatever the alien equivalent of this thing is."

"Check," said Serise taking the tool from him. "Splunger."

"Check," said Carlos accepting the flat plastic tool in return. "Where'd you get the power source?" he asked.

"Umm. Let's say that I visited the galley and now one of the food machines is down. Consider that a blessing," she said. "I tried reprogramming the database so we could get decent food but it's coded in binary language and the library lessons weren't helpful in figuring it out. I got some of it decoded but it translated into a weird foreign language. I copied part of the code and fed it through a program I set up on my laptop and all I got were sounds like boop, beep, boopity beep beep. Not even Morse code."

Carlos laughed. "Bummer. Probably a trick to keep nosy kids out. Or team members on strict menu plans who want real food, not sacrificial proteins and vegetables. Those meals are enough to make me ask for double portions of the green glob formula. I could use another one of those chocolate things, though."

Serise reached into the replacement backpack Kavera bought for her and pulled out a wrapped container and a spoon.

"Ask and you shall receive. It's the last one so we have to split it five ways. Or until we can convince Kavera or someone on my team to go get us something else."

"So where is Grace anyway?" Ben asked, peeking up from a pile of authentic graphic novels Kavera brought back from Japan. He was just at the part where some bicycle dude was challenging another guy to a bike race. Although it was sometimes confusing having to read the pages from right to left instead of left to right.

"Meditating with her team," Serise said. "She's been gone all day. And April's in the garden to try to get us some food the chef hasn't altered. Right now I'd settle for a tomato."

"Did Grace tell you what she's doing in training?"

"Not a peep," said Serise. "At first she used to come back with a headache. She tried hiding it but she'd go into the room and sit on her bed with her hands on her head. But now? Nada. She seems fine. Just sits there and meditates before she goes to bed. Can't pry it out of her. When your uncle said her team won't talk about what they're doing, he wasn't kidding."

Ben frowned and looked at the pile of computer parts on the table. "Need some help?"

"Nope," said Carlos. "Almost done. We'll check it out first then make back-up copies to Serise's computer just in case."

"How'd you get the parts?" Ben asked.

Carlos laughed and gave Serise a high five. "We took April's advice and wore people down until they gave us stuff. Even Orin got sick of me and told me to take whatever I wanted if I would get out of his hair and let him concentrate." He held his hand up to Serise. "Torx screwdriver?"

"Check!" She handed him a tiny tool with a star shaped end.

He screwed a rectangular block into the computer's cavity, then placed the cover back on the white dome.

"What do you think, Serise. Ready for launch?"

"Beats me," she said. "I code, I don't build."

"Well," said Carlos. "I've never done major surgery on a computer. It will either work, not work, or explode." He hit the power button and, clearly holding his breath, backed away.

The computer chimed followed by the sound of the ancient drive crunching data.

"So far so good," said Serise.

The monitor, which still looked a little wobbly, turned on as well, showing the hoped for boot up sequence. Even Ben was holding his breath. In seconds the desktop was revealed. Carlos clicked the finder and yelled, "Score!"

"What'd you find," Ben said, looking over his shoulder.

"Not sure, but it's got a file with floor plans of the Harbor, an alien browser and what looks like some video games."

"Anything useful?" Serise said? "Like dialer software, clues to what the teams are looking for? Anything?"

"Nothing I can read," said Carlos. "Just machine code. Want to practice?"

Serise blew a raspberry.

Ben pointed. "Fire that up. Looks like game software."

Carlos turned to face him. "Remember the last time we activated software without knowing what we were doing?"

"I plead the fifth," said Ben. "But since we're not connected to the internet, what's the big deal?"

Carlos frowned. "You're right. Let's see what this bad boy can do."

Unable to read the language, he clicked on a map of the world. A window opened revealing continents and several avatars.

"Looks like a game to me," Ben said. "We've got time on our hands. Want to play?"

"Looks like my father's Art of War game. Let's pick the Middle East. Lots of stuff going on there." Carlos navigated to the region. Video clips of explosions, fighting and rioting streamed.

"You sure this thing isn't connected?" Ben asked.

Serise pointed to a wall just to the left of the couch. "See that hole there? Fiber optic connection. We need a cable to hook into it, and I haven't managed to "why" my way to getting one. I think the warriors are catching on. The last one, whose name I can't pronounce said, 'I wrote that book long before you read it, young warrior'."

"What does that mean?" Ben asked.

Serise laughed. "He said it meant he was our age once and it didn't work on adults when he tried it either. Guys, I think our reputation is out. Even Mansurat said no and I pulled out all the flattery I could think of. He's still mad about the Smithsonian."

Chuckling, Ben pulled a chair next to Carlos and sat down. "Okay. You take the country on the left and I'll take the country on the right. It will be like Battleship, only you keep my bombs out and I'll keep your bombs out."

When they tried to launch an attack the computer asked for a password.

"Uh oh!" said Carlos.

They tried every name and code they could think of. The names of their home planets, the fake identities their parents used, the name of the neighborhood they lived in and their own names. Nothing.

"Well, that was a bust," Carlos said.

Ben watched the action unfold on the screen. A massive war with fighting among civilians and terrorists.

"Kind of gets old," He pulled the keyboard closer, typed something and hit enter.

The fighting stopped suddenly.

Thirty seconds later, Ben's uncle stormed into the apartment. "What do you children think you are—"

Before he could finish, his tablet lit up. "Jemadari," said a voice on the other end. "The fighting in Syria has ceased temporarily. A message from an old communication unit appeared in the sky."

"What did it say?" Ben's uncle asked in a low growl.

The voice on the other end cracked. "It said, 'Stop fighting. You are a disgrace! This is God speaking!'"

Ben covered his mouth to stifle a laugh. In the monitor he could see Sonecian teams rushing into the area to retrieve fragments of a religious temple. No one on the ground noticed. Everyone was still looking at the sky and pointing.

Ben heard another loud growl but when he turned around his uncle was gone. Minutes later, and thousands of miles away, his uncle was on the scene directing the teams.

Carlos and Serise looked over his shoulder.

"That's a good thing right?" Serise asked.

CHAPTER THIRTY-TWO

State of Grace

The Shakrarian compound was comfortable but not lush. The team members rarely spent time here because they were almost always working in the field. Even their living quarters were spare. Only the essentials were provided: a table, chairs, a couch and bed for when they returned for meditation. No tapestries or paintings. Just simple woven rugs to warm their feet. Grateful to be living in the Xenobian compound with her friends, Grace worried about why she'd suddenly been summoned to this section of the complex. The weaving room was normally off limits to her.

She sat beside her mentor, a thin man with a long gray beard, as he prepared a large loom placed in the center of the floor. Nearby, a window displayed their planet's environment, with its mountainous terrain, large waterfalls and three moons.

In this room, nearly empty except for millions of golden orb spiders, the sacred cloth worn by the team was woven by hand. It was their only indulgence.

"This will be your meditation," Tenzin said. "When I am feeling uncentered, I find solace in the work here."

"You could use machines to do this," Grace said. "There are ones that can extract spider silk and spin it into threads automatically. I saw a beautiful gold shawl made from their silk at a museum in New York."

"The value is in the meditation," Tenzin said quietly. "Not in the end result. Your parents taught you the tenets of our culture?"

Grace nodded.

"Explain," Tenzin said, his voice quiet and low as he moved a shuttle back and forth to start the first rows of the cloth.

"To identify the cause of suffering. To defeat darkness and bring light. To achieve nirvana by following eight paths: vision, aspiration, truthful speech, action, livelihood, effort, awareness and concentration through meditation. It is part of Buddhism."

"And it is our way as well," Tenzin said. "The same tenets, similar paths to achieve them. Enlightenment is the highest state of being. Achieved by meditation and service to others."

"But what we do," Grace said. "What we keep secret—"

"Allows us to help others achieve the same goals. A rebirth as it were, as energy is passed from one soul to another. And so you will keep this part of our practice to yourself."

"The spiders?"

"And their purpose." He smiled and placed the shuttle in her hand. "Be mindful to practice your faith every day. Enlightenment is a journey. We do not expect it to occur so early in your training. We are, however, impressed with your progress. It must have occurred to you that the Harbor would register my presence in two places on the planet at one time and raise alarms about a possible breach."

Grace's stomached turned into knots. "I'm sorry."

"Why apologize? The deed is done. Did you accomplish your goal in Kansas City?"

Grace nodded and diverted her gaze to the window and its view of an unfamiliar landscape she should be calling home.

Tenzin put his hand on her shoulder. "You are very young, and yet your journey and your ingenuity revealed you are ready for greater responsibilities."

On the far side of the chamber hung a wall of new cloaks, all gold.

Soon they would be dyed in a bath of white liquid to conceal their origin and purpose. A tenet: forgo luxury to achieve a higher calling. After she wove the required length of cloth, someone would help her fashion it into a cloak for herself. Grace pressed the treadle with her foot causing half the warp threads to lift so her shuttle could pass through to the left. She repeated as she brought the shuttle back to the right. Two golden rows completed. A thousand more to go. She would also have to master a complex pattern that would uniquely identify the cloth as her own.

"You are adjusting to your new environment?" Tenzin asked.

Grace shrugged. "I feel guilty. Keeping secrets is not my thing."

Tenzin's brow furrowed. "Your thing?"

"It's an Earth term. It means not something I like to do. Keeping secrets from my friends feels like I'm violating their trust."

"And yet it maintains their safety," Tenzin said. "If people were to know what we do—what you are learning to do—it would sow seeds of distrust and throw the Council into chaos. It is sufficient that they know we have mastered translation and can be called upon to mediate conflicts when needed."

Grace pursed her lips and let the silk-wrapped shuttle rest on top of the loom. She stood and walked to a wall filled from floor to ceiling with compartments of large spiders resting quietly. Slowly winding spools collected the yards of golden silk they produced. Each spider was half the length of her hand. "Why don't you use silk worms? I hear they're easier to raise."

"Why not these spiders?" Tenzin answered. "We all have a role to play in the life of the universe. These spiders are fulfilling theirs."

"They are slaves. Trapped behind glass for life."

"They are kept behind glass because they like to bite, not because they are enslaved. As it takes tens of thousands of Madagascar spiders to produce a few ounces of thread, we cross bred the golden orbs with sacred Shakrarian spiders as an experiment. It prevents having to deplete our planet's supply for the mission. We are pleased to say the hybrid's output has increased a thousand-fold. They seem content to serve. In the wild, the females are a warrior race. If we were to release them, they would eat both the males and the weaker females. What good would that do either? Here they are well fed as they are harvested, and when their silk is depleted, we indulge them to play and hunt in their habitat."

He guided her to a glass enclosure on the other side of the chamber. Inside, millions of spiders traveled across webs at least eight feet in diameter. Mist and steam poured from vents near the ceiling creating a tropical environment. The glass felt warm to Grace's touch.

"Shakrarian spiders are intelligent and can be reasoned with. That dominant gene was passed down to the hybrids. We find that once their silk regenerates most return to their stations. Those that do not, remain in the habitat to replenish webs and produce offspring. We do not force them to return, but if the need arises, they can be enticed."

"How do you manage that?" Grace noticed she could not see the end of their habitat. Was it hundreds of feet long? Thousands?

Tenzin pointed to glass tubes overhead, all teaming with spiders crossing from the habitat to the silk collectors. "The spiders are mostly blind and use scent and touch to find their way back to their stations. I believe the nourishment we provide is tastier than the heads of other spiders they would be forced to eat in the habitat."

"It wouldn't be if those green chefs were making the meals."

Tenzin slid his hand over his mouth to conceal a smile. But his eyes twinkled. "I believe you are correct. I think the spiders would mutiny and all would be lost. Luckily, their food stocks are supplied from Earth resources, not Sonecian galley chefs. These lucky spiders have achieved a food nirvana we have not been as fortunate to experience."

Grace laughed and returned to the loom. "So this means I'm going on a mission?"

"You are," Tenzin said. "We considered a delay, but time is of the essence and there were few alternatives." He tapped the necklace she wore. "This will protect you and prevent tracking."

"Like the one Serise wore when she traveled with her team."

"Correct. Only this has other properties. Be mindful that it stay in your possession at all times. It cannot be replicated. Your family is one of few granted permission to own it. And no other exists on Earth."

Grace frowned. She was only thirteen and despite all she'd gone through, a "scary" mission was still not her thing. "Do I have a choice, Tenzin?"

"Indeed, like the spiders, you do."

She stroked the golden threads he wrapped around her wrist like a bracelet. "Can you tell me why I was chosen?"

Tenzin took in a deep breath and blew it out. Grace could tell he was struggling with his answer. Finally he said, "I cannot."

"Does Commander Kurosh know," she asked, clutching the necklace tightly, "what you are asking me to do?"

"He does." Tenzin bowed, then headed for the door. "The Council, however, does not."

CHAPTER THIRTY-THREE

The Gift

⁘ The hydroponic garden was a paradise. Flowers grew in rotating columns that spiraled toward the ceiling. Vegetables and herbs requiring full sun grew in long horizontal troughs stacked like a pyramid. Plants requiring shade sheltered beneath them. The garden was one of the few areas that every team except the Solai maintained as a shared space. And like April, everyone nibbled at the food they tended. Aris stretched lazily beneath a skylight exposing his now cat-sized body to the simulated sunlight.

"So let me get this straight," April said, munching on one of the green beans she'd stashed in her pouch as she headed for the rare plant section of the garden. "The galley chefs take something this good and turn it into the most disgusting food on Earth?"

"I'm afraid that is an accurate assessment of the situation," said Danine as she filled vials with flowers from a 40-foot Bolivian plant. "Be grateful for the gift of this assignment. What is grown here may be the only palatable food you receive each day. Although I am aware of Kavera's breaches in Harbor dietary protocol when he obtains unauthorized treats for you."

"Oops," April said. "Sorry."

"Not to worry. I turn the other cheek as long as it is not a frequent occurrence."

"Look the other way," April corrected.

Danine turned in the direction of the cat. "I am looking. To what do you refer?"

April chuckled. "No. I meant you're supposed to say 'I will look the other way'. When you 'turn the other cheek' it means you're ignoring someone who slapped you or hurt your feelings."

Danine's eyebrows crinkled. "I am supposed to ignore a person who hurts me? Human rules of combat are mystifying. However, I stand corrected. I will metaphorically look the other way when Kavera strays from galley protocols. The new Harbor chefs are an acquired taste. In time I pray they can be persuaded to adjust to our dietary preferences and not their own."

"Uh. Wait. They're not robots?"

Danine laughed. "The Osmaru are sentient beings with a vested interest in the mission."

"Because if we blow up, the universe and their home planet goes with it," said April.

"An unfortunate but accurate assessment," said Ayotunde, walking up behind them. "They will improve, but for now we honor their service by not telling them the food tastes like it has already been eaten and regurgitated." He laughed. "Many blessings, young princess and Danine."

April's mouth hung open in shock because the tall and lanky warrior rarely said more than a few words. His deep velvety voice was much too gentle for someone who was part of a warrior fighting team. "What are you doing here?"

"Why would I not be here?" Ayotunde asked, rolling up his sleeves.

"Because you're warrior class."

"Should that preclude other aspects of my life?" Brown eyes sparkling, he grinned as a hummingbird flew over his shoulder and hovered near the flowering plant. "On Xenobia, I am a botanist. Like your mother I like to feel rich soil beneath my fingertips. It is gratifying to grow something that might bring joy to another, or nourish them. As for the team, Berko is a chemist. Zadra is an astrophysicist. Your uncle—our Jemadari is—"

Danine cleared her throat loudly.

Ayotunde stopped, grimaced and then continued. "To be warrior is a way of life, not the definition of our passions and professions. When a mission calls, I answer. Otherwise, I am the grower of beautiful and delicious botanical delights."

He examined the spiked leaves protruding from the base of the new plant. He winced in pain, pulled back his hand, and squeezed his finger. Danine put her basket down and rubbed a device over his finger to stop the bleeding.

"Take care with this new addition, Ayotunde. Its rare blooms appear only once every Earth century." She handed him long metal tweezers. "This Queen of the Andes, as it is known on Earth, is somewhat Casmirian in temperament despite its beautiful flowers. It can shred skin when handled incorrectly."

"Ah!" he said, winking at April before using the tweezers to pluck a white flower from the stalk, "I am intrigued by the challenge this Queen presents."

April pulled another green bean from her pouch and debated eating it.

"Enjoy the bountiful gift, young princess" said Ayotunde. "We have an abundance of this bean species."

"I have a question," April said.

"I am happy to answer if I have the ability," said Ayotunde.

April paused as water began misting the plants. "Uncle Henry said everything here is recycled."

"That is correct," Danine said. "What is your concern?"

"Does that mean we're watering the plants with our pee and fertilizing it with—"

Danine laughed, picked up her basket of vials, and plucked an apple-like fruit from a nearby tree. "Harbor water is purified to remove the salts and solids. It is cleaner than what fills your water glasses at a restaurant. The process is not unlike that of Earth's International Space Station. However, the excrement is incinerated. Some of our teams found its use as fertilizer distasteful as a concept. And now I take my leave of you, dear warriors. May your day be blessed."

"It would be," said Ayotunde, taking the green bean from April's hand and biting into it, "If the Osmaruvian galley chefs could be persuaded that food serves a greater purpose than mere survival."

Danine turned white, which April assumed was her version of a blush. "That would, indeed, be a blessing and a much needed miracle," she said heading towards the door.

"Where's Nandi?" April asked, looking around for her tutor. "I want to see if she'll let me grow strawberries in one of the empty spiral columns."

"She is checking on team availability for a short mission. I'll be part of the triad today. We'll need two more."

"I could be one of them," April said hopefully.

"You would indeed be an interesting addition." Ayotunde smiled and gestured for her to follow him towards the vegetable garden.

"So how come you always travel in groups of four?"

"I don't understand," Ayotunde said, pulling a spinach plant from the soil and inspecting its roots. "Is four not a logical number?"

April shrugged.

Ayotunde furrowed his eyebrows, then brightened. "Look straight ahead, young warrior. Don't adjust your eyes. Tell me when you stop seeing me."

He moved to April's left. She lost track of him when he was perpendicular to her arms.

"I can't see you anymore," she said.

"You may look now." Ayotunde said, waving his hands and turning in a circle. "How well could you see my movements?"

April frowned. "I couldn't."

"And now you have your answer. If danger presents, three can stand together, and be aware of activity surrounding us. But to do so would require peripheral vision and there would be blind spots. If there were only two of us, it would be impossible to visually track activity to the left and right of us. So it is decreed that we travel with a compliment of three people. Like the pyramid above us, the team leader and the triad form a sturdy foundation with four corners. And if a member is hurt, the others can form a triangular shield around them. The fewest we are allowed on a mission is three. Always depend on your team, and choose them wisely. Never travel with less than an optimum compliment which can, as you say on Earth, have your back."

"Makes sense," April said. Like Aris she let the sunlight bathe her face. A sprout appeared as her fingers brushed the soil above it. "I still don't understand how we get so much sunlight down here."

Ayotunde nodded in approval as he examined the sprout. "Kavera is right. You are as inquisitive as my daughter of your age."

April's mouth dropped wide open.

He winked. "There is life beyond missions, little one. As for the light, it is created in abundance by your star. The sun, like most stars, is a giant nuclear fission reactor. Heat and light is released when the hydrogen atoms collide and fuse. Much of what is produced never reaches Earth. It bounces off your atmosphere. If it did not, all life would die on the surface. Our solar arrays collect what would normally be wasted energy and repurpose it for use at the Harbor."

"Oh," said April, suddenly at a loss for words.

"We are ready," said Nandi, accompanied by Nzingha and Idris, who were usually assigned with Kavera to Uncle Henry's triad. "Apologies for my late arrival, April. But I bring good news. I have received clearance for you to accompany us."

April's eyes lit up. "Really? Where are we going?"

"To the Millennium Seed Bank in Earth's United Kingdom, and the Doomsday Vault in Norway. We can replenish seeds we lost when the Sonara was destroyed. There are two million stored there. We must also recover seeds inadvertently collected that are not from Earth."

April smiled but in her heart she was groaning. She'd heard about those trips. Searching through endless jars of seeds wasn't her idea of a party. But she kept smiling.

"I sense your discomfort," said Nandi. "When I was your age, I would not have considered such a trip to be a highlight of my day. However, for our botanist warrior friend, it will be nirvana. Rest assured we know the locations of the seeds we require and shall be there only a brief time. Afterwards we'll travel to Western Sumatra. With your help we hope to recover a few specimens of *Amorphophallus titanum*."

"I don't know what that is," April said.

Nandi pulled up a photo on her digital pad.

April's mood brightened. "Oh! Mom had one in the greenhouse. It's a corpse plant."

"Yes. It is with regret that the specimen your mother cultivated was destroyed. With your help, we believe that we can replicate her experiment and accelerate its growth. You've shown quite a gift with Sonecian plants. It appears those under your care are thriving and growing much larger than the others. All teams have taken notice and requested your assistance."

"The corpse plant isn't the secret ingredient in the breakfast drink, is it?" asked April. "Because if it is, I'm not helping."

Ayotunde laughed. "Have no worries, young botanist. The plant is not edible. It is, however, quite interesting."

CHAPTER THIRTY-FOUR

Chi Sau

Ben leapt into the air and landed clumsily. He concentrated and tried again. Still no progress. Try as he might he could not duplicate what he saw during Aurelia's demonstration with his uncle's guards. If Aurelia was from Xenobia, he was from one of the deserted moons caught in its orbit.

"What are you doing?" asked a familiar voice.

"Nothing," Ben lied. "Just playing around."

"I see," said Aurelia, removing flight gloves and placing them on the table. She was wearing a flight suit, which meant she'd traveled somewhere off the planet. "Would you like assistance? You cannot start out at the advanced level. It is necessary to start at the beginning." She offered her hands, but Ben was reluctant to accept.

"Start with a simple exercise. I will move my hands in a circular motion. Try to follow them. When you are ready, change the pattern and I will follow you. We will each be in control."

It sounded stupid to Ben. He had done an exercise like this in gym class. It was like working with a Ouija board. It wasn't real because you knew someone was pushing the dial around to spell out the message they wanted to fake. But he had time on his hands now that he was essentially back on lock-down. What did he have to lose?

Ben touched her open palms with his own. Her hands were soft. Too soft for someone involved in the grueling work she did.

"Maintain an air space between us," she said. "We will generate the necessary electric current to track each other."

Ben backed off and held his palms about two inches above hers. Aurelia moved her arms in a slow, circular pattern. Ben followed easily. In a short time, however, her rhythm changed. The pattern became more complex, less predictable. Ben looked at his hands and tried to follow.

"No," said Aurelia. Her voice was firm, but kind. "Don't look at your hands. Keep your eyes fixed on the center of my face. Concentrate on a single point and don't waver from that spot."

Ben tried, but that just made things worse. He found himself concentrating on her exotic brown eyes and their piercing stare. He thought of a million questions he wanted to ask about her training, her clan, how she chose to be a warrior. He wondered about her relationship to Kavera. And what faraway planet she might have just visited. He lost his focus and with it, his ability to follow her hand rotations.

"You are too easily distracted, Benjamin. Try closing your eyes." Aurelia said. "They deceive you. Close them and allow your remaining senses to focus on the energy field I'm generating. Let that focus take you to a heightened sense of awareness. There will be plenty of time to talk about my brother and Xenobian job opportunities."

Ben grinned sheepishly, did as he was told and immediately felt the difference. As Aurelia moved her hands in different directions, light currents of electricity flowed across his arms. He followed her hands with more accuracy than when his eyes were open. With practice, he was able to take control of the pattern by altering his direction. Aurelia changed with him, but increased the pace. Soon their hands and arms were rotating rapidly in midair like windmills. Ben found it difficult to keep up but only once did his hand slip away from hers.

"Don't open your eyes," she cautioned. "Find me, feel the energy field around me and how it fits with yours. Use your senses—the scent, the sound, the touch—to find me." And then she was gone.

No! She wasn't.

Ben could sense her presence.

He heard a door open followed by a muted giggle.

"Focus!"

She was behind him. He reached backward and touched an arm. It was too small to be a woman's. Ben opened his eyes and turned around. It was April's hand.

"Where'd you come from?" Ben asked.

"Got a message that there was a surprise," she said with a mischievous grin. "That's all I know."

Aurelia placed her hand on top of theirs and squeezed lovingly. "Should you become separated, you will be able to find your sister, even when there is no light to guide you." Aurelia said. "I am leaving for a mission tomorrow. We can continue when I return."

"So that's not the surprise? We're not going with you?" April asked, suddenly looking deflated.

"I am headed to a region that is not safe. Kavera and Danine have petitioned Kurosh for you to have a brief respite and, in light of your stopping the destruction in Syria, even if by accident, he has agreed. We now realize that you are each tender shoots in the ground. To not be allowed to play in the fresh air and sunlight may cause you to wither. Or continue inadvertently hacking into Harbor systems. You and April will travel with Kurosh and Kavera. I will see you when you return. If not . . . your uncle possesses much more knowledge than I. He is committed to seeing you grow to your full potential."

"You think you might not be coming back," Ben said.

"There are no guarantees in life, Benjamin. Only service in the face of destiny. How we die is as important as how we live. Death in the midst of service is an honored tribute to both the living and those who have passed on before us. I don't fear death. I only hope I am worthy when it comes."

Ben shuffled his feet. "I hope you are safe. Akoosh vera . . . ," he stopped, unable to remember the rest.

Aurelia's face brightened. "The phrase is 'Akoosh sakur vera inna.' It means 'Return safely to me." She bowed and touched her hand to his cheek and to April's. "And I appreciate your blessing."

CHAPTER THIRTY-FIVE

Arecibo

Observatorio de Arecibo, Puerto Rico
18.3442° N, 66.7528° W

"Whoa!" was April's unscientific observation when she and Ben stepped into the control center of the Arecibo Observatory.

"You might recognize this location, Ben," said Uncle Henry. "As it was tied into the Casmir Array the day you and Carlos shut down all of Earth's deep-space satellite systems."

"When did that happen?" April asked. "You never told us about that!"

"Long story," Ben said, still embarrassed about hacking into Arecibo when he lived in California. He stared out toward the largest radio telescope on the planet. It was at least a thousand feet across and made from thousands of aluminum panels. Three huge towers held—he paused and counted—eighteen cables that kept a platform suspended in the air about five hundred feet above the dish. The receiver dangled from it like a giant diamond. Up until now the largest satellite dish he'd seen was the one Carlos's family had installed behind their house in Sunnyslope. It was several stories high before it disappeared. Now he knew it had been cloaked by holographic trees to keep him from finding it again. But this thing. Whoa was right. The tiny picture he'd seen on Dr. Lopez's computer didn't do it justice.

"We appreciate your coming," said a technician. "As you can see, a recent earthquake caused one of the cables to snap. The receiver is in danger of collapsing."

"The dish remains operational?" Uncle Henry asked.

"Within tolerances," said the technician. "But with hurricanes predicted to make landfall in this area, we may only be days away from a collapse. I don't care to discover how deep that sinkhole is underneath the dish. If it goes, we lose most of our capacity to reach the Casmir array. The facility on the moon is not nearly as effective as this one."

Ben's heart beat a little faster. "There's an outpost on the moon?"

"Yes, placed in a precarious spot to prevent detection by Earth satellites. Not an optimal location but we make do."

Ben choked. "So can we go see it when we're done?"

His uncle's eyes narrowed. "No. The moon outpost is currently unmanned."

"But, Aurelia just— "

"No moon trip," his uncle repeated with a sideways glance.

The technician grimaced then winked at Ben, giving him a glimmer of hope of an unauthorized mission sometime in the future.

"Kurosh, perhaps the Hayoolkááł could be persuaded to lend assistance with inspection," the technician said. "Using a Casmirian team would result in too much weight on an already fragile suspension system. And we both know my new commander lacks finesse."

Kavera coughed, abruptly, then cleared his throat. The technician stopped talking.

"April? Ben? Would you like to tour the facility while we work?" Kavera pointed towards a brochure with floor plans. "They've got a hands-on visitor's center where you can play with a spectrometer, or simulate the Doppler effect. It's quite interesting and as it is after hours you'll have full access to the equipment."

Ben shook his head and focused on the control panel.

"You want to operate the telescope?" his uncle scowled, one eyebrow raised. Ben thought he should just keep it there since it was his "go to" expression whenever Ben was around.

Still, he nodded rapidly. "Not as good as going to the moon, but yeah. I mean, yes. You tell me what to do and I won't mess up."

Kavera laughed. "Don't count on it. I did. The first time I was at the controls. The Casmirians are a bit twitchy about their array. Like you and Carlos, I accidentally replicated a solar pulse that knocked out power to the Eastern Seaboard."

"Whoa! For how long?"

"A matter of seconds," said Kavera. "But scary nonetheless. Lucky for me, the news reports suggested it was a brown-out due to heavy air conditioning use in the area."

"How deep is that thing?" April asked, pointing at the dish.

"Oh, about one hundred and sixty-seven feet, give or take an inch," the technician said. "I believe Kavera said you used the Lopez computer to search for E.T."

Ben grimaced.

"That is what we do here. We track planets and asteroids but we also broadcast signals to test for extraterrestrial life."

Ben shot a worried look at Kavera.

"Not to worry, young curious warrior. Samuel here is Casmirian. There are a number of Sonecian teams working undercover at satellite installations around the world."

The man winked. "My real name is Seti. But you understand how, with the Earth-based SETI program searching for extraterrestrial life, I got sick of the jokes from the human scientists. After a while they'd call me E.T. and joke that the search was over. Little did they know how close to the truth they were. So I switched to Samuel."

"I like Samuel," said April, giving him a thumbs up.

"I do too," he said. "And although I am very serious about my Earth-based job performance rating, you'll understand if sometimes, the signals don't land where they are supposed to go."

"What does that mean?" Ben asked, still staring at the massive dish.

"A good example would be Earth year 1974 when Arecibo was progammed to broadcast a signal at the M13 cluster of stars. It was the equivalent of a 20-trillion-watt signal. Of course that is easily intercepted by pirates as the cluster is twenty-one thousand light years away. To prevent that, one of my predecessors bounced it off a Casmirian satellite one thousand light years out, altering the signals and directing any who might encounter it to explore the vast wealth of Alpha Centauri and other planets that create problems for us. Routing the world's telemetry through the Casmir array has its advantages. Right now we are monitoring what is known as the Kepler mission. It has recently detected habitable planets outside this solar system."

"Is that a problem?" asked April.

"Not at all. Earth's technology isn't advanced enough to reach them. Or even see the surfaces with clarity. Pluto is as far as they've gotten in terms of detailed images. NASA's current focus is on putting people on Mars. We are safe for now. But it is fun watching humans speculate. Like a glimpse back to our own technical evolution I think."

Ben liked Samuel. He was more like Carlos and less like the ruthless leader running his team.

"Can that dish search for things on Earth?" April asked.

"Like what?" Samuel asked.

"Our parents? The beacons they were carrying?"

Samuel placed his hands on her shoulder. "Only what is in space, little one. If I could find your parents, I would make it my priority." He frowned then brightened. "Perhaps I can offer a diversion. While Kavera and your commander study the structural damages, I'll take you out to the receiver. If you are scared of heights, let me know."

"I want to go!" April said. "Heights don't bother me."

Samuel looked to Ben's uncle for approval. He sniffed and then waved them off.

"Go. I promised Aurelia and Danine that the children would get some natural sunlight. I will call in reinforcements to fix the cable."

The technician passed out hard hats and led them out a door and down a long walkway. When they arrived at the first catwalk, Ben sucked in his breath. Samuel wasn't kidding. Standing at the edge, the dish looked even bigger. Reaching the center meant walking 500 feet, about a city block, to reach the triangular platform holding the receiver. But it also meant traveling across a suspension bridge forty-five stories in the air. A sign read, "Maximum capacity: 5 people." There were only three of them. That still didn't make Ben feel any safer.

"Is this thing safe?" Ben asked, taking one tentative step before fully committing to putting his weight down on the mesh.

"Oh, yes," Samuel said. "The structure weighs 900 tons. Your weight will be like a mosquito landing on it."

"And what if that broken cable snaps?" April asked.

"Well," said Samuel, "let's hope your uncle is quick with his fingers in dialing us to safety. The platform and suspension bridge are connected to Harbor transport circuitry. In case of trouble, you could say we are able to dial home. "

"So technically, we could get to the moon outpost from here," said Ben.

"Yes, technically. But it would not be practical," said Samuel. "The trip is not one for the faint of heart given the distance."

"But what if we just went and came right back," April said, jumping in.

"I believe that subject is closed," Samuel said, grinning.

"Why?" she asked.

"Because the outpost is close to four hundred thousand kilometers away, or approximately two hundred and fifty-thousand Earth miles. A very rough ride without a vehicle. And even if it were not, any remote chance of my taking you there died with your uncle's refusal to allow it. He has ultimate jurisdiction."

Ben frowned and snapped his fingers. "Well, you can't say we didn't try."

"I'd be disappointed if you did not. For what it is worth, you are not missing anything, young warriors. It sounds exciting until you take the trip and discover it is just a giant rock in space with earthquakes that ring it like a bell. The vibrations can be as high as a six on Earth's

Richter scale and last for quite a while. Getting assigned there is not—"

They were interrupted by a sudden "whoosh" and a gale force gust of wind that nearly knocked them over. Seconds later the bridge was occupied by twenty Hayoolkááł warriors, all carrying equipment and cables, along with one very terrified Serise.

"Not happy, not happy, not happy," she said. "Don't like heights. No heights!"

"Sorry, Serise," said Micique. "Emergency repairs. Thought you'd enjoy the satellite tour."

Serise blushed, then returned to her original expression of terror.

Ben was having trouble wiping the shocked look off his face. "You flew here?"

"Don't get it twisted. Was flown here," said Serise, her eyes still wide with fear. "With my eyes closed. We were supposed to go check out the Northern lights."

"Then don't look down," said April. "Because it's like looking at the Grand Canyon without the 'Grand'."

"No kidding," Serise said, looking instead at the clouds.

"Could be worse," Ben said. "Grace is climbing Mount Everest—"

Micique frowned.

"I mean, Chomolungma," Ben corrected, "and she doesn't have your flying pals to get her there."

"Oh, but she does," said Micique. "We can withstand the cold and the atmospheric changes. We were able to give her team a lift into the death zone and back down to the village known as Namche Bazaar in a matter of hours. Grace stayed in the village while we worked, as we would not risk taking a Shakrarian child to that altitude. No tourists are on the mountain this time of year. Only Sherpa, with whom we have a kindred relationship. A small team leant assistance with the Shakrarian mission, and while they waited helped the Sherpa bring down tourist waste and tidy up the mountain range a bit. It is a pity. The mountains are sacred yet tourists treat them as a receptacle for their refuse." He frowned, then joined his team.

The Hayoolkááł flew from one concrete tower to another, inspecting and pulling new cable as they went. Occasionally Micique waved back at Serise who was still shaking like a leaf.

"I think we should continue to the central platform," Samuel said. "It is a bit more stable."

It took five minutes to walk to the triangular deck. It began vibrating as hydraulic jacks moved the dangling receiver into a new position.

"Why is it moving?" Serise asked, her pitch rising. "Why are WE moving?"

Samuel raised one finger for silence, listened to something in his ear piece, then smiled. "Nothing to worry about. It appears that there is a message being received in response to the SETI signal that was broadcast. We are moving the receiver into alignment to get a fix on the origin. Your uncle is sending back the equivalent of a 'no one is home' beacon before it is intercepted by NASA. Or as it is commonly known, we are bouncing the message back with static."

"And how are you going to explain the cables suddenly getting replaced? Aren't there going to be construction crews coming to check?" April asked

Samuel nodded. "It will be just another mystery. My approach, as with everything is not to explain it when asked." He raised his hands towards the heaven in prayer and laughed. "I just say, it's a miracle. Hallelujah!"

Once the cable repair was complete and the telescope was stabilized, Samuel signaled approval of the work, then pointed towards the observatory in the distance. "Now, let's go play with the controls. We've got a few asteroids that look to be a problem. I'll let the three of you pulverize them with lasers from the Casmir array if you promise to avoid hitting Earth satellites or the International Space Station." He winked. "And only if you don't tell Pendon or his second in command. Mean temper on those two, for sure."

CHAPTER THIRTY-SIX

Competitive Advantage

Carlos collapsed on the bed and proceeded to snore. Pendon had taken him on a mission to examine Olmec ruins and he returned covered with more cuts and bruises. His upper lip was swollen. His damp, matted hair stuck up at odd angles. After weeks of training he was losing weight and developing a more muscular build, but as his skill increased so, it seemed, did whatever violent training techniques Pendon introduced.

Aurelia walked into the room. "You summoned me?"

"I think we need to call Danine but he won't let me," Ben whispered. "He's a mess. I'm worried about him. He's more banged up than usual. He won't tell me where he went on the mission and he won't talk about what's going on in training."

"As is the rule in his tribe," said Aurelia. "Do you speak openly of your own training?"

Ben knew better than to lie to her. "Yes, but—"

"Then you are breaking a covenant," said Aurelia. "A sacred trust. Some things are not to be shared. It is what gives your tribe a competitive advantage."

She looked from Ben to Carlos then back to Ben again. "However, these are unique circumstances. I sense a powerful bond among you and your friends. I do know that your fathers often shared strategies which allowed them to be stronger as a team than the sum of their skills as individuals. Unusually defiant men, those two. Their pranks are legend in the galaxy, as was their skilled alliance. We felt the loss when they joined this mission."

She paused and thought a moment. "I will make an allowance in this case. However, I would ask you to remember to be discrete in your 'sharing' outside of these walls. Neither Kurosh nor the Counsel will be as tolerant or forgiving."

Ben sighed. "Doesn't sound like the Counsel is any different than Earth's leaders."

Aurelia smiled. "We are advanced. That does not mean we are perfect." She walked toward Carlos's bed and studied him. "Ben, would you leave us a moment. I need to talk to Carlos privately."

Ben was disappointed but stood and headed for the door.

"And Benjamin? Your uncle would like to have a word with you." She placed something in the palm of his hand and closed his fist around it.

He opened his fingers a micron to peek at what she'd given him, then closed his eyes and wondered if Serise could find codes to dial him to another planet.

Aurelia wiped the sweat from Carlos's forehead then perched on the edge of the futon. She removed a small jar from her pouch and began rubbing a salve into his back.

Carlos stirred, flinched instinctively then relaxed when he saw who was attending to him. His head flopped back into the pillow and sighed. "I told Ben not to call anyone."

"As I'm sure you have guessed, I am not just 'anyone'." Aurelia pushed the hair out of his eyes and stroked his head gently.

Carlos sighed. "Sorry. That wasn't what I meant." He shuddered from her touch and relaxed.

"I will talk to Pendon," Aurelia said. "He needs to understand that you were raised as human and will need time to adjust to your training."

"No!" cried Carlos." I can handle it."

"I fear it will kill you," said Aurelia. Her voice was calm and soothing. She rolled up his sleeves and began to rub the ointment into his arms working from his shoulders down to his finger tips. "Perhaps moderation is in order."

"NO!" Carlos moaned. "I can do it. Isn't this what my father had to do when he was my age?"

"Yes," said Aurelia. "But he began his conditioning shortly after birth."

"Then I can do it," said Carlos, rolling over on his back and letting out a tiny cry of pain in the process. "I can do it. If I can't, I'll tell them myself."

Aurelia gently rubbed salve into his cheeks and forehead with her fingertips. The bruises faded.

"I will respect your wishes," Aurelia said. "For now."

She pulled a thin mesh blanket from her pouch that pulsed with electricity. She placed it over Carlos then pulled his blanket over it to conceal it. "A gift from Danine."

She placed the jar of ointment on the table at the head of Carlos's bed. "A gift from me. Both, if used sparingly, will ease the pain and accelerate your endurance. You will have to learn the techniques of your tribe over a long period of time, but there is no shame in having a hidden advantage of your own during the journey."

Carlos nodded. "Thank you."

"Are you sure you don't want me to intervene? Kurosh and I have ultimate jurisdiction on this mission."

"I'm sure. I don't want to make things worse between Kurosh and Pendon. I know they hate each other."

"That is not something you should feel a need to address yourself," said Aurelia. "Their history is a long one."

"I know," said Carlos. "But I can do it. The training, that is. And if I can't I promise I'll stop it before it goes too far. I have to do this—for my father. It's what he would want. Or at least I need to try to honor his memory."

Carlos pushed up on his elbows and examined the rapidly healing wounds on his hands. "But I'll keep the blanket and the cream. Pendon doesn't need to know everything."

Aurelia nodded. "As you wish."

"Oh, and Aurelia?"

"Yes, young warrior?"

"When I'm better I'd like to train with you too. I'd like to learn a few tricks so I can kick Peng's butt next time he insults my family." Carlos managed a weak laugh then moaned and collapsed.

"I'd be honored." Aurelia stood and smiled as she headed for the door. "And your father would be proud."

CHAPTER THIRTY-SEVEN

The Apprentice

⁘ "Sorry."

Ben had been sitting in his uncle's apartment for a half hour, with only the man's disapproving scowl and the Dogon's blue diamond for company. He supposed this was the Harbor equivalent of a time out.

"I promise I won't try that again."

"Don't make a promise you don't intend to keep." His uncle's normally booming voice barely registered on the decibel scale.

"Okay. But I thought I . . ."

His uncle's sideways glance told him to just shut up.

Ten more minutes of silence passed between them according to the desk clock. Holographic images of whales flashed above an open silver box he'd received from Calamar, each accompanied by graphs of sound waves. Small whales, killer whales, humpback whales, and a few that looked like the blue whale at Atlantis.

"I promised to take it back to the Dogon," Ben said shuffling his feet against the floor and clasping and unclasping his hands. "I was just trying to help. I didn't know you were planning a field trip. I can take the diamond back."

"Kavera will return it."

Ben brightened.

"With my team," his uncle continued. He fixed his attention on a large blue whale whose frequency was above the others. His eyes narrowed but the edge of his lip creased upward.

Ben brightened. "Good news? Is that the whale you were looking for?"

"Perhaps," his uncle said.

Silence.

"Can I ask why?"

"No."

"Why not?"

Uncle Henry's nose flared as he turned and glowered.

So much for April's 'why' game.

Ben listened to the whale song as his uncle played it over and over again.

"I think I know something . . . "

His uncle raised his hand. "What about time out do you not get? Be still and meditate on why you are here."

"But I saw . . . "

His uncle slammed the lid. "Saw what, exactly?"

Ben took in a breath. What did he see exactly? A whale? Moby Dick? A hallucination? He was panicked while he was waiting for Serise to get the transport codes right. Telling his uncle about something that might lead to a false trail wasn't going to make his current predicament any easier. And it was as much as putting salt on a wound to rehash going off base, let alone all the way to some undiscovered rock in the middle of the Pacific Ocean. He decided to quit while he was ahead.

"Any signs of my parents?" Ben asked, changing the subject.

Uncle Henry shook his head. "No, but we have not lost hope."

"What about those eight beacons we found when we first got here?"

"They were a false trail," said his uncle.

More silence. It was killing Ben. Uncle Henry not talking to him was worse than being yelled at.

"Are you still searching for what blew up the transport?" he asked. "Was it a whale?"

"No," his uncle replied, his brow suddenly furrowed. "I know the cause."

Ben was stunned. "You do? What was it?"

Ben's uncle paused and pursed his lips as he returned to the images in front of him. "The captain activated a self destruct sequence."

Ben's breath caught in his throat. "Why?"

"To keep whatever was on the ship with him from returning to Earth. Or making its way home with them. It was a choice. A horrible, painful choice made easier by duty and knowledge of one's place in the cosmos." Uncle Henry's face was expressionless as he looked Ben directly in the eyes. "Everything happens for a reason. I will not question the meaning of it."

"Still feels awful. All those people."

"They died doing something they loved. Never forget that. If death is the result of a noble cause, it is not something to mourn. It is why we honored their passing."

Ben wasn't sure he wanted to know the answer to his next question. He couldn't read his uncle's mood. "Are there more out there?"

There was a very long pause. "Yes."

"So if we find those keys will that take care of the problem? Will we go home?"

"Possibly," said his uncle. "I'm not sure what will happen when we activate the Guardian. I assumed you would want to stay. Isn't there a basketball career in your future?"

Ben shrugged. "I don't think so. Seems kind of lame now."

Uncle Henry pushed the silver box aside and crossed his arms, his prayer beads clicking against the case that held his knife. "Why would you not want to play again? It has always been your passion. Do you not enjoy the challenge?"

Ben felt his mood lighten with his uncle's acknowledgement but nothing had changed about his future. "Not now that I know I have an unfair advantage. These aren't human skills that allow me to hit a basket every time. When I thought it was just me and all that practice it was exciting. Now it just feels like a cheat."

"No more than those who are genetically destined to be seven feet tall at maturity. Why not develop your gift without taking undue advantage? Control it. Manage it. There are many applications beyond a basketball court for what you are learning. Perception, heightened awareness, accuracy. They are your birthright on both planets."

"But I would get on the court and annihilate the other team. It wouldn't be any fun, not much of a challenge." After seeing his uncle in combat with Aurelia, Ben decided that basketball seemed more like child's play.

"Ben, there is a difference between defeating your opponent honorably and stripping them of all dignity. Having power is not license to unleash its energy unwisely. You only end up diminishing yourself in the end. An opponent, allowed his dignity, may capitulate. An opponent, humiliated, always comes back more determined and better prepared."

Ben sighed. He didn't understand.

"Your test, " his uncle continued, "is not how many baskets you can make, but how you grow as a person. That you can tip the scales in your team's favor is not a sin. That would be like telling a man who is naturally seven feet tall that he has an unfair advantage because he is closer to the net. Use your superior control to shift the spotlight to your teammates. Support them but don't overshadow them. That is the greatest honor."

"But you said we were warrior class."

"It is a state of mind, not a job description. Besides, many of our skills are not uniquely Xenobian. They are simply honed from years of practice. Be proud but be gentle and subtle. Did you notice that Aurelia never hurt anyone during her training session? Do you think she could have performed like that if she had not also practiced control and restraint?"

Ben had to think about that comment for a while. What would have happened if she had not fought back, or someone made a mistake? Could she have been killed?

"Maybe, but not likely," answered Ben's uncle without waiting for the verbal question. "Her team is very advanced in their training. I would not have needlessly put her life in danger."

"But those weapons!"

Ben's uncle pulled the knife from its case. It grew in size threefold.

"Whoa!" Ben gasped and stepped backward. "What's—"

Without warning Uncle Henry spun in a 360 degree arc and swung the knife full force at Ben. The tip of the blade touched his neck but did not penetrate the skin. Paralyzed with fear, Ben perspired profusely.

"Did you think I would hurt you?" his uncle asked, one eyebrow raised.

Ben couldn't answer. He was still trying to coax his spirit back into his body.

"Prepare to defend yourself," Uncle Henry ordered before jabbing the knife towards him. Ben tried to block the attack but missed. The blade stopped, barely touching the pull on his zipper.

Ben was breathing heavy now. His heart strained against his chest as it beat well above its normal rate. His uncle handed him the knife which he took gingerly. It was twice the size of his hand, but lacked weight. Its silver surface was polished to a brilliant shine. He gripped it tightly. The handle molded firmly in his grasp. Ben could hardly feel it in the palm of his hand and yet it felt a comfortable part of him, an extension of his arm. He had seen a pair of knives like this before.... locked in a drawer in his father's den. "My parents— "

"Jakaravite. A rare precious metal," Ben's uncle interrupted. "You won't find it on Earth's periodic table. It is sacred and will only extend when yielded by a Xenobian warrior. No one else. But don't be fooled. Even in its retracted state it can slice through all known materials. Now attack me!"

Ben froze.

"I ordered you to attack!" His uncle's booming voice reverberated throughout the room.

Ben took a deep breath and jabbed tentatively in the direction of his uncle. Uncle Henry didn't flinch. *"Is that the best you can do? I said ATTACK!"*

The telepathic command screamed inside Ben's head. He swung the knife full force at his uncle and found himself instantly on the floor. He didn't know how he got there. He had not felt himself go down. He didn't even see his uncle move to block his attack. And yet there he was, on his back, his uncle once again wielding the knife which was touching his Adam's Apple. Ben wasn't hurt, but his ego was sorely bruised.

Uncle Henry retracted the blade, returned it to its case and helped Ben to his feet.

"As your Uke, your sparring opponent, it is my job to assist in your training but not exploit your weaknesses or mistakes to my own advantage. I am only qualified to train you if I possess superior focus and control. However, some measure of risk must be involved if the training is to be effective. A real enemy will not stop himself, will not hold back. None of the guards would have penetrated beyond a superficial nick here or there. Even with their speed, Xenobian warriors can stop their weapons short of the target. The ability to disable without harm is the ultimate achievement. Aurelia has mastered this even beyond the level of our best trainers."

"But you seem so upset with her," said Ben once he regained his voice.

"I did not expect to see her leading Sondar's team. I had requested a senior, more experienced officer."

"She's awesome! From what I've seen, she's the best person for the job. I don't understand why you wouldn't want her help."

"On the contrary. I am honored that she chose to join the mission. She is a flawless strategist. And now a fierce warrior. In battle, she will be a formidable ally."

"But still, didn't it bother you when you couldn't defeat her?"

Ben's uncle paused and looked past Ben to something far away. "I will admit to being caught off guard. Her skills have progressed far beyond my expectations. She is very headstrong, independent and impulsive. A lot like you, I think. It is highly unusual for someone leading the religious caste to choose a warrior's path. She was only beginning her apprenticeship when I left for Earth. I had hoped to train her, but the missions required my presence here. It appears a great deal has changed in my absence. According to Sondar, the casualty rate on the team has dropped to zero under her leadership."

Ben frowned. "You've been gone a long time, huh?"

His uncle eyed him thoughtfully, his eyes softening as the slack in his jaw released. "Perhaps too long."

"So why do you hate her?"

Uncle Henry's eyes narrowed. "Hate her?"

"Yes! You ordered ten guards to attack her!"

Ben's uncle seemed almost amused by the question, but the glint in his eye quickly disappeared. "You misunderstand. I sought only to assess her current skill level. Ten guards is a light workout. A full test would have involved the entire team."

Ben wasn't convinced. From his uncle's reaction when she arrived, there had to be more to the story. "So you don't resent a woman being in charge?"

"Her gender is not an issue. Surely you've noted I often have women in my triad."

"Then what's going on?" Ben asked. "I can tell you two don't get along."

Ben's uncle huffed and shook his head. "Your eyes and ears deceive you. Aurelia and I share a common bond."

"Huh?" said Ben.

"We are bonded." Ben's uncle rolled up his sleeve to reveal a small tattoo on his shoulder blade. It depicted two intertwined rings pierced by a dagger. Above each ring was a tiny hieroglyphic word. In the handle of the dagger was a symbol . . . an Ankh. Ben had seen it before and thought nothing of it. Now Ben remembered seeing a similar pattern tattooed on Aurelia's shoulder and on his parent's.

"Is that to show you're from the same caste?"

"No," said Uncle Henry, setting his jaw. "It is to show that we are married."

Ben's mouth dropped to the floor but before he could ask another question, his uncle opened the apartment door and stood indicating it was time for Ben to leave.

"By the way, I have decided that your punishment will be to reorganize the supply closet and scrub the training room floor."

"Okay," Ben said thinking his exile could be worse. He'd been cleaning the floors anyway.

"With this," his uncle continued, reaching into a drawer and pulling out a toothbrush. "It appears you have too much time on your hands and this should correct the problem. When you are done, Kavera has made modifications to the training facility. I expect you to test the equipment and give him a full report before you retire for the evening."

CHAPTER THIRTY-EIGHT

Defeated

Ben bounced the basketball from side to side, eyeing the hoops installed in the training center and trying to think of a way he could thank Kavera without embarrassing him with a hug. This was perfect. He messed up and Kavera still had his back. Like the big brother he'd always wanted.

If he squinted, he could imagine himself in an arena, surrounded by thousands of adoring but silent fans. He closed his eyes, took in a deep breath, then shot the ball from center court.

Woosh! Nothing but net!

He was good. No. He was better than good. If life had been different he was destined to be an all-time great with an unbreakable record.

He tried one of Uncle Henry's trick shots, slamming the ball backwards without looking. Not even close. He ran after the ball and tried his father's shot.

His father.

All those years wasted when he could have been learning at the feet of the master. Geek science nerd was just a cover story. Okay, part of that story was true. Jeremiah Webster WAS a geek science nerd, but he was also a fighter pilot and a lead warrior.

Ben tossed the ball over his shoulder and tried to visualize hitting the basket as his father had done when he thought Ben wasn't looking. The sound of the ball swishing through the net warmed his heart. He closed his eyes again and tried to conjure images of laughter and clumsy— apparently faked—games of one-on-one on the driveway.

"Are you in need of assistance?" A hand settled on Ben's shoulder.

Ben jerked around. Berko was only slightly smaller than his uncle.

"Hey! No. Just thinking about my dad."

The warrior nodded appreciatively. "What is it you hold in your hand?"

Ben tossed the ball to Berko. "A basketball. It's an American game."

"And how does one play this American game?"

Ben gestured towards the basket as he explained the basic rules. "Want to play a game of one-on-one?"

Berko shook his head. "We are all curious." He pointed toward the balcony. Warriors were filing into the room for the start of evening training. "We would like to try a real game. Perhaps it will make you feel less homesick."

Ben straightened as his adrenaline kicked in. "Perfect. We need five people on each team. Within seconds, volunteers were on the floor while the others took seats in the balcony. Because women were on both teams, Ben opted not to suggest shirts versus skins.

"Ok," said Ben. "It's shirts against sashes. Calisthenics are usually an hour. Let's play 'til it's quitting time or until a team reaches twenty -one, whichever comes first."

"Deal!" said Berko. "That is the proper response for this occasion?"

Ben grinned. "Works for me!"

At that moment, Kavera walked through the door. "Ah! Young diamond-borrowing warrior! Seems you have found my surprise and are in need of a referee. Would I do?" He reached into his pocket and produced a small silver device. "I've even got a whistle for when you foul out!"

Ben was elated. "Foul out? You wish! And hey, thank you!"

Kavera winked. "No problem, little dude. I know being cooped up at the Harbor is tough on you. Just remember. It is for your own safety that we keep you here in our care. I thought, perhaps, some creature comforts were in order to lighten your burden."

Kavera took possession of the ball, moved to center court and quickly explained the rules. The warriors cheered and hooted like a real American crowd. Ben felt instantly at ease. Berko's team narrowly won the toss-up. Within minutes the game was in full play. Instead of dribbling, Berko simply tossed the ball across the court and hit the basket. Ben rushed to rebound but was beat by Zadra, who was on his own team. She shot the ball from full court but it was blocked by the opposing team which shot the ball back in their direction. The ball was then blocked by Zadra who, seeing an opening, shot again and hit the basket at the other end of the room. Tie game. The teams were evenly matched. No one ran up or down the court. They simply stood by their respective baskets and took turns blocking and shooting.

Kavera blew his whistle and called the teams over. "At this rate no team will ever score twenty-one."

Berko said, "I am confused. There is not much challenge to this basketball game. Is there a random element of chance involved that we do not understand?"

Kavera chuckled and shook his head. "Earth people have a lower level of skill. For them this IS a challenge. Given the circumstances, I think we need to add a few rules. No shooting from farther than center court. The ball must change hands on each team at exactly five times before shooting. No more. No less. Also, each player must dribble—which means bounce—the ball at least five times before they pass the ball. No player may have the ball more than once per turn. Only the person assigned to an opponent may block that opponent's shot. But any member of one team may attempt to gain possession of the ball from a member of the opposition at any time. So keep track. Let's try this again."

Ben raised his eyebrows in horror. He had barely registered half the new rules, but the warriors laughed and agreed. Once the game was in full swing Ben found it difficult to keep track of who had the ball. The warriors moved at lightning speed. Kavera's rule of five's made things more difficult. When a warrior rebounded he was down court in less than three dribbles, which meant that they had to dribble up and down the court just to run out the requirements. In the middle of play, someone would steal the ball and the sequence would start again. Despite the confusion, the warriors gave high fives to each other or shook hands as they passed, whether they were dribbling or not. The ball passed from one person to another as the five dribbles grew so rapid the ball was barely visible. Ben tried counting and when, on rare occasions, he got the ball in time it was intercepted by an opposing warrior who ran by in a blur before he could get to his second dribble. The warriors leapt effortlessly through the air, executing forward and back flips over one another to escape the person who was guarding them. Ben blocked a shot, and then, forgetting the rules, took possession of the ball and took aim from half court. He hit the basket.

Kavera blew his whistle again. "Foul! Can't block any shot other than your own man. Even so, there were no dribbles and no pass. It's the other team's ball."

Ben shot him a dirty look.

"It's that or I can give them a shot from the free throw line." Kavera made a goofy face at him and winked. *"Does it look like they'd miss that easy shot?"*

Ben was ready to blow a gasket. The new rules were too hard to follow. "I can't keep up."

"Yes," Kavera said sternly. *"You can. Stop thinking like an Earthling. Think like your tribe."*

Ben nodded begrudgingly and tried again. All of his shots were blocked. He didn't make a single basket. Then he noticed something. Now his team only passed to him on the second, third or fourth pass. Never the fifth. He didn't have a chance to shoot and when he didn't dribble fast enough, the other team stole the ball, only to have Ben's team steal it back.

"Pass me the ball!" he yelled.

The ball passed rapidly between teammates. The dribbles were so fast they barely had time to register.

Ben waved his arms in the air. "Over here! I'm open!"

Someone tossed him the ball but it was intercepted mid-flight by a warrior who was halfway down the court before Ben realized the ball had been taken.

"That's not fair!" Ben groused silently.

"Life isn't fair," Kavera answered. *"And it's also not always about winning."*

Ben gulped. He didn't know his private thoughts had been overheard. Telepathy was going to be a liability until he learned to block them. It didn't matter. He couldn't keep up. He couldn't block shots. He was a liability to his own team. They didn't seem to mind, they started passing to him more often anyway. And, as the end of the hour neared, with the score tied, Ben finally got to take a shot. It was blocked despite his best efforts and his sky high jump. Ben's opponent rebounded, dribbled five times in a rapid fire sequence, passed the ball to his teammates who did the same as they circled center court to get through the five passes needed. Each time they shook hands or extended high fives. Ben tried to intercept as he counted:

Fourth pass - 1, 2, 3, 4, 5,

Fifth pass - 1, 2 . . .

He reached in to grab the ball before it could be shot but was off balance as Ayotunde dribbled twice with one hand, twice with the other then switched and bounced one more time all at lightning speed. Ben tripped. Ayotunde turned to face Ben, grinned and shot over his shoulder. The ball soared like a missile and hit the basket dead center.

Kavera's whistle blew. The game ended with a score of 21 to 20 in favor of Berko's team. The warriors still looked as if they were fresh out of a shower. Ben felt he'd been worked over by a lawn mower and only begrudgingly shook hands.

"Fun game," said Zadra, pulling her braids loose from their ponytail. "And great work-out!"

Ben wiped himself with a towel then, thinking everyone was gone, threw it at a basket in disgust.

"You need to learn humility," Kavera sighed, patted a nearby column and left the room.

Serise squeezed past him. "You okay?"

Ben didn't answer. He wasn't in the mood for her sarcasm or insults.

Serise picked up the ball, stared at it for a few seconds, then shot from the three point line. The ball swooped through the net without a sound. She rebounded, dribbled, then shot again with the same results. She retrieved the ball again, looked at Ben then raised her eyebrows before going to center court. She dribbled the ball in a 360 degree arc around her body, switching from one hand to the other while maintaining a steady cadence, then shot.

Whoosh!

"Didn't know you could play like that," said Ben, accepting the ball she held out to him. He took a shot from the same place.

Whoosh!

"Well, you weren't exactly nice to me back in Sunnyslope," she said, rebounding, "so why would I tell you? And when you weren't around, I tried helping Carlos. Operative word is 'try.' But he's as clumsy as your father pretended to be. Not one basketball playing gene in his entire body." She aimed.

Whoosh!

"I was watching the game from the balcony. I figured I'd get kicked out but no one said a word so I stuck around. The movements were syncopated. Almost choreographed. Then I figured out why. The teams had an advantage, so don't feel bad. You couldn't beat them. I wouldn't have been able to beat them either." She took another shot.

Whoosh!

Ben was awestruck. He and Serise were evenly matched. "What do you mean by advantage?" he said, rebounding and taking his own shot.

Whoosh!

He tossed the ball to Serise.

"If you'd been paying attention, you'd have figured it out by now. By the way, it's time for dinner." She shot the ball one last time, then walked out of the room.

Whoosh!

CHAPTER THIRTY-NINE

Special Request

After dinner, Carlos crept silently down a corridor, ducking between columns so he wouldn't be seen by the people passing by. He remembered the location of the room where he'd seen Ben's uncle practicing a fierce kata, and navigated there mostly by instinct. But the door didn't open. He wasn't authorized. Like everything at the Harbor, tribal sections were limited to the warriors on that team. So much for Kumbaya and let's all get along. The teams, for all their advanced knowledge, were still separated by planet and keeping their trade secrets hidden from everyone else. No wonder they couldn't solve the Guardian problem. His own team's idea of working together was sending a representative to a Council meeting once a day to pick a fight.

He wondered if he could knock when the door suddenly swung open.

"You appear to be in the wrong place, young AWOL Casmirian warrior." Kavera leaned against the door jamb, crossed his arms and looked amused.

"I need help," said Carlos.

Kavera tilted his head and lowered his voice. "Is that not an issue for Pendon to resolve?"

"The problem IS Pendon," Carlos said, "and Peng, and . . . "

Kavera frowned. "Surely Peng is not paired with you for combat training?"

Carlos nodded. "Your sister said she could teach me some pointers."

"Did she?" Kavera's eyebrows raised in surprise. He moved to the side and gestured. "Well then, enter young learner!"

Carlos frowned and stayed put.

"I assure you, we don't bite," said Kavera.

"My team does," Carlos sighed. "Sorta."

He found his courage and entered as far as the other side of the doorway, remembering the large wall of lethal weapons Ben's uncle had used. But the wall was sealed and no weapons were in sight.

"What ails you, young warrior?" asked Aurelia, looking up from holographic displays of team members and their physical readouts. Beyond her, every wall streamed with Sonecian hieroglyphic symbols and rotating DNA strands as light beams crisscrossed over a mountain-ous region in the Middle East.

"What are you looking for?" he asked.

Aurelia smiled, then shut off the monitors, although the computers still beeped as data was downloaded. "Nothing that need burden you, my young friend."

Carlos frowned again and shuffled his feet.

"You are in need of assistance?"

He nodded.

"Then I am honored to serve," she said warmly as Kavera placed his hand on Carlo's back and guided him into the training center. The door closed behind them.

CHAPTER FORTY

The Returned

Rockpoint, Arizona, Dinétah
36.7194° N, 109.6250° W

Serise looked into the face of her mother's friend, Johana, as the woman whispered to Kyloria in a language Serise didn't understand. She felt exposed even as Micique and Dazal smiled and tried to make her feel at ease. Kyloria slipped a device into the woman's hand, silver with black engravings, and a tablet. Johana nodded and placed both in the pocket of her skirt.

Her granddaughters, Nya and Leandra entered with heaping bowls of stew, roasted corn, and a plate piled with bread. Once the food was placed on the table, Johana bowed her head, folded her hands and recited a prayer. Serise's first thought was to be thankful she would get her first decent meal since living at the Harbor.

"Welcome back, Serise," the woman said, gesturing for the others to begin their meals. "We did not expect to see you returned so soon. If I remember, you were not interested in learning your mother's ritual when you were last here."

Serise sighed. "I was afraid. I didn't understand what she was doing."

"And now?"

"I've changed. I'm not the same person you knew before."

The woman scoffed, tore a piece of bread in half and offered part to her. "What could you have changed in such a short time? You are who you are."

Serise was tempted to explain that she couldn't have known about her own origins. "I'm going to adopt more traditional ways."

"You can change the outside, dress more modestly, soften your voice. But those changes are superficial. The universe doesn't much care how you dress or what jewelry you do or do not wear. That has nothing to do with who you are on the inside."

Embarrassed and at a loss for words, Serise looked across the table at one of the girls. Nya had always been nice to her. She, in turn, not so much. Nya caught her eye then quickly looked back down at her food, leaving Serise even more embarrassed.

"I'm sorry," Serise said. "I apologize."

The woman shrugged and spooned stew onto her plate. "Eat. I'm sure the Harbor food is not nearly as good as my granddaughter's."

Nya beamed, pushed her long braids behind her shoulders and waited until everyone was served before she helped herself to the food she'd prepared.

"I saw you born, Serise," The woman continued. "And studied your behavior while you were here visiting with your mother. You watched our customs, our ceremonies, but you did not join in spirit. You wore the jewelry and the symbols but you didn't understand them." The woman's voice was quiet, but stern. "We helped provide a foundation for you when your parents could not reveal their true selves. Your tribe's spiritual core mirrors many of our own. We are one family even if raised by separate nations."

"I'm so sorry. I want to learn. I can't go back but I can go forward. I will change myself to honor my parent's memory."

"Your parents wanted that for you. Cheryl poured her hopes into you. David tried to teach you. But you would not listen. Even now, you do not quite believe you have a place in your world and in ours."

Serise wiped at her tears but couldn't keep them from flowing.

"Your parents are proud people. They made a great sacrifice to bring you into this world. I myself was there to welcome you at your birth."

"My parents are dead," Serise said, hugging herself.

Micique reached out to console her, but Kyloria held him back. "This is her task to complete," she whispered. "We cannot do this for her. We can only be present to support her."

"Her parents are not dead," Johana replied.

"Are you sure?" asked Kyloria, looking up in surprise.

"We have prayed on it," Johana said. "Their spirit is strong."

Serise wiped at her tears. "Then I will find them."

"Sonecian teams are searching for them. You must first find yourself. You must first learn prayer and healing from within. To do that you must grow up. As you have learned, life is not fun and games."

"But—"

The woman raised her hand but not her voice. "You have not yet been molded or completed the purification rituals needed to become a woman. Because of this, what gifts you possess will not develop. Do you know our story of Changing Woman?"

"Yes. It's a legend."

"Aren't all legends based in part on truth? Explain to your friends."

Serise wiped her tears with the sleeves of her shirt, looked off into some faraway place and began.

"Changing Woman is the mother of the Diné. She was born at the boundaries of darkness and light. She is the guardian, the source of energy that nourishes and protects the people. She is the source of medicine's power to heal and provides for the Dine in the bounty of the Earth. She was adopted by First Man and First Woman and raised in the ways of the holy people."

"Just as our religion tells of a first family," said Micique. "We've learned some Earth cultures have another version. I believe they were called Adam and Eve."

"I guess every religion has their own version of the beginning," said Serise.

"You are closer to the truth than you believe," Johana said. "If you can do this thing I will ask of you, then I will sponsor you upon your return. You will know peace. You will find the answer your mother sought."

"Do you know what it was?" Kyloria asked.

"We have always known," the woman said. "Even as the government forced us from our land, and thousands of us died, ripped away from our ancestral grounds, we have protected it with our lives."

"But we need it now," Serise said. "We don't know how much time is left before this whole Earth thing blows up."

"We are prepared to meet our destiny," the woman continued. "But the key will not reveal itself until the time and conditions are right. You cannot rush what will not be rushed."

"What can I do?" Serise asked.

"First you must work with your Sonecian tribe. Learn their ways. There are many parallels with our own. After a time, with your tribe's permission and ours, you can come back and work with our girls to go through the steps towards Kinaalda."

"When you have completed those steps," Kyloria said, "you will be asked to perform the ritual assigned to your mother."

Johana smiled and nodded. "It is your birthright. No one else can do it. Cheryl Hightower was a strong, proud woman. She produced a strong, proud daughter. But you do not fully understand the task or its risks. You have not faced enough hardship."

"But I have. You wouldn't believe what it took to get here. I've seen all kinds of things."

Johana sniffed. "Apparently, not the right things."

"What do you mean?"

"You don't understand that you hold a special place in the world. Once you complete this task you will be changed forever. There are no merit badges, no awards, no public recognition, no expensive designer clothes. Just your obligation to further the nourishing spirit of the Earth and become one with it. To experience the power of the healing, you must first heal yourself."

Panicked, Serise looked to Kyloria. "How do I do that?"

"We don't have those answers," Kyloria said. "The records are unclear, otherwise we would guide you along the path. But if we did, you would not strengthen your wings in the process. The clues your mother uncovered were lost when their outpost was destroyed."

Johana became quiet.

"You know, don't you? What she found?" asked Kyloria.

"Her mother was not specific, but I have my suspicions," Johana said. "Nothing more."

Serise reached across the table and took her hand. "Please? Could you give us a clue?"

Johana sighed. "Our own history tells of two sons given to Changing Woman by the Sun God. Twins. The first is the Monster Slayer. His spirit has returned to the Earth although he does not yet understand his destiny. The second is the Child Born of Water. His spirit has also returned to us. He is aware of his place in this miracle and is waiting. You must locate the second child and return with a symbol of his connection to us. Together, when all of the elements of the Earth are properly aligned, the brothers will be part of a circle that clears the world of evil."

"Where do I find this spirit?"

"Finding the answer is part of the challenge. You have good friends. They will assist you. Once the task is completed, your return to your faith and your mother's ritual will be an easier path. We will consult with our Medicine Man and your own to determine where you go from there." She removed her turquoise necklace, and placed it around Serise's neck. "A gift from your mother that I return to her daughter. When you complete your task, come back and I will tell you stories."

"And if I fail?" Serise asked.

"Come back anyway," said Johana, grasping Serise's hand and smiling. "You are family and I will still tell you stories."

"Who is the Monster Slayer?" asked Micique.

"That is not for me to say," Johana said. "When the time comes, he will reveal himself.

CHAPTER FORTY-ONE

Uke

"On my mark!" said Aurelia. "Roll!"

Kavera swung a large Casmirian rod in Carlos' direction. Carlos tucked his chin and rolled on the mat, missing the swing.

"Better. Again!" Aurelia said, her voice forceful and gentle at the same time.

Kavera swung from the other direction, and Carlos missed his timing and got whacked on the shoulder. Only it was a tap, as if Kavera knew how to hold back on his force.

"Again!" Aurelia shouted.

Exhausted, Carlos rolled one more time then lay flat on his back. "I can't do this. It's hopeless."

"It is only hopeless if one is no longer breathing. Until then, the future is always filled with possibilities," said Kavera.

Aurelia smiled and nodded. "A competitive advantage is not the creams and blankets, but your birth here on Earth. Had you been born on Casmir you would be trained in their ways. Although you believe you are powerless, your advantage is your unpredictability and acute powers of observation."

Carlos cocked an eyebrow and pulled himself up.

"Peng, for instance, is quite predictable," said Kavera. "He uses brute strength. That strength is your team's asset in battle, but it is also their weakness. He has, what you call, a 'tell.' Sometimes it is a change in his foot position or a shift in his shoulder. So why train in their weakness when you can develop your own strengths? The ability to determine each member's 'tell' and use counter measures. Is it not a common Earth phrase forewarned is forearmed?"

"In honor of your father's alliance with our team our gift will be to teach you to be fluid. Use your weakness as an asset," Aurelia said.

Carlos sighed and rolled up his shirt. "This welt is the result of me trying to do that."

Aurelia examined the mark and stroked it with her thumb. Her touch was firm but gentle and the bruise began to fade. "The mark is not from yielding. It is from your failure to yield. You choose to brace instead of relax. Ben talks to you of our daily exercise?"

"He said you dance like Alvin Ailey, throw in some hip hop and do yoga poses."

Kavera burst out laughing, then quieted when he saw the stern look on his sister's face.

"We practice the art of yielding. Developing the flexibility needed to avoid injury and to react quickly to danger," Aurelia said, nodding toward her brother.

"Defend yourself." Kavera flattened his hand and threw a ridge hand strike at Carlos.

Carlos instinctively threw up his arm and blocked the move. Kavera winced and hit his arm sharply.

"Sorry," said Kavera. "It was necessary for the demonstration."

"That hurt, did it not?" Aurelia asked.

"Uh, yeah!" Carlos frowned and rubbed his arm.

"Principles of Physics. You met brute force with an immoveable object. Kavera held back."

"That was holding back?" Carlos pulled cream from his pocket and the small red mark on his arm disappeared.

Aurelia input a code on her console. The wall of weapons opened.

"Carlos, please retrieve a stone block from the stack to the right of the spears."

It took both hands for Carlos to lift the top stone from its resting place. He waddled back to the center of the arena, straining under the weight.

Aurelia took the stone from him as if it were weightless and placed it on the floor. Placing her hand in the same ridge hand strike as Kavera, she raised and lowered it as if trying to gauge the distance and power needed. Without warning, she brought her hand down on the stone. It broke cleanly in half.

"As I said, Kavera's strike was not at full strength otherwise your arm would be in the same condition as the stone."

Carlos frowned. There wasn't a mark or bruise on her hand. He wondered what other superpowers she had.

"Strength is not always the best course of action. You are smaller. You cannot win with that strategy against Peng or any other Casmirian," Kavera said. His tone was kind and nonjudgmental.

"I'm just trying to survive," Carlos said.

"Try this instead," said Aurelia. "Kavera, please allow Carlos to throw a strike in your direction."

Carlos paused then tried to duplicate the technique Aurelia and Kavera had used. Instead of blocking the shot Kavera stepped to the side, swept his arm around and under Carlos's arm locking it at the elbow.

"Did that hurt?" he asked.

"No," Carlos said, unable to get out of the hold.

"I did not need strength to do that," said Kavera. "And as my attacker, you also remain unharmed."

"So I can learn how to do that?"

"Absolutely. Although I don't recommend the strategy. With your tribe it will work only once and you will be unable to do it a second time. It's just an example. Save it for emergencies."

"Then what can I do?"

"You can bend like a reed," said Aurelia. "An old branch will break under stress. A new branch retains its flexibility and the ability to snap back in some circumstances."

"I'm confused," said Carlos, shoulders slumping.

Aurelia glanced at Kavera.

"If you block your team's attacks it might break your bones," Kavera said. "The force is that great. Instead, I will help you with techniques that are similar to Brazilian Capoeira and Aikido. To you, it will appear to be dance moves. But it will surprise them. They are unfamiliar with the style and their bulk will make it hard for them to master it at this late date. In time you will become lightning quick. But if we train you, we insist you adhere to our philosophy. You don't strike unless it is to save your life. Agreed?"

Carlos smiled. "Agreed."

"And our training remains a secret. Not even Ben or Kurosh will know, understood?" said Kavera.

"And how do you propose to hide this from me?" said Ben's uncle as he entered the room, his robes flapping behind his long strides. His booming bass voice echoing as usual.

"Kurosh, we—," Aurelia started but Ben's uncle abruptly put his hand up to stop her.

"Are you prepared for this training, Carlos?" he asked.

"Yes, sir, Commander Kurosh, sir," Carlos answered, wishing he could hide behind Kavera as he braced for a lecture.

His eyes darting from Aurelia to Kavera, Ben's uncle remained silent for several minutes. Carlos knew it was a telepathic debate and hated he couldn't listen in, but Ben's uncle didn't seem angry. Carlos unclenched his teeth but remained wary. After a few minutes, Ben's uncle asked, "You prefer I not intervene with Pendon?"

"No, sir. I don't want to dishonor my father. I want to handle this myself."

As typical, Ben's uncle didn't smile, but a glint appeared in his eyes and his expression softened. "Then I grant permission for my subordinates to continue."

Carlos nodded and suppressed the overwhelming urge to hug the man. He finally felt like he had a fighting chance.

CHAPTER FORTY-TWO

The Plan Redux

"Okay, team. There's an eight hour time difference between here and Palenque," Ben said.

Having studied Mayan myths they narrowed their first search to a couple of temple complexes including Chichan Itza which had a humongous ball court, Tikal and Palenque. The Palenque temples were the most intact and rumored to be built on top of even older ruins dating back to 900 BC. Plus Ben thought it looked cool. Couldn't rule out the fun factor. His uncle said *"don't break a promise you don't intend to keep."* So in his mind, this excursion was an 'expected' development in his adolescent growth. He laughed, then refocused.

"If we leave Egypt at midnight it will be 4pm there. We'll need to get there and back before breakfast, and you KNOW our training starts at the crack of dawn."

"That doesn't give us a lot of time," said Serise. "According to the website the park shuts down at 4pm. Allow an hour for tourists to take their sweet time leaving and it means we can go in at about 5pm. Which means leaving here at 1am."

"Make it 2am," said Carlos, yawning. "You know tourists. They don't exactly leave on time."

April shook her head. "The website says no one is allowed after hours."

"Right, and that worked so well for the British Museum when I went there." Ben chuckled. "Okay, we'll leave at 2am."

"All of us?" asked Grace.

"It will go faster if we're searching as a team," Carlos said. "Why? Do you have somewhere to be that early in the morning?"

Grace bit her lip. "No. It will be dark. That's all."

Ben furrowed his brow and pantomimed. You okay?

Grace shrugged and nodded.

"That gives us five hours to get there and back before training starts," Carlos said. "And we have to include time to get some sleep."

"Hello!" Grace protested. "It took us a week to find artifacts in the game. You think we can pull this off in a few hours?"

"It only took Ben and Carlos an hour to get a diamond," said Serise, "and that put Orin in a great mood. Imagine what perks we can get if we find something else useful?"

"Right. We want to prove we're as good as the rest of the teams," Ben said.

"I read in the archives that there might be something in the tomb of the Red Queen," Carlos said. "But we should check the Emperor's tomb first. His sarcophagus looks like he's communicating with space aliens."

Grace waved her arms. "No! Not going there. No tombs."

"The mummies are both gone, I think," Carlos said. "I know for sure the queen is stored at a museum. They couldn't put her back because once they broke the seal on the sarcophagus there was no way to keep out the moisture. So this will be like that whole mummy in Sunnyslope Museum adventure but without the hidden portals, weird passwords and dark holes."

Grace looked skeptical.

"I can get the coordinates," said Serise. "And there won't be any teams there because they're back in Llactapata. Guess Carlos's father was on to something, although they haven't found diddly squat yet and as your uncle says 'the clock is ticking.'"

Carlos laid a tourist brochure on the table, looking over his shoulder as if he still didn't trust that there were no cameras watching them.

"Where'd you get that?" asked Ben.

"The librarian printed it for our research. I asked for a paper copy instead of a digital one. She said it was a waste of resources but I said it was what Earth people do, so she made an exception." He stopped and laughed. "Score one for being raised human. And look. The ruins fit the pattern. The ancient name of the city used to be Lakaham, meaning 'Great Water.' It's got a lot of temples, a palace, and a ball court to keep Ben happy while we look for clues."

Ben punched him in the shoulder. Carlos winced.

"You okay?" Ben asked.

"Yeah, fine," Carlos said looking him straight in the eyes. "How come?"

Ben shrugged. "You've just been gone a lot after dinner."

"Working extra shifts with Orin," Carlos shrugged. "Keeps me out of Pendon's way."

Ben had a twinge of jealousy. From what he heard, Orin was working on cool technology and he'd give anything to play in that lab too.

"So back to the plan," Carlos said, "Twins," he stopped and gave Ben a fist bump, "and water. Most of the creation myths involve both those things."

"And animals," April said. "The myths all say the ancient people were animals."

"Right. Animals," Serise said. "But technically people, even outer space ones, are animals, so it still fits. Remember? The librarian said some myths use metaphors and analogies to describe real events."

"Okay," said Carlos. "To get to the tomb we've got to walk through Templo Del Calavera which stands for Skull Temple.

There was a loud groan.

"It's just a name," said Ben, excited to be going to see it.

"Up until a few weeks ago Safe Harbor was just a name too," Grace said.

Ben rolled his eyes. "Where do we go next, Carlos?"

Carlos studied the map and pointed. "We need to get to the Temple of Inscriptions. That's where the Emperor is buried. If that doesn't work, we'll go to Temple Thirteen. That's where the Red Queen's tomb will be."

"And she's called red why?" asked April.

"Because when she was put in the tomb she was covered with cinnabar—it's kind of a rock. But we have to be careful because it says here that it's also mercury sulfide. We don't want to touch it."

"Does anyone not see the connection?" Serise said. "Chinese emperor tomb: mercury booby trap. Mayan emperor tomb covered with mercury. Hint? Booby trap. That stuff is poison if it gets on your skin or you breathe it."

"Then we need some gloves," said Carlos.

"Got that covered," said Ben. "I got five sets from the Xenobian storage room. They're heavy duty because they're only used when the team is transferring from one distant space gate to another. Aurelia's back from some secret mission and now no one is traveling outside of the atmosphere for a while. They won't be missed. I can put them back when we are done. Grace, you sure we can use the transport pads in your team's compound?"

Grace nodded. "My team's hardly at the Harbor and when they are, they're in their quarters meditating. We should be fine as long as we go at night."

"One problem," April said. "We still can't get out of our apartment, remember? After we got caught sneaking out they locked down the library portal but they also put a fingerprint lock on our door."

"Not a problem," said Carlos. He pulled out a rubbery pad, placed it on the table, then pulled a glass from behind the couch.

"What's that?" Ben asked.

"Watch and learn." Carlos smashed and molded the material until is was thin and transparent. He wrapped the material around the cup, careful to keep it smooth as he went. He pressed tight, then slowly peeled it off.

"I helped bus plates the day the teams were called to an emergency somewhere in the Ukraine. Your team can read your mind but they can't read mine. So I didn't want to tell you in case they were nosing around in your head. I figured your team is authorized for access, so I snuck out some of their water glasses." He pointed behind the couch. "I knew we'd eventually need to hack the lock. Since we have to clean our own apartment, who would find them?"

He placed the clear material near the window, and turned the display to simulate one of the uninhabited planets closest to the Sonecian sun. The bright rays raised the room temperature to a scorching degree, but the material began to cure in minutes. Carlos turned the display back to Sunnyslope and waited for the material to cool off. Then he walked to the door and pressed the material to the keypad.

"What was that word your team uses for 'open'?" he asked.

"Fungua!" said April.

It didn't work.

"Fungua!" Grace said in an almost perfect parrot of Uncle Henry's voice.

Ben narrowed his eyes and wondered how Grace was getting so good at imitating voices. But it worked. The door opened.

"Problem solved," she said, avoiding his stare.

CHAPTER FORTY-THREE

Palenque

17.4839778 N 92.0463278 E

The Mayan complex was dark. Darker than the Egyptian corridor they'd found after their home was destroyed. Darker than the caves under the Vatican and they were outside this time. The fragrance of orange trees blanketed a jungle alive with the sound of wild animals. A light mist shrouded everything around them which made it just that much more spooky to be there. Something small and dark skittered in the trees.

Ben froze and allowed his eyes to adjust in the low light. A troop of howler monkeys continued on to their destination without taking notice of the rogue mission on the ground. According to the librarian, the monkeys were considered descendants of the wood people. The ones made by the Mayan gods after the first group was destroyed by a flood.

"I don't know if this is such a good idea," April said. "I mean, this isn't a game anymore. The Smithsonian was safe for humans. But look at this place. What if the booby traps are real?"

"That's why we started with this one instead of the one in China," said Carlos. "No booby traps."

"That we know of," said Grace. "You have a lot more faith than I do. Any chance we could just run down and find replicas of artifacts in the gift shop?"

"Gift shop is closed and I don't think the Guardian will open with fake plastic stuff made in a Chinese factory. Besides, we don't even know what we're looking for, so just follow the plan," said Serise, "and we'll be back before breakfast."

They trudged up a staircase toward the first building. A giant skull was carved into one of the pillars at the top.

"Okay," said Carlos, pointing to the map. "This is the—"

"We know what it is," said April, stepping closer and inspecting the stucco sculpture. "Just don't say it."

"I was going to say it's a sculpture of a rabbit skull, not a human one, so we should be good to go unless you're fluffy and have a cottontail."

They continued across the courtyard to the Temple of Inscriptions. The staircase rose nearly ninety feet into the air leading to a rectangular building punctuated by five rectangular doorways.

"You have got to be kidding," Serise said. "The sarcophagus is way up there?"

"According to the map," said Carlos.

Ben grumbled and lead the way. The steps were smooth from centuries of weathering so he stepped gingerly, stopping occasionally to wait for the others.

Serise huffed. "About now I wish I had I had my team's flying skills."

"That would come in handy," Ben said, his thighs straining from climbing. "You could fly up and do a reconnaissance for us."

Once at the top, Serise froze. Ben turned to see what had scared her. On the way up he had not noticed the incline. But now, at the top, it was frightening. The steps looked like they were only inches apart and at an impossibly steep angle. Getting down was going to be hard and he didn't have a blindfold for Serise like he did when they were lost beneath Rome.

"Don't look down," Ben said, holding her shoulders and turning her to face away. "We'll come up with a plan when it's time to go.

Maybe we can get back to the storage room from here."

They walked down a narrow stone corridor with a pitched ceiling.

"Look at these stones," said April. "At home they use cranes to put up a building. Wonder how they built this thing without equipment."

"Probably the same way the people on Easter Island moved the heads," Carlos said. "Create a fulcrum, use trees for a conveyor belt. Then maybe create ropes from vines."

"But you'd need pulleys," said Grace. "To lift them in place. Look at this. How even the cuts are on the rocks. Like they had lasers."

"Teams have been visiting for years," Carlos said. "Might have helped them out. Plus, there's a theory that this temple complex is built on top of an older city. Kind of like the Pyramids being built on top of a secret space outpost." He studied the map again. "Oh!"

"Oh what?" Ben said, bracing. "Booby trap?"

"No. The sarcophagus is not up here. Look for an opening in the floor. We have to go down to an inner chamber. Anyone got a flashlight?"

There was a collective groan. April was the first to find the opening and went down. "Not a good idea, not a good idea, not a good idea," she repeated for most of the sixty-plus steps it took to descend into the darkness. Damp and slippery stone steps followed by a turn and more steps. But there at the bottom, in low light, sat the sarcophagus of the Mayan ruler, Pakal. It rested behind iron bars, well out of reach.

Bats hung from the ceiling twenty feet above them. An odor clung to the air of something best left unknown.

"Dead end?" asked Serise, looking closely at traces of red substance on the walls. "Blood?"

"Paint," said Carlos. "I think it's worn off paint."

Serise frowned and nodded, but didn't touch them.

"Serise, really. It's paint. I read it in one of the books the librarian gave us."

Grace whipped out a pair of glasses and studied the sarcophagus lid on the other side of the bars.

"It looks like a spaceship," Ben said. "Look at the way he's sitting. Tilted, like he's in an old fashioned space capsule."

"That would make sense," Carlos said. "Because according to the legends, only the rulers could talk to the gods in the divine world. If they thought our ancestors were gods, then the bird at the top of the lid makes sense. But it also looks like a scene from Alien. You know, where they find the giant space traveler only he's been dead for thousands of years."

"No!" April said. "We don't. You KNOW my mom didn't let us watch those movies. Talking about movies we haven't seen is kind of mean."

"Sorry," he said. "Dad couldn't get enough of them. It just reminded me of that scene. That's why it looks like he's going into space."

"I saw it," said Ben, feeling sheepish. "At a friend's house after basketball practice."

"Awe!" said April. "How come you always get to see the good stuff?"

"Trust me," Ben said. "That movie was so scary I had my eyes closed most of the time."

"Grace," Serise said. "You've been quiet. Kavera get you new glasses?"

Grace looked up suddenly embarrassed. "Umm. No. Picked up the wrong pair after training. But they work. I'll return them to Tenzin when we get back." She tapped her finger against her thigh.

Another lie? Ben wondered.

"It could be a space ship," said Grace, her fingers tracing an invisible line around the carving on the other side of the iron bars. "But I think it's something else. I did some extra reading and some people think this isn't a ship, but a tree with roots that lead to the underworld. Carlos, didn't the Mayan twins have to go to the underworld to get their father back?"

"Yes. How come?"

"I think we have to go there too."

"Anyone got a dialer code for the underworld?" April asked.

"No," said Ben, standing near an opening in the wall that wasn't there before. "We've got something better."

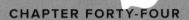

CHAPTER FORTY-FOUR

The Red Queen

⁚⁖ The portal lead directly into a smaller chamber. It was dark, but not as ominous as Pakal's chamber. And they could touch the sarcophagus.

"I'm getting deja vu," said Carlos.

"But the Queen's sarcophagus in Sunnyslope was safe," said Grace. "It was just a way to another chamber."

Ben looked into the empty stone box. "What if this is the same thing?"

April put on her gloves, and touched the surface. "Better look for a code," she said, "because this thing is solid. No portal in there."

They scanned the plain walls of the chamber, searching for a magic door, a secret button, or any other abracadabra device that would give them a clue. Nothing.

Serise tapped her fingers on the edge of the coffin.

"Careful," Carlos said. "That red powder is mercury. It's toxic. Put on your gloves."

Serise searched her pockets and frowned. "I think I left them back at the apartment."

"Then use one of mine." Carlos handed one over but let go before

Serise had a firm grasp. It dropped into the coffin. Reaching for it with his gloved hand, he hit nothing but solid stone. He frowned.

"What's the matter?" Ben said.

"The glove. It's not there."

Ben reached in and found nothing but a solid limestone surface. He patted the walls and checked the corners kicking up more red dust. "Where'd it go?"

Grace checked the sarcophagus. "He's right. It's not there."

"It has to be," said Carlos. Using his gloved hand again, he checked the sarcophagus. Solid stone. No glove.

"Try putting your other hand in there," said Serise.

Carlos tried switching his left glove to his right hand."

"No," Serise said. "Without the glove."

Carlos' eyes grew wide. "Are you nuts? This stuff is poisonous."

Serise shrugged. "When all other options are ruled out, whatever is left is the truth."

Carlos smiled. "Mr. Spock. Star Trek."

"Whatever," said Serise. "I mean, umm, yes! Precisely! Mr. Spock."

Everyone held their breath as Carlos reached in with his ungloved hand, careful not to get any of the mercury dust on his skin. There was a void. A beautiful, wonderful, welcome void.

He grinned. "I think we've found our portal!"

Carlos held his hand to the side so his friends could step through. As expected, there was a staircase allowing them to descend farther into the temple. The stories were true. The current buildings were constructed on top of a much older stone city. Once at the bottom, there was light, although he didn't know where it was coming from.

They stood inside a narrow corridor, surrounded on three sides by stone walls rising two stories high. Ahead of them, a doorway lead to an outdoor courtyard. All around them were Mayan hieroglyphs as sharp as if they'd been carved the day before. "This might be it," said Carlos. "The mythical courtyard where the twins had to play basketball to defeat the great evil."

"Then we've got this!" Ben said. "Easiest puzzle to solve. I'll play!"

"And I'll play back-up," said Serise, grinning.

"By the way, Serise," Carlos asked. "How'd you know my hand would open a portal?"

"Your uncle gave us a clue when we first arrived at the Harbor. He said that the original Sonecians had programmed the ancient portals so they'd respond only to specific DNA patterns. Kind of like the Libyan desert portal working when Grace or Ben touched it. We didn't find any other clues on the walls. There were no charts or dialers, so that was the only thing left."

Everyone nodded in appreciation.

"Okay," Carlos said. "Let's rock and roll." He lead the way out of the corridor. But when he turned around the others were pushing up against an invisible barrier.

"We're trapped," Grace yelled. "I think it's a booby trap!"

Carlos rushed toward them, finding it impossible to get through. The invisible barrier felt like cold glass. He took off both gloves, hoping his DNA against the surface would bring down the barrier or open a portal. Instead the sound of stone against stone rang out across the courtyard. Four large balls flowed out of a hole in the wall. High above it, a stone ring slid out. Inside the corridor, on the other side of the glass, the walls began moving towards each other. It WAS a trap and his friends were about to be slaughtered.

And then a deep booming voice echoed across the courtyard. It was almost mocking in its tone.

"What did it say?" Ben asked.

Carlos froze, his face a mask of terror.

"Carlos?"

Carlos didn't answer. Instead he banged his fists on the barrier as if his life depended on getting them out.

"Grace? Did you catch what the voice said?" Ben asked.

Grace nodded, her face now ashen. "If we can't find a way to help Carlos, if we can't get you out there with him, we're dead meat. That voice? Loosely translated it said—," she choked, then recovered.

"It said, 'Play Ball!' "

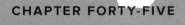

CHAPTER FORTY-FIVE

Play Ball!

"Shoot, Carlos! Shoot!"

The walls advanced towards the middle of the chamber. In a few minutes everyone but Carlos would be pressed into the limestone like fossils.

"Carlos!" Ben yelled while looking for a rock he could use to shatter the glass barrier. "Hurry up!"

Carlos grabbed the first ball, lined up his shot and froze.

"Be a math nerd," Ben shouted. "Visualize the arc, gentle, sweeping, line up the angle of trajectory."

"Shut up! You're making me nervous. These balls are solid rubber and must weigh twenty pounds." Carlos steadied himself, fell into a crouch and then sprang into action. The ball flew up and out of the court and disappeared.

"On this planet," yelled Ben as he dug in his feet in a futile attempt to keep the massive ten ton walls from advancing. "Next time try aiming for a hoop on EARTH!"

Carlos aimed again. This time the ball fell well short of its target and landed with a dull thud to the right of the main entrance and disappeared.

233

Now only two balls remained.

"Carlos!" yelled Grace. She pressed her back against one wall and her feet against the other. "I wasn't planning on meeting my ancestors so soon."

The third ball landed on the rim of the hoop, fell to the ground and shattered against a sharp rock before disappearing. Only one chance left.

"Concentrate," yelled a chorus of frightened voices.

"Don't use your hands," April said. "Remember. In the stories the librarian told us? It's like soccer. You have to hit the goal without using your hands."

Carlos stopped, looked at April, then gave her a thumbs up. He put his arms together, let the ball run from his fingers to the cradle formed by his elbows, then launched it straight up. As it fell he butted it with his head.

"Ouch!"

The fourth ball flew through the air, rolled on top of the rim and fell toward the ground. Carlos ran like his friend's lives depended on it, which it did. He caught it before it landed. It didn't disappear like the others.

"Try again. You can do it," said Serise.

"Pretend you're aiming for your dad's satellite dish!" said Ben.

Carlos shot an angry look in Ben's direction.

"It's a joke!" said Ben. "To help you relax."

"You can do it," yelled April. "I don't want to die. I haven't gotten to drive a car yet. I want to see outer space. Go on a date."

"I hear dates are overrated," said Serise, laughing nervously.

Ben looked at Serise incredulously.

"If I'm going to be crushed to death, at least I can go out with a sense of humor!"

Carlos took the ball, wiped the sweat from his eyes and stared at the hoop, testing the weight of the ball in his hand. He crouched and poised for the shot. He hesitated.

"Carlos! Daydream later, okay? Shoot the stupid ball already!"

Carlos straightened and eyed the hoop. Eyes narrowed, he backed up thirty feet then began running towards it.

"What are you doing?" Grace shouted. "Don't use your hands, remember?"

Carlos kept his eyes on the target as he picked up speed. Six feet from the hoop he launched the ball forward and high into the air. Tilting his body, he shot one leg straight out and kicked the ball straight through the opening.

Carlos had never ever hit a basket despite a lifetime of trying. Today, however, he nailed his target with a flying soccer kick.

With a groan, the massive walls came to a dead stop, reversed direction and retreated into the walls.

CHAPTER FORTY-SIX

Discovered

⸭ "Greetings, young disobedient warriors," Kavera chirped as he poked Ben with his foot. Following his normal morning ritual, Ben resisted getting up, hoping for just twenty more minutes of shut eye and clutching the sides of his mattress. Also following habit, Kavera blew up the bed, only this time twice as fast causing Ben to be launched into the air. He scrambled to right himself just before his feet landed with a whomp.

Carlos scrambled out of bed on his own.

"Is there something you both would like to tell me?" Kavera asked, arms crossed.

Ben looked him straight in the eye. "Like what?"

Kavera slid his hands across the edge of Ben's blanket. His fingertips were tinged with red. He slid a device from his belt, scanned the laundry basket and frowned.

Ben stood sheepishly near the bathroom. "I was . . . "

"Don't say it," said Kavera. "I was young once. I am lucky your uncle put up with me. Wild and impetuous and not ready for prime time. But he put me on his team anyway. I think it was because he wanted to impress my sister. But yes. I know what it is like to be young and incredibly stupid."

He grew serious. "Ben. Carlos. These are dangerous times. Very dangerous. I don't think you comprehend the risks we take every day."

"But we can help and you won't let us! Besides, we found something!"

Carlos pulled a jade stone and a fragment of a stone tablet with a spiral pattern similar to the fringe on the canopic jars from beneath his mattress, along with the four pairs of Xenobian flight gloves they forgot to return.

Kavera scanned the artifacts, his eyes narrowing as data streamed above his console.

"Where did you get these?"

"At Palenque," Carlos said. "We were researching Mayan myths and had an idea."

"That's not possible," Kavera said, shaking his head in disbelief. "The teams have searched that complex thoroughly. Even studied the glyphs and the artifacts in museums and the unrestored ruins still hidden in the jungle. You need to come clean and tell me where you obtained them."

"On a hidden ball court at Palenque," said Ben. "I swear we're not lying about that."

"Across the river? Near the Sun Temple?"

"No," Ben said. "There's a portal under the Red Queen's tomb. It lead to a different court. Carlos sank a basket and this was the reward. Kind of like an arcade. If you win you get a prize."

Kavera's eyes widened in alarm.

"We'll need a debriefing from each of you." He produced a biohazard bag from his pouch and opened it. Carlos dumped the gloves inside.

"We are missing five pairs. Where is the other?"

"In the girl's room, I think," Carlos said.

Ben pointed to the jade object in Kavera's hand. "But it worked out, right? See? We wanted to help and we did!"

Kavera blew air out of his lungs in exasperation. "And it is appreciated. You and your friends are a blessing. Truly. But your trips off site without authorization have become a distraction. It is imperative that we know where you are at all times. It is also necessary to keep this location secure to keep whatever breached our barriers from launching another attack. Perhaps, if I were to offer an incentive. Say a trip to an amusement park of your choice?"

Ben grinned. "Our choice? Anywhere?"

"Hold on," said Carlos. "Let's negotiate."

Kavera shook his head but did not smile this time. "You grow more like your Casmirian team members every day. I would say, however, that you do not have grounds for negotiation."

Ben made a slashing motion across his throat. "Don't push it. Last time I got a time out with Uncle Henry. It's like solitary confinement at a Supermax prison only worse."

"He will not be informed of this breach," said Kavera. "At least for now. Danine and I will cover for you while I find an appropriate way to explain this discovery. In the meantime, I am ordering all young rule breaking warriors to report to Medlab."

Carlos looked stricken with horror. "Why?"

"Your visit to the Red Queen's tomb has exposed you to mercury and other contaminants. You'll require a dermal scrub and a vaccination against any bacteria or virus you may have stirred up."

Ben groaned. "No other options?"

"Afraid not," said Kavera. "The decontamination procedure will be done manually. Think of it as a human car wash with bristle brushes. We cannot afford to expose the cleaner wrasse to the mercury. And now that I am also contaminated, I will be forced to undergo the same process. To say I am not pleased is an understatement. I'll have a team decontaminate the bedroom using robotic equipment." He took a cloth out of a pocket in his robe and used it to retrieve a tin box from another pocket without getting mercury on it. "In repayment for keeping your secret, would you do me a favor and hide this for a short time? It is for Danine. A surprise. Just tuck it in your closet. I'll retrieve it in a few weeks."

"Sure," said Ben, turning the box over in his hand. It was only a few inches long. "What's in it?"

"An inside joke between me and the doctor. But as I share my quarters, I would rather this be stored where it cannot be found until I am ready for the surprise."

Ben put the box on the closet shelf. Curiosity was getting the better of him but he'd broken enough rules for the day. He needed to re-earn Kavera's trust. He wouldn't look. Even if it killed him not to do it.

CHAPTER FORTY-SEVEN

Missing

After a long day in Medlab, Ben trudged back to the apartment where he found Serise trying to reload information from the old iMac she and Carlos reconstructed.

"Where is everyone?"

"Don't know about Grace," Serise said. "She headed for the Shakrarian compound when we were through. She still won't tell me what she's doing there. April's in the hydroponic garden. She said something about getting permission to grow strawberry plants. I hope it works. I'm craving some right now. And Carlos? Probably in Orin's lab working on some weird top secret thing to get his mind off that weird car wash decontamination Danine dreamed up."

Ben frowned. "Any luck with the computer?

"No," said Serise. "The bad thing about super smart people from space is as soon as we open a loophole, they find a way to close it."

"Didn't you make back-ups?"

"Well, duh!" she said. "But the laptop's not compatible and the tech team reconfigured the iMac so information can't be uploaded to the hard drive without an encryption password. I tried a brute force algorithm but it's so long it will take a hundred years to crack. The only thing we're allowed to do is download lesson plans from the library and duty rosters. They took the good stuff off too. No more messages from God in the air. I think we're at a dead end."

"Well, keep trying," Ben said. "That Middle East hack was kind of funny. And the team got what they wanted, so they can't stay mad at us for too long. I'm going for a walk to see if I can find where Warrior Lopez is hanging out these days."

⋮

Ben put his face in front of the scanner and waited for permission to enter. The door dissolved.

"Hi!" he said.

Orin looked up briefly, then returned to his work, a large weapon in his hand and a pile of blue diamonds at the edge of the table. Ben flinched as Orin aimed it over his shoulder, blasting a large hole in a chuck of twisted metal behind him.

"Something I can do for you, boy?"

"I was looking for Carlos," Ben said, stepping out of his line of fire.

"How should I know of his whereabouts?"

"He said he was working extra shifts."

"He is not."

"You sure? He's been doing it for weeks."

"Boy, do you have eyes? Does it look like he is here? Go away. I do not have time for your nonsense."

"Well, if you see him, could you tell him I was looking for him?"

"Perhaps you should leave that message with his—" Orin paused and scrolled through a series of translations on his computer and said, "—secretary."

Ben paused at the door.

"Something else I can do for you?"

"This your first time on Earth?"

"No, why do you ask?"

Ben stared at man's stumps which stopped at the knees. Resting against the table where two prosthetic legs. Thin strands of polymer wove in and out to form a shell with a hollow core. If he had not known what they were he'd have assumed the legs were an abstract sculpture. Too beautiful for a man so gruff.

"You're the guy who called Calamar a slimeball?"

Orin stopped and eyed Ben for a long while, tilting his head from one side to the other sizing him up the way Calamar did at Atlantis. "I was young then."

Ben paused and frowned. "I don't trust Calamar,"

"Then you are wise," said Orin, returning his attention to his experiment.

When Ben didn't answer, Orin said, "Something else I can do for you?"

"I thought you were healed."

"I was." Orin's nose flared but he continued tinkering.

"Then how—"

" Calamar did not do this," Orin said, cutting him off.

"But Danine cured you, right?"

"She did."

"So why—"

"This was an unavoidable consequence of a battle best forgotten. I chose not to undergo treatment."

"But why? Kavera said Danine can heal just about anything."

Orin growled. "That is for me to know, boy. You test my patience. Best you return to your own section of the facility."

"I'm not afraid of you," Ben lied.

"You should be." Orin narrowed his eyes and Ben half expected laser beams to shoot out of them. Just then, the door opened with a loud whoosh.

"Orin! I have need of —"

Ben looked up and froze. The Casmirian leader was not tall, but what he lacked in height he made up for in sheer bulk. His red and black tunic stopped just short of the floor. Beneath it, a tight black shirt showed rippling muscles beneath the fabric. The silver tips on his leather boots looked sharp enough to be weapons of their own.

"What is your business here?" Pendon asked, his voice like the slow growl of a tiger.

"I was—,"

"He was lost," Orin said, cutting him off. "Nothing more. He has been informed of the gravity of his error."

Pendon's eyes burned in intense hatred. He slapped one hand on his weapon then turned his head from side to side as if sizing up an opponent. Orin sat expressionless but kept his own eyes trained on his leader.

"This sector is considered sovereign territory. Like one of your Earth Embassy locations. Understood?" Pendon continued.

Ben wanted to flee but the door was blocked. "Yes, sir. I was just—"

"Spying? For your uncle? That is typical. We would not be in this predicament if it were not for your Xenobian family." Pendon flicked his wrist extending the blades on his weapon, then stepped to the side and swept his hand towards the door. "Do not let me find you here again, as my blades have need of a target," he whispered as Ben passed. His breath was as hot as dragon's fire.

Ben hurried into the corridor, hearing Pendon bark at Orin as the door closed. Now he was worried about Carlos more than ever.

CHAPTER FORTY-EIGHT

Jealousy

:• Ben wandered into the corridor, thinking of how Carlos looked sometimes after training. He was getting better, and the harmonic blanket made quick work of the bruises, but still, he wondered what kind of man Pendon was to let a kid get beat up like that. Or why Orin didn't help him after they'd gotten him a diamond. Even Carlos's father had never once hit him. Growled? Check. Blew a gasket a few times? Check. Frank Lopez, or whatever his real name was, had facial expressions that would scare Godzilla. But never once did he get physical or insult his son. So Ben was sure that whatever Pendon was doing, wasn't entirely about being Casmirian. It was more like being a super villain on a power trip.

He walked to the outer sector toward the Casmirian training compound. If Carlos wasn't helping Orin, then where was he? He hated to think of him hurt somewhere but Ben had been warned to stay out of the Casmirian wing of the complex so that left him few options other than sneaking around. Something he was getting quite good at. There was always the possibility Carlos was going on missions off the base. Ben was sure Grace was doing the same thing. A shot of envy hit him in the gut. Everyone had missions except him. Even April went to Indonesia to retrieve corpse plants like the one his mother had grown in her greenhouse. But him? Ben Webster was exiled at the Harbor with no hope of reprieve.

The Casmirian training facility was empty, so he checked the hydroponic garden, the galley, the control room and then the library. No sign of Carlos. He shot out of the library just as the librarian materialized. He didn't want to chance her asking if he'd completed his homework.

Ben headed for his own training center to see if he could look for the transport pad used to transfer equipment. Finding it would make it easier to get in and out of the Harbor undetected. It was late afternoon, the teams would still be out in the field, or sleeping so they could take the next shift. A few would be coming back for evening practice and dinner. He had to work quickly.

He slipped in the door and froze. Aurelia's voice rang out from the right side of the complex.

"Again!" she ordered. "Better! Your skills improve each day."

"Agreed," said Kavera. "You have come far in such a short time."

Ben heard grunting and, thinking he could catch some pointers on self defense, slipped farther into the room but remained in the shadows. All around him monitors processed data streams from teams working around the world. The Xenobian computers chirped and beeped, masking his approach.

"Okay," said Kavera. "Remember, anticipate the tell, then adjust. Don't assume each strike will follow the same path. Stay focused."

Ben heard a whoosh and inched closer to see Kavera swinging a large Casmirian battle sword at an unseen opponent who was panting hard. The warrior's identity was concealed by another set of columns.

Aurelia studied a monitor. "Control your breathing. Deep breath in through your nose. Exhale through your mouth."

More grunting.

"Yes!" she said. "Close your lips a bit. Force the air to work on its way out. Keeping your blood oxygenated will help your brain maintain its focus. Don't starve it. Feed it."

Panting, then more controlled breathing.

"Yes! Much improved."

Ben wondered about the warrior being trained. It was unusual for anyone on the team to struggle this way except maybe himself. And he had not heard of anyone being hurt in the field. He tried moving forward but there was too much light. They'd be sure to see him.

"Now," Aurelia said, "Kavera will create ten different offensive moves. They will come in rapid succession. You will have little time to think. See if you can anticipate them and develop a counter strategy. He will intentionally create a "tell" before each one."

Kavera dropped the weapon, dropped low in the knees and began to generate what looked like Capoeira moves at the unseen warrior.

Ben heard grunts and puffs as the person tried to defend themselves.

"Slow your breathing," Aurelia said. "Better. Now, bend your knees to gain more distance as you approach and retreat. Find your rhythm and then vary it to keep your opponent off guard."

"Yes! Perfect!"

Ben couldn't help but feel a tinge of jealousy and found himself mirroring the breathing instructions Aurelia ordered. He drew breath into his lungs, then released it through pursed lips as he mentally walked through the training exercises from that morning. He imagined himself moving across the room, felt his muscles tense as they responded to an imaginary battle. He didn't see why they wouldn't train him. What if he were out and needed to defend himself? Even here it was clear that the Casmirians didn't like him, or the rest of his family. How do you defend yourself against people like that?

He sighed. While he was daydreaming in his own self-pity he'd missed the next drill.

Aurelia's device beeped. "Your heart rate is improving. Much better muscle tone. Now, try the other techniques we taught you. Fluid. Don't respond, only yield and avoid the attacks."

Ben couldn't wait any longer. He took a chance and stepped a few inches forward. Pressing his head against the column he pivoted just enough to see which one of the team members was undergoing training. Maybe if he asked one more time, Kavera or Aurelia would relent and train him too.

Kavera looked almost as if he were dancing as he rotated in and out of view. Soon he pivoted and shifted his position. Ben froze as Kavera's opponent spun forward.

Angry, he stormed out of the room, not caring if they heard him or not.

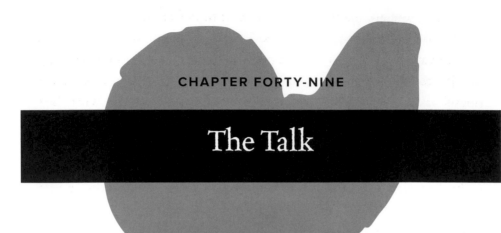

CHAPTER FORTY-NINE

The Talk

⁝ "Ben!"

Ben didn't stop or even look behind him.

"Ben!" Kavera said louder, suddenly beside him. "What ails you, my young friend?"

"Do I have to say it?" Ben struggled to keep his rage in check. He supposed he should meditate, but he just wasn't in the mood. He felt betrayed.

By two of his closest friends.

Kavera grabbed his arm firmly and spun him around. "Let's talk."

"I don't want to talk. There's nothing to talk about," spat Ben. "I'm family! You and Aurelia are the only family I've got left besides April and Uncle Henry. You won't train me, but you'll train Carlos?"

Kavera closed his eyes. "This is a private matter. We need to go to Temple."

Ben resisted.

"Now!" Kavera ordered, tightening his grip as he guided Ben forward. Once inside he said, "Sit," pointed to a stone bench, then took a seat beside him.

Ben slammed down as hard as he could to make a point.

"Ben, there are many things you don't understand."

"I understand that I'm always odd man out," Ben said, lowering his eyes toward the floor. "I made a mistake and I'm stuck doing clean-up and janitor stuff. Serise gets to go out with her team even though she doesn't like to fly. April went on a trip. Grace won't tell me what she's doing but I'm betting she's going out too, right?"

When there was no response he continued ranting.

"And Carlos is going on missions and learning about what it means to be Casmirian. But all I get is a trip to a giant satellite dish and a bunch of secrets and half truths. I'm not welcome in the Casmirian wing of the complex, but Carlos comes to ours and you give him the one thing I wanted most?"

He looked up, but Kavera had his hands clasped, eyes closed and appeared to be meditating. Ben could tell from the rise and fall of his chest that he was breathing deeply. But he made no sound either on inhale, or when exhaled from his pursed lips. All around them, water cast a wavy reflection on the walls of the sanctuary as it trickled around an outer viaduct. After a minute or so, Kavera opened his eyes and turned them towards Ben.

"Carlos is not learning to fight. Fighting . . ." Kavera paused, "only invites more conflict. I have never seen a confrontation in which a person being attacked simply gives up and the attacker follows suit."

Ben scowled. "But I saw it. You're teaching him how to fight!"

"We are not," said Kavera. "We are teaching him to yield."

"What's the difference?" said Ben, tempted to get up. "I saw what I saw with my own eyes."

Kavera took in another, much deeper long breath. This time with an audible sigh. "Your eyes deceive you, Benjamin. Carlos is at risk. Pendon was once bested by Carlos's father in battle. Carlos's father has always held a favored position for his ability to form alliances outside of Casmir. And now Carlos has chosen to live with you and your friends rather than his own tribe. I believe Pendon is, how shall I say this, picking on his rival's son. He's a bully and his team doesn't dare object. A mutiny would be punishable in the most extreme way."

"Then why is Carlos training with you if it will just make Pendon angrier?"

"He sought out Aurelia for help."

"But I asked her for help, too."

Kavera put his hand up to stop Ben. "You are not in mortal danger. Carlos is. Aurelia consented to the breach under the condition he keep his training a secret. Even from his friends. He honored her request even though I'm sure it pained him to keep it from you. To discover that he was being trained by us might destroy the fragile alliance we have with his team."

Ben followed joints in the stone floor they snaked toward the altar. "Pendon said it was the Xenobian's fault that the mission is in trouble."

Eye's widening, Kavera lowered his voice to a whisper and seemed to check to make sure they were alone. "You saw Pendon? Today?"

Ben nodded, "And Orin, while I was looking for Carlos. What did he mean by that?"

Kavera's jaw tightened. "Nothing. Pendon is mistaken We all bare some responsibility for the difficult task at hand. It cannot be laid at the feet of a single tribe."

"But if the Casmirians are holding a grudge, then I might need to learn to fight like Carlos."

"Carlos is not learning to fight. He is learning to duck. Literally. We are teaching him flexibility so he can avoid the blows. Exhaust his opponent. I believe my sister explained to you our philosophy. That the highest order of attainment is to defeat your enemy without harm. To leave them with their dignity. You cannot control what others do to you. Only how you allow yourself to react to the stimulus."

Kavera stood and gestured for Ben to join him.

"Throw a punch."

"What?"

"Throw a punch," he ordered. "Hardest one you can throw."

Ben braced his feet, then took a swing. He hit only air and nearly fell off balance. Kavera was now behind him.

"Want to try again?"

Ben repeated the exercise, but anticipating that Kavera would move behind him, he punched while he pivoted to the back. Again, he hit nothing but air. The exact same result when he was challenged by his uncle.

"Understand? Carlos has not once been taught how to punch. We would never teach him something that might lead to his death at the hands of Pendon's second in command. Only how to avoid them."

"But YOU know how to fight!"

"I know how to protect myself. There is a difference. And that is the second level of training. I spent years learning the art of avoidance first. Avoiding conflict. Walking away. Not escalating a difficult situation. And later I was allowed to train in techniques similar to Aikido where you gently guide your opponent where you want them using their momentum against them. And like you I was angry that I could not be taught the sparring techniques of my mentors. It was years before I learned more advanced martial arts and I must admit, now I find the idea of escalating a dispute or taking a life distasteful."

"Okay," Ben turned to leave. Even in sanctuary he struggled to get grounded. He understood the point intellectually. And Kavera was the closest thing to a big brother he had. But emotionally he still felt betrayed.

He stopped at the door, careful not to turn around so Kavera wouldn't see the wetness forming in his eyes.

"Does Uncle Henry know?"

"He does," said Kavera. "But only because he, like you, discovered our subterfuge. It was unintended for him to be so informed."

"But he let you do it, anyway?"

"He granted the exception because he understands the alternative of not teaching Carlos would be worse. You have seen Orin, have you not?"

Ben nodded. "He's the guy who insulted Calamar. I thought you said Danine fixed him."

"She did. Healed him completely. But he defied Pendon on another matter. In retaliation, Pendon ordered the guards to teach him a lesson. Orin survived. Defeated every warrior that complied with the order. But not without sustaining injuries that were permanent. So you must understand our concern that Pendon returned on the transport bringing with him a larger, more loyal squad."

Ben froze.

"I will teach you," Kavera said, letting his hand settle on Ben's shoulder. "Let me finish up with the current mission, and I will train you. It will just be the two of us. We'll start with the same techniques. Aikido. Capoeira. Fluid styles that lend themselves to your current training. But until then, everything you need to know is already being taught to you in morning exercises. Honor them. Practice and commit the movements to memory until it becomes second nature."

"You promise?" Ben turned and looked at Kavera through the blur of his tears.

Kavera nodded and rubbed Ben's shoulder.

"Okay, thanks," Ben took a cleansing breath, nodded, then toward door.

"And Ben," said Kavera. "I will change the authorization codes. Your friends, as long as they are discrete, will be welcome in our compound at any time."

CHAPTER FIFTY

Flash Mob

As the glorified outpost janitor, Ben swept the training room. Again.

The room was spotless but his uncle told him to clean it anyway. He still had four steel crates to unpack and organize. He tried to move the largest crate so he could sweep underneath it. It looked like it hadn't been moved in a thousand years and scraped against the floor before catching on something. Ben groaned and, seeing nothing obvious, got on his hands and knees and swept his hands back and forth.

It couldn't be!

Adrenaline pumping, he wedged his feet against a wall for leverage and forced the crate to the side. Yes! Cut into the floor was a pattern he recognized. Not the modern platforms and gleaming tubes used by the warriors to travel around the country. Nope. He'd found the holy grail of discoveries for future Ben Webster excursions. A long forgotten transport pad like the ones he used in the game. If he could find the old codes to activate it, he'd be back in business and without having to "borrow" badges to get out of the complex. He rushed to move the crate back in place. No use having the secret discovered.

"Benjamin?"

"Be there in a minute, Berko!" Ben checked to make sure the dialer was completely covered and rushed into the training room. Berko and Zadra stood in the middle of the floor arms folded and looking stern. The male warriors were lined up on one side of the room, April and the women on the other. Everyone except April was frozen in a military stance, hands behind their backs.

"Uh oh. This isn't going to be good."

"What's up?"

"Kavera called an emergency meeting and requested we retrieve you," Zadra said.

Ben braced and tried to block out images of the hidden dialer as he walked toward them. Kavera was nowhere in sight.

He shot a look at April who lifted her hands and shrugged.

"What'd I do now? And I apologize in advance just in case."

Music filled the room. Berko grinned and began performing a precision routine in time with the drumbeats. Soon all the men were strutting across the floor synchronized with Berko while the women laughed and hooted. Their massive muscles rippled as they performed a syncopated pattern, part tribal ritual, part urban hip–hop. The women began a dance of their own.

Ben was confused. Emergency meeting and they were dancing?

A woman known as Letria gestured for Ben and April to join them. Ben declined, but April jumped right in. She moved awkwardly at first, but soon found her footing and kept up with perfect rhythm. It was obvious the women had lowered the complexity of their dance for April's benefit, but soon returned to the original pattern. April had no problem following. She was a natural.

Ayotunde broke from the group and waved Ben forward.

"No thanks. I'm good just watching," Ben said, staying put near the storage room door.

"It was not a request." Ayotunde said, his voice firm.

At least a foot taller then Ben, Ayotunde pulled him to the center of the floor. The men slowed and showed him what to do. Pump his arms in the opposite direction of his hips while stepping with his heels and waving his feet back and forth between the beats of the music. Left, right, left, left, right with his legs. Only his arms were supposed to move in a completely different pattern. Like morning calisthenics, Ben was forced to access the left and right hemispheres of his brain. Unfortunately, both refused to acknowledge the request. Still sore from training he couldn't kick as high or move with the grace and fluidity of the warriors.

"Begin at the beginning," Kavera said telepathically. He appeared on the balcony with Ben's friends. *"It takes time. There is no shame if you make a mistake. Just give in to the music."* Ben tried and found himself having fun despite his aching muscles and his clumsy rendition of the routine.

Carlos, Grace and Serise laughed before producing tablets on which they displayed numbers ranging from 2 to 5 out of a score of 10. They hooted and hollered and embarrassed him.

"Hey Ben, how can you play basketball with so little rhythm?" asked Grace.

"So much for stereotypes!" yelled Carlos.

There was no comment from Serise. She was doubled over with laughter.

Ben sneered and ignored them.

Two Osmaruvian chefs marched on to the floor pushing a table filled with sparklers, a large cake and an enormous silver tub of chocolate ice cream.

Ben caught himself. "What is this?"

"Happy day of your birth, Benjamin!" Everyone cheered, still dancing.

Stunned, Ben was speechless. His friends clapped from the balcony and yelled, "Flash mob!"

"I knew you missed the creature comforts of home, young long suffering warrior," Kavera said. "We just needed to wait for a break in our schedule. I realized that today held a special meaning. A perfect reason to break nutritional protocol. I hope you don't mind gelato. I prefer it to ice cream."

"The chefs didn't bake the cake did they?" Ben asked, eyeing it suspiciously but almost not caring.

Kavera laughed. "We are not cruel. The cake and gelato were imported from Italy for the occasion."

The music stopped abruptly as Ben's uncle and Aurelia entered the room and eyed the teams warily. Ben wondered if they'd had ever heard of the word "fun." April ducked behind Zadra. Carlos, Serise and Grace hid behind a column.

Hands on his hips, Uncle Henry stepped up and down the line inspecting the team, his boots clicking on the floor as his cloak flapped behind him. Each person looked straight ahead, their faces a blank slate while Kavera stood to the side and winced.

"Benjamin? Do you have any clue what you were doing out there?"

Ben frowned and said, "No, sir."

His uncle ran one finger over the top of the gelato, tasted it, then snapped his fingers. The music returned.

"Aurelia's team has never heard contemporary American music. I think they have taken a liking to it."

His expression still stoic, he extended his hand toward Aurelia, who was staring at the cake and its mounds of icing with disapproval. Ben could swear he saw an electric arc pass between them and braced for another combat demonstration. Instead, Aurelia's eyes closed. She placed one hand in his, the other on his shoulder. Her face was a mask of concentration. Without warning they erupted into the oddest kata Ben had ever seen. Their speed surpassed anything Ben had witnessed from the team. Their legs whipped in and out as they traveled across the floor at light speed. He swiveled suddenly and pushed forward with his right leg causing her to fly into the air before landing and spinning in to start again. The warriors seemed delighted and took a step backward to give them more space. Kavera's eyes grew wide with shock.

The music changed and his uncle switched to a pattern that reminded Ben of a Salsa. Uncle Henry spun Aurelia so fast it even made Ben seasick. Carlos, Grace and Serise came out of hiding and clapped loudly.

Kurosh signaled for the troops to join in. It was the first time Ben had seen the team break ranks in his uncle's presence. Feet flew across the floor, sashes whipped with energy. Ben was unable to keep up.

Aurelia broke away. "A gift on this special day," she said touching his temple before squeezing his hand. His aches dulled as she transmitted the dance patterns. So this was how the team shared data so fast! Ben joined April and danced alongside the team, now able to keep up. Laughter rang out from the team.

Ben's uncle and Aurelia returned to the perimeter where they streamed the team's biometric data as if this were just another training exercise.

Carlos, Grace and Serise joined the flash mob but it didn't look voluntary. Kavera was prodding and herding them onto the floor.

"No shortcuts for you three," he laughed. "You will have to learn the old fashioned way." He took Serise's hand. Carlos chose Grace as his reluctant and skeptical partner.

Ben couldn't wait to return the teasing. But after a few missteps, Carlos moved through the routine, flawlessly positioning Grace at each step. Grace grimaced but managed to keep up.

"What?" said Ben. "How?"

Carlos grinned. "Mom and Dad liked to dance. They made me practice with them."

Kavera winked at Ben then raised his hand, transmitting a change in routine. The tempo reverted to African tribal movements. Carlos was hopelessly lost. He flailed about clumsily. Only Serise was able to keep up. Now it was Ben's turn to laugh.

"Thanks Kavera," Ben said.

Kavera smiled and gave him a thumbs up. "Happy Birthday, Ben."

After a half-hour of gorging on desert and more dancing, Ben and his friends were near exhaustion. Everyone else looked refreshed and rested. Serious to the bone, his uncle and Aurelia where still pouring over data streams on a bank of monitors.

"Wow! That . . . was incredible!" Ben said to his uncle in between pants. "You were . . . amazing. . . . I can't . . . believe . . .you can dance

. . . like that. And the team . . . I thought . . . you were going . . . to punish them . . . for . . . goofing off."

"Of course not," his uncle replied, his voice as dry as the Sahara. "They are quite disciplined. Life on Xenobia is not all business. It can be quite joyful. When the team is working, they are focused solely on their tasks as they should. They have made the ultimate sacrifice to join this mission. If we are unable to find a solution we will all most certainly die, why deprive them of any remaining pleasure?"

Uncle Henry knew how to strip the joy out of any situation.

"By the way," Ben paused to catch his breath. His heart was still beating in time with the frenetic African drum beats. "That first kata you did. The one where your legs were . . . whipping around like crazy. What . . . was that?"

"Not kata," said his uncle. "Tango. Aurelia has never seen it before. I thought I would surprise her. Xenobians love to dance."

Ben's jaw dropped.

"The teams will return to mission protocols tomorrow," his uncle continued. "Until then, enjoy your party." He dipped his finger into the gelato one more time before disappearing through the door.

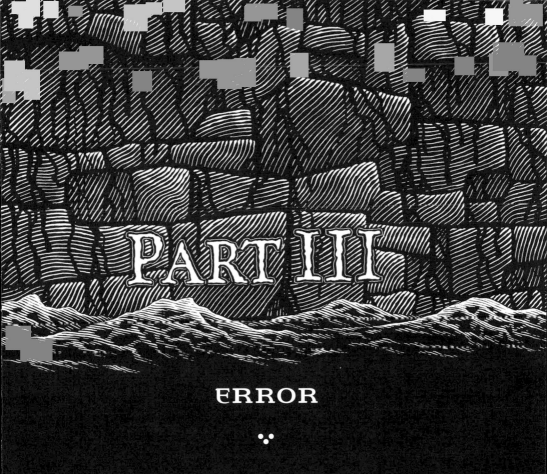

Part III

ERROR

⋅•⋅

In the end, only three things matter:
how much you loved,
how gently you lived,
and how gracefully you let go of things not meant for you.
—*Buddha*

CHAPTER FIFTY-ONE

Secrets and Lies

•᛫• The computer chimed as the ancient iMac booted up. Harbor technology probably lasted for years but it still surprised Ben whenever the computer turned on since they didn't have a way to recharge the power supply Serise borrowed.

The software he used to stop the Syrian fighting was gone, along with the software that connected them to Harbor systems remotely, replaced with homework assignments, maps of the Sonecian solar system, and training schedules. He slipped the Atlantis flash drive into a slot in the back. Like the day he hacked into the Lopez computer, a screen with Sonecian symbols popped up. Only one file was loaded on the drive. He clicked and held his breath in case it backfired like everything else. Instead it showed pods of whales along with their last known locations and migration patterns.

Boring, Ben thought. Until he remembered that the missing whale was seen in the Devil's Sea and Barakas had given him codes to go there.

And he'd found a dialer, hadn't he?

Like his uncle's research, the graphs above each pod showed frequencies of sound. He remembered the whale that charged him when he was stuck on a rock in Argentina. One that sounded a lot like the frequency his uncle had focused on while Ben was in his apartment. He searched for a migrating animal with the highest frequency. It only took minutes to find it. One whale in the entire world with a frequency of 47 hertz. The others were between 10 and 40 hertz.

Ben clicked on the photo. A blue whale almost 100 feet long. A graph showed it had been spotted by the US Navy's sonar equipment in 1989 at 52 hertz. But the Atlantis data showed it was now at 47 hertz. Its location? Near the Devil's Sea.

Serise told him she had to find a Child Born of Water. She thought it was Volari. But in the game a whale had given the girls a pearl. Could it be that simple? Find a real whale, get a pearl or a rod with DNA patterns like they got in Palenque?

Ben smiled. He had to find Serise quick. Another mission was forming in his head.

•••

"How's it going?" Ben asked as Serise broke away from her console.

"Temporary setback," she said. "I lost my authorization to access the mainframe, so I was stuck manually decoding messages as they came in. Their mainframe is bigger than a hundred Cray supercomputers, so making me do it by hand was a punishment to slow me down."

"Not working is it," Ben said as more of a fact than a question.

Serise grinned and shook her head. "You know me so well. Mansurat is a tough nut to crack, and forget about Grace's tribe or mine. They cannot be nudged. Not even Micique would give up his secrets. But you know what? The Mondavi guys came back from New Zealand with new war chants and tattoos. Tell them how hot they look, or get some the green beans in the galley to give the Solai extra helium and they all crack like an egg." She laughed, put her flash drive into her laptop and it spit out translations instantly. "Well, would you look at that? I'm as fast as a supercomputer at decoding when I use someone else's security codes!"

Ben cracked up, then swiveled his head as the Libyan doors opened. The endless tubes continued flashing, only this time the ones nearest the door were frosted.

"You're in here a lot. Any hints about what they're doing in there?"

Serise shook her head. "Everyone has representatives going in there now but no one, and I mean NO one, will say what's going on. But watch the tubes close to the doors. It's small, but focus on the pattern. It won't be long before someone else comes out."

Ben nodded. The doors opened and this time Ben saw what Serise was talking about. Every filled tube had a DNA helix rotating in front of it.

"That makes sense," Ben said. "Remember, he said he was looking for descendants that matched the DNA patterns in the Guardian jars."

"But why so many?" Serise asked. "They're full sometimes, and then empty the next day."

"Uncle Henry said no more ships were coming so it can't be more animals for an ark."

"Right," Serise said. "Most of the teams transport out from the Control Room so we can monitor their status." She pointed to the monitors overhead which streamed live shots of the teams in action, mostly doing boring archeology digs or scanning people as they walked down busy streets. "But now there's a Shakrarian group that goes out every day —usually mornings but not always. And always from inside that room. And get this, those trips didn't show up in any system I could access before my clearance got taken away."

Before Ben could tell her about his idea for a new mission, the door to the Libyan facility opened again. Two Shakrarian warriors walked out covered from head to toe in their white robes.

Ben gasped as the hood on the shorter of the two shifted just enough for him to catch the profile of the person beneath it.

Grace.

⁘

Ben slumped in his chair, put the Atlantis flash drive back into the computer and pulled up the whale files again. The revelation that Carlos was being trained in secret still made Ben feel like a cast-off. He tried to shrug off his feelings but he couldn't. Carlos had apologized and Ben forgave him. It wasn't his fault they made him promise. But now Grace was going on missions to Norway. And even when he pushed her, she wouldn't tell him anything else other than she meditated and slept a lot. There had to be more to it. She looked like she was going to burst from not telling him. Even Serise and April couldn't pry it out of her.

There were other things nagging him. There was no word about his parents. Not even a status update. He wasn't even sure anyone was really looking for them any more. And although Kavera had offered to train him, he'd been gone for two weeks with his sister's team, coming back just long enough to reload on supplies. And always through those Libyan doors. So while he waited for his turn at training, Ben was stuck in the equivalent of Harbor lock down.

He focused in on the Atlantis II location, writing down the longitude and latitude indicated in the window. As he was about to log out, he spotted the eight blips he'd seen when he was talking to Barakas. The same eight blips he'd seen on Serise's computer when they first arrived at the Harbor. And always in the same place. Everyone said they weren't real. Then why weren't they turned off?

Ben was going on one more mission. And he was going to do it alone.

CHAPTER FIFTY-TWO

The Beacon

•͙• Ben slipped off his futon, careful not to make a sound. It wasn't necessary. Carlos slept like a log and snored so loud it sounded like a room full of warriors was being tortured. A sonic boom could go off and he wouldn't wake up.

Tiptoeing into the living room he attempted to open the apartment door but, as expected, it was locked. It would be years before his uncle trusted him again. Kavera was forced to reveal Ben's side-trip to the Palenque ruins and despite their success it just made his uncle more agitated.

He was going to prove once and for all he was as good as his father had been. Or the other team members. He didn't have brute strength. He didn't have years of training. But he'd helped find two important clues and now he was going to find another one. One that might even help Serise get what she needed.

Ben pulled the last remaining fingerprint copy from his pocket. The only one Carlos made that the teams had not found when cleaning the apartment.

"Fungua!" he whispered in as close to his uncle's gruff voice as he could get.

The panel lit up with a stream of hieroglyphics, but the door did not open. Ben pressed the rubber against the glass panel for a fingerprint identification and held his breath.

"Fungua!" he said again, this time trying to imitate Kavera.

"Askar."

The door dissolved. Ben gasped and remembered to breathe, then slipped into the corridor. Dressed in a borrowed flight suit, he felt like a ninja as he looked to the left, than to the right before continuing with his plan. It would only take one slip up — one mistake — to put him back where he started—in lock-down until calisthenics. But if all went well, he'd be long gone before anyone noticed. His translator and badge were on the bed. No use giving his uncle a head start in tracking him.

Blissfully, the corridor was empty and he made his way to the first level of the storage room without being detected. Before he dialed, he retrieved a handful of purple capsules, a tracking device and a jakara-vite knife from the shelves. The knife wasn't his so it didn't extend to its full length in his grip. But it was still sharp and he needed protection. Just in case. He chewed a purple pill, blew a bubble and dialed.

⁘

Atlantis II was eerily quiet. Ben gave his eyes a moment to adjust in the low light. Fish swam over him but seemed to take no notice of his presence. Oddly enough Ben didn't need the capsule. An air pocket surrounded him as soon as he emerged from the transport beam.

He switched on the tracking device. It still showed eight strong life signs and a series of hieroglyphic notations. He muted the sound level just in case. He was entering the main diplomatic building uninvited and didn't know how Calamar would react. On the other hand, he'd overheard his uncle say that the main pyramids in both complexes were used primarily for meetings and visiting dignitaries. Theoretically, this section of Atlantis II should be deserted. Still, Ben wasn't taking any chances.

He paused. The hairs on his neck stood on end. He had the feeling of being watched. Again. This time it seeped into his pores and he couldn't shake it. He pushed his back up against and wall and worked to recover his nerve. This was stupid. His parent's wouldn't be here. His uncle had come to Atlantis II several times since they'd had gone missing. Calamar had skeleton screws stationed here. If his parents had transported here, someone would have seen them by now. And yet the tracking device didn't lie. There were eight signals in this location. When Ben adjusted the device to eliminate all teams that arrived within the last few months, only a handful remained. And these eight signals were the same ones he'd seen the day the Sonora arrived. It had to be them. If it wasn't, he'd know soon enough.

The tracking device didn't provide a layout of the complex. This hunt would have to be manual. Luckily, the air bubble was mobile. Where Ben went, so did a constant supply of air.

The Atlantean complex was a labyrinth of endless corridors branching off of each other. Everything looked the same. He wondered how the Atlanteans were able to navigate and how they were able to get to the upper levels, then realized Atlanteans didn't need stairs. But Ben wasn't a fish. Some rock climbing equipment would come in handy about now.

Whoosh.

Ben stopped dead in his tracks. Had he been followed? The last time he heard that sound Calamar had entered the building. He sucked in his breath, closed his eyes like Aurelia taught him and listened. He felt tiny impulses of electrical energy flow through the air barrier. He pushed on the sides of the bubble and concentrated.

Whoosh.

He wasn't alone.

Heart pounding, he steadied himself, slowed his breathing and focussed. He could sense the gentle vibration of the Atlantean power plant. He felt the changes in water current as schools of fish swam by. He concentrated and waited to sense something larger.

Minutes passed. No other sounds returned. No unusual or ominous sensations. And thankfully, none of the foul odors that greeted him when he first discovered the desert entrance to the Libyan facility. Still, he couldn't shake the feeling of dread.

Atlantis outposts were second only to the Harbor in security protocols. The disturbance was probably just a fish or small squid or some other aquatic being. Possibly a sentry. Wearing black helped him to blend into the dark surroundings, though he wished he had something to completely cover his face. When he opened his eyes again he noticed a light shining beyond the third level balcony. How to get up there?

Ben pondered the question, then remembered an earlier comment his uncle made about his abilities once he began dumping his mother's habitat mix in the backyard bushes at home:

"This explains your ability to perceive a physical thing and perceive it. . ."

He crouched, visualized the balcony, then jumped. As his feet left the surface, he waved his arms in a modified breast stroke, and found he could propel himself in the water. As he passed the second level, he used its balcony for leverage to propel himself upward. Seconds later, he was safely on the third level. Piece of cake!

Ben!

Startled, he took a visual sweep of the chamber. Schools of fish spiraled around him then swam over the balcony and vanished. He prayed they weren't sentinels. Ahead, stone columns rose upward and out of sight. Unlike the Harbor—the carvings included no humans and no lettering. He touched the figures and tried to make sense of the story they told. None of this had been covered in the librarian's books.

Ben!

A woman's voice. It was so soft as to only be a whisper but something primal resonated deep inside him—like a connection at the cellular level drew him to it. The scent of lavender permeated the oxygen flooding his bubble. Yes! He was on the right track. He was close. He would show his uncle he could be just as valuable to the team as the other members.

To the right, beyond an archway, a light glowed softly in alternating hues. Like the tubes in the Libyan facility.

Stasis tubes?

Fleeting movement—a shadow—crossed the doorway and vanished. He crouched, narrowed his eyes and waited. No other movement detected. Optical illusion? Light did play tricks on the eye under water.

Convinced he was on the right track he pushed off, launched towards the entry and found himself inside an empty room filled with more aquatic hieroglyphic carvings.

Whoosh!

Ben froze as he sensed movement behind him.

"It's about time!"

CHAPTER FIFTY-THREE

The Envoy

•᛫᛫ Barakas chuckled, the sound muffled by the water barrier between them. The octopus glided twice around Ben before landing.

"I can understand you," said Ben. "How is that possible without a translator?"

Barakas sighed. "Let's not waste time on idle discussion of our technology, shall we? Did you find your uncle's whale?"

Ben shook his head. "No. I didn't"

"Pity," said Barakas. "I was almost hoping you had. Elusive fellow, that one is. I guess, as land bipedals say, your trip was a bust."

"No!" Ben said, brightly. "I found some other signals—the team locator beacons."

"Ahh. I see. So your mission is not a total loss." He glided to within inches of Ben's face. "And where is your back-up? Xenobian teams are forbidden to travel without a triad."

Something about the octopus' tone and demeanor seemed odd. Ben felt for the security of the knife tucked safely inside his shirt. "They're on their way. I assumed it was okay to get here first. Kind of scout things out in advance," he bluffed. "I thought you worked at Atlantis I."

"I do," said Barakas. "But I had business to attend to here. And as you've noticed, transport makes traveling between portals instantaneous. I'll be back before I'm missed."

"Then I apologize for disturbing you. I should have waited for permission."

"None is needed. That is why I gave you the codes. The Sonecian teams have clearance for both facilities and they've never abused that privilege. Although Calamar still harbors a slight grudge against a particular Casmirian tribesman. But that doesn't diminish his respect for your tribe or the mission in general." He gestured towards a corridor that lead off to the left. "You say you are tracking those elusive locator beacons? Perhaps I can help you find what you seek."

Barakas lead Ben down a series of corridors until they arrived at a chamber on the outer edge of the facility. "Is this what you are looking for?"

Ben's heart leaped, but he entered the room cautiously. Eight pulsating stasis tubes.

Eight.

Whatever was trapped inside was the size and shape of a human. But the tubes were frosted blocking any view of who or what might be trapped inside. His mind raced through all the possible outcomes. His uncle had visited the complex several times in the last month and Calamar didn't make him aware of the parents. The signals had been in this location since his parents had disappeared. On the other hand, what safer place to go than Atlantis II? Sunnyslope was off the Pacific Ocean. If his parents were trapped in the garage and with limited power in their crystals for transport, this location was closer than the Harbor in an emergency. Perhaps they'd transported to a different location—close—and were moved here. He couldn't be sure this location was exactly the same as the ones he'd found when he reached the Harbor, or on Barakas' flash drive. It could also be a trap.

"Young warrior? Is this what you seek?" Barakas asked, his tentacles tapping impatiently.

Just outside a window a vent glowed and bubbled angrily. Heat seeped inside his air pocket making it hard to breathe. The temperature here was hotter than Atlantis I. He flipped on the tracking device. It pinged a confirmation at one second intervals.

"Yes." He touched the first glass container but found no controls to deactivate them. "Thank you."

"Well then. It appears your mission is successful. I'm surprised, though, that Kurosh let you out of his sight."

"He trusts me." Ben tried scanning the tubes again. It couldn't penetrate the glass to confirm the identities of the people inside. Something was wrong.

"You are lying, young Xenobian warrior in training. Kurosh trusts no one. These are dangerous times."

Ben steeled himself and tried to think and respond like his uncle. Always cold and serious during negotiations. "And yet we are both here alone."

Barakas paced back and forth in the water. "Like you, I am waiting for my own back-up." The octopus gave him an appraising glance as the room filled with the most foul creatures Ben had ever seen.

CHAPTER FIFTY-FOUR

Surrounded

•.• Translucent like jellyfish, the creatures were hard to see when they weren't moving, impossible to see when they were. Ben backed-up but found himself surrounded on all sides by new creatures: grey and decaying. All bone and sinew. He'd seen something like this before—the day the Sonara was destroyed. The day his uncle pitched a black stone into the transport beam. Trapped, Ben took stock of his situation. One knife he had yet to master—a stolen one at that—against hundreds of beings. All looking like they were once . . .

. . . human.

So he waited. According to their tribal beliefs, Xenobians never attacked first.

Barakas swam in and out of gaps between the stasis tubes, tapping a tentacle against the glass.

"What do you want?" asked Ben when he couldn't take the silence any longer.

"Hmm. That's not so easily answered. What I want is not something you are in a position to grant."

The water suddenly rushed out of the room, and Ben's air bubble collapsed. An overpowering odor of death and decay filled his nostrils. He nearly choked from the sudden onslaught and struggled to keep his hands and his voice from shaking.

"My team will be here any minute."

"Don't bother with this ridiculous charade," said Barakas. "No one is coming. I could smell your fear and your lie, even when you were in your protective cocoon. I'm here to offer you a trade."

"A trade for what?"

Barakas uttered an unintelligible sound and the glass frosting of each stasis tube dissolved. Resting inside, all eight parents stood in suspended animation. Ben rushed to the closest tube and collapsed on the floor in relief. They were alive!

He gasped for air, tasting the essence of rotten meat settle on his tongue. "What do you want?"

"I propose a trade. The security codes to your Egyptian facility."

"The Harbor?"

"I believe that even with my crude translation I was perfectly clear. They've been changed since the last breach. Give me what I want, and you shall have what it is you have been seeking. Give me what I want and I'll spare the life of these poor deluded souls and give them back to you."

Ben slumped to the floor in defeat. Placing his temple against the stasis tube containing his mother, he tried to feel her soul through the thick layer of glass. He reached out with the other hand and touched the tube containing his father. Nothing —no impulse, no sensation. He'd found a chance to save them but at what cost? His heart ached, but he couldn't betray the Xenobian team to save his parents. "I can't give you the codes."

"Free will, Benjamin. You can do anything you set your mind to do."

"I can't." Ben tried to sound strong but he choked on the words even as his mind worked through options. He had a jakaravite knife. It could cut through anything even in its small size. But would breaking the glass cause his parents to come out of cryogenic freeze too fast. Would that result in their death? "I won't sacrifice hundreds of people to save eight."

"They're going to die anyway, one way or another. Why prolong the inevitable? The planet is breaking up, all life topside will be destroyed. We have agreements with the revered one to maintain all life below the surface."

Ben was confused. "We?"

"The Atlantean Council. Calamar brokered the deal."

Ben spun around. "You're lying! He's an ally."

"Allegiances are meant to be broken, young warrior," Barakas purred. "Given the right incentives." He aimed a laser at the last tube— the one containing Serise's mother.

"NO!" Ben stood abruptly, whipped the knife from its hidden sheath and sliced through one of Barakas's tentacles.

The creatures advanced on Ben. Barakas uttered a sound and they retreated.

"Someone wasn't paying attention in class," said Barakas, quickly growing a replacement. "You're trying my patience and I need to get back to my delegation. Perhaps you need a better incentive" He swiveled and aimed his laser above Ben's head—at the tube containing Ben's mother. Outside, a vent bubbled furiously. The temperature rose to uncomfortable levels. "Shall we try this again?"

Ben's heart stopped and all the memories came crashing back. Soon the overpowering stench of the room was replaced with the scent of jasmine and lavender. He felt as if the weight of the world was crushing him. Save his mother? He couldn't allow Barakas to hurt her. But if he saved her, what would happen to the Harbor? To his friends. To April?

"I'm counting on you to take care of your sister. Keep her safe. You can't help us here. I need to know you are both safe . . ." his mother had told him when she sent them into hiding.

"I can't do it," spat Ben, his heart breaking. He rose to his feet and searched the chamber for an alternative. "I won't do it."

"No," sighed Barakas. "I didn't suppose you would. Pity. But as with everything I have a contingency plan. I've made a little trade of my own."

The tubes began to dissolve. Ben leapt at the first, hoping to transport with them and fell to the floor. *Not solid. Holographic?*

"Where'd you send them?" he demanded. "Where'd they go? Take me instead. I dare you, you coward!"

"Ahhh. So it's truth or dare is it? Interesting top-side, bipedal game. Tell you what. I'll accept your dare and as a bonus, I'll tell you the truth. He tossed eight beacon markers on the floor at Ben's feet. Ben scanned them with the tracker. They were the same beacons he'd followed to Atlantis II.

"What's this?" he asked, dreading the answer.

"The truth," said Barakas. "Don't know where your parents are. Don't think I haven't tried to locate them. No matter. This is better. These decoys were quite effective don't you think?" He placed his tentacled arms around Ben tightly. "And I accept your dare. In trade for these useless markers, I'll take you instead."

"What? Why?"

"Let's just say you've been sold to a collector of rare treasures and these are your escorts."

"Sold me? For what?"

"Power," said Barakas. "Isn't that what it's always about?" He tightened his grip until Ben could barely breathe. "Don't worry. You'll just lose consciousness temporarily. Trust me, I've been where you are going and it's better not to be awake on the journey. Just in case."

Ben's stomach lurched. "In case of what?"

Barakas sighed. "In case you die on the way. We've taken precautions. The bounty is for dead or alive but believe me, the payout is enormous if you are delivered alive."

Ben surveyed the room. He was outnumbered. He felt himself getting light-headed. With no other option he would go out fighting. If he was going to die he'd take a few souls with him. Then it hit him. Did these creatures have souls? If they did, would he lose his own for taking the life?

Barakas's hot breath scorched his neck and something else—stronger now—mixed with his foul scent. lavender. He swiveled.

"Mom?"

Barakas tossed a cannister on the floor. A purple mist sprayed from the nozzle.

"Told you, boy. Decoys can be so effective." His laughter echoed throughout the chamber.

Ben let the scent take him back to a happier time and felt his mother's essence course through his body. Summoning every ounce of strength, Ben pushed outward then contracted his muscles and relaxed. He dropped to the floor before Barakas could react, sprang to his feet and attacked, landing a blow to Barakas's head. As he did, the creatures launched an attack of their own. He closed his eyes and tried to emulated Kavera and Aurelia in using his senses to detect movement.

There were too many creatures to track. Instead of distinct sounds and vibrations in the energy field, all he got was a jumble of confused signals, as if they possessed no energy at all. He swung wildly and was knocked to the floor and pinned again.

The creatures' stench was overpowering. Ben tried breathing through his mouth, tried channeling his mother's scent again, but his panting blocked any coherent sensory data. He needed to defend himself the old fashioned way. Time to street fight. He opened his eyes, swung in rapidly reversing arcs and managed to cut off another tentacle. As before, a new one grew in its place.

Barakas chuckled. "Strategic advantage. Trust me, boy. Join our alliance and know what real power can mean."

"Never," said Ben gagging in the stifling heat. "If I'm going to die, I'll take you out with me." He swung again, rolled out of the way and sprang to his feet. As fast as Ben cut off the octopus's arms, they grew back again.

Barakas seemed bored and did not defend himself. "Enough of this foolishness. Restrain him."

Foul slimy limbs grasped at Ben. He struggled, twisted and turned and managed to take large chunks out of several as he fought them off. But there were too many. The harder he fought, the more that materialized. The heat increased to intolerable levels as the vent outside the window began spewing lava. But Ben kept swinging and soon began trying to duck like Aurelia and Kavera had taught Carlos to do, all the while looking for a source of escape. There was no hope. He was exhausted and felt his energy draining.

Game over.

CHAPTER FIFTY-FIVE

The Triad

❖ A roar the strength of a sonic boom rocked the room. Barakas screamed out in pain as two of his tentacles disintegrated in a spark of blue flame. Ben froze in terror as two enormous prehistoric creatures launched into the room, their iridescent and heavily armored bodies gleaming even in the low light. Towering almost seven feet high, they moved so quickly they appeared to be blurs of black smoke. Ben was only able to track their movements by the bodies being ripped apart and their terrifying snarls.

"Aris! Bastet! Clear a path to Ben!" Kavera shouted, appearing out of nowhere and aiming Orin's experimental weapon at the octopus.

Released from the Baraka's grip, Ben dropped to the floor and rolled as the arms of the octopus continued to dissolve. He tried to process what he'd heard. The enormous monsters wiping out half the room were Aris and Bastet?

Kavera moved with stunning speed and unleashed a rapid fire barrage, reloading with glass cartridges strapped around his chest.

Barakas didn't have time to regenerate between shots. "What trickery is this!" he asked writhing in agony on the floor.

"Holy water," said Kavera letting loose another salvo. "Pretty potent, don't you think?"

"You lie. I'm not affected by top-side religious iconicity."

"Not human holy water," growled Kavera. He rolled to avoid a blow from a nearby creature and took a shot of his own. "Ours."

"I thought Xenobians didn't kill."

"You're not dead," Kavera said, through clenched teeth. He continued firing his weapon while tossing something to Ben. A transport badge.

Phone home! Now!

Ben tapped the badge.

"It's not working," he said, tapping it over and over again, hoping for a signal that would get them both home. He ducked and rolled backwards as more creatures came after him, landing with his back against a wall. Barakas struggled to right himself, but with no remaining tentacles the effort was futile. Kavera aimed his weapon at the octopus's head. Barakas collapsed in a heap and fell silent.

"Is he dead?"

"No," said Kavera in disgust, running to Ben while he continued to dispatch everything that came near him. *"Coward just fainted. I cauterized his wounds so his tentacles can't grow back."*

"I can't let you kill because of me," transmitted Ben. He covered Kavera's flank and took out two chubby demons that reminded him of the flying monkeys in the Wizard of Oz.

"You can't kill what is already dead."

Kavera let loose a stream of blue mist which vaporized the demons surrounding Ben, creating a path to escape.

The suddenly room fell silent. Aris and Bastet stood at the entrance, their long sharp teeth extending past their muzzles but their glowing eyes trained on Baraka's limp body. Ben couldn't stop staring at them. "How many different forms can Aris and Bastet take?"

"This is their true form," Kavera said, trying to activate the remote transport. He hissed. "Signal's jammed. Need to get to a transport pad and hope Barakas didn't deactivate them."

As they ran toward the entrance, a new round of demons appeared, this time more than ever.

"Ugh oh," Kavera said. He shot Ben a sideways glance and then a sly grin. Suddenly drumbeats filled Ben's head. He understood immediately. Drop and roll. Swing. Turn. Flip. Within seconds Ben and Kavera were fighting side by side performing a synchronized training exercise.

Swing! Don't use the same move twice in a row. Keep them guessing.

Ben lowered his body to avoid a blow then swung to kick the demon behind him.

"Time for a crash course on self defense!" Kavera grabbed Ben's hand and squeezed.

Techniques and strategies slammed into Ben's prefrontal cortex. He fought to recover from the brain freeze. Everything Kavera had ever learned about self-defense transferred in a matter of seconds.

"Rock and roll!" Kavera said.

Ben began using the demon's momentum against them. They advanced and Ben swerved to the left. As the creatures collided, Ben slashed off a limb here, a tentacle there, careful to avoid major arteries and organs. Cripple but don't kill.

"You can't kill what is already dead."

But he couldn't be sure. When in doubt . . .

"Namaste?"

"Always," transmitted Kavera.

Ben was covered in a slime. He tried to put that out of his mind.

Not human.

Not human.

Not alive.

Aris and Bastet cleared the perimeter. The sound of their ferocity was deafening as hundreds of bodies fell to the ground in motionless heaps and dissolved.

Score one for the Xenobians. They had won against insurmountable odds.

Ben's elation didn't last long. Within minutes, they were surrounded by a new set of creatures which regenerated as soon as he and Kavera took them out.

"*Remember, what we teach in training, Ben. Yield. Use momentum against the enemy!*"

Even with his new knowledge, Ben's muscles weren't developed enough to keep up with Kavera's superhuman speed. Kavera continued firing until the mist was depleted, then dropped his empty weapon and pulled multiple knives from their sheaths. All the while he continued coaching Ben.

"*Your training is a version of kata.*"

The knives spun in his hands as he twisted from side to side. He stayed within the boundaries of Xenobian tenets. He didn't attack first and he sent the creatures scurrying without limbs.

"*Keep your patterns fluid but unpredictable. Be a reed, not a redwood. Use muscle memory.*"

Kavera looked like he was dancing. There was a rhythm and pattern to his movements that was similar to morning training exercises but different at the same time.

He WAS dancing!

Everything within arms reach was down in an instant.

Despite his best efforts, Ben soon found his wrists pinned by multiple demons, his knife gripped useless in his hands.

Whoosh!

The demons dragged Ben towards a nearby window where a volcanic vent gurgled angrily, spitting out lava in streams of orange and red. The sulfurous odor overwhelmed him. He splayed his arms and legs and wedged them against the ledge, using every ounce of strength to keep from being pulled through.

Kavera rolled as multiple demons advanced, causing them to crash into each other. "*Hang on, Ben!*"

Blam!

A loud explosion rocked the room as creatures fell away. The Royal Guard burst into the room bearing long sabers and more of Orin's weapons fueled by blue diamonds.

"*Kavera!*" transmitted Aurelia. "*Are you hurt?*"

"*Never better, my sister!*" he said with a defiant grin. He was cut badly, but it didn't slow him down. "*Get our boy out of here!*"

Whoosh!

Volari, in dragon form, arrived with an army of giant squid and other Atlantean teams. Demons fell to the floor like dominoes but regenerated as fast as they were defeated.

Uncle Henry slashed his way to Ben's side and pulled him from the window. "*Boy, when we get back to the Harbor, you and I are . . . .*"

A black tentacle curled out of vent and wrapped around Ben's waist. Ben's uncle caught a blow to the chest before slicing the tentacle through. It writhed on the floor before dissolving. Ben touched his own chest. His uncle had cut the monster's tentacle but had not even nicked Ben's shirt in the process.

Whoosh!

An army of Aculeatus octopi tackled Ben and held him securely as his uncle returned to the fight. He struggled to break free but then he remembered, the Aculeatus were the good guys. He stopped struggling long enough to catch glimpses of the action through the phalanx of guards that now surrounded him. The warriors fought tirelessly, but even Ben could see that the Xenobian and Atlantean teams were outnumbered. He'd lead them into a trap.

Aris and Bastet cleared a path for Aurelia as she took hold of the wounded. In an instant the warriors were up and back in the fight.

"We need a transport now!" Uncle Henry growled as he immobilized his attackers two at a time. His massive muscles swelled as he took blows without wincing and returned the force ten-fold.

"Jemadari, signal is jammed!" yelled Berko.

"Zadra! Adjust the harmonic frequency!"

"No time for transport! Need manual extraction!" shouted Kavera, increasing the tempo of his kata and taunting the demons gleefully as he fought them. "I can hold them off!"

"We don't leave one of our own behind," yelled Aurelia. "Aris! Bastet! Akoosh!" The cats surrounded and protected Aurelia as she pulled orbs from her belt, warmed them in her hands, then pitched them into the volcanic vents. Explosions rocked the room and the light extinguished as the vents sealed.

In the darkness, Ben heard a jumbled chorus of voices flooding his senses. Despite the battle, Kavera transmitted English translations so Ben could understand what was happening. Orders to form a phalanx against the onslaught. Battle mode. Concentric circles with attacks in the upper, middle and lower quadrants. Armor up!

That was a problem. Kavera had arrived without armor, a breach in protocol. That meant he and Ben were unprotected.

"Where's that transport?" yelled Uncle Henry.

Whoosh!

More warriors arrived on the scene. Even in the dark, he recognized the accents Casmirians, Mondavi, Hayoolkáál, Solai, Shakrarian, and more. The room was filling with teams from the entire Sonecian contingent. Xenobian telepathic discussions revealed that Harbor teams could beam in, but outbound traffic was being blocked by some unknown source.

The team's uniforms began glowing, bringing much needed light into the room. Still, his uncle and the other guards were fighting so hard and so fiercely Ben could only see whirling blurs. He could hear sabers swishing in the air and wondered how so many warriors could be using them without hitting each other. Even with the vents sealed and no more demons arriving there were too many to defeat. Surrounded in a crush of the foulest creatures Ben had ever seen, Kavera was isolated and badly wounded. The team couldn't get to him. More importantly—Aurelia couldn't reach him even with Aris and Bastet quickly dispatching anything in the way. But Kavera kept fighting as if he had the strength of ten men.

"No!" Ben screamed, struggling to push past the circle of Aculeatus that surrounded him. He had to get to Kavera. "No!"

His uncle turned angrily to the Aculeatus and yelled, "Get Ben out of here!"

"No!" Ben summoned all his energy and broke free of his restraints.

In the corner, Barakas revived. "Get the boy, you idiots! Get the boy!"

The demons turned from Kavera and focussed their attention on Ben.

"Kill the others, but take him alive," continued Barakas. "And that Kurosh trash if you can. But I'll settle for the body if—"

Volari rocketed across the room and crushed what remained of Barakas in his muzzle.

Kavera dove through the air, and landed in front of Ben. Kavera took repeated blows as he shielded him.

Something took hold of Ben with a vice-like grip as a monster pierced Kavera through the chest. A fierce look of defiance on his face, Kavera turned and cut the head from his attacker before collapsing to the floor.

"Man down! Man down!" yelled Uncle Henry.

"Get him . . . out . . . of here! You know . . . what's . . . at stake!" Kavera gasped, his voice weak and labored. "Protect him . . . at all . . . . costs."

Kavera's body glowed bathing the room in a bright light.

"NO!"

Aurelia rushed across the room, suddenly glowing in the same hue as her brother. Volari swooped in, picked her up mid stride and flew her to her brother's side while Aris and Bastet suddenly disappeared, then reappeared in front of Kavera, forming an impenetrable armored wall.

"Man down! Repeat! Man down!" yelled Henry as he and the Royal Guard formed a second barrier around the cats.

"Jemadari, transport connection re-established," yelled Zadra.

"Harbor Control! Emergency transport to Medlab now! Repeat. Emergency transport NOW!"

As Ben was whisked out of the room he saw Aurelia collapse on Kavera's body as they both disappeared into a transport beam.

And then everything went black.

CHAPTER FIFTY-SIX

Paradox

Atlantis III
Location classified

•̇•̇ Ben woke with a start. Nearby, a small fire bathed his face in warmth, but he shivered violently, then choked and coughed up water. He steadied himself against the icy floors until his lungs were clear. Except for the fire and a phosphorescent pattern of binary code on one wall, the room was pitch black and freezing.

"Hello?"

"Hello? Hello? Hello? Hello?"

He coughed again. More water spewed from his throat. Despite the air bubble surrounding him, he felt as though he were drowning. His clothes were damp. His lungs burned. Had he been in water? For how long? He raised his hands and warmed them on the fire. But his back was cold. He curled into a ball and tried to conserve his body heat.

"Hello?"

"Hello? Hello? Hello? Hello?"

"Is anyone out there?"

"Out there? out there? out there? out there? out there?"

"Where am I?"

"Where am I? "am I? am I? am I? am I?"

"Kavera?"

This time no sound returned. Or maybe he just blocked it out. Short images flashed through his mind. Barakas. Those creatures.

Creatures?

Barakas had said he'd made a trade. For Ben. That was before the triad stormed in.

Was this the trade?

Where was he now?

Footsteps echoed in the chamber. Ben couldn't see beyond a few feet. His head was killing him.

"Kavera?"

The echo did not return as a voice, only more footsteps in the distance growing closer.

"Uncle Henry? Aurelia?"

Ben drew himself up from the floor and braced to protect himself. But his strength was gone. The air warmed around him. His clothes began to dry and the humidity dropped. But ice still formed at the core of his body and he felt numb. If this was the end, then so be it. He closed his eyes and waited for death to claim him.

"Sorry about the water," said a familiar voice. "I needed to get you out of there quickly. A transport beam would have been detected and therefore traceable. I used temporary stasis to get you here, but unfortunately, although we can travel through water, it's a hard route for humans —especially at light speed."

Ben opened his eyes and saw a puddle of shimmering cloth at his feet. He slumped back on to the floor and felt dizzy.

"We?"

Calamar nodded to his right where an enormous blue whale floated in the shadows.

"Thank you, my friend," he said.

The whale emitted a low base tone before swimming away. Ben had heard his song before, both in Uncle Henry's apartment, and when he was in Argentina.

"That's the whale my uncle was looking for?"

"Indeed it is," said Calamar.

"You've known the whole time where he was?"

"I have," said Calamar. "But as a sentient being, he has elected to stay hidden from the Harbor teams for the time being. Perhaps when the time is right. I was able to get you out of the Devils Sea facility but needed his assistance to get you the rest of the way. He was kind enough to oblige."

Ben coughed more water out of his lungs and looked around again. The temperature was too cold to be Atlantis I. "Which outpost is this?"

"Classified location," said Calamar as he knelt beside him. "How are you feeling?"

Ben groaned. "Sick to my stomach. Where is everyone?"

"Securing the Devil's Sea facility." Calamar hesitated. "Do you remember what happened?"

Ben nodded, but the memory was too painful to discuss. He'd messed up this time. Badly.

"Why were you there?" Calamar pressed.

Ben choked again - this time not on water, but on the grief. He'd been a fool and it almost cost him his life. "I thought my parents were there. I was trying to rescue them."

Calamar sighed. "I don't understand. Why would they be there?"

"I found eight beacons," said Ben. "I couldn't get anyone to investigate. Now I know why."

"And why is that?" asked Calamar, his voice suddenly devoid of emotion.

Ben hesitated. "Don't you know?"

"This isn't a question of what I know. I'm not on trial here."

"They were decoys."

"Yes," said Calamar. "They were."

His heart went cold. "You planted them?"

"I did not."

"You're lying," spat Ben. "Barakas told me everything."

"Did he?" asked Calamar.

Ben knew the question was rhetorical. "The whole thing was a trap. You sold me out in exchange for power."

"Is that your final assessment?" asked Calamar, a hard edge creeping into his tone.

Ben shivered. "I don't want to play mind games. I need to go home. My uncle will be looking for me."

"No one is looking for you," said Calamar. "I suspect Kurosh would be content if you remained hidden here until the end of the mission. I know of many who'd be content if you simply disappeared."

Ben massaged his throbbing temples. "I need to go. My uncle said something is tracking the teams. I need to go back to the Harbor."

"Pity you didn't think about that before you breached the security measures Kurosh put in place for you." Calamar paced back and forth, his tentacles wrapping into knots then untying again in agitation. "Not to worry. Whatever might be looking for you can't penetrate these shields. Or the cold."

"How'd you find me?" said Ben. "I left my translator on the bed."

"Kavera asked Danine to inject you with a subdermal tracker after you returned from Palenque. For insurance."

"He told you that?"

"Yes. When he called for emergency transport to Atlantis II. We change our access codes hourly."

That bit of news caught Ben off guard. He'd used codes to dial there. The codes were weeks old. Then why did they still work?

"Where's Kavera? I need to explain. Did he make it back to the Harbor?"

Calamar remained silent.

"He got back, right?"

Again, Calamar didn't answer, but his eyes burned with hatred.

Ben froze. "No! He's not—."

"His body was transported back to the Harbor. There was nothing that could be done."

Ben collapsed and vomited. Thousands of small fish emerged, each encapsulated in their own pocket of water, cleaning the area and leaving the floor spotless in an instant. Wracked with grief, Ben began sobbing uncontrollably. The tears froze as they hit the floor and shattered into millions of glittery pieces—like stars in an endless ocean of space.

Please don't let it be true.

He rocked back and forth, unable to find the right words, unsure of who or what he was asking, but he kept asking, hoping for a miracle. A sign that Calamar was wrong. He opened his eyes to find himself in no better position and felt his hope draining. But he continued his silent quest—hoping to reach some open channel in the heavens—some sympathetic spirit who could turn back the clock and let him start over.

"A little late for that, don't you think?" asked Calamar, his words slow and accusing.

Ben continued to rock and focus with every fiber of his being, using Aurelia's technique to connect with another Xenobian soul, trying to connect with Kavera. But no one was in range. He was alone. In minutes, his sorrow turned to anger, then anger turned into rage. He forced himself to his feet and stared up into Calamar's eyes. Instinctively he grabbed for his knife. The sheath was empty.

"Is this what you seek?" Calamar held up the knife for Ben to see, then tossed it across the room. "Surely you had no intention of using that pitiful device against me?"

"You killed him!" said Ben, beating his fists against Calamar's robes. "You set me up! You killed him!" He collapsed again, realizing the futility. No weapon, and Calamar could morph back to his original size in a nanosecond. "Why?"

"Me?" said Calamar, unfazed by the blows. "It was not I who went off on an unauthorized mission to chase beacons everyone else knew to be a decoy. This is not the first time you put yourself and your team at risk, is it not? Were you not locked into your apartment for your own safety?"

Ben spat at him. "You're a traitor!"

Calamar sighed. "To whom? To you? It was not I who was attempting to make a bargain with an agent of, shall we say, the devil. I believe the Council referred to you as a liability. It appears you are bound and determined to prove their point."

"Barakas said you sold me out for power. Why would he lie?"

"Why indeed," said Calamar.

Ben was exhausted. Calamar was as frustrating as his own uncle. But he had one more question to ask. "Are my parents—"

"Dead?" said Calamar. "I don't have an answer for that question. But I am curious as to what you felt you would accomplish on your own."

"I thought I could save them."

"Instead, you put yourself and your uncle's entire mission at risk. For the equivalent of eight magic beans as the fairy tale goes. Would your parents have made the same tradeoff?"

"To find me? Yes."

"But your parents were highly trained. And even they could not withstand the attack on your outpost. What did you hope to accomplish at your skill level?"

"My father said to be prepared to make a choice. I made a choice."

"One that had consequences for us all," said Calamar. "Your friend is gone. Do you ever think about the consequences before you act?"

Ben faced away. There was nothing left to feel. Kavera was dead. His friend . . .

. . . was dead.

"No. I don't suppose you do," said Calamar. "You are impetuous. Rash. Immature. And the results seem to leave death in its wake. The Sonara, for example—"

Ben wheeled around. "I didn't cause the explosion! I didn't cause it!"

"Is that what Kurosh told you?" Calamar's voice was laced with disgust. "Xenobians. So good with semantics. One of your most endearing qualities. You never lie, but you'll get as close as possible without crossing the line." He pushed his face into Ben's for emphasis. "No, Ben. You didn't push the button, that much is true. You ARE, however, the proximate cause of the explosion. As a result, the Council ordered Kurosh put you in stasis for your own good."

Ben stared.

"That's right. I sit on the Council." Calamar circled Ben in a slow arc. "Your uncle has gone soft where you are concerned. He refused our request, a decision I'm sure he'll live to regret."

"He lied? Those stones were explosives?"

Calamar blew air into the room, causing the water around the perimeter to ripple violently. "The problem with you, Ben, is that you continue to think in such finite terms. No. Not explosives. The captain activated a self-destruct voluntarily. I suspect it was the only way to contain the damage and eradicate any remaining contamination. It would not have been done without the unanimous consent of those on board. They sacrificed themselves for a greater good. Something you have yet to do I'm afraid."

"But I wasn't on the ship. I wasn't responsible for what happened!" said Ben.

"I HAD FAMILY ON THAT SHIP!" Calamar's angry response nearly shattered Ben's eardrums.

"I'm sorry," whispered Ben. "I didn't know."

"Didn't know? You intentionally sent the stones to the ship, did you not?"

Ben's answer came out in a miserable whisper. "Yes."

"Without showing them to your uncle."

"Yes." Ben could barely contain his grief. "If it wasn't a bomb, what was it? What was in those stones?"

"Something you couldn't possibly fathom. The purest essence of evil in the known universe - or its surrogate. Worse than the creatures working with Barakas."

"NO!" shouted Ben. "NO! You're lying. Barakas said you sold us out!"

"And yet, if he is a liar, then the lie you accuse me of telling must, in fact, be the truth, n'est pas?"

Ben clutched his head. He didn't know what to think. This was worse than the puzzles he'd tried to solve back at Sunnyslope – a grade school paradox.

> *Barakas claims Calamar is a liar. Calamar refuses to answer, but implies Barakas is a liar. If Barakas is a liar and says Calamar is a liar, then is Calamar, in fact, a truthteller?*
>
> *But if Barakas is a liar and Calamar is also a liar, then Barakas would have said the Calamar was a truthteller. So Barakas must be the liar.*
>
> *But if Calamar IS a liar, is Barakas the truthteller?*
>
> *What question should you ask to determine the truth?*

Ben's head hurt as he wavered back and forth. Barakas wanted to kill him, but clearly Calamar wasn't entirely honest. And if he were lying then Kavera's death was also a lie. Ben felt a glimmer of hope. That was it. Ben wouldn't listen to any more of Calamar's lies. He'd search for a way to get out. But how could he get out when he didn't know where he was? Why did his uncle let Calamar take him?

"No one is looking for you . . . "

"All this is about power?" asked Ben, his voice barely a whisper.

Calamar paced the floor. "You don't know what real power is. Everything is a game to you. Dismissive of teams possessing knowledge that is centuries old. Power, young man, is learning to control what can be controlled and leaving others to do that which is in their purview." He strolled across the room and sat on an enormous throne that materialized in the center of the floor. The jewels adorning his clothing glowed in alternating patterns. "Power, is knowing when to act and when not to. Power, is not something meant to be in the toolbox of the weak." Calamar paused as a panel on his chair lit up.

. . . I know of many who'd be content if you simply disappeared."

"Is that why I'm here?" Ben asked. "So you can kill me?"

Calamar sighed. "Sonecians don't kill children. Not even the impetuous ones. Some lines even I don't cross."

"You're . . . you're Sonecian?"

"Does that surprise you? Our species were visiting Earth long before the others arrived to colonize." Calamar stared at a pattern on the far wall. It had changed since Ben first arrived. "No matter. I don't expect you to understand. Time's up. The Harbor will be expecting your arrival. I did promise to get you there once the danger had safely passed."

"You never explained what was after me."

"Indeed," said Calamar as the light on his console extinguished. "Given the circumstances, I believe that continues to be a prudent course of action. You might try trusting that some of us are a bit older and wiser on these issues." He reached across the room, grasped the knife, and tossed it back to Ben. "Next time I suggest leaving this at the Harbor — in the hands of someone who knows how to use it."

As a transport beam and took hold of Ben, Calamar turned towards him one last time and converted to his full height. He towered above Ben, his face hidden in the murky water five stories above. But his booming voice resonated throughout the chamber.

"By the way, young warrior. Just to be clear. I have plenty of power. I don't need any more. But if I did, I wouldn't need you to get it."

CHAPTER FIFTY-SEVEN

Alone

•.• Like his previous refuge, Ben's apartment was eerily silent. He'd been gone for hours. Were the others at calisthenics? Or breakfast? A warm plate of food and glass of water waited for him on the table.

He couldn't bear to eat. His stomach contracted into tight knots and all he could think to do was sleep and hope that, when he woke, he'd find this was just a bad dream. He trudged into the bedroom. Carlos's bed was empty, all the linens removed. Ben groaned and closed his eyes. Laundry day. He had to remember to get up later and change his sheets before he got a lecture from Danine on the dangers of bacteria and dust mites.

His head throbbed violently. He closed his eyes and tried to will the pain away. Kavera wasn't dead. He couldn't be. It was a mistake. A simple mistake. He'd fix it in the morning when he woke up. Calamar had tried to trick his uncle on the first trip to Atlantis. Why trust him now?

"Why indeed?"

Calamar's voice crashed into his brain.

"I HAD FAMILY ON THAT SHIP!"

Ben covered his head with a pillow, trying to shut out the memories.

Streaming images of the Sonara exploding. A holographic annihilation playing out over and over again above his uncle's head in three dimensional clarity. His mind raced forward. He could still feel the fake stasis tubes dissolving beneath his touch. The grip of Baraka's tentacles tightening around his throat.

Kavera.

He gasped as he remembered the essence of Kavera's spirit rising even as Aurelia worked to bring him back. Golden. Shimmering. Kavera smiling back at him even as he lay dying.

"You don't get it do you?" His uncle had said the day he decided to stay on Earth instead of going back to their home planet. *"This is not some make-believe computer game. The stakes here are real. You cannot select 'new game' from a pull down menu if you get hurt or killed. There is no convenient 'undo' function to retrace your steps if you make an error. No 'escape' key to beam you back to reality."*

Ben had caused the explosion. He'd caused Kavera's death. And his parents were gone. What was left to to live for?

April.

Despite the temperature —a stable 70 degrees—Ben shook violently, unable to keep his body warm. April was better off without him.

The painful throbbing reached migraine proportions. He rolled off the bed and headed for the bathroom. On the way he stopped to shut the closet door. It made a hollow sound as it closed. Ben paused, then peeked inside. All of his clothes hung neatly in a row. But Carlos's clothes were gone. Startled, Ben searched Carlos's cabinet drawers.

Empty.

His heart sank as he rushed into the living room and burst into the girl's room without knocking. The beds were empty, the linens gone. He searched the closets and dressers.

Empty.

All traces of his friends were gone. No notes. No goodbyes. Nothing to indicate they'd ever shared the space with him. Immediately he went to the comm panel. It didn't light up by touch or on voice command.

Deactivated.

He pounded on the door until his fists were sore, hoping someone would hear his pleas for release. But no one answered. No one came.

This was worse than stasis. Xenobians operated in triads, on a sense of community. This was their equivalent of purgatory—solitary confinement—exiled. Ben was left to suffer with the memory of what he'd done. No telepathic voices to help him.

He was alone.

That was more than he could bear. He collapsed on the floor and waited for sleep to take over and hoped, in the morning, it would all be over. His only serenade, the mournful chorus of his own sobbing reverberating throughout the empty apartment.

CHAPTER FIFTY-EIGHT

The Stand

•.• Ben woke to a loud rumbling. The room vibrated with the sound of engines building up to a cataclysmic explosion. He slumped and re-laxed. His head still throbbed but he was never so relieved in his life to hear that sound.

He glanced at the couch where Carlos lay bruised and snoring under Danine's harmonic blanket. A half empty jar of ointment lay on the floor near a pile of his clothing.

He wasn't alone, or abandoned. The thought made tears well up in his eyes. And sometime during his sleep, Carlos had covered him with a blanket. He bowed his head in prayer and thanked whatever divine spirit blessed him with a friend like that. The noise stopped abruptly.

"Hey." Carlos struggled to sit up but collapsed.

"Hey," said Ben, his head pounding. "Thought you were gone."

"I was, but now I'm back."

Ben smiled and nodded, but didn't know what to say or where to start. "I'm sorry."

"Yeah," Carlos's scratchy voice gained strength. "I know. Tough break. What happened? No one's talking, not even my team, but everyone's taking it pretty hard."

Ben sighed and shook his head. He didn't want to break down in front of Carlos. "I can't talk about it either. Not yet. Okay?"

Carlos nodded. "Okay. But if you had told me what you were planning I'd have gone with you."

"Didn't want you—."

"I know," said Carlos. "But I wish you had trusted me anyway."

"Sorry."

"Me too."

They sat there in silence for a while, Danine's blanket providing the only sound, gentle background noise against a bleak day.

"Ought to try this," he said, laughing, then coughing.

"Tough workout at calisthenics, huh?" asked Ben.

"Day of mourning," Carlos answered. "Whole complex. All teams are in. No one's working today."

"Then what happened to you?"

Carlos gestured around the room. "We were ordered out of the apartment. Council decided that we should live with our own tribes."

"Thanks for coming back for a visit," said Ben.

"Not a visit. I came back to stay. April's staying with Aurelia. Grace and Serise are sharing an apartment on the other side of the complex. You'd have been proud. April told off the Council representatives. Man, she's got a mouth on her and she did it without a translator. Serise put up quite a fight of her own. She can't fly yet, but you should have seen her do the flying round kicks that Grace and she learned from watching videos in the library. The Hayoolkail warriors kept dematerializing to keep from getting hit in the face when they ordered her out. Finally they gave up and called in that warrior, Micique, the one Serise is crushing on. He snuck up behind her and pinned her arms behind her back until she calmed down. The leader of the Shakra alliance finally said she and Grace could live together since they were practically family anyway." Carlos laughed, then groaned and wrapped the blanket around himself tighter.

"What happened to you? Why'd they let you come back?"

Carlos hesitated. "They didn't exactly let me. Kavera said our dads were inseparable, right? So we've got to carry on the tradition. We have a pact. Can't leave a bud hanging out there alone, can I?"

"Betting Pendon's not happy about it."

"He isn't," Carlos said in a voice that was almost proud. "But I stood up to him in front of the whole team when he ordered me to live next to his quarters. I said, 'No'."

Ben gulped. What Carlos had done would usually result in a death sentence. "No? To Pendon? And he let you live?"

"Yeah. Kind of cool, huh! Probably the first time in Casmirian history!" said Carlos. "We got into an argument so I demanded it be settled in combat. As usual, he told Peng to fight me."

"Okay, now I know you're crazy," Ben said, his stomach suddenly going sour. "He's the size of a bull elephant."

Carlos nodded enthusiastically. "All that stuff Aurelia and Kavera taught me came in handy, though. He telegraphs his moves. You can tell when he's going to attack. Pretty predictable once you know his tricks. Nothing but brute force. All I did was wait until he was past his center of gravity, then ducked or moved out of the way. He kept stumbling and falling flat on his face."

Ben smiled, it was the most he could muster under the circumstances. Carlos did make him feel better. "So you won?"

Carlos chuckled and winced. "Does it look like I won? He totally lost it when the other warriors started laughing. But I managed to get a lot of licks in and gave as good as I got. Just when I thought he was going to finish me, I stood up and told him to go ahead and do it. Told him I was my father's son and I'd die like a warrior. Didn't even close my eyes. Just stared right back at him and wiggled my fingers—the ones that weren't sprained—to taunt him."

Ben choked. "Are you nuts?"

"Guess so," said Carlos. "I pretty much figured it was over and I was toast what with some of the warriors taunting him to do it. Instead, Orin came in and said something to Pendon I couldn't hear. Pendon looked like he was going to blow a gasket, but he stopped the fight and said something about admiring my impudence and earning the right to choose my own living quarters. Then Peng collapsed. I guess I kicked him in the wrong place during the fight. You could say it was a 'low' blow. Peng's in the medical wing getting patched up." He coughed, then laughed. "Danine's in a foul mood. She said no harmonic blankets or ointments for him. He'll have to heal the regular way. It'll take days before he's back on his feet." Carlos laughed again, holding his sides in agony and collapsing.

Overwhelmed, Ben shook his head in admiration. "You did that for me?"

Carlos nodded. "I did that for us. Told you, we're a team. Buds for life. I won't leave you out there hanging alone. So next time, don't go on a mission without me or I'll kick your butt too!"

CHAPTER FIFTY-NINE

Sanctuary

•⁝• Ben sat in a corner of the courtyard and watched as people poured in and out of the sanctuary in preparation for the funeral. Warriors passed him all day long without glancing in his direction. Ben was effectively an outcast, shunned by everyone in the complex but his own small group of friends. Even his sister felt pressure to avoid him in public places but kept finding him in private.

Danine, who had treated Ben warmly in the past, avoided his gaze as she rushed into the sanctuary. Her skin color was midnight blue. Ben had never seen her that color before and assumed it was the sign of mourning in her tribe.

Ben's uncle exited the chapel, dressed in elaborate ceremonial robes.

"Uncle Henry?"

"You require something?" he answered out loud.

"I want to help. Is there something I can do?"

"The preparations are complete. You will attend service when the time comes. That is all that is required."

"I wanted to say I'm sorry," said Ben. "To the team."

His uncle looked through him, as if he wasn't there at all. Ben could see the anger mixed with a profound sadness in his eyes. "What you want is absolution."

"I don't understand," said Ben.

"You seek forgiveness?"

"Yes," said Ben.

"That is not their job today. The warriors have their own grief to deal with."

"I thought, maybe, I could explain."

"There is nothing to explain. What is done is done."

"I thought maybe I could talk to Aurelia."

"She is tending to Danine."

"Danine?"

"Kavera's wife."

Ben gasped. "I didn't—"

"Know?" said his uncle. "It appears that is a constant theme in your life. If you want absolution, best find it in yourself."

He turned his back on Ben and walked away.

CHAPTER SIXTY

Saying Goodbye

•• Sitting in the front row of the sanctuary—the section reserved for family—Ben felt exposed. It was suddenly dawning on him, the enormity of what he had done. Kavera had sacrificed himself for Ben. He wasn't just a friend. He was family. And now he was . . .

he was . . .

. . . gone.

The Council delegation arrived, including those from Atlantis who sat, protected, behind a wall of water. Next came the tribes, all dressed in ceremonial regalia. April sat next to Ben, her eyes red and puffy. She reached out, held his hand and didn't ask what happened. Her touch helped. His breathing stabilized. His muscles relaxed.

"Love you," she whispered telepathically. *"It will be okay."*

"Love you too," Ben answered, surprised she had developed the ability.

He looked across the room to see Carlos sitting next to Pendon, Orin and the still recovering Peng. Carlos gave a subtle sign—a fist of solidarity tapped against his heart, nodded once, then focused his attention on the center of the room. Like Carlos, Serise and Grace were seated next to the Council representatives from their own tribes.

Each glanced quickly at Ben, gave him a quizzical look like, *"What happened?"* Ben shook his head to indicate he didn't—couldn't say. Grace nodded with understanding, but Serise arched her eyebrows searching for more meaning. Again, Ben shook his head and wiped at a tear with his thumb. Serise finally shrugged, nodded in acknowledgement and left it alone.

Last to arrive, Danine led the Xenobian contingent bearing Kavera's body on an alabaster platform that floated in the center of the color guard as they walked to the center of the room. Aurelia stepped forward as the platform was placed on the altar. She raised her hands in prayer:

"In the beginning, the universe sprang into existence, bringing with it life and sustenance. We are individuals, and yet we all spring from the same substance as the stars. Our energy, our life force is neither created or ended, simply blended and repurposed where it can serve a greater good. Today we come together to send our brother . . ."

She paused but didn't cry. Instead she smiled broadly, her cheeks flushed.

"We send my brother to a higher plane of existence where he will join with our ancestors, bringing light and prosperity to those he leaves behind. He is not gone. His spirit nourishes the universe. As we are touched by his gifts and his love, so has he been touched by ours also."

"We say!" she called.

"This is a time of joy!" the audience responded in a blended chorus.

"We say!"

"This is a time of love!"

"We say!"

"Peace be with Kavera on his new journey!"

The outpouring of voices from every person in the room nearly swept Ben away.

Next, each team told a tale of Kavera's heroic adventures, and only then did Ben realize the enormity of the loss.

The Casmirians talked of a battle on the planet Taug in an outer galaxy where a Sonecian expedition to mine rare minerals was confronted by pirates from another planet who arrived shortly after.

While the Casmirians preferred settling the dispute with brute force, Kavera negotiated the transfer of one hundred metric tons of freshly mined ore to their ship instead. It gave the Sonecians time to load the real minerals on the four transport ships in orbit with no loss of life. It was only after the Sonecian ships were underway and had safely cleared two jump gates that the pirates were likely to discover they had procured worthless gold rocks that would lose their lustrous and hastily applied coats of paint upon the first rain.

Everyone laughed. The Casmirians raised their fists in salute and shouted, "Kavera!"

The Shakrarians told of his ability to negotiate with any species, regardless of origin. Sometimes with just an impish smile and a slight nod of his head. On their planet, he was revered and often welcome among their ranks simply because of the joy that surrounded his aura.

The Hayoolkail talked of a young warrior who slipped in his training and in his fear did not position his body correctly for flight. During a recess in a diplomatic mission, Kavera, who accompanied Kurosh as part of his triad, had been climbing the steep rock face of Minus Verga, the tallest mountain on their planet. Lashed to a rope, Kavera pushed off with his feet, swung outward and caught the warrior as he tumbled past, clipping him to the last remaining carabiner on his line. Thus risking his own life and in the end saving the warrior as the rope went taut. They nicknamed Kavera, "He who flies without wings."

The stories continued for nearly a half hour with everyone confirming that Kavera had been adopted by every Sonecian tribe as family, a rare honor. Several Xenobian warriors explained how Kavera came to be their brother, even though he was the smallest among them. One told of how he trained his sister in secret after she joined the holy order and even though it was forbidden at the time. How Kavera found the wild animal now known as Bastet, injured in a jungle on the equatorial band of their planet. He freed the beast who was nearly crushed in a landslide then brought him home where Bastet took up residence as a protector of his sister after she healed his wounds. Bastet growled, but seemed content with the tale as he and Aris stood next to Aurelia.

Finally, Ben was asked to tell his story. His uncle's face was blank as he stared ahead at nothing and no one. Even with the passive expression, Ben could see how wounded his uncle was by the loss. Kavera had been part of his triad for the last two missions. Probably longer than that. And he was family. Choking back tears, Ben told how Kavera became like a big brother. He told of the smuggled chocolate and the basketball court. He talked about having a big brother he could look up to. And then he found his courage and told the story of how Kavera fought hundreds of monsters and in the process saved Ben's life. It was gut wrenching and agonizing and he diverted his gaze from the shocked looks on the faces of his friends. But the Xenobian team hooted in appreciation and were soon joined by the Casmirians, who enjoyed a good battle tale and kept shouting "Kavera!"

At last, when Ben's testimony was completed, all Xenobian warriors stepped forward, crouched on the floor, then raised their hands to heavens. Ben searched for meaning. His uncle joined Aurelia and Danine at the head of the altar, stretching his massive arms towards the sky. Aurelia transmitted a telepathic explanation.

"We are sending the soul safely on its journey. It is the sign of a bird in flight. He has gone, but his essence remains. We must release it. It cannot return to the body."

Ben understood and mirrored the actions of his tribe as they intermittently dipped, crossed their arms across their chests, raised them as if unfurling wings, then turned their faces upward towards a golden light streaming from the center of the chamber.

Kavera's body glowed as Aurelia chanted and the team sang in praise. Her hands caressed his face as his body dissolved in a beautiful golden light. A beacon of silver appeared in the center of the altar, then split like an Atlantis transport beam. But this time, in the space, was Kavera smiling and nodding approvingly at Ben.

The warriors increased the pitch of their singing and began to circle the altar, touching the rods that surrounded his body. Their words indicated they'd been touched by his spirit, guided by his wisdom, and now were adding his collective energy to their own and returning it through the rods to give him strength for his new journey as a celestial warrior.

Ben's uncle stepped aside and refused to join in the dancing. He folded his hands and did not touch the rods. Ben assumed, given the tragedy, that he should do the same. April circled twice with the team and then, following Ben's lead, joined him to the side. She held his hand in support and gave it a gentle squeeze. He felt a jolt of energy course through his body, as if another piece of Kavera had just transferred to him. His family members were dwindling. First his parents, now Kavera. The only two people on the planet that carried his blood line were his uncle and his sister. It was clear from his uncle's expression that anything good between them was damaged beyond repair.

Kavera, now floating above his body, saluted his tribe one last time, and they saluted him in return. Stepping forward, Danine's color shifted from midnight blue, to purple, to maroon, to a golden copper as the last of Kavera's essence floated around her before rising out of sight on a beam of light. And through her tears Danine was—

—smiling. She blew him a kiss as he disappeared.

It was beautiful and devastating.

And as his tribe continued to sing and dance in celebration, Ben felt worse than ever.

CHAPTER SIXTY-ONE

Ajamu

•••"Tell me what happened on our planet."

Ben's uncle didn't answer, instead he focused on the data streaming from his tablet. His fingers flew across the keyboard as every wall of his apartment filled with binary code. Beams crisscrossed a digital globe, comparing DNA patterns to eight templates spinning in the middle of the room. Ben knew immediately what he was searching for. The tablet beeped continuously as strand after strand was rejected. Ben had learned enough code to understand the two words repeating over and over again.

01001110 01101111 00100000 01001101 01100001 01110100 01100011 01101000

01001110 01101111 00100000 01001101 01100001 01110100 01100011 01101000

01001110 01101111 00100000 01001101 01100001 01110100 01100011 01101000

01001110 01101111 00100000 01001101 01100001 01110100 01100011 01101000

No match.

He pulled out a chair and sat down.

"Uncle Henry. Please. Why won't you talk to me?"

Silence.

"Pendon said the problem was caused by Xenobians."

His uncle looked up abruptly.

"Please," Ben pressed. "Will you tell me what happened?"

Uncle Henry sighed and typed more commands into his tablet. "It is not something I wish to discuss."

"I made a mistake," Ben said, tears forming. "I thought I could help you and prove I could be part of the team and I screwed up."

When his uncle didn't respond Ben took a risk and continued. "Kavera said that everyone was to blame, not just us. But Pendon was specific. He said it was my Xenobian family. So did that mean the tribe? Or us?"

His uncle pursed his lips then looked him straight in the eye. "What is it you are asking?"

"I want to know what happened that caused the mission. Why people think it's our fault."

Silence.

"Uncle Henry, I know I messed up. I can't take it back. I can't bring Kavera back. But maybe if I knew what happened I could help fix it."

"What is done is done. It serves no purpose to revisit it."

"I'm not the only one who made a mistake." Ben said. From the pained look that crossed his uncle's face he already knew the answer. "It's not the first time someone died."

His uncle set his jaw hard, then looked past him at the spinning globe.

"No."

Ben's heart leapt into his stomach but he kept his voice calm. "You made a mistake too."

It was minutes before his uncle responded.

"Yes."

Ben paused. He didn't expect that answer, but saw it as an opening. "Did the Tribe forgive you?"

His uncle took in a deep breath, then gave a single nod. "They did."

Ben relaxed his posture and wiped the moisture from his face. "And now everyone's got this hard job to try to fix it. And they're not happy about it. And you're stuck with the hardest job of all. To hunt this thing, this beast the Atlanteans talked about, right?"

"That is my mission," his uncle confessed still looking out at nothing and no one.

"Then let me help. We both messed up and now it is up to us to make it right again."

Uncle Henry closed the tablet, and then his eyes, letting his hands rest in his lap and breathing as if he were meditating. Ben waited, trying hard not to push him. But when his uncle stayed in that state he felt there was no choice.

"I want to help."

"No."

"Why not? I could help you find the whale. I saw —"

"I know where the whale is," Uncle Henry said, quietly. "I've known for a while."

"I don't understand," Ben said. "How could you know?"

"The box I gave Calamar. It had a listening device. I knew he was hiding the whale's identity. Volari was able to find and tag him without being detected."

A holographic window opened in front of Ben. A single blue beep showed the whale's location in the Pacific Ocean off the California coast. "We can track him now."

"I didn't know," said Ben, thinking that everything that had gone wrong in his family was because, like the other Sonecian tribes, no one was willing to give up their secrets. No one talked to anyone. Everything went through the Council and all of them protected their own.

"The whale's important because he's a genetic match for one of the jars in the Guardian room?"

"In all likelihood," said his uncle. "Danine is running tests on samples Volari obtained."

Ben studied the data streaming on the walls. No change. No matches found. And then something jolted him.

"Protect him at all costs. You know what is at stake." Kavera had said when Ben was rescued.

"The jars reacted when we first got here. Danine ran a scan of our DNA during the physical. And we found artifacts at Isla Ballestas and Palenque, two places the teams had already searched." He paused, his next sentence too horrible to contemplate. "We're a match for the jars too."

A loud sigh rushed from his uncle's lips as he opened his eyes and looked directly at him. "Yes."

Horrified, Ben sank deeper into the chair as his world began to collapse.

"The Council will not know of this, understood?" his uncle said, his voice hardened.

More secrets.

"Who else knew besides Kavera?"

"Danine, Aurelia, Tenzin and Calamar. And it will remain so. You felt distress that your friends were forced to keep secrets from you. Now you must do the same. To reveal what you now know will put them at risk."

"Because we're the keys you're looking for."

Uncle Henry tapped his fingers on the desk before answering with a single nod.

Ben sucked his breath in so hard he was forced to settle all the way into the chair. "Did my parents know? Is that why they had children? To use us as human sacrifices?"

His uncle's expression softened. "Of course not. Your parents, at their core, are human. They desired offspring. You were born out of love."

Ben's tension eased a micron. "And those stasis tubes? There are hundreds of them."

"Millions," said his uncle.

That knocked the rest of the wind out of Ben.

"The teams are scanning every human on the planet looking for genetic matches using mitochondrial DNA as a marker. It is passed from mother to offspring and survives intact even after several millenium."

Ben paused. "If the planet is destroyed, what good will the tubes do?"

His uncle didn't respond but the answer seemed obvious. April had spent time at a Doomsday vault and said the Harbor was always accessing it after hours but they weren't growing any of the seeds. Ben's father was collecting animals for an ark before he disappeared. If they were now collecting people that could only mean . . .

"Another ship is coming."

"Yes," his uncle said. "But it may not reach us in time. In the event we do not complete the mission we can transport two million people in stasis and seed another planet using the Casmir Array. But only if the Sonecian Council is successful in locating a wormhole to a distant part of the universe. We're going to try to outrun the explosion that is coming. That is why we couldn't allow Arecibo to fail. It is the largest dish on the planet with the capacity needed to transfer that volume of specimens through the array."

"So people are in tubes at night for testing, but gone in the morning before they wake up. You're tagging the ones you hope to save."

"The United States military maintains thirty-six GPS satellites in orbit," Uncle Henry said. "Only twenty-four are in use at any one time. With the reserve capacity tied into Arecibo we can track and retrieve descendants within seconds if the Council votes to abandon Earth. The Casmir array is being prepped for the transfer."

Ben did a quick calculation in his head. The librarian said there were seven billion people on the planet. "If the planet is destroyed you can save maybe two out of every seven thousand people." He stopped and projected the outcome as the horror of what his uncle was implying washed over him. "That's twenty out of every seventy thousand? Three hundred people out of every million?" His voice dropped. "Uncle Henry, that's hardly anyone."

His uncle frowned. "It is not a choice we prefer to make. But it is the only remaining option in the event our mission fails. The Council continues to negotiate the terms and criteria for who will be saved."

Ben tried to process the information. He was still in shock. He was a key. That's why they couldn't go to the Guardian or the Libyan facility. "You don't want the Council to know we're keys because they'd use us to brute force the combination to the Guardian lock. Even without the whale, Sunnyslope kids are half the equation."

Ben's uncle nodded again, his eyes narrowing. "Pendon cannot know what I've revealed to you. Do you understand? He'd have no issue with having Carlos or any of you killed if that is what it took to break that lock."

"You and Kavera have been protecting us the whole time. You've been looking for descendants who can take our place."

"Once Kavera saw the jars change we restricted access to the Guardian. Danine erased the memories from those technicians present at the time. We couldn't risk the information leaking to the Council until we had a contingency plan in place."

"Then I went on a mission by myself. Because I didn't know. And Kavera died trying to save me." Ben wiped at the new tears that formed.

"He died in service to you. It was an honorable act," his uncle said quietly.

"Then let me help. To honor his memory. I promise, I'll follow the rules. I'll work with Aurelia on my training. I'll help Berko and Zadra and Ayotunde and everyone until I'm good enough to go out with them. I can hunt with you."

"No."

"But so many people on Earth will die. We can't let that happen. All of us could help if you let us."

Uncle Henry's eyes flew open in rage. "NO! I will not lose another member of my family to this mission. Do you understand me. I will NOT take that risk!"

"But I can do it. Kavera showed me everything he'd learned when we were fighting. I'll practice until I'm just as good. I get it now, everything you've been trying to teach me. What he tried to teach me. I can do it. I swear."

Uncle Henry raised his fist then slammed it down, stopping just above the table. He let it hover there a minute, then drop back into his lap.

"Uncle Henry," Ben pleaded. "I'm so sorry. So so sorry. Please forgive me."

They sat in silence, his uncle not meeting his eyes, looking as if he were reliving those painful memories. Finally, not getting anywhere and watching the sun go down in the window, Ben rose and walked toward the door. He stopped just inside the threshold and looked back.

"Why won't you forgive me?"

"I have forgiven you," his uncle said, his voice soft with resignation. He opened his tablet and returned his focus to the data streams. "It is myself I cannot forgive."

CHAPTER SIXTY-TWO

The Healing

•⦁• Seeking escape from his suffocating sadness, Ben entered the sanctuary. A tiny sunbird flew down from an avocado tree to light on his shoulder. Ben didn't flick it away. Instead he looked for a place to meditate, finally deciding on the fountain at the far end of the garden. The bird pecked at Ben's growing locks, removed a strand of hair and flew off to add its new treasure to an unseen nest.

His sister and aunt were sitting beneath a balcony. *His aunt.* It had such an odd ring to it. April lay on a floor pillow, her chin and arm resting on Aurelia's thigh. Unlike the bimonthly complaints that always accompanied her braiding sessions at home, she made no other sound beyond deep sighs.

Aurelia unraveled the braids and ran her fingers through the tangles. She hummed an unfamiliar melody as she worked. Other than the rise and fall of her chest, April didn't move a muscle. She just stared out at simulated landscapes as tears streamed down her face. Both were bathed in the light of a pale orange sunset. Ben could have sworn they were glowing.

After Aurelia applied cream from a small jar, her comb flowed easily without catching a single knot. Watching Aurelia work, twisting

April's hair into a complex geometric pattern, Ben realized that this place was the closest thing he would find to a real home. An ache gnawed at him, nestled in a place deep inside. A place that no amount of prayer or meditation could touch.

Aurelia leaned over and looked sideways at April who did not return her gaze. She placed the comb on the table and gently stroked April's head in a downward motion then ran her long delicate fingers across the tips of her ears.

Shuddering under Aurelia's gentle caresses, April shut her eyes and went to sleep. Aurelia smiled, kissed her softly, and then returned to her work, twisting and braiding until April's hair was transformed into a work of art. When she was done, she lowered April to the floor and positioned her body against large pillows scattered around them.

"Shir, shidana" she whispered softly. At her command, the lights above them winked out. Aurelia removed her outer robe and placed it over April. In the dim light Ben could see a faint golden shimmer that lingered around his sister after Aurelia walked away.

"She will be safe here for the night. No need to move her," Aurelia whispered. "She is missing her mother."

"What did you do to her?" asked Ben.

"I gave her peace. She will still grieve, but it will not hurt as much."

"But that glow . . . "

"That is not my doing," said Aurelia. "Her aura is coming from inside. She is not yet aware that she is doing it. That is a good sign. She is becoming Shaman. Like your mother. It will take years of training, but she is gifted. Her genetic structure suggests the makings of a great healer."

Ben didn't respond. His sister looked so peaceful and so beautiful bathed in the light. "Thanks," he said before turning towards his original destination.

"You have never witnessed a death?"

"No. I wasn't there when my parents . . ." The last word caught in his throat.

"It is not a time of sadness. It is a time of rejoicing," Aurelia said.

"Kavera no longer inhabits his physical shell. But his energy surrounds us and nourishes the cosmos. That is why we danced in celebration of his new life."

"I . . . " Ben stopped. He didn't know how to continue. No words could adequately describe his sadness.

Aurelia finished his thought "Could not have prevented his death."

"He would still be alive if I had gone home on the Sonara."

"And you would be dead in his place. I suspect the fates had other plans. Destiny wanted you to remain on Earth or it would have found a way to put you on the transport."

Ben clenched and released his fists. Kavera's death played over and over in his mind in a continuous loop. He closed his eyes and tried relieving his anxiety through a series of deep inhalations and slow, controlled exhales. His efforts only made things worse. Guilt consumed him and there was no running away from it.

"Kavera died an honorable death. He died doing something he had a passion for. He lived to serve. He died serving you. It is a disservice to mourn his death. You must celebrate it."

"Celebrate? How do you celebrate a mistake?"

"By living an honorable life. By discovering your destiny and pursuing it passionately. It is the ultimate tribute. A way to continue his legacy and honor his sacrifice."

"Okay, thanks." Ben didn't want to continue. Every ounce of him wanted to flee from the room. He turned and walked towards the door.

"It is not a sign of weakness to ask for help," Aurelia said gently.

"I don't need help." Ben stopped in his tracks, but kept his back to her. He hoped it would make it easier to keep his thoughts private. "I'm fine."

"It is not a sign of weakness," Aurelia repeated, "to admit that you are also missing your parents. Or perhaps that you need to be hugged. Touch can be healing. Energy flows from the strong to those who need it. Why carry this burden with you? Who does it serve if you choose to bear it alone?"

Ben looked up at the stars projected on the glass surface of the ceiling. He struggled to be strong for his sister's sake. For his uncle. But it was too hard. He had lost faith in himself. How could he have thought that he alone could find his parents when hundreds of scientists couldn't do it? How could he have been so stupid? And now there was this new revelation. He and his friends were the keys to saving the world. He had the weight of an entire planet filled with seven billion people and a few trillion animal and plant species resting on his fourteen-year-old shoulders. And it was a secret he couldn't reveal, not even to his friends. Ben wanted more than anything to return to the days when basketball championships were the only challenge he dreamed of. But he remained stoic. He would not embarrass his uncle by showing his vulnerability.

"Being stoic is your uncle's way. It is not necessarily the way of a Xenobian tribesman," Aurelia said.

Ben hated that she could probe his mind whenever she wanted. "I don't want to be a burden. It was stupid to think I could do this."

"Burden? You are a blessing. A gift. What you consider to be a mistake helped reveal the identity of a traitor in our midst and perhaps advanced the mission in doing so. You can't see that because you allow your pain to consume you. Ajamu, a single drop of boiling water can cause an injury that takes months to heal. That same drop of water, dropped into an ocean, will lose its power to injure but retain its positive energy to nourish the whole."

Ben shrugged in defeat. "Why do you call me Ajamu?"

Aurelia smiled. "It is a term of endearment. It means 'He who knows what he wants.' It suits you."

She held out her hands. Ben hesitated. She didn't insist. She sat on a bench but kept her hands outstretched. After several minutes, Ben yielded. He placed his hands in hers but would not look into her eyes. Instead he stared at the intricate mosaic floor. Aurelia stroked the backs of his hands with her thumbs and hummed. This time the song was familiar. His mother sang it to him when he was very young. She would stroke his hands when he resisted sleep, tell him she loved him, and hum this simple, exotic melody. She continued stroking his hands, but the tempo changed as if Aurelia were distracted.

"What if I had a way for you to say goodbye to Kavera. To make your peace and know he is at peace as well," she said finally.

Ben frowned and shook his head again. "He's gone. I know it."

"If there were a way? Would you accept that opportunity?"

"Yes," Ben said, his heart slowing as if it were trying to give up. "I would."

"Please wait for me." Aurelia rose and left the garden, leaving Ben alone.

CHAPTER SIXTY-THREE

Forgiven

•ᵉ "Hello, young grieving warrior."

Ben froze.

Aurelia nodded toward her brother. "We must be brief, for his spirit cannot remain with us for more than a few seconds. And we will never speak of this outside of the sanctuary. Am I understood?"

Ben nodded. He'd paid the price of violating someone's trust. He wouldn't do it again. He reached out to touch Kavera, to make sure he was real, but Aurelia pulled his hand back.

"Time is of the essence, Ajamu."

"How?" Ben asked.

"It isn't the how that matters, young warrior," the image of Kavera said. "I am here now. Don't grieve for me. It is to a glorious place I go. The start of my new mission."

A single tear formed on Kavera's cheek.

"I'm sorry," said Ben. "So sorry for not having faith. For not protecting you the way you protected me. For not following the ways of a warrior. For—"

"I forgive you," Kavera said. "Now you must forgive yourself. I died with honor, so you could live and continue our legacy."

"But . . ." Ben stopped.

"Dance in my honor," Kavera said. "Rejoice in life. You have friends that love you. Don't live your life looking back, only forward."

"I'm sorry," Ben repeated, trying hard to hold back his tears. "So, so sorry."

"I forgive you," Kavera said, his voice catching, his eyes moist. "And I love you."

That was all it took. Sobbing, Ben collapsed on the floor and buried his head in the soft folds of Aurelia's robes. Her clothing was infused with the scent of lavender and jasmine. His mother's scent. The ache he had worked so hard to suppress finally revealed itself to be a huge gaping hole in his heart. Aurelia rocked him as if he were still a small child, stroking his back and humming his mother's song. Something round pressed into the small of his back. A jolt of static electricity engulfed his body. And then, without warning, all his grief poured out of him as if someone had opened a faucet on full.

CHAPTER SIXTY-FOUR

The Dawning

∴ In the Xenobian courtyard, Grace lowered her hood, wiping at the tears that flowed down her cheeks. She placed Kavera's knife in Aurelia's hands.

"Is he going to be okay?"

"With your help, yes," Aurelia said. "But I was wrong to request your assistance."

"It was important," Grace said. "And I know my team would have forbid it."

Aurelia paused. "I am aware the risk and the physical sacrifice that was required for you to breach Shakrarian protocols. I fear I can never repay you."

"I saw what you did for him. So it was worth it. But I miss Kavera too. And your orbs don't work on my tribe. So I can't ever do that again, okay?"

Aurelia nodded, then wrapped Grace in her arms and healed her the old fashioned way.

∴

Ben woke to birds chirping and a familiar voice whispering in his ear.

"Gonna sleep the morning away?" asked Carlos, looking mildly amused. "This your new room? Never pegged you for the camping type."

Ben sat up, wiped the sleep from his eyes and looked around. He thought he'd been dreaming, but he was, in fact, still in the sanctuary covered in tribal blankets and resting on a bed of large pillows. At least Aurelia had spared him the indignity of being carried back to his room by one of her guards. He stretched. The dark grief that had plagued him was gone. He felt . . . hopeful.

Carlos held out a glass of green juice. Ben winced. "No thanks."

"Taste it. It's pretty good. I made it up myself in the galley."

"No thanks," Ben repeated. "I'm not drinking any more of that stuff."

"Suit yourself," said Carlos, downing the entire glass in one gulp.

"Ugh." Ben groaned. "How can you drink that?"

"Easy," said Carlos, pulling a flask from his pocket and offering it to Ben. "It's kiwi juice. Freshly made from the hydroponic gardens. Your uncle said we're off the green glob for good!"

CHAPTER SIXTY-FIVE

Two Against Nature

•• Ben returned to his duties, cleaning the equipment room. The dialer was gone, replaced with a plain stone floor. He focused on the task he'd been avoiding. Opening crates and sorting equipment onto the shelves. He returned the knife he borrowed to its case with the others. He welcomed the solitude.

"Woman, you can't dance at all!"

Ben froze as music and Kavera's laughter filled the outer room. He peeked out the door and saw nothing. Maybe Aurelia's healing didn't last long. He'd need more sessions and maybe time in Medlab if the doctor was still willing to talk to him.

"I confess I do not understand your criticism," said a voice that sounded like Danine. "There is a pattern. I am following it."

"Don't move your feet if there is no beat. It's as simple as that," said the man who sounded like Kavera. "Use the beat to guide you!"

"It would appear as if we are following different beats," said Danine.

"It would help if you just followed the drums. Or the bass. Or the guitar. But you can't follow every instrument at the same time," Kavera said, unleashing a loud chuckle.

"I most certainly can," said Danine, her voice rising several notes to mock him. "And it appears I am quite proficient at this skill you call dancing."

Ben inched out into the room and saw Danine looking at a holographic monitor. She swayed along to a recorded projection of her doppelgänger attempting to follow Kavera in a line dance. The on-screen Danine jerked around like she was having a seizure.

"Perhaps you are not correct in your instruction!" On-screen Danine laughed, the first time Ben had heard her do so, and turned light pink.

"Perhaps you have no rhythm, my love," said Kavera, taking her hand and attempting to do the Salsa instead. "Your dancing resembles a person whose brain synapses are not firing correctly."

The normally stoic doctor glowered, but continued dancing and tried to keep up. She failed miserably. It was if she had two left feet and her arms were made of gelatin. She continued jumping around as if she'd had ten cups of expresso and had been set loose in a bouncy castle. If this were a battle her enemy would be beaten to death just from the spastic flailing of her head, arms and legs. But the holographic couple and the real Danine laughed and kept dancing and Ben laughed inside too, grateful the Danine didn't have his tribe's skill for reading his mind.

He was about to give her privacy when he remembered the box Kavera had given him to hide from her. He slipped out the door and sprinted towards his apartment.

"What's up?" said April, when he burst through the door. She sat with Aris curled in her lap reading one of the Manga novels Kavera had smuggled in.

"Not sure," said Ben, running to his bedroom. The small iron box was still on the shelf undisturbed. It didn't look like a present since it wasn't wrapped in paper or a bow. He peeked inside and found a flash drive with Danine's name written on it and the words "Two Against Nature."

April poked her head in the door. "You sure you're okay? Aurelia has those little silver orbs. Apparently they draw bad energy out and let the good energy in. I can go get her if you want."

"Huh?" said Ben. "No. I'm good. She and I talked. She did the ritual. It worked okay. But I forgot Kavera asked me to hide something for Danine. Want to come with me?"

He and April rushed back to the training room with Aris following close behind. Danine was still there, but no longer dancing. Just staring at the video clips of her and Kavera laughing while attempting to find a rhythm in common.

Ben cleared his throat. Danine turned, her cheeks tear stained.

"I am sorry for the intrusion," she said, her voice cracking inside of a whisper. "I feel closer to Kavera in the Xenobian complex. I will allow you privacy to attend to your chores."

"Don't go," Ben said. "Kavera had something he wanted to give you. I don't know what it is, but thought you might." He handed her the flash drive.

She turned it over and over in her hands, then slipped it into the side of the console. Kavera suddenly appeared in the holographic projection. "Dearest one. In honor of our second anniversary I wanted to bless you with a gift."

Music started and Kavera began dancing. Only he wasn't dancing a normal cadence. He was flailing his arms and laughing and kicking his feet from side to side in perfect time to the music. "At last, my love. The only song on this planet that fits the unique Danine rhythm!"

Danine covered her mouth, then laughed as she watched Kavera act like a goof ball. Ben turned to leave and pulled April with him.

"Don't go," said Danine, wiping tears away with the back of her hand. "I am alone as a species until we return home. Kavera became my family. Now you are family. Would you both dance with me? Perhaps I will fare better this time with your assistance."

Ben froze, not sure what to say.

"Please?" she said, her hand outstretched for them both to join her.

Aris nudged Ben forward, pushing gently on his wobbly knees.

As he and April walked towards her, Danine said, "Let us celebrate his life together in dance. It seems fitting." She turned. "This means you must honor him too, Aris."

Aris growled but joined them, not exactly dancing, but weaving in and out of their circle in his own unique cadence.

Ben began dancing to the beat in the only way that made sense. Like no one was looking. To a song filled with bongos and squeaking horns, minor chords, clapping, organ interludes and piano riffs. It wasn't the type of music a person was supposed to use for dancing and the lyrics made absolutely no sense. But it fit Danine's style perfectly. In his last act, Kavera had found something she could remember him by.

Whatever grief remained in the corners of Ben's mind disappeared as his two left feet found a rhythm they could follow and the three of them bounced around the floor, occasionally colliding with each other. Danine's color glowed a fiery vibrant red. And when her laughter rang out, so did his and April's.

EPILOGUE
Changing of the Guard

Ben took a few tentative steps into the chamber. He stood with his back against the door as warriors performed their own warm-ups. He felt out of place there. Like he was standing on the edge of a giant hole left behind by Kavera's absence.

The door slid open and he nearly fell backwards.

"Good morning, young warrior!" Berko chirped in his deep bass voice.

Ben nodded and tried to hold his emotions in check.

"Greetings," said Zadra, giving Ben a pat on the back and then a bear hug before she joined the others.

As more people poured into the room, Ben noted that they were smiling, giving each other handshakes and hugging affectionately. Several turned and did the same to him. One woman held his hand, kissed his cheek, then joined the others in formation. The funeral was held yesterday and yet everyone was joyful.

The room grew silent as Aurelia entered. She looked around thoughtfully, then said out loud, "Ben. Please take Kavera's place and lead the teams. I am required elsewhere."

Ben froze. "I can't."

"Yes," said Berko, "you can. It would honor the memory of Kavera for you to replace him."

Ben felt as if his feet were bolted to the floor. He could never replace Kavera.

Never.

He looked into the smiling faces of the team and saw only acceptance.

"Kavera would have wanted you to step up so that his sacrifice would have meaning," Zadra said, her eyes sparkling and her hands outstretched. "Come. Lead us."

"And perhaps if you crave challenge, we can honor him by playing a game of basketball. Only I think we shall now call it, Kaveraball!" Ayotunde grinned, then took his place in line. "It is decreed. You shall lead us young warrior!"

Ben nodded. "Okay. I'll try my best to make him proud."

Aurelia gave them a weak smile. "Short work out today. Then return to your duties." She turned and hurried out of the room.

"Something's brewing," said Grace, giving her own tribe a wide berth. Several Shakrarian team members stared and frowned as they walked by. Grace ignored them. She was under orders to stay away from Ben unsupervised. He was to be shunned. But like his friends, she continued to break the rules and take her lumps for the breach in protocol. Grace waved back in greeting and scowled. "What ever happened to "Namaste?" she muttered under her breath.

"I don't want to get you into any more trouble," said Ben.

"Don't worry about us," said Serise, sneaking up behind them. "Hey, what's going on in that room?"

"Emergency Council meeting," said Carlos. "I overheard Orin talking about it."

"Yeah, something's up," said April. "The whole Atlantis team came back last night. Couldn't see who, but the control room was lit up like a Christmas tree while they were transporting in."

"I heard there's even an emergency link to the Sonecian home worlds," Carlos confirmed.

Serise nodded. "They're draining a lot of power from the Casmir array to do it. Think we're in danger?"

Ben knew it was too early for an evacuation, but his instincts told him that this meeting was bad news. He attempted to establish a telepathic link, but the room's harmonic barrier returned nothing but static. "How long have they been in there?"

"All night," said Carlos. "Can't hear what is going on, because the room is soundproof. They've been at it non-stop without food. Tried to get Orin to spill the beans, but he was suddenly called into the meeting too."

The group huddled on the balcony, partially hidden by shadows. Within minutes the door opened and the Tribal Council streamed out in silence. The chamber filled with bright flashes of lights—the Atlanteans were transporting back to their base on a private frequency. The mood was somber.

Uncle Henry emerged, accompanied by an equally stoic Pendon. They split and headed in separate directions. Pendon stopped at the entrance to the living quarters and looked up toward the balcony. Ben pressed closer to a column but he could swear Pendon was looking straight at him. Pendon placed one hand on his weapon, narrowed his eyes and gave a slight nod before turning on his heels and exiting the room.

Aurelia and Danine were the last to leave the Council chambers. Danine's colors shifted through a rainbow of colors from white to black. The two women hugged, then split up as well. Ben took the stairs three at a time and caught up with Aurelia in the corridor. Her face was drained of color.

What happened? he asked.

She didn't answer. Instead she picked up her pace.

"Aurelia! Please! What happened!"

She stopped in her tracks and turned, her face expressionless, her voice barely audible. "Kurosh has been relieved of command . . . "

Ben staggered backward as Aurelia finished her sentence.

. . . Pendon is now leading the Harbor."

THE LOST TRIBES

Trials

Don't Miss Book 3
The Science-Fiction/Adventure Continues
Coming Fall/Winter 2017

Safe Harbor has a new leader and the stakes are more dangerous than ever—from a mission to a forbidden Emperor's tomb to a top secret outpost in Antarctica. To salvage the mission Ben and crew are slammed into their new powers! But is it too little? Or too late?